More Praise for Hugh Holton

"Fast moving. . . . A compelling read about the seedy underworld of crime and the crime fighters who wage wars against it."

—*Indianapolis Star* on *Chicago Blues*

"Holton writes with the stark, gut-wrenching realism of a cop who knows the slime pit cops work in."
   —William J. Caunitz, *New York Times* bestselling author of *One Police Plaza*

"Where in the world did Hugh Holton come from? He is a true, immensely talented writer."
   —Dorothy Uhnak, *New York Times* bestselling author of *False Witness*

"The most exciting storyteller I've encountered in a long time. His novels have everything—suspense, mystery, fascinating characters—and an insider's knowledge of the streets of Chicago. He is extraordinarily talented."
   —Andrew M. Greeley, bestselling author of *Irish Gold*

"A shivery, grisly read that's bound to add to Holton's growing reputation as a first-rate crime writer."
   —*Booklist* on *Windy City*

"A macabre thriller about the underbelly of Chicago. . . . Holton has written an imaginative first novel."
   —*Kirkus Reviews* on *Presumed Dead*

Forge Books by Hugh Holton

VIOLENT CRIMES

HUGH HOLTON

A TOM DOHERTY ASSOCIATES BOOK
NEW YORK

This is a work of fiction. All the characters and events portrayed in this book are either products of the author's imagination or are used fictitiously.

VIOLENT CRIMES

Map by Mark Stein Studios

A Forge Book
Published by Tom Doherty Associates, Inc.
175 Fifth Avenue
New York, NY 10010

Forge® is a registered trademark of Tom Doherty Associates, Inc.

ISBN:0-812-57187-8
Library of Congress Card Catalog Number: 96-47195

First edition: February 1997
First mass market edition: August 1998

Printed in the United States of America

0 9 8 7 6 5 4 3 2 1

In Memory

For Lt. William F. Caunitz, retired, of the New York Police Department; a good cop, a good friend, and a tremendously talented writer. You will be missed.

—Hugh Holton
July 1996

I would like to dedicate the novel *Violent Crimes* to my friends Silvernail, Julie, Susan, Bea, Sandy, Carol, Tim, Norman, Jeanne, Jack, and Kim-Jennifer. To Adele, Veronica, and Warren with love. To all of the members of the MWA Midwest Chapter, especially Barbara D'Amato, Mark Zubro, Michael Allen Dymmoch, D. C. "Debbie" Brod, Marilyn Nelson, Buddy Vogt, Bill Spurgeon, and Dave Walker.

A special dedication to the memory of Police Officer James T. "Tom" Ford, my father's partner, who was like an uncle to me and served as the model for Blackie Silvestri.

For all the members of the St. Columbanus Church and School community, which has been my spiritual home for the past twenty-eight years.

And for all the members of the Chicago Police Department, living and dead, who have made the CPD the best police department in the world.

—Hugh Holton
June 1996

Acknowledgments

I've noticed that my acknowledgments tend to remain pretty much the same from book to book, for which I am grateful. So I would like again to thank: Mrs. Barbara D'Amato, for her constant help, wise counsel, and encouragement; my agent, Susan Gleason, who is always there when I need her; and my editor, Robert Gleason, who continues to amaze me with his genius and publishing savvy. Thanks, too, to Tom Doherty and Linda Quinton and all the great people at Tor. I shudder to think where I'd be without you.

—Hugh Holton
June 1996

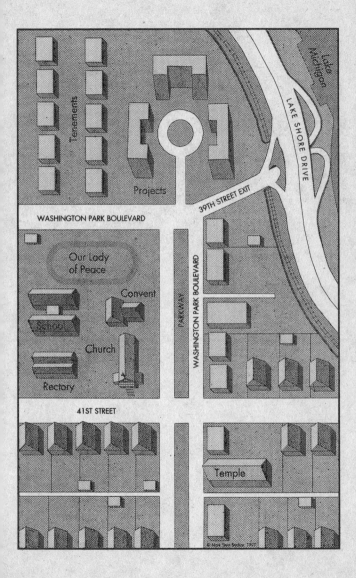

1

"First the cops, then you, Sister."

—Steven Zalkin

CHAPTER 1

APRIL 17, 1991
6:45 A.M.

It was a cool, overcast spring morning in Chicago. Comdr. Larry Cole of the Chicago Police Department drove his unmarked police car north on Lake Shore Drive. Rush-hour traffic was increasing, but as yet there were no bottlenecks as he passed McCormick Place, Soldier Field, and the Shedd Aquarium. At the Field Museum of Natural History he made a left turn to enter Grant Park. He picked up Columbus Drive at Roosevelt Road and again swung north.

The traffic became more dense, slowing his progress. Reaching beneath the dash, he flicked the switches to activate his flashing emergency headlights and electronic siren. Cars cleared a path, enabling him to pick up speed.

Cole was on his way to a homicide scene. Murders were not infrequent occurrences in Chicago, as the city averaged two a day every year. At least during slow years. Detective division commanders weren't routinely called out for homicides unless there was something different about them—something extraordinary, calling for command expertise in order to give the detectives assigned to the case a leg up on solving it. The homicide he was going to now was unusual in that the victim had been a soldier.

Cole turned west onto lower Wacker Drive, which took him under Michigan Avenue, State Street, and LaSalle. The streets above him in the Loop were clogged with traffic. Down here was not as bad and he made the run to the western end of the central business district in less than three minutes.

He swung back to street level four blocks north of the Sears Tower and continued west. He was now traveling away from the Loop into a neighborhood that had once been populated by small factories. Now the area was being rapidly turned into a high-priced residential area. A block from his destination, Cole cut the siren.

He saw the knot of police cars—marked and unmarked—along with the mobile crime-lab van and a police van, at the mouth of an alley behind a vacant building bearing the sign SPACE FOR RENT—CALL DEARBORN REALTY AT 555-0101. He pulled to a stop behind a marked Chevy and got out.

Larry Cole was six feet, one inch tall and weighed a trim 195 pounds. He was a medium-complexioned African-American and his hatless head was covered with curly black hair beginning to show traces of gray. As he clipped his gold commander's star to his trench-coat lapel, a stirring went through the cops gathered at the murder scene. He was brass—and when the brass arrived, it was best to watch yourself. But Cole wasn't what was known in the vernacular of the street cop as an "asshole." He was a good cop whom luck, brains, and a penchant for hard work had enabled to rise to the rank of commander with only twenty years on the force. For command-rank he was young. He was also black, which was still enough of a rarity in Chicago to cause some of the old-timers to stare.

He walked to the barrier tape strung across the alley. Detective Lou Bronson, a stocky black man of fifty-five, stepped up beside him. "Good morning, boss."

Cole returned Bronson's greeting before turning his attention to the corpse lying on the floor of the alley, fifteen feet inside the barrier tape. The soldier was dressed in starched, neatly pressed fatigues. Cole noticed the stainless-steel watch on his left wrist. The black combat boots still held a mirror sheen.

Bronson opened a pocket notebook. "His dog tags say he's Bryce A. Carduci, male, white, born March 4, 1953. Blood type O. Officers Benton and Garcia on Beat 1-13 found him at 0517 hours."

"There was no call?" Cole said.

Bronson shook his head. "The beat cops said it was a slow night, so they were cruising the alleys looking for burglars. That's how they came across the soldier."

Cole looked around. There were high-rises a few blocks away, which towered over the murder scene. In the dim early morning light it would be unlikely anyone there could have seen what happened in this alley.

Cole looked back at the body. The soldier was propped up against a trash Dumpster behind the warehouse. On the other side of the alley was a vacant lot.

"It doesn't look like a robbery or that the body's been disturbed by any of the local street people," Bronson said. Using his pen as a pointer, he added, "That watch and those shiny boots would have been gone if they had."

The dead man's face was completely hidden by congealing blood and brain matter leaking from a large wound in the skull. The commander accurately guessed the cause of the wound as a large-caliber bullet.

"Well, one thing's for sure," Cole said. "He couldn't have been here too long."

"Why is that, boss?"

Cole shivered in the cool morning air. "Because the rats would have gotten to him. There are a lot of them around here. They come up from the river."

Bronson nodded.

* * *

Lou Bronson's partner was Detective Manfred Wolfgang
Sherlock, who at the age of twenty-three was one of the
youngest detectives on the force. Manny, as he was called,
was white, six feet, four inches tall, and Abe Lincoln lean.
He had the face of a choirboy and a head of wavy hair with
a tendency to do just the opposite of what his comb and
brush intended for it. During the five months since his
graduation from preservice detective's school, Sherlock
had been teamed with Bronson, who was considered by
many, including Commander Cole, the best detective in
Area One. Some even thought the best in the department.

Blackie Silvestri, Sherlock's sergeant, had given the
young detective some advice when he was assigned to
Bronson. "Keep your ears open and your trap shut, kid, and
maybe in twenty years or so you might be half the detective
Lou Bronson is."

This did not bolster Sherlock's professional self-image.
So he listened and watched, but wasn't sure whether he
was learning fast enough to meet Sergeant Silvestri's
twenty-year timetable.

Now Manny was returning to the North Side alley crime
scene with twelve cups of coffee for the cops and lab technicians assigned to the case of the murdered soldier. A uniformed sergeant from the First District had asked for a
volunteer to go get the coffee and when there were no takers,
Manny had stepped forward. For this he had drawn a sour
look from Bronson, who accompanied him to their squad
car after Manny had collected the money.

"You don't volunteer to be a runner for beat cops,"
Bronson scolded. "You're a detective now. You're a grade
up on them."

"Oh," Sherlock said innocently. "Did I do something
wrong?"

Bronson sighed. "I guess not, but don't forget to make
mine black and easy on the sugar."

When he returned, the cops surrounded him to get their

coffee. The lab technicians had finished with the crime scene and came over to grab their cups. Manny saw his partner on the other side of the barrier tape conducting a close-up examination of the body. When Sherlock saw Cole, he froze. The young detective was pathologically terrified of bosses, and Cole was the highest-ranking officer in his immediate chain of command.

At that instant Bronson turned around, spied his partner, and yelled, "Bring the coffee over here, Manny."

Sherlock hesitated. He hadn't bought a cup for the commander. Maybe he should have anticipated Cole's arrival. When they had gotten the call, Bronson had told him that area commanders were required to respond to all homicides involving military personnel. This procedure had been put into effect after six sailors' throats were cut during that past Christmas season. Bronson had also told Manny that even though they had caught the psychopath responsible, some idiot in the chief of detectives' office figured a good way to make sure the detective division command staff stayed busy would be to have them on the scene of all GI slayings.

Sherlock wasn't so sure that this was a good procedure, as he didn't think many sailors, or, for that matter, soldiers, were murdered in Chicago annually. One thing he was certain of was that he didn't want to go stumbling around a homicide crime scene with his commander present. He was too afraid of making a mistake.

Bronson was waiting. "Manny, would you come on?"

Cole turned to look at Sherlock. The commander's expression was merely curious; however, Sherlock could have sworn he was scowling.

Carefully, balancing the remaining cups in the cardboard tray, Manny tried to bend down low enough to go under the barrier tape. When that didn't work, he swung one leg up and straddled it. The tape became jammed tightly in his crotch, making him come close to crying out.

Quickly, he swung the other leg over and managed to get to the other side without falling.

The other cops stared at him with barely concealed amusement. Remembering his partner's words about his position, he haughtily turned his back on them and ran head-on into Bronson. He lost control of the coffee tray.

Manny Sherlock was not only Lou Bronson's partner, but also his self-proclaimed responsibility. Whereas others thought Manny awkward and stupid, Bronson could see the diamond-in-the-rough qualities hiding behind that gangly, lingering adolescent appearance. So when he saw his partner's distress he guessed that it was because of Cole and knew with the premonition of a mother that disaster would soon strike.

When Sherlock straddled the barrier tape Bronson quickly excused himself and crossed the alley just as the skinny detective turned around with the coffee tray. When Sherlock dropped it, Bronson's hands were less than an inch beneath it. He caught it without spilling a drop.

"Thanks, Lou," Sherlock whispered.

Bronson smiled and turned around to Cole. "Coffee, Commander?"

Cole silently witnessed the vaudeville act between the two detectives. If he hadn't known Bronson better, he would have sworn they'd rehearsed the coffee tray drop and catch. But Cole had better things to do than ponder the pros and cons of their comedic talents.

With the crime-lab technicians having finished collecting available evidence and photographing the body and surrounding area, the detectives were free to move SFC Bryce A. Carduci, deceased. His wallet, keys, and a Zippo cigarette lighter were found in his trouser pockets. In one of his shirt pockets they found a half-empty pack of Winstons and a laminated identification card bearing the sergeant's typed name,

Social Security number, signature, and the name "Astrolab."
The detectives and their commander were surprised when
they found two thousand dollars in cash in the soldier's
wallet.

They retreated outside the barrier tape, as a First District
squadrol crew entered to remove the body. Cole, the detectives, a lab technician, and First District patrol officers
Benton and Garcia gathered around the commander's car.

"He was shot in the head at close range," Cole said. "It
looks like the bullet went right through his skull."

"I don't think he was killed here," the lab technician
added. "I'd say it happened someplace else, because
there's not enough blood on the floor of the alley." The
technician took a moment to blow on his coffee before taking a sip and putting it down on the hood of Cole's car. "He
was dumped less than an hour after death, but there's nothing I can find to tell me who or what he was dumped from.
No tire tracks. No spent cartridges."

"There's nothing around here that a soldier would be
interested in," Bronson said. "His being in fatigues does
raise some questions."

"Like what, Lou?" Sherlock said. Manny crossed his
long arms over his chest to keep them out of the way.

"You've never been in the service have you, Sherlock?"
Cole said.

The commander addressing him directly caused
Sherlock to stiffen in a less-than-authentic imitation of
coming to attention. He had never been in the military.
When he dropped his arms, his left hand knocked over the
lab technician's cup. Hot coffee spilled over the hood of
Cole's car. All Bronson could do was close his eyes.

"So we can assume, Detective Sherlock," Cole said
tightly, "that you haven't seen military service in this
peace-time world. So you would have no way of knowing
that fatigues are only used for work details. If the soldier
was in town on a pass or some other business, he would

have been dressed in a different uniform. Do you follow me?"

Sherlock's strangled "Yes, sir" was barely audible.

Cole turned to Bronson. "Lou, I want you and . . ." he paused, "your partner to check Carduci's dog tags through the Department of Defense. They'll be able to tell you where he's stationed. That's as good a place as any to start."

Cole shot Sherlock a parting glare. "I'm heading for the station, after I see if I can find a car wash open this early. Let me know what you turn up."

As the commander pulled away with coffee dripping from the hood of his car, Bronson said to his downcast partner, "Manny, sometimes I really wonder about you."

"Lou," Manny said, "sometimes I wonder about myself."

It was routine. The Military Police provided Bronson and Sherlock with background information on Sergeant Carduci's duty station. With Sherlock behind the wheel of the squad car, they headed south on I-94 into Indiana. Their destination was Astrolab Industries, outside of Gary.

Bronson noticed his partner still looked glum after the incident with the commander's car. "Why don't you forget about it, Manny? Cole will get the car washed and the whole thing will be a thing of the past by the time we get back."

"It looked like he'd just had it washed, Lou."

"Well, coffee's good for the finish anyway," Bronson said, checking his notebook.

"Really?" Sherlock said, brightening.

Bronson changed the subject. "The Defense Department says Carduci was assigned to Fifth Army Engineers out of Fort Sheridan, but detailed to the Defense Personnel Support Center at this Astrolab place."

"Astrolab," Sherlock said, reflectively. "Sounds like a toy manufacturer."

"It probably is," Bronson said, lighting a cigarette and ignoring his partner's disapproving frown. Sherlock didn't smoke. "Top-secret toys for the military."

"But what has the military got to do with toys, Lou?"

"I was talking about weapons, Manny. Real sophisticated weapons."

CHAPTER 2

APRIL 17, 1991
8:18 A.M.

As Sherlock and Bronson drove into the Indiana countryside, the Chicago rush hour ebbed. Cars traveling inbound on South Lake Shore Drive were still moving at a pace ten miles below the posted speed limit; however, the outbound lanes were deserted. A black van pulled off the southbound drive at Washington Park Boulevard and turned west.

The van, its windows tinted to limit visibility from the outside, drove down the boulevard toward Our Lady of Peace Catholic Church and School located at 948 East. Long before the van reached the complex, the driver could see the spires of the huge church. The van pulled to a stop across from the school and parked.

The school day began at nine, and there were children playing in front. The school was next to the parish convent. The van stayed parked with its engine idling. No movement came from inside.

CHAPTER 3

Astrolab Industries consisted of three brick buildings on seven acres of well-tended grounds in the northern Indiana countryside. An electrified Cyclone fence ran around the perimeter of the property. As Sherlock pulled the squad car up to the guarded entrance he noticed armed sentries leading huge German shepherds patrolling the inner grounds.

The information officer they were directed to see was Capt. Robert Lee Watkins of Lafayette, Louisiana. Watkins, a thin, humorless man in an immaculately pressed uniform, had been raised in a racially limited environment that caused him to direct all his answers to Sherlock despite Bronson asking all the questions.

"When was the last time Sergeant Carduci was seen here at Astrolab, Captain?" Bronson asked.

Watkins looked at Sherlock as he answered with a southern drawl, "He went off duty from building C at 2400 hours last night."

"Does the army provide round-the-clock security for this installation?"

"We do." Watkins squinted at Sherlock. The skinny policeman was pantomiming Bronson's words by moving his head and eyebrows, while keeping his mouth shut.

"What do you do here? Some type of military research?"

"That's classified, Officer . . ."

"He's Sherlock. I'm Bronson." As Bronson spoke, Sherlock pointed first at himself and then at his partner.

With annoyance, Watkins turned to look at the black cop.

"Could you tell us who was the last person to see Sergeant Carduci?"

"That would be Sergeant First Class Kenneth Glass."

"We'd like to talk to him before we leave."

"Of course."

CHAPTER 4

APRIL 17, 1991
8:20 A.M.

The driver of the black van remained parked across the street, staring at Our Lady of Peace Convent. He was wearing a black-visored motorcycle helmet with the shield down, a black jumpsuit equipped with multiple pockets, thin black leather gloves, and black combat boots. The jumpsuit fit the figure snugly, revealing a muscular body beneath it.

A few of the children playing in the schoolyard noticed the parked van, but gave it no more than a passing thought.

The driver wasn't interested in them anyway. The door to the convent opened and a nun, dressed in a knee-length blue habit, stepped outside before turning to lock the door behind her. As she started down the steps, the van driver tensed. The helmet's visor jutted forward to touch the driver's side window.

The nun reached the bottom of the steps and turned toward the school. She did not notice the van.

The driver waited until she entered the building before he put the van in gear. The tires screeched on the asphalt as he executed a sharp U-turn and drove back the way he had come.

CHAPTER 5

APRIL 17, 1991
8:30 A.M.

Capt. Robert Lee Watkins remained at his desk until the cops had left the Astrolab grounds. Then he went to Dr. Orlov's office.

Orlov was a small man with hair plastered to his skull and effeminate mannerisms. Watkins was a West Point graduate. They did not get along well.

After telling Orlov about Carduci's death, Watkins asked, "Have you checked the equipment inventory in building C this morning?"

"That's a military responsibility, Captain," Orlov said.

"I make it a point never to interfere in military matters unless I'm forced to."

"Well, we'd better take a look. Carduci was up to something. Him being found dead in Chicago proves that."

"Oh, for God's sake, Watkins, the man could have simply gotten a hard-on a hand job couldn't fix and gone off on a fling." To emphasize his words Orlov waved a limp wrist through the air. This caused the muscles in Watkins's jaw to tighten. Orlov continued, "He got mixed up with the wrong people and they cleaned his clock for him. It's been known to happen."

"Carduci was a tough wop from Brooklyn," Watkins pressed. "He wasn't going to let no Chicago punk get the better of him. . . ."

"If he could help it," Orlov interrupted.

The captain's face darkened in anger. "I want to check that inventory and I want you to go with me right now."

"Anything you say." Orlov sighed.

There were eight soldiers assigned to building C. Carduci had been their NCO. They were basically part of a research team, but also required to perform periodic guard duty. On this spring morning, a PFC was assigned to such duty outside the building's equipment vault. His rifle was propped up against the wall behind him and his helmet liner was tilted back on his head. He was examining the centerfold of *Playboy* magazine when Captain Watkins and Dr. Orlov approached.

Quickly, the soldier discarded the magazine beneath his chair, jumped to his feet, straightened his helmet, and picked up the rifle. When they reached him he was more or less at attention.

Watkins had better things to do than chew him out. At least at that moment.

The vault was secured by an electronic locking mechanism,

which could only be deactivated by application of a numbered code. Watkins typed the code into the digital mechanism and the vault sighed open. He and Orlov entered alone.

The captain noticed the discrepancies instantly.

CHAPTER 6

APRIL 17, 1991
8:45 A.M.

Washington Park Boulevard was L-shaped. From 400 to 1200 East it ran in an east-west direction. Then, at 1200 East, it turned at 3900 South to become a north-south thoroughfare down to 5100 South. The black van made a right turn and cruised down the boulevard. On the north-south leg a wide parkway with trees, a walkway, and park benches bisected the street. The houses in the area had once been grand old mansions, but had been allowed to deteriorate into rat-infested slums.

The black van traveled four blocks down the boulevard before pulling to the curb. The driver remained motionless, staring through his visor and the tinted windows at a building on the opposite side of the boulevard.

The building under scrutiny rested alone between two vacant lots. It had once been a movie theater. Now the marquee was corroded and the lobby area bricked shut. What it had been over the years from the theater's closing in 1962 and its present incarnation beginning in 1988 was an urban mystery. What it had become in 1991 was emblazoned on a carelessly painted sign hanging from the marquee: TEMPLE OF ALLAH—ABDUL ALI MALIK, MINISTER.

The driver of the black van was waiting for Minister Abdul Ali Malik to arrive.

CHAPTER 7

APRIL 17, 1991
9:17 A.M.

The house was in Hyde Park, a short distance from the Temple of Allah. It was white, sand-blasted brick and had a wrought-iron fence surrounding it. A driveway ran along the side of the house to the rear garage. A black Cadillac pulled out of the garage and rolled to a stop at the side entrance of the house. The engine of the Cadillac remained idling in the morning stillness.

The Cadillac was driven by a young black man dressed in a dark suit, white shirt, and dark tie. On his head he wore a bright red fez, which was the symbol of the members of the Brotherhood of the Mosque—formerly known as the Satan's Saints street gang. The chauffeur clutched the steering wheel tightly, tension radiating through his wire-thin frame. The reason for this tension was that he was a heroin addict and was in dire need of a fix. However, his first responsibility was to make sure Minister Abdul Malik got to the temple. Then he would make a connection on the street near the temple and get his much-needed fix.

The chauffeur wasn't worried about the minister finding out about his habit, as this Temple of Allah–Brotherhood of the Mosque line was no more than a front for the former street gang's narcotics and extortion operation. Minister Malik and the rest of the Brotherhood had been threatened many times by legitimate Muslim sects in the city, but they had as much muscle as the true followers of Allah did, so the threats meant little. The chauffeur was also not worried about Malik finding out about his heroin addiction, because the minister had a serious cocaine habit of his own.

The front door of the house opened and the minister's bodyguard, General Jack, stepped outside. The general was dressed in the same dark suit, white shirt with tie, and red fez uniform as the chauffeur. However, the bodyguard weighed over three hundred pounds. The general didn't have a narcotics habit. He lived for only two things: women and food. He usually enjoyed vast quantities of each. And his dedication to the minister was fanatical.

Satisfied that the front of the house was secure, the general turned and waved an "all clear." Then Minister Abdul Ali Malik stepped outside.

The chauffeur remarked to himself that, for a man so obsessed with security, the minister wasn't very smart. He had General Jack, who carried a nine-millimeter pistol in a shoulder holster to supplement the Uzi in a hidden compartment under the front seat of the Cadillac. He had the body of his car reinforced with steel, along with the installation of puncture-proof tires and bullet-resistant glass. But any one-eyed sniper with a BB gun could hit him because he was such a visible target.

This was because Minister Abdul Ali Malik, phony preacher and gang leader, always dressed in white. White suits, white shoes, white socks, and all-white accessories. His only exception to this sameness of ensemble was the full-length capes he wore, which were usually bright red. He was never without a pair of prescription sunglasses shielding his eyes. The obligatory fez he wore was encrusted with jewels. Standing in the driveway of his Hyde Park house, Malik stood out like a searchlight in the dark.

Minister Malik was a medium-complexioned black man of below-average size and weight. He always wore lots of jewelry on his fingers, wrists, and around his neck. As he came down the walk and swept toward the Cadillac's back door, which General Jack had dutifully standing open for him, the street-gang leader sparkled.

When his passengers were securely seated, the chauffeur put the car in gear. General Jack opened the double gates leading out to the street with a remote-control device, and they headed for the Temple of Allah.

CHAPTER 8

APRIL 17, 1991
9:20 A.M.

Chicago police officers Ralph Kessler and Jerry Brick were assigned to the beat car in the Washington Park Boulevard area where the Temple of Allah was located. Kessler and Brick were white, six-foot-three-inch, two-hundred-fifty-pound bookends who had worked together for over a year. During that period they had watched the fez-wearing members of the Brotherhood of the Mosque stride in and out of the temple with infuriating impunity.

"Twenty-one twenty-seven," the walkie-talkie attached to Brick's belt crackled.

Activating the microphone fastened to the epaulet of his nylon jacket, he responded, "Twenty-one twenty-seven."

"We have a complaint from the alderman's office about an illegal peddler in the 4900 block of South Cottage Grove."

"An illegal peddler. 4900 Cottage. Ten-four," Brick said.

Kessler turned a corner and began driving west in the direction of their call. "You know what the politicians are doing with this illegal peddler crap, don't you?"

"No, what?" Brick asked, as he recorded the address and nature of the call on their Patrol Incident Log.

"They're charging the peddlers for making calls to the License Bureau. If the alderman don't call, they don't get a license. Of course, there's a charge for each call."

"You're kidding. That sounds illegal as hell to me."

"Tell me about it," Kessler said, laughing. "But it just goes to show you, Chicago still ain't ready for reform."

Brick also laughed.

"Well, look what we got here," Kessler said with a tight grin.

Brick followed his partner's gaze through the windshield. Crossing the intersection in front of them was Minister Abdul Ali Malik's Cadillac. Kessler took a sharp right and fell in behind the luxury car.

"We got a call, Ralph," Brick said, as he recorded the Cadillac's license-plate number on their log.

"It's just a peddler, Jerry, and you don't have to write every fucking thing down."

Brick shrugged. Their sector sergeant always made a big deal about filling out the logs properly. "You gonna stop them?"

"They haven't done anything yet," Kessler said, pulling the police car to within less than a car-length of the

Cadillac's rear bumper. "But maybe we can make that little junkie driver nervous."

Brick didn't know about the driver, but he was starting to get a bit nervous himself. He could see the back of Malik's head through the rear window of the Cadillac. The phony minister was ignoring them. The big bodyguard had turned completely around in his seat and was staring at the squad car.

"Maybe we should just let them go," Brick said. His mouth had gone dry. "We have a call anyway."

"You already told me that, Jerry. Now just sit back and relax. That fat bodyguard won't pull nothing and the driver is probably ready to shit in his pants about now."

Kessler eased the car closer to the Cadillac's bumper. Brick could see the bodyguard glaring back at them. The bodyguard turned around and said something to the driver. It looked like, "Speed up!" But the Cadillac's speed did not increase one centimeter.

Brick was tense. Last September the department had organized a raid on the Temple of Allah. First Deputy Superintendent Raymond Schmidt had been in charge. But despite battering rams and all the rest of the sophisticated equipment the police had at their disposal, they had been unable to get in through the steel-reinforced double doors at the entrance. After the raid, Malik hired a slick, LaSalle Street attorney who had gotten an injunction against the CPD barring further harassment of the members of the Brotherhood of the Mosque.

Kessler's and Brick's watch commander had warned them to stay away from Abdul Ali Malik and the Temple of Allah unless they had indisputable probable cause. At that point Brick had considered transferring to another district. However, he liked it over on Washington Park Boulevard. That is, until Ralph Kessler pulled something stupid and got him a civil-rights-violation beef.

They continued three blocks in this bumper-to-bumper

fashion. A red light halted them. Brick felt a trickle of sweat run from under his arm down his rib cage. Kessler had a cruel smile pasted across his face. Brick hated it when his partner got this way.

The light changed and the Cadillac crossed the intersection. The police car stayed right on its tail.

"They're only a couple of blocks from the temple," Kessler said. "I bet our fat black friend's carrying an illegal piece."

Brick blanched. "C'mon, Ralph. They've got a court order barring us from harassing them."

"What in the hell's the matter with you? They have guns in that car and you know it. That's not harassment; it's good, effective law enforcement!"

"Twenty-one twenty-seven."

Brick answered.

"We're getting a second call on your peddler. The ward committeeman is on the scene waiting for you."

"Shit!" Kessler pounded the steering wheel. They were less than a block from the Temple of Allah.

"C'mon, Ralph," Brick said, feeling a relief he hoped his partner wouldn't notice. "We can always come back and check them out after we answer the call."

"Yeah," Kessler said, as he accelerated to roar past the Cadillac and then take a hard left at the next intersection.

The three members of the Temple of Allah watched them go.

CHAPTER 9

The man in the black van watched the Cadillac and the police car approach. The muscular figure stiffened momentarily with apprehension until the police car veered off, crossed the boulevard, and was gone. The Cadillac pulled up to the temple alone.

The van driver slipped a .357 Magnum six-inch-barrel Python revolver into a leather holster attached to a thick belt. He strapped the belt around his waist, checking to make sure each of the ammo pouches for the four-speed loaders he carried were in place and secure. Then he climbed into the back of the van.

He unlocked an olive-drab footlocker, which had been secured with a padlock. On top of the footlocker was the stenciled legend, PROPERTY OF ASTROLAB INDUSTRIES. From the footlocker he removed a number of items, which he placed in a cloth sack. He removed his helmet and also placed it in the sack. The sack was attached to a long strap, which went easily over his head to hang across his right shoulder. The sack itself rested against his left hip, opposite the holstered revolver.

There was a brown hooded parka hanging on a hook in the back of the van. The parka was worn and dirty. But the garment went on easily over his black jumpsuit, the holstered gun, and the cloth sack. From another hook he removed a brown plaid cap with floppy earpieces. He placed the cap on his head and pulled it down over his forehead. The last items he retrieved from the back of the van were a black plastic garbage bag and a stick from which a sharp nail protruded. Then he exited the van by way of the back door.

CHAPTER 10

APRIL 17, 1991
9:23 A.M.

Abdul Malik's chauffeur was shivering although he was bathed in sweat. He had been certain that the minister would let him go after they arrived at the temple, but the two cops made the minister change his mind. Now the chauffeur was forced to wait because the minister and General Jack wanted to be driven to their attorney's office on LaSalle Street downtown. The minister and the general had gone inside the temple to call the lawyer and notify him that they were coming.

The pain of the chauffeur's addiction coursed through his body like a raging virus. With each beat of his heart, which sent blood pounding against his temples like sledgehammers, his condition worsened. He needed a fix badly. There was no way he could drive downtown in the shape he was in.

He was about to get out of the Cadillac and go inside the temple to make his plea to the minister when he saw the man in the ragged coat and floppy-eared hat picking up trash on the parkway. The fact that this man was out of place here on the boulevard could not penetrate the chauffeur's drug-ravaged nervous system. After merely glancing at the ragged man, the chauffeur returned to his own pressing problems.

CHAPTER 11

APRIL 17, 1991
9:28 A.M.

The man posing as the trash collector made his way slowly to the side of the parkway closest to the Temple of Allah. Only once had the chauffeur in the Cadillac glanced in his direction. This was good. As the man had hoped, he had managed to blend in with the surroundings of the financially and socially depressed Washington Park Boulevard area. However, he realized he could never withstand a close inspection by anyone taking more than a passing interest in him. This meant that he didn't have much time.

Before leaving the van, he had placed the items he would need to deal with the chauffeur in the pockets of his worn coat. Now he removed one and held it in his left hand. It was a metal tubelike device, which was open at one end. There was a black button on top of the device, which the man was careful to keep from touching until the time was right.

At that instant the chauffeur got out of the car, closed the door behind him, and started around the hood of the Cadillac en route to the front door of the temple. A momentary despair gripped the phony garbage collector, as he wasn't quite ready to begin his operation against the chauffeur and his master. But then the junkie driver stopped to brace himself against the car's hood.

This was the chance the man needed to regroup. He checked Washington Park Boulevard in both directions. There were a couple of people walking north about three-quarters of a block away. Their backs were to him. There was no vehicular traffic in evidence, but the cop car earlier had frightened the man. He realized that they could return at any second.

The chauffeur was still leaning against the Cadillac's hood, but making an effort to stand upright. Once the attack began, the man understood, there could be no turning back. Once he pressed the black button on top of the metal tube he would have to move very quickly to complete the job. He'd been waiting for this moment for fifteen years, and now that it was here he hesitated.

The chauffeur stood up. Taking in a deep breath, the man pressed the black button.

A small projectile erupted from the end of the metal tube and rocketed toward the chauffeur. The man's aim was not very good, but it didn't have to be. The projectile, which was about the size and shape of a disposable ballpoint pen, struck the Cadillac and detonated on impact. The explosion was so violent it completely obliterated the car and the chauffeur. The concussive blast rocked the foundations of the Temple of Allah and rattled windowpanes up and down the boulevard. The concussion also knocked down the man who'd fired the projectile.

Amazed by the force of the blast, he got shakily to his feet. Snatching off the cap and ragged coat, he yanked his helmet from the canvas sack, put it on, and started for the front of the temple.

CHAPTER 12

APRIL 17, 1991
9:30 A.M.

The peddler sold socks off a card table. He moved from place to place along the business strips intersecting the boulevard and peddled his wares for anywhere from a dollar to three dollars. Basically, he was harmless, but in this ward the alderman demanded a cut of the action. To get the appropriate telephone call to the License Bureau in City Hall cost two hundred dollars. The peddler didn't have two hundred dollars and the alderman didn't take IOUs, give credit, or allow constituents to pay on the installment plan. So, as the slick-looking ward committeeman wearing the lavender suit looked on, Jerry Brick wrote the peddler a citation.

Brick tore the citation from the book and handed it over. The peddler took it and looked sadly at the two officers before beginning to pick up his merchandise and card table. The ward committeeman waited until the peddler walked away before saying, "The alderman's real interested in keeping these guys off the street. He wants you to chase them any time you see them."

Kessler looked hard at the wormy little man. "Suppose they have licenses?"

"Well, then," the committeeman chuckled. "If they have a license, they're legal. We're just interested in those who violate the law."

"Ha!" Kessler took an aggressive step toward the committeeman, forcing him to back up. "Wouldn't you call extortion breaking the law, or do you politicians have another name for it now?"

"Ralph!" Brick warned.

"Now see here . . ." The committeeman never got the chance to finish his protest, as the roar of an explosion swept through the neighborhood.

"What in the name of God?!" Kessler said.

"Something sure as hell blew up," Brick said. "Sounded like an ammo dump exploding."

"Let's go." Kessler headed for the car followed by Brick. The committeeman remained rooted to the sidewalk.

"It came from the northeast," Brick said once they were rolling.

Kessler came to an intersection and turned north. They were driving along the boulevard toward the Temple of Allah.

"There!" Brick said, pointing down the block to where the still-burning shell of the Cadillac rested on its rims.

Kessler was opening his mouth to speak when the temple exploded. The concussion rocked the police car, making him lose control. The car bounced up onto the parkway, sideswiping a tree before coming to rest with the front wheels hanging over the curb in the opposite lane. A black van was parked directly in front of it.

"Are you okay?" Kessler asked his partner. Brick nodded.

The two cops got out of the car. They stared at what had once been the Temple of Allah. It was now nothing but a flaming pile of debris. Heat and burning pieces of ash drifted through the air, giving the scene a hellish, surrealistic appearance. They were attempting to figure out what could have happened when they saw movement coming from inside the wall of flame.

Initially, it looked like no more than a distortion of the atmosphere caused by heat from the fire. However, it possessed a regular silhouette. They were able to identify the shape as something two-legged moving in their direction.

"What in the hell is that?" Kessler whispered in a voice choked with fear.

Brick opened his mouth to answer, but no sound came out.

The man stood unscathed inside the wall of flame. His helmet, suit, gun belt, and cloth sack were not affected by the conflagration raging around him. This was due to an anti-thermal spray called CS-12, which had been developed at Astrolab. It enabled anything that it was sprayed on to withstand incendiary temperatures. However, it would only do so for 180 seconds.

Sgt. Bryce Carduci had warned the man when he'd sold him the spray, which had to be kept in a metal refrigerated container. "This stuff is pretty good, but I wouldn't trust it for more than ninety seconds. Two minutes at the most. If you're exposed to fire longer than that, you might end up with your ass burned off."

The wall of flame made it impossible for the man to see, so to insure that he didn't stay exposed to the heat for too long he had an audio, computerized timer installed in his helmet. It counted off the seconds in five-second increments. Now, it recited in a mechanical voice, "One minute . . . one minute and ten seconds . . . one minute and fifteen seconds . . ."

After disposing of the chauffeur, the man had rushed over

to the front wall of the temple. He removed two of the square devices from his sack and placed them flush against the wall of the building. They stuck there because of an adhesive strip on the back of each. He'd pushed buttons on them to start the countdown to detonation. The first one was timed to go off in fifteen seconds; the second in five seconds.

Carduci had told him a thing or two about these devices as well. "They're compact thermal bombs. Look like something out of a James Bond movie, but once they ignite they'll start a blaze going that'll consume everything within fifty yards of it. Now if you use the CS-12 spray, you'll be all right for a minute or so, but if I was you I'd hit the deck when they go off. They detonate with more of a hiss than a bang, but you gotta watch things like gas mains and other explosive stuff going up."

It was the gas main servicing the temple that had been responsible for the second explosion that had rocked the Washington Park Boulevard area. However, this explosion had blown up and out, leaving the man in black, who was lying on the ground, unharmed.

"One minute and thirty seconds . . . one minute and thirty-five seconds . . ."

He got to his feet and walked through the wall of flame. The black suit, protected by the CS-12 anti-thermal spray, was not even emitting smoke. He paused for a moment to glance back at his handiwork. Astrolab's hardware had done the job well. Now was the time for him to return to the van and make his escape.

He stepped into the street and was about to cross to the parkway when he saw the two cops.

"It looks like a man," Brick said.

"Let's get out of here." Kessler started back toward the police car. "Something is very wrong with this, Jerry."

"Ralph, look!" Brick shouted, but Kessler had already turned to run.

Without hesitating the assassin pulled the Python and fired at Brick. The bullet struck him in the center of the forehead. The cop's expression changed from awestruck to terrified in the millisecond before he died. Brick's head exploded in a pink haze.

Kessler had almost reached the police car. With arm extended, the assassin adjusted his aim and sighted in on the small of the fugitive's back. He didn't aim for chest shots, because most cops wore safety vests. Again, he squeezed the trigger.

The Magnum round shattered the base of Kessler's spine. Screaming, he was thrown forward to slam against the side of the car with such force that he cracked one of the windows. He fell to the ground, writhing in pain. He lost control of his body from the waist down.

The assassin walked over to Brick. The head shot had torn away most of his skull, but the killer was taking no chances. He fired another round into the cop's face. Then he hurried toward Kessler.

The big cop was lying on his back with his feet under the squad car. He mumbled rapidly in a pain-filled voice, "Please help me, God. Please help me, God."

The assassin stood over him. The black helmet and large gun terrified the policeman. Like a wraith from hell, the man in black had materialized out of the flames of what was left of the Temple of Allah. The cop tried to beg for mercy. The assassin silenced him with a bullet through the head.

The man in black walked away from Kessler toward the van. Through the visor he could see people emerging up and down the block to investigate the explosions and gun shots. The numbers increased rapidly and gawkers were crowding the sidewalks and front porches of the tenements.

The assassin crossed the boulevard and reached his van

when someone shouted, "That's him! That's the one who did it!"

A short black woman screamed, "He killed those two cops! You know they gonna come down here jumping on everybody if we don't get him!"

A burly man with huge arms and a gut hanging over his belt started walking rapidly toward the assassin. Others followed.

The assassin turned and faced them. For a moment his appearance made them hesitate. Then a thin man shouted, "What're you people waiting for? Get him!" The crowd broke into a run toward the assassin.

The man in black knew he only had two rounds left in the Python, but that wasn't a concern. He slipped a speed-loader into his free hand and raised the revolver with the other. He shot the burly man in the throat. The bullet went completely through his body to strike a balding man behind him in the chest. Quickly, the assassin picked another target and fired. A gangly young man with corn-rowed hair bent double as the bullet tore through his stomach. Without waiting for a reaction, the assassin ejected the spent rounds and reloaded. In seconds he leveled the Python again and opened fire. Bodies dropped on the boulevard as the mob fled. The assassin took aim at the skinny man who had incited the crowd against him. He was running down the street, looking back over his shoulder while keeping the short, fat woman between them. The assassin shot her in the back of the head to get her out of the line of fire and then killed the man with a bullet between the shoulder blades.

The assassin was about to reload again when sirens echoed off in the distance. He dropped in a fresh speed-loader before scrambling inside the van.

Now the boulevard was deserted except for the dead. The survivors were ghetto dwellers. They wouldn't be hanging around to take license-plate numbers after the shooting. There were no license plates on the van anyway. He drove down the block at a good clip, but not recklessly. He kept going to the first red light. The cross-street would take him back to Lake Shore Drive. He quickly went over his list of options in case he was stopped by the police.

A marked car with blue lights twirling and siren blaring crossed the intersection and made a right turn onto the boulevard. An instant later the assassin's light changed and he made a left turn. He waited for the light on the east side of the boulevard to change. The thirty-second interval seemed to take forever. Before he could move, two more police cars screamed past him.

He turned on a police scanner preset to the frequency Twenty-first District police units operated on. He kept his hands gripped tightly on the steering wheel as he listened.

A flurry of vocal activity choked the channel for the next few minutes. Ambulances were ordered and backup units put in place. The investigation slowly began taking shape.

The assassin passed under McCormick Place at Twenty-second Street as a description of a possible wanted offender was broadcast over the police radio.

"Wanted for the murder of two police officers. A dark-colored van, license number unknown. There are two possibilities as far as the description of the driver. One is a muscular black man wearing a dark hat and clothing. The other is a man wearing a motorcycle helmet, who was also clad in dark clothing. The offender is armed and believed to be extremely dangerous."

Still clad in his helmet, the assassin laughed. He glanced at his watch. It was exactly 9:35 A.M. "A black man wearing a dark hat," he said out loud. Then he began laughing louder. He laughed for a long time.

CHAPTER 13

APRIL 17, 1991
10:10 A.M.

A three-ring circus would have attracted less attention to the boulevard in front of the wreckage of the former Temple of Allah. Twenty-two police vehicles clogged the streets on both sides of the parkway, forcing traffic to be rerouted. Television minicam vans from all the major stations had mixed themselves into the jam of police cars before the streets were closed. Now their crews, dragging cables across the crime scene, attempted valiantly to obtain interviews from any cop who would stand still long enough to permit a microphone to be shoved in his or her face.

But no spectacle would be complete without spectators. In this regard the event qualified as a success. People lined the sidewalks on both sides of the boulevard. They strained all the way up to the yellow barrier tapes designating three areas of the boulevard as crime scenes. One such designation was the heap of smoldering ash, which was all that remained of the Temple of Allah. Another was the thirty-foot stretch of barren ground on the parkway island where the bodies of Officers Kessler and Brick were found. The last was the sidewalk opposite the temple, where six people had been shot to death.

Sgt. Blackie Silvestri stood in the middle of the parkway. He had a cigar stuck in the corner of his mouth and a frown of supreme annoyance plastered on his face. The official investigation was going nowhere fast, and with each passing second, things got progressively worse.

Blackie had a receding hairline and a dark-jowled face. He could be considered handsome in a strictly masculine manner characterized by screen personalities such as Anthony Quinn and Sean Connery. At the age of fifty-three his affection for pasta and a few beers after work had settled in his middle, but he was still capable of cracking the skulls of street punks half his age.

Lou Bronson and Manny Sherlock crossed the parkway toward him. Between them they escorted a seedy-looking black man. Blackie waited for them without changing the position of his cigar or the ferocity of his scowl.

"This is Tom Patterson, Sarge," Bronson said. "Claims he saw our assassin before the fireworks started."

Silvestri stared at the witness. "Bum" was written all over him. He hadn't shaved in a week, his coat could probably defeat a delousing attack, and he smelled as if he'd been pickled in a vat of muscatel. But those things didn't matter. If Bronson thought he was reliable enough to bring in, he had to have something to offer.

"Take him into the station and get a formal statement, Lou. It doesn't look like we'll get much more from this place anyway."

"Manny, take our friend to the car," Bronson said. "I'll be along in a minute."

Although he looked far from happy about having to put the wino in the back of their nice new Chevy, Sherlock did what his partner instructed.

"We're having a problem with witness statements, Sarge," Bronson said. "No one saw our perpetrator until he opened fire on Kessler and Brick."

Blackie nodded and listened. He had found, during the

years he had been a cop, it was always best to listen first. There was always plenty of time to talk later. "That is, no one except Mr. Patterson. He saw the perpetrator get out of the van before the fireworks started. Then no one saw him again until Kessler and Brick went down."

Blackie looked around the area. The number of witnesses who had actually seen the killer was limited, due to most of them being dead. Blackie could only hope that one of the ones still walking around would remember seeing him later. But a lack of witnesses at this point didn't seem to be what Bronson was getting at.

"What's on your mind, Lou?"

Bronson turned and stared off down the parkway. "It's the two cops who were shot, Sarge. Brick got his in the head and face. Kessler caught one in the back—it looks like he was shot while running away. It was as if something frightened him, and that doesn't sound like Ralph Kessler."

Although Blackie didn't buy it completely, he said, "Cops can get scared just like anyone else."

"I don't think so, Sarge. You been in Area One now what, five years?"

Blackie nodded.

"You never heard of Ralph Kessler before?"

"No."

Bronson slipped off his cap and scratched his receding hairline. "Kessler used to lead the department in brutality complaints. Was so trigger-happy a few years ago, a lot of cops were afraid to even back him up on calls because they might get shot in the bargain. He's had four sustained findings of brutality. Been to the department shrink twice and up for separation both times. The police board gave him a break, so he stayed on the job."

"So he was a bad cop, Lou," Blackie said patiently. "That doesn't mean somebody couldn't get the drop on him. Bad cops are prone to make more mistakes than usual anyway."

"Not Kessler. He wouldn't have run from anyone unless something strange happened out here."

"Something strange, like what?"

"I don't know, Sarge, but give Manny and me some time and we'll find out."

CHAPTER 14

APRIL 17, 1991
10:15 A.M.

Comdr. Larry Cole was having a bad morning as he drove toward the Washington Park Boulevard crime scene. He could see the smoke cloud above the Temple of Allah from a mile away. As he got closer to the area, the already-overcast day darkened to an eerie pretwilight haze from the heavy accumulation of smoke and ash in the air. The acrid burning smell intensified to the point that it began irritating his eyes and throat.

Cole was forced to leave his car a block from the crime scene and proceed on foot. He could see the Mobile Command Vehicle, referred to as the MCV, parked on the boulevard. First Deputy Superintendent Ray Schmidt was on the scene. Whenever he left headquarters to go out into the field, he used the GMC motor home.

The MCV was painted in the same blue and white colors with identifying logos as Chicago Police squad cars. It also had Mars lights affixed to the roof and was equipped with a siren. The interior of the motor home had not been altered from the original, factory-equipped GMC recreational vehicle that had rolled off a Detroit assembly line in 1987.

Cole knew that he would have to check in with Schmidt—whose nickname in the department was Captain Bluto because of his pronounced resemblance to the nemesis of Popeye the Sailor—but first he'd have to be briefed by Blackie Silvestri.

As Cole approached Blackie—who was still standing on the parkway—the wind shifted, causing the smoke shrouding the area to dissipate. The sun peeked through high-altitude clouds and the temperature rose. The on-scene investigation at the former Temple of Allah was winding down. Most of the police cars had returned to their normal duty and the remaining fire truck present was parked on the vacant lot north of the former temple. A steady stream of water spewed from a hose onto the still-smoldering debris.

"What have we got so far on this thing, Blackie?"

"Bronson and Sherlock took a witness into the station just before you arrived, boss. This old wino is the only one we can find who actually saw our offender before the explosions."

"We have any motive or suspects?"

Blackie shrugged. "Abdul Ali Malik and company weren't popular with a lot of folks, including us. But whoever torched the place used state-of-the-art explosives. The perpetrator didn't intend for Abdul or any of his boys to walk away."

"What about the two dead officers?"

"I'm still working on that one, but Lou Bronson's got some ideas. I want to talk to him again before we lay it all out."

"Stay on top of this, Blackie," Cole said. "I want daily reports on what you find."

"What do you think went down here, boss?" Blackie asked.

Cole took a moment to study the steaming mound of ash the fire truck was still dousing. "I don't know, but somehow I've got the feeling that there's more to this than what we can see at this point. I'd be willing to bet that whoever did this has something else planned."

"Well, I can tell what you've got planned next," Blackie said, firing up his cigar.

"What?"

"An interview with 'Channel Six On-the-Scene News.' "

Cole turned to see a minicam crew, led by one of the city's more aggressive female reporters, heading straight for him.

"Why didn't they go and talk to Schmidt?" Cole said.

"They wanted to interview someone who would know what they were talking about."

Blackie walked away, leaving Cole to the press.

CHAPTER 15

APRIL 17, 1991
11:11 A.M.

First Deputy Superintendent Raymond Schmidt got out of the chauffeured MCV in front of police headquarters at Eleventh and State. He boarded the first available elevator and rode up to the sixth floor. He walked into his outer office and passed the police officers and civilians working on the various tasks it took to run the largest bureau of the Chicago Police Department.

As he passed his administrative lieutenant's cubicle, he struck his head in the door and said, "Pat, I need to see you."

Lt. Pat Roberts grabbed a steno pad and pencil before following Schmidt into the first deputy's private corner office.

Lt. Patrick Michael Roberts was a small man with bland features and a balding head. He had spent four years in a seminary before opting for the secular life. He married and promptly sired seven children. Between offspring one and three, he became a police officer. By the time the seventh came screaming into the world, he had risen to the rank of Lieutenant Roberts had spent very little of his career on the street. His typing and bookkeeping skills, learned as a minor to his theological studies, made him a permanent desk-officer. When Schmidt had become first deputy, he had looked for someone who could keep him on an even keel administratively; Roberts had proven to be the man.

The lieutenant entered the first deputy's office and closed the door. Schmidt had taken a seat behind his cluttered desk. The lieutenant carefully affixed his eyes on a spot just below the second button of the first deputy's shirt. He was not afraid of Schmidt. Submission was simply Roberts's way.

First Deputy Raymond Anthony Schmidt was a man of meager intelligence and limited social skills. He was cunning, however, and could be as devious as the criminals he'd hunted for most of his adult life. Schmidt was chronically paranoid, and believed that half the officers on the force were goofing off while the other half were engaged in acts of covert corruption. He was also a closet racist—that is, he was openly fair toward blacks, Hispanics, other minorities, and women, but secretly believed that white males were genetically superior and therefore made the best cops.

Now, Schmidt had a certain detective commander named Cole on his mind. But first things first. Although he trusted Roberts to an extent, he didn't want to let on what he was really up to.

"We're not getting anywhere fast on what happened to Kessler and Brick."

"From all indications, sir," the lieutenant said, "they were not the target of the attack, but merely innocent bystanders. Abdul Ali Malik and his gang were who the offender or offenders were obviously after."

"Hmmm," Schmidt said, leaning back in his chair and rubbing his fingers across his perpetual five-o'clock shadow. "Then maybe we should give the case to Gang Crimes." The commander of the Gang Crimes Unit was Dan Sullivan, who was a personal friend of Schmidt's.

"Begging the first deputy's pardon, but we can't do that."

Schmidt glared at Roberts.

The lieutenant did not flinch. "The investigative responsibility for the Temple of Allah rests with Commander Cole of Area One Detectives."

There was silence in the office for a time, and then Schmidt said, "What do we have on Cole?"

Roberts closed his notebook. He had an excellent memory and made it his business to learn the ins and outs of the headquarters building along with collecting any gossip drifting around about the current command staff. Generally, he kept his discoveries to himself until Schmidt asked for specifics.

"He's been on the job for about twenty years, sir. Worked the tactical unit in the old Nineteenth District for a while. Made a reputation for himself by killing Frankie Arcadio, Paul Arcadio's nephew, and arresting the top Arcadio family enforcer Sal Marino on the same day."

"That was Cole, huh?" This information did not sit well with Schmidt.

"Yes, sir. Won the Blue Star Award and the Medal of Valor. Cole got Marino in the apartment where he killed former Chief of Detectives John T. Ryan."

Schmidt groaned. It was all coming back to him. "Go ahead."

"Well, after Riseman became chief, he pushed for Cole to receive a meritorious appointment to detective. There's not much else except that he made sergeant, lieutenant, captain, and commander under Chief Riseman in the Detective Division. Riseman's his clout, but the last three superintendents, including our current one, have openly praised Cole's work to the press."

"What about his private life?"

"He's married with one child, but the rumor mill has it that he and his wife are separated."

"Does he drink, gamble, chase women?"

"There's nothing going around about him in that regard. He has a narrow circle of friends, I've been told: his case management sergeant, Blackie Silvestri, and some of the detectives under his command."

"Anything else?"

"Not that I can recall, sir."

"Okay, keep your ear to the rail on Cole. Anything interesting comes up, you let me know."

"Yes, sir. You do remember your luncheon appointment at the Press Club? It's at noon."

Schmidt frowned. "It's with that guy who gave a million bucks to the Cops for Education campaign."

"Yes, sir," Roberts said. "If you'd like I can call and cancel it for you."

"No. I'm going. Who else is supposed to be there?"

Roberts recited, "Deputy Superintendent Baldwin, Chief Racozzi, Chief DeStefano, and Chief Riseman are some of the command officers who were invited."

"Riseman will be there, huh?" Again Schmidt rubbed his chin.

"Yes, sir,"

"Get him on the phone for me. I think I'll offer him a ride."

CHAPTER 16

APRIL 17, 1991
NOON

Schmidt and Riseman were dropped off in front of the canopied entrance to the Press Club. They crossed the sidewalk and entered the lobby, which was wood-paneled and lined with the portraits of men who had made their marks in the newspaper publishing business in Chicago. No women were represented. In fact, prior to 1979 and the election of the first female mayor in the city's history, women were not allowed in the club.

"May I help you, gentlemen?" a stern-faced male receptionist in a black tuxedo said by way of greeting.

"Yeah," Schmidt snarled. "We're Mr. Zalkin's guests."

The receptionist gave him a tolerant smile. "Of course, sir. Mr. Zalkin's party is in the Hemingway Room on level two. If you'd like, I will get a page to escort you."

"We'll find our way, pal," Schmidt said. "Save the help for someone who needs it."

Riseman silently followed Schmidt to the elevators.

When they were out of earshot, the receptionist said, "Fucking heathen!"

The second-floor dining room was elegantly appointed with antique furniture, Oriental rugs, white-linen table-cloths, and sterling silverware. Waiters carrying trays of food hustled back and forth between a large buffet table and the seated guests. A maître d' clone of the receptionist downstairs met Schmidt and Riseman and said, "Mr. Zalkin is waiting for you gentlemen."

As they followed him across the room, Schmidt asked, "How'd he know we was with Zalkin?"

"Must be ESP," Riseman said, deadpan.

Steven Zalkin's table was set for eight. The other guests were already seated. Going clockwise from the two empty seats for the latecomers, there was: Edward Baldwin, Deputy Superintendent of the Bureau of Community Services; Phillip Racozzi, Deputy Chief of Patrol Division Administration; Franklin Lewis, Deputy Chief of the Organized Crime Division; Thomas Flaherty, Commander of the Finance Division; John DeStefano, Chief of the Patrol Division; and their host, Steven Zalkin.

Zalkin stood as his final luncheon guests approached. "How are you, First Deputy?" he said, extending his hand.

Schmidt took Zalkin's hand in his own paw and squeezed until his host winced.

"Wow," Zalkin said, rubbing the spot where Schmidt had crushed a gold signet ring between two of his fingers, "You ever cracked coconuts with those hands?"

Schmidt laughed. He enjoyed these periodic shows of strength, which at one time or another he had practiced on everyone present. He might not be the smartest guy invited to lunch today, but he was sure the strongest. He also out-ranked the rest of them. He studied Zalkin for any signs of annoyance over having his hand crunched, but the kid had a pretty good grip of his own and had taken the bone-crusher in stride.

Riseman stood by until Schmidt's act was over. Then he stepped forward and said, "Bill Riseman, Steve. It's nice to meet you."

"Yes," Zalkin said. "You're the chief of detectives. This is a real honor for me. I've been following your cases for years."

"Yeah," Schmidt said, plopping down in one of the upholstered chairs. "Bill's been chief of dicks since old John Ryan got axed . . . what was that, guys? Fourteen, fifteen years ago? Hell, I was just a patrol sergeant working out of the old Wood Street station back then."

Zalkin indicated the chair next to his own for Riseman. "Something to drink, gentlemen?"

Riseman ordered white wine, Schmidt a double bourbon on the rocks with a beer chaser.

When everyone was settled, Zalkin said, "I don't want to keep you from your jobs any longer than necessary, but having lunch with you was the only recompense I asked for my contribution to the Cops for Education campaign."

In unison, the cops present smiled. They were there by force, not choice. Zalkin's contribution of one million dollars demanded this.

If the Press Club could boast of nothing else, it could say with a degree of certainty that the food rivaled the best in the city. The menu was small, but the items on it fresh and prepared to a certifiable perfection by the chef.

Zalkin ordered for them and they enjoyed one of the best lunches in memory. Riseman was finishing a cut of chilled salmon, which was the most delicious fish he had ever eaten. Then his cop instincts began acting up.

Zalkin was talking to Chief DeStefano. "What would you say is the biggest problem facing the Chicago Police Department today?"

DeStefano wiped his mouth with a white napkin and began the textbook answer. It generally went drugs, street crime, lack of public involvement, and lack of resources. Riseman had thirty-five years of service with the department and had never known those issues to change substantially. They were always there and cops learned to deal with them as best they could.

But to Riseman, Zalkin's questions during lunch did not seem like simple civilian inquisitiveness. The millionaire was looking for specifics.

"Well, I guess that phony Temple of Allah operation being blown up this morning takes quite a load off of you guys' minds," Zalkin said. There were a few nods of agreement around the table. "Somebody did the department a favor after that raid failed last year."

"It didn't fail!" Schmidt snapped. He was halfway through a thick porterhouse steak and had not said a word since he started eating. But the raid on the Temple of Allah had been his operation. And as Zalkin had said, despite Schmidt's protestations to the contrary, it had failed miserably.

As Schmidt began defending the aborted raid, Riseman studied their host. There was money there. A great deal of money. Hair styled, perpetual tan, tailor-made clothing, gold Rolex. He was young—at least by Riseman's standards. Not a day over forty. Seemed smart enough, but nobody knew where his money came from. The city didn't care, as long as Zalkin wasn't a criminal and his name had checked clear of all warrants both local and federal.

So, Riseman thought, we took his million dollars and agreed to come here and play in this little sideshow as payment.

"Abdul Malik's real name was Richard Kenneth Johnson," Chief Lewis said. "Was nothing but a small-time pusher and local fence before he got hooked up with the Satan's Saints street gang. Was known as Slick Rick Johnson before he hung on the Abdul Ali Malik moniker. Got to give it to him though—he was smart enough to turn that bunch of street punks into a bona fide criminal organization. Somehow he got involved with both the Cuban and Mexican narcotics connections. Rumor had it the Mafia was scared of him. Of course, I wouldn't be surprised if they're the ones who had him hit."

"Old Rabbit Arcadio's not afraid of a punk like Johnson," Deputy Chief Racozzi said. "But the Rabbit was never the same after a couple of Bill's boys put his organization through some changes a few years back."

"I don't think the Mafia was involved at all," Zalkin said. "This was much too sophisticated. It sounded more like a commando raid. A military-type operation. Very precise. Very well-organized."

More than one wary glance was exchanged around the table. Riseman didn't know whether Zalkin's popping-off was arrogance or simply civilian stupidity. However, he did have to admit that the millionaire had a point about the military-operation part.

The cops had little to say for the rest of the luncheon.

CHAPTER 17

APRIL 17, 1991
12:25 P.M.

Francis Xavier "Frank" Delahanty was drinking his lunch. He was in the Bard's Tap on the second floor of the Press Club. His third martini with four olives rested at his elbow. His worn notebook, with the initials *FXD* in gold leaf on the cover, was open in front of him on the bar.

He was scribbling ideas for Friday's column, but so far nothing worked.

Delahanty sipped his martini. When he placed the glass back on the bar he noticed with some annoyance that it was half-empty. He was watching his daylight consumption of liquor, so he planned to stop at three. But then he didn't *feel* anything. A good martini was supposed to be like a cloud in a glass that tickled the palate and, if properly handled, sharpened the wit. Who had said that? He remembered that he had—in his August 4, 1990 column. The one that had gotten him all that mail from AA members and teetotalers. He printed most of their letters in his August 11 column, and did he have a ball with them.

Recalling those columns made him feel good. He smiled, reached out, and polished off the rest of his martini. There goes number three. He raised his hand for the bartender.

"Another one, Mr. Delahanty?" The bartender stood six-foot-five and towered over the seated columnist. Delahanty didn't like people who towered over him.

"Why not," he said.

The bartender began mixing another double vodka martini.

When it was served, Delahanty took a sip. He could taste the vodka, which was a bad sign. That meant he was getting stiff, and he didn't want to get stiff. At least, not until he had Friday's column written. But he hadn't the slightest idea what to write about.

Frank Delahanty was a celebrity in Chicago journalism circles. He had won a Pulitzer Prize for his column when he was at the *Tribune*, and his work was studied in journalism schools nationally. He was said to be one of the sharper wits in the newspaper-column field. He was a celebrity, but he had his problems.

Delahanty was an alcoholic. He knew he was an alcoholic, but he wasn't going to do anything about it. He drank because he liked to drink. He drank when he got out of bed in the morning, he drank periodically during the day, and he drank continuously after the sun went down. He had lost two wives, two jobs, and a driver's license over his drinking, but he didn't intend to stop. Booze meant more than anything else in the world to him except his writing, and he wrote better when he was drunk. At least, he thought so, and there wasn't an editor alive with the nerve to touch a Delahanty column.

"What?" The columnist was startled out of his stupor to find the bartender standing over him.

The bartender emptied the last of the liquor from the martini shaker into his glass. Delahanty knew his drinking well enough to realize that he was entering his belligerent stage. He had gotten a lot of ass-whippings while passing through this stage of inebriation. That is, before he became Frank Delahanty, syndicated columnist.

The bartender graced him with a smile and moved down the bar to wait on someone else. Delahanty stared at the full martini glass. This was his fourth, and it wouldn't be dark for hours. He tried to concentrate on his notes, but none of what he had written made any sense. He was also starting to get that bloated, sick feeling that generally didn't occur until he was ready for bed.

I'm shit-faced, he admitted to himself.

The bartender was again standing in front of him. "Would you like another, Mr. Delahanty?"

Five martinis in what, half an hour? Maybe he should write a column suggesting that they add martini-drinking to the Olympic Games.

Ignoring the bartender, he stood up. He would now have to do something he hadn't done since he was in the navy. He was going to eat to sober himself up. He'd probably puke it all back up later, but by then he'd be half-sober. Or should he consider himself half-drunk?

He slapped the empty glass back on the bar and said to

the bartender, "Put it on my tab." There was a slight slur to his speech, but he didn't think it was that bad. He always sounded like that after he had five martinis for—he corrected himself—*before* lunch.

Delahanty made his way slowly, but steadily, to the Hemingway Room.

"Good afternoon, Mr. Delahanty," the maître d' said. "Table for one?"

He managed a nod.

"Right this way, sir."

As the maître d' led him across the room, Delahanty followed and kept his eyes fixed on the bald spot on top of his escort's head. He didn't notice Zalkin or his guests as he passed their table. A few "Hiya, Franks" came from other tables, but he didn't acknowledge anyone.

The table the maître d' gave him was set for four and too far out in the middle of the room for Delahanty's tastes. All he wanted was a bowl of chili and an Alka-Seltzer. Maybe a Heineken if the chili was really hot.

"Would you like a menu, sir?" a waiter said, hovering over the columnist.

"You got chili?"

"Chili, sir?"

The little prick of a glorified hash slinger looks offended. "Yeah. Beans, meat, and peppers. Mix it together and have a Mexican girl piss in it and there you have it. Chili!"

Delahanty's voice rose and a number of heads turned in his direction. The waiter looked around nervously before smiling and saying, "We have Hungarian goulash on the menu today, sir. But no chili."

"Okay, *garçon*, bring on the stew and a Heineken and be quick about it, because I've got a column to write."

"Yes, sir," the waiter said, hurrying away.

A glass of water was set in front of him. The silverware and napkins were removed from the other place settings. A green beer bottle and chilled glass were placed in front of him. Finally, the columnist snapped out of his trance.

Delahanty's mind had gone blank, which happened from time to time, but he was okay now. It was like being asleep with your eyes open. In fact, he felt as if he had just awakened. He was a bit groggy and it took him a moment to remember where he was and why he was here. The bottle of beer on the table in front of him brought it all back.

He finished the beer before the waiter set the goulash and a basket of hot bread down in front of him. He ordered another beer and tasted the goulash. It was good, but he wasn't hungry. He tried the bread. It was good, too, but he would have preferred peanuts or pretzels.

The second beer came and he left the bread alone. As he gulped beer he looked around. The place was crowded because it was the lunch hour, but some of the diners were starting to trickle out. He hadn't paid any attention to the people who had spoken to him when he walked in. But he never did. However, no one except the maître d' and the waiter had approached the table since he sat down. He was alone in a room full of people. Moreover, he was alone in a room full of fellow journalists.

He was Francis Xavier Delahanty—senior columnist for the *Chicago Times-Herald*. He was a Pulitzer Prize winner; a best-selling author. A man whose words were read by millions of people, six days a week, forty-seven weeks a year. But nobody here cared. He was in the Chicago Press Club in downtown Chicago and no one was paying him the slightest attention.

He felt like standing up and screaming his name. He felt like taking the empty beer bottle and hurling it against the wall. He felt like writing a column about the insensitivity of the Chicago media. A column that would stand this town on its collective ear. He would tell how the press, with the exception of his own exalted personage, were nothing more than a bunch of whorish vultures, who invaded privacy for the sake of a few lousy lines in the morning edition. He would tell—

"Mr. Delahanty?"

The columnist snapped out of his angry contemplation with a start. He looked up at the man standing at his table.

"I wonder if I could talk to you a minute?"

Delahanty sized up the newcomer. *Nice dresser, styled hair, lots of money there, but he didn't earn it. Limited education from his speech patterns and too damned flashy. Wears as much gold on his wrists as a black pimp with a stable of white whores.*

Delahanty liked that line. He pulled his notebook out and jotted it down while the man watched.

"Mr. Delahanty, my name is Steven Zalkin and I've got a story you might be interested in."

Oh, sweet Jesus, not another asshole with a story. Everyone had a story for his column. Everybody wanted to tell him what to write.

"May I sit down?" Zalkin asked, taking the seat across from the columnist before he could respond.

The waiter came over and asked if he could bring Zalkin anything. Delahanty ordered another beer. Zalkin declined and told the waiter to put the columnist's beer on his tab. In Delahanty's book, that rated him two minutes.

"You a journalist?" Delahanty's words came out without a slur now. His voice was gravelly, but he had hit an alcoholic tolerance plateau that he could maintain for hours. That is, if he continued to drink.

"No," Zalkin said. "Why do you ask?"

"Because this is the frigging Chicago frigging Press Club, lad."

"Oh, that," Zalkin said, laughing. "I'm an associate member."

Delahanty's beer came and he took a long pull before saying, "Isn't that expensive?"

"Costs a thousand dollars a year."

He has a lot of money, but he's not used to it. Said "Costs a thousand dollars a year" like he was talking about winning the Congressional Medal of Honor. Bought his way in. Everything's for sale these days.

A column idea loomed in Delahanty's mind.

"Well, the idea I had," Zalkin continued, "concerns my luncheon guests over there." He indicated the table behind them. Delahanty was surprised when he saw the men seated there. He knew all of them from stories run in the *Times-Herald.*

"You an associate cop, too?"

Zalkin laughed again. It was a forced laugh, which was another item of information Frank Delahanty filed away about his table companion.

"No, but I do admit that I support the police. I gave them a million dollars for the Cops for Education campaign."

"I'm impressed," Delahanty said, but his mind was racing in a completely different direction.

"These guys are doing a helluva job in this town, Frank. They've got dope dealers, mad-dog killers, and all manner of psychos running around out there, yet they still manage to hold the line."

Delahanty looked from Zalkin to the table of cops. "Is that why they can enjoy two-hour lunches with you?"

Zalkin looked surprised. "Their coming to have lunch with me was part of the deal I made with the superintendent for giving the department the money. They deserve a break."

"Tell me," Delahanty said, while scribbling furiously in his notebook, "you ever take any crooks to lunch?"

Zalkin's face darkened. For an instant there was a glint of fury behind those blue eyes. A look of insane fury, which died suddenly.

"I was hoping you could see the importance of what I was trying to say, Frank."

"You said your name was Steve, right?"

Zalkin nodded.

"Well, let me tell you something, Steve. You bought me a beer so that entitled you to bend my ear for a couple of minutes with your bullshit. You're about a minute over the limit now. As far as your flat-footed friends over there go, all I see them doing is goofing off on the taxpayers' time with an overdressed jerk who's trying to buy his way into polite society. So why don't you trot your ass back over there and leave what I put in my column to me?"

This had been one of Delahanty's best put-down speeches in years. He hadn't been this good since the time he'd made the gay movie star cry on a local late-night talk show. But Zalkin didn't cry. He didn't smile, frown, or give any indication of what was going behind those blue eyes.

"You just made everything much easier, Frank," Zalkin said.

"What in the hell is that supposed to mean?" But Zalkin had already gotten up from the table and was walking away.

He called over his shoulder back at the columnist, "Have a nice day, Frank."

That son of a bitch ain't right. Delahanty stared at Zalkin as he sat back down with the cops. The columnist started making notes for Friday's column. It would be about gold-bricking policemen. Suddenly he found it difficult to hold his pen. Extending his fingers, he found that his hand was trembling. The booze? But he only had the shakes in the morning.

He turned once more to look at Zalkin's table. The man had scared him. A waterhead like that had actually frightened him. He was Francis X. Delahanty. Who was this Steven Zalkin compared to him?

He flagged the waiter and ordered a vodka martini to calm himself. He then proceeded to write Friday's column in its entirety. The subject: "Steven Zalkin and Part-Time Cops."

CHAPTER 18

Steven Zalkin drove his silver Porsche west on upper Wacker Drive away from the Loop. His luncheon guests had parted with him amiably in front of the Press Club a short time before. He had noticed that Schmidt was slightly tipsy as he got into his car. Riseman's disapproval was masked, but evident. The first deputy had proven to be everything that he was rumored to be and then some, Zalkin thought.

He crossed Wells Street a block from the alley where Sergeant First Class Bryce Carduci's body had been found that morning. The body, along with all signs of the police investigation, had long since been removed. A block farther on, he swung the car into an old but clean cobblestoned alley. He drove down the alley to a three-story factory. Using a remote control he switched off the alarm system and opened one of the overhead doors leading to the rear loading dock. After making sure that there were no prying eyes hiding anywhere in the alley, Zalkin drove inside.

As the door closed behind him he got out of the car. He had parked the Porsche beside a black van. The van bore no license plates. The windows of the overhead doors that opened onto the loading dock had been blacked over to prevent anyone from seeing inside. Resetting the alarm system, he climbed a short flight of steps to the top of the dock. Removing his wallet—which contained every gold and platinum credit card available—from his suit coat pocket, he took out a digital plastic square. He inserted it into an access slot beside a steel door. The security unit hummed softly before stopping with an abrupt click. Slowly, the door slid open.

Zalkin stepped through into a well-equipped machine shop, which had been purchased intact from the prior tenants. Drill presses, a lathe, a large electric saw, and small blast furnace occupied most of the space. A worktable against the back wall was littered with tools. Beside the table was a metal cabinet secured with a heavy combination lock.

Zalkin crossed to the cabinet and worked the combination. He swung the double doors open to reveal an arsenal inside. There was an impressive assortment of weapons—from fifty-caliber machine guns to twenty-five-caliber automatic pistols. There was a small flame-thrower and a light anti-tank weapon. There were hand grenades and timed detonators containing plastic explosive charges capable of producing the same effect as a hundred-pound TNT bomb. And there were two CS-12 anti-thermal-spray canisters. Before closing the cabinet, he removed the six-inch .357 Magnum Python from its holster and placed it on the worktable. He planned to clean it later.

Zalkin walked toward the side wall of the workroom. The wall itself was of solid brick. A levered switch protruded from a green metal case constructed into the facing. He pulled the lever down and a large section of the wall swung inward.

On the other side was a gymnasium laid out with the complete equipment for a Gold's Gym franchise. There was also a dry sauna, wet sauna, and steam room, along with cold, warm, and hot whirlpool baths. The gym could have accommodated thirty people. In fact, it only serviced one.

He crossed the gym and exited through a carved-oak door on the far side of the room. The door was an antique, which had originally been constructed without keyholes. The designer with the matchstick figure and heavy makeup that reminded him of the Joker had told him the door had once graced the Humboldt Boulevard mansion of a German meatpacker, who had lived a century ago. Back then, she had explained, there was no need for locks, as there were always servants to open doors for visitors.

On the other side of the antique door were Steven Zalkin's living quarters. He had the entire first floor to himself. Occupancy of the two floors above him was being considered by an interior-decorating firm and a temporary-employment service. However, the real estate agent Zalkin used was prohibited from showing the prospective tenants the space unless he was present, and lately he'd been too busy to be bothered.

The living space was separated by partitions into three areas. The ugly designer had clucked over every detail and charged him a fortune. He had been here more than a year and he liked it. He really could never figure out why, but he decided that it probably had something to do with the six-figure price she had charged him.

The office space contained a reception area with a couch, easy chairs, and a cocktail table. A large curved lamp hung from the ceiling to provide ample light over these furnishings. As Zalkin seldom received anyone, he seldom turned the light on.

There was also a desk with a high-back leather easy chair behind it and two comfortable armchairs in front. The lighting here was from antique reading lamps salvaged from a remodeling job at the old main branch of the

Chicago Public Library. An antique metal safe was positioned beside the desk.

Beyond the desk, against the partition wall, was a kitchen alcove with sink, refrigerator, microwave oven, and gas range. In front of the kitchen, beginning at the opposite wall, was the living room. This area contained a sectional sofa, matching armchairs, a glass cocktail table, and a console-model television in a hand-carved mahogany cabinet. A very expensive, state-of-the-art VCR-cable hookup and stereo system were also contained inside the cabinet. Surrounding the living room was a three-sided bookcase, which was filled with magazines and paperbacks arranged in a haphazard fashion.

The designer, after determining Zalkin's unique needs and total lack of taste, arranged the entire living space into one large room. In fact, Zalkin needed lots of space. This had been the only restriction he had placed on the designer. It was a strange living arrangement, almost like the various scenes in an in-the-round stage play. It was also very new. So new that the designer was able to get a full six-page spread of her work exhibited in *Decorator's Monthly*.

Zalkin picked up a remote control and turned on the television set and VCR. Taking a seat on the couch, he pressed the rewind button. He began playing the videotape he had made earlier after he had returned from his mission of destruction on Washington Park Boulevard.

The tape began playing. A plump male reporter with styled hair stood on the parkway a hundred yards south of where Zalkin had killed Kessler and Brick. The tape began partway through this segment of the broadcast.

". . . self-styled Minister Abdul Ali Malik and at least thirty of his followers were known to have been inside the building at the time of the explosions."

The tape switched to a different channel. A thin-faced woman with lank hair blowing in the breeze said, "The identity of the assassin remains a mystery; however, the police are mounting a massive manhunt for the perpetrator or perpetrators of these horribly violent crimes. . . ."

Zalkin liked that. *Violent Crimes.*

"Behind me," a pinched-faced reporter—whose horned-rimmed glasses made him look like a bad imitation of Clark Kent—was saying, "is the Chicago Police Department's mobile command vehicle. It is called the MCV. At this moment First Deputy Superintendent Raymond Schmidt is conducting a strategy session with top-ranking police brass. There are high hopes that this meeting will lead to the arrest of those responsible for the holocaust that has occurred here."

Holocaust. He liked that word, too.

Zalkin freeze-framed the shot and studied the MCV. He doubted whether anything of any merit, or rather anything that would prove to be a threat to him, would come out of there. Especially with his buddy Ray Schmidt running the show.

Zalkin started the tape running at normal speed again. The scene switched back to the thin-faced female reporter. She was standing beside a man whose appearance made the assassin stiffen. Zalkin activated the volume control and turned up the sound.

"Commander Larry Cole of Area One Detectives will be in direct command of the investigation. Commander Cole, what can you tell us about what happened here this morning?"

Zalkin closely studied the image of Cole on the screen. He hadn't seen him in a long time—years, in fact. Then the cop had been younger: not so heavy, not so gray. Zalkin wondered if Cole would recognize him after all this time had passed. Probably not. It was unlikely to the point of being impossible. No one would recognize Zalkin now.

"There are a couple of theories we're checking out about what happened here," Cole said. "We've already got officers working to see if we can piece together the events that occurred around the temple and on the boulevard after the explosion. I think we'll have it in place very soon."

"Do you think that this was the work of one man or a group of men?" the reporter asked.

"At this point I wouldn't want to speculate. I'm sure with the physical evidence and developing leads we'll have something of substance shortly."

This was the part that worried Steven Zalkin. What leads? He was aware that he had left physical evidence. There was no way that he could have engaged in such an operation and not done so. But there was nothing they could latch onto. He'd left a few shell casings, but he'd worn gloves whenever he'd handled the Python and the speed-loaders. Perhaps there was a boot print or two. But he'd purchased the boots from Carduci, who'd bought them, in turn, from an army post exchange in another state.

On the screen Cole had run out of answers and the reporter moved on to another interview. Zalkin switched off the set.

Seated in the silence of his isolated living area, Steven Zalkin stared at the blank television screen. With a fanatical assurance he realized that neither Larry Cole's police department or the God they worshipped at Our Lady of Peace Catholic Church would be able to stop him now.

CHAPTER 19

Sister Mary Louise Stallings was teaching the seventh-grade history class at Our Lady of Peace grammar school. There were thirty-five students in her class. All were black: eighteen boys and seventeen girls. They were inner-city youths who came from depressed backgrounds. Some of them were from homes where they were frequently exposed to alcoholism, drug abuse, and incest. Many of them had relatives who had been killed in gang wars or by the police. Others had relatives—fathers, brothers, sisters, and mothers—in prison.

They were a tough group. A group that could be as collectively or individually vicious as any adult. A group possessing only two things that bound them together: their respect for and allegiance to Sister Mary Louise.

"Who invented the first system of electronic traffic signals, Shirley?"

Shirley Rogers was a pretty girl with red hair. She had a razor scar across her forehead, inflicted when she was nine by a female member of a rival street gang. There was just a trace of a ghetto snarl in her speech as she answered, "Benjamin Banneker."

Sister Mary Louise stared at the student with a gaze as

sharp as the razor that had sliced her skin open. Shirley lowered her gaze to the desktop and said an almost lady-like "Benjamin Banneker, Sister Mary."

The nun would have smiled, but this would display weakness at the wrong time. These children could neither respect nor tolerate any form of weakness. In the streets they came from, being weak was fatal. However, Sister Mary Louise was not angry with Shirley. She understood that the razor cut had left more scars than the one on her forehead.

"In what city did Mr. Banneker first install his traffic lights, George?"

George Green was six feet, two inches tall and weighed three hundred pounds. At sixteen, he was the oldest member of the class. He also tried the hardest to succeed. "Washington, D.C., Sister Mary."

The bell rang. Not one student moved.

"So, you're ready for the history final on Friday," she said, closing her book. "This final will decide who takes this year's first, second, and third place scholarship medals for the seventh grade."

They stirred. An anticipation ran through them, charging the atmosphere of the classroom. Fourteen of them were in contention for the top academic honors given each year to classes at Our Lady of Peace. This was a phenomenal percentage out of any one class. But then they had a phenomenal teacher.

"I suggest that you leave the TVs off tonight and hit those books." She paused. "Class dismissed."

They rose quietly and went out the door in single-file order. They did not talk until they were well out into the hall and then their voices rose barely above whispers. This was not her rule but Father Ken's. He was the principal and pastor of Our Lady of Peace. He was the architect of what *Times-Herald* columnist Frank Delahanty had proclaimed "the ghetto miracle."

After the last student filed out, Sister Mary Louise collected her books and papers and left the room. As she walked along the corridor, boys and girls went rapidly to their final class period of the day.

"I'm through for today, Sarah," Sister Mary Louise said, as she stepped in the door of the school office. "Do you need me for anything else?"

Sarah had been the school secretary since 1965. She had seen many things change at Our Lady of Peace, most of them bad, but she was still amazed at the changes for good wrought by Father Ken and the nun.

"Nah, Sister," Sarah said. "Ain't no problems I can't handle. If I need anything I'll call over to the rectory."

"I'll check back with you before time to lock up."

As Sister Mary Louise made her way out of the school she noticed how similar Our Lady of Peace was in structure and basic appearance to Saint Agnes, where she had gone to school in Kellam, Iowa. Our Lady was old, but maintained in a flawless state of perfection. The floors were varnished, the paint fresh, and the heating-and-air-conditioning system only two years old. Besides "the ghetto miracle," it was also known as "the miracle on Washington Park Boulevard." She knew that the miracle-worker was Father Kenneth Smith. Father Ken—with a lot of help from God.

Once she was outside, her habit billowed behind her as the wind blew a pleasant spring breeze across the city. It was a chilly day, but sunny now after an overcast morning. Sister Mary Louise could feel summer in the air.

She made her way along the south side of the school, which bordered on an alley. Beyond the alley was a block-long stretch of vacant lots, which now belonged to the parish. This area was slated for a youth center—one to be built by 1993. She had seen the plans and knew it would be the crowning achievement of Father Ken's career.

She detoured from the rectory toward the church. She

decided on a few minutes of prayer before her daily meeting with Father Ken.

The side door of the church facing the school was left open during the day. Except during scheduled masses, the other doors were locked to keep out thieves and derelicts. No one had stolen anything from Our Lady since Father Ken had taken over in 1981, but the pastor didn't believe in tempting fate. He could also understand the need for the homeless to seek refuge in the house of God. However, he had formalized arrangements with a halfway house in the neighborhood to provide not only shelter but food and blankets for the less fortunate. So there was no need for anyone to sleep in the church.

She blessed herself at the holy-water font and stood inside the door. The church was as big as any of the cathedrals downtown. It had been built in 1919 when the boulevard area was one of the most exclusive in the city. The ceiling paintings and sculptures of saints rivaled anything found in the Vatican. The marble and gold metal of the main altar gleamed in even the dimmest light. But what Sister Mary Louise found most impressive about the church was the silence she encountered when she was alone there.

She knelt in a pew in front of the side altar dedicated to the Blessed Virgin. She crossed herself and waited. The silence became so intense it took on a physicality of its own. Then the feeling of peace that always came, whether she was here alone or when the pews were filled to capacity on Sunday, descended on her.

She let her mind focus on the doubts and fears that haunted her. She always worried about failing the kids. They looked up to her, respected her, and in some cases even emulated her. Most of them had nothing but Our Lady of Peace. Outside these walls their lives were a hell the likes of which she couldn't even begin to imagine. Often, perhaps too often, she was afraid she couldn't measure up to their expectations. That if she revealed one weakness or one chink in her armor of perceived invincibility, they would see that she was no more than a weak, mortal woman. A weak woman whose existence was nearly as fragile and uncertain as their own.

She looked at the elaborately sculptured main altar. There was a time, back when the church was first built, that a black person would have been barred from entering this house of God. Now this place was the mainstay of a black community barely hanging on under the siege of drugs, gang violence, and fear.

She shook her head, marveling at the mysterious ways in which the Lord worked. How he had brought her to the convent and then this place was equally mysterious. Her life flashed quickly before her: good times, bad times, and that one terribly horrible time that had nearly destroyed her and had shaken her faith in the Almighty.

She felt goosebumps spread across her arms. She rubbed her flesh beneath the habit and forced the disturbing images from her mind. She composed herself in the stillness of the huge church. The feeling of peace returned once more. For a moment, she became one with it. Her strength and resolve were renewed. She roused herself and walked out.

She let herself into the rectory with her key. She passed through the kitchen, where Mrs. Turner was preparing dinner. She opened the pot and looked in.

"The spaghetti smells heavenly, Mrs. Turner."

"It's good and filling," the severe-looking woman said. "Made a pan of cornbread with it. 'Course, won't do one smidgeon of good if Father Ken and you don't eat it, Sister."

Mrs. Turner was a white-haired black woman who would never tell her age and seldom smiled. When Sister Mary Louise first arrived at Our Lady, she thought Father Ken's housekeeper simply didn't like her—that is, until she found out that the woman treated everyone in the same rigid, uncompromising fashion, including Father Ken.

"That smells good, Mrs. Turner," Father Ken said, walking into the kitchen. "Why don't you fix me and the good Sister a couple of plates with a pan of your cornbread? I think I've got a jug of red wine in the pantry, which will go real good with the spaghetti."

Sister Mary Louise and the housekeeper stared at the priest in shock. He almost never ate dinner this early, if he ate at all. They looked at each other, then back at him. He lit another Merit menthol from his Zippo lighter with the black onyx crucifix on the side. The lighter had been a gift from a parishioner this past Christmas.

Father Ken entered the walk-in pantry and began rummaging around in Mrs. Turner's neatly stacked shelves. This galvanized the housekeeper into action.

Entering the pantry, she grabbed him by the arm and pulled him back into the kitchen. Then she hurried Sister Mary Louise and Father Ken into the dining room with, "I'll find your wine for you, Father. You and Sister just make yourselves comfortable."

Ken Smith was fifty-two years old on this spring afternoon, but he could have passed for a man ten or even fifteen years younger. He was slender, but had the lean, strong muscles of a basketball player or track star. He had been outstanding in both sports at Quigley Seminary. His hair was wiry with a spreading bald spot. He usually tried to go without his glasses, but his eyes were getting worse so now he was forced to wear them almost all the time.

He possessed a medium-brown complexion with a skin texture that would wrinkle slowly, if at all. His features were regular and set in a cast that spoke accurately of the keen intelligence continuously working behind those intense brown eyes. Father Ken found it difficult to sit still very long because of the tremendous energy constantly coursing through him. In his private prayers he sometimes referred to himself as "the Lord's live wire," and every ounce of that energy, directed twenty-four hours a day, went to doing God's work. Although he didn't begrudge others their inability to keep up with him, he felt that being idle was a sin.

They sat down at the huge dining-room table. Sister Mary Louise sat at Father Ken's left. Despite her blue habit and the sternness she usually exhibited in the halls of Our Lady of Peace School, she was still a very pretty woman. The blond hair she always tried to keep tied rigidly back under her headpiece was curly. After half a day in the classroom, it would twist out of the confining bobby pins to form tiny curlicues of gold around her face. Her eyes were a deep blue under long lashes. Her nose was well chiseled and her lips full. She was slender because she ate as sparingly as Father Ken and drove herself almost as hard.

Now, as they sat at the table, Father Ken said, "Today has been a truly glorious one, Sister."

His manner was infectious and she smiled. "I guess it must be good for you to eat dinner at three o'clock in the afternoon."

He blew smoke out of his nostrils. "Remember I told you I needed to raise another five hundred thousand dollars to cover all the costs for the youth center?"

She nodded.

"Well,"—he tried and failed to mask his self-satisfaction—"a man called today and said he would give us the entire thing."

Sister Mary Louise's eyes widened in surprise. They had figured they would need at least another fund-raiser or two before they could break ground. Even then, they still wouldn't have all the money needed to complete the project. But Father Ken had a couple of schemes up his sleeve. Now they were unnecessary.

She laughed. "That's wonderful. Who is this generous benefactor?"

Mrs. Turner came through the door from the kitchen carrying a tray laden with so much food that she could barely walk. Before either of them could rise to help her, she set the tray down on the table.

There was spaghetti in a silver serving dish, a plate of buttered squares of cornbread, two tossed salads with creamy garlic dressing, a decanter of Chianti, and a pitcher of water along with silverware, plates, and glasses. Mrs. Turner began serving them.

Despite their protests, she heaped mounds of food on each plate. Then, with a strict order for them to eat, she hurried back to the kitchen.

Sister Mary Louise asked again, "Who's our generous benefactor, Father?"

Father Ken had a mouthful of spaghetti, which he took a moment to swallow and chase with water before saying, "His name is Zalkin. Steven Zalkin."

"How did he make his money?"

The priest continued eating. "I really don't know, but he's legit."

"How do you know?" There was an edge in her voice.

This surprised him. He stopped eating, put his fork down and looked at her. "I don't know, Sister. Any man who would want to give that much money to the church couldn't be a crook."

"Abdul Malik offered you money."

"That was different," he snapped, but quickly lowered his voice. "Malik was trying to bribe me to stop putting him down in the community. That was obvious."

"This Zalkin could also have an ulterior motive, Father. We don't know anything about him."

Father Ken pushed his chair back from the table and lit another cigarette. He blew smoke through his nostrils and said, "You want to tell me what this is all about?"

She looked down into her plate. She couldn't answer him, because she really didn't know. Maybe it was because his last name began with the letter Z. She didn't trust people whose last names began with Z.

"You've done so much good work here. It would be a shame to jeopardize it all because you took money from the wrong person."

Father Ken smoked in silence for a time. "You want me to check him out?"

"How could you do that?"

"You've met Detective Bronson at Sunday mass."

"I don't think so."

"Sure you have. You just didn't know he was a policeman. His son's in the third grade. He was the poker dealer at the last Las Vegas night."

"Oh, the man who took in all the money for us. I know him."

"Well, he's a police detective," Father Ken said, as the front doorbell rang. "I'll have him make sure Mr. Zalkin isn't a crook and then"—he rose to answer the door—"I'm going to take his five hundred thousand dollars."

Alone in the dining room, Sister Mary Louise Stallings began feeling very foolish. She silently scolded herself. Who was she to question the charity of one of the more materially fortunate of God's children? Suspicion was warranted if there was evidence to support it. Here she had no evidence. She would let Father Ken's detective check Mr. Zalkin out and just forget about his last name beginning with the letter Z.

Father Ken returned to the dining room, his face bloodless with shock.

"Sister, did you hear what happened on the boulevard this morning?"

"No, what?" She stood up.

"Two policemen were killed—"

"Oh, bless us, Jesus," she crossed herself.

"—and Abdul Malik's temple was blown up. He was supposed to have been inside. It must have been some type of gang war. A number of innocent bystanders were also shot. Jim and Barbara Price were killed."

Sister Mary Louise's legs went weak. Jim and Barbara Price had been taking instructions to become Catholics. They had three young children. Expectantly, she looked at the priest.

"Grady Johnson has the children with him. He wants us to put them up for the night until he can locate their next of kin."

Grady Johnson was the County Department of Child and Family Services worker who served their area.

The knowledge that the three young children were here and needed caring for strengthened Sister Mary Louise's legs and straightened her spine. She had work to do. Groundless worries about benevolent benefactors whose last names ended with the letter Z could wait.

CHAPTER 20

APRIL 17, 1991
5:45 P.M.

Detective Lou Bronson sat at his desk, entering the results of their investigation into the events surrounding the destruction of the Temple of Allah into his laptop computer. Across from him, Manny Sherlock sat at the adjoining desk correlating lab reports and photographs into three neat piles to serve as references for Bronson's narration.

Bronson finished the report, did a quick proofread, and pressed the print button. As each page came out of the printer, Sherlock grabbed it, dashed to the copy machine, and made copies. He then returned to his desk and added pages to each stack.

They finished, stapled each set together at the left-hand corner, and carried the original and two copies to Sergeant Blackie Silvestri for approval.

Blackie was chewing on the butt of a cigar and occasionally flipping ashes into an ashtray overflowing with the remains of other cigars. His desk was at the back of the room in front of Commander Cole's office. The desk was ten feet from the nearest detective's in the open office bay. Now, with the sergeant having spent the afternoon chewing and puffing on one stogie after another, there was a haze enveloping him like a fog. As Bronson and Sherlock passed through it, Manny held his breath.

Bronson's report was five pages of single-spaced typing. While the sergeant read, Bronson sat in the chair beside his desk, a cigarette adding his own contribution to the smoke cloud. Sherlock perched on the edge of the desk and hoped he wouldn't contract a case of lung cancer from secondary smoke.

When Blackie finished, he placed the report down and stubbed out the remains of the cigar. "That's good work, Lou, but we've still got nothing to go on. No leads to a rival gang or who iced Kessler and Brick."

"There is one good thing, Sarge," Sherlock said. "All the witnesses now agree that the cop-killer was a man wearing a black motorcycle helmet and driving a black van."

Blackie stared hard at the skinny detective. "Why is that good, Manny?"

"Well . . ." Sherlock paused, as he tried to think of how this would be specifically good enough to please the sergeant. "It helps us to narrow down our field of suspects."

Blackie looked from Sherlock to his partner. Bronson was quick to defend. "Manny's got a point, Sarge. His outfit was almost like a uniform, and what happened resembled a commando operation."

"Okay," Blackie said, "but I think that's quite a long shot, even if it does narrow the field of suspects." He gave Sherlock a hard look the detective returned with a bland expression.

"Detective Bronson?"

They turned to see Capt. Robert Lee Watkins, the information officer from Astrolab, standing just inside the perimeter of Blackie Silvestri's smoke cloud. He was in full Class-A uniform and his posture was parade-ground erect.

"Well, hello, Captain," Bronson said. After introducing Sergeant Silvestri, he added, "What brings you here?"

Watkins looked different than he had when they saw him earlier. There was something in his manner—a hesitance, or perhaps a barely concealed anxiety. Blackie caught it before his detectives did: Watkins was afraid of something.

"I'd like to talk to you about Sergeant Carduci," the captain said.

"Sure. You want to step over to my desk?"

"No," Watkins said. "I saw a McDonald's across the street. Maybe we could go over there and have coffee?"

"Sarge?" Bronson looked at Blackie.

"Fifteen minutes—then I want both of you back here. We've still got a lot of work to do."

Bronson and Sherlock sat down in a booth after Watkins volunteered to buy them coffee. Sherlock declined the coffee in favor of a strawberry shake and a large order of fries. Bronson constantly marveled at his partner's slender waistline.

"What do you think of this guy, Lou?" Sherlock said. "Wouldn't you say that he's acting a bit strange?"

"He's different than when we saw him before, but let's play it out. He didn't travel all the way into Chicago to pass the time of day over a cup of java."

Watkins returned and sat down across from them. He placed his saucer cap on the table and straightened his uniform blouse. He began to meticulously add sugar and cream to his coffee. Bronson was sipping black coffee and Sherlock was halfway through his shake when Watkins completed the blond-colored mixture.

He left the cup on the table and looked up. Now they could see the worry on his face. A great deal of worry.

"I understand you talked to a C.I.D. investigator about Bryce Carduci's death?"

"That's standard procedure, Captain," Bronson said. "We liaison with C.I.D. on major crimes involving the military as a courtesy. It's still our jurisdiction and our case."

"Oh, I didn't mean to imply otherwise. You're probably the best suited to hunt for the sergeant's murderer."

"Probably?" Sherlock punctuated his question by popping a couple of french fries into his mouth.

Watkins let the remark drop. For a moment he stared at his West Point class ring. Then he took a sip of coffee, placed the cup back in the exact spot it had occupied before he picked it up, and said, "You need to know a couple of things about what Sergeant Carduci was doing for us out at Astrolab."

"Sergeant Glass told us Carduci's duties were classified, but the C.I.D. investigator is supposed to give us some additional information," Bronson said.

"What you'll get from C.I.D. about Astrolab won't help you at all. Even they won't be able to find out."

"Can we assume that you're going to tell us?" Sherlock said.

"Astrolab is funded by the Defense Personnel Support

Center. In conjunction with the army, they've been doing research on improving the combat equipment of your basic infantry soldier.

"We've looked at higher-powered, lighter-weight weapons that will hold more ammo in each clip, at a lightweight body armor that will not only protect against bullets but also flamethrowers, tropical heat and Arctic cold, and at various types of anti-thermal devices."

The captain stopped, took a sip of his coffee, straightened his uniform, and continued.

"Bryce Carduci worked on everything and you could say he'd been around the army long enough to know how to make an illegal buck. We were top secret, but that wouldn't mean anything to a smart noncom, who logged his twentieth year in the army last March."

"So Carduci stole from the army and sold on the black market," Bronson said. "Soldiers have been doing that since before the time of the Romans."

"The Romans crucified soldiers for stealing," Watkins drawled. "Nowadays, we're lucky if they get general discharges under honorable conditions. Carduci was too smart to get caught, even when we knew he was responsible for important hardware that came up missing."

"What kind of hardware?" Sherlock asked.

Watkins hesitated before continuing. "Any number of things, but we were mostly concerned about the weapons. We lost a couple of nine-millimeter sidearms, an experimental M-29 rifle with a few hundred rounds of explosive tip ammo, and a few CS-12 anti-thermal canisters. We think he was peddling these things in Chicago, but we could never prove it."

"What's a CS-12 anti-thermal canister?" Sherlock asked.

"Didn't C.I.D. investigate him, Captain?" Bronson said angrily. "I mean, that's heavy-duty equipment."

"What is a CS-12 anti-thermal canister?" Sherlock said more insistently.

"Did you ever bring Carduci in and sweat him? Make him tell you what the hell he did with that stuff?" Bronson said.

"He isn't like your common criminal out here in the streets," Watkins argued. "He is—or was—a Sergeant, First Class in the U.S. Army. He has rights according to the Uniform Code of Military Justice."

"Would somebody please tell me what an anti-thermal canister is?" Sherlock pleaded.

Bronson looked at his partner, as if seeing him for the first time and then back at the captain. "Okay, what is an anti-thermal canister?"

Watkins leaned forward to place his green-clad elbows on the table. His voice dropped an octave as he said, "That's the real reason I came to see you."

Bronson and Sherlock exchanged wary glances. Neither of them liked the way this conversation was going.

"After you left this morning, we took an inventory of our anti-thermal canisters. There were three of them missing. Although they're experimental, they are very efficient."

"Efficient at doing what?" Bronson asked.

Watkins took a deep breath, looked around to insure they could not be overheard and said, "It can allow anything sprayed with it to withstand an open flame generating up to one thousand degrees."

"Jesus H. Christ," Sherlock said.

CHAPTER 21

The superintendent of police sat at the head of the conference table in his office. Around the table sat First Deputy Superintendent Schmidt, Chief Riseman, Commander Cole, two agents from the Chicago office of the FBI, two agents from the Treasury Department, and Capt. Robert Lee Watkins.

Watkins sat at the foot of the table opposite the superintendent. His posture was ramrod straight, but he kept his eyes riveted to the surface of the table. His complexion was pale and he looked sick. This was not the best day he had ever spent, either in or out of uniform.

One of the FBI agents, who was also a Southerner, spoke to Watkins. "Cap'n, I can't understand why you didn't report these acts of pilferage right away."

Watkins had been over all of this. First with Detectives Bronson and Sherlock, then with Commander Cole and Sergeant Silvestri, and only a few minutes ago with those present. He understood that they liked to go over things again and again, but for some reason he didn't consider this straw-haired hayseed, in the Sears wash-and-wear suit, a real cop.

Watkins reverted to type as a defense against this assault

on his military competence and snapped, "We required time to complete the inventory, sir. The inventory was still in progress when I heard about the two policemen being killed."

"How did you make the connection between them and the missing equipment?" Riseman asked.

"It was mostly conjecture, sir. The explosion of this temple place appeared to have been accomplished by CX-14 detonation units."

"What?" Schmidt bellowed.

"CX-14 thermal detonation units, sir," he repeated.

Schmidt opened his mouth to shout at Watkins, but the superintendent stopped him with an upraised palm. "How do you know they were these detonation units you mentioned, Captain?" the superintendent asked.

"A case of them is missing from the installation, sir."

The West Point, parade-ground responses were starting to get to the superintendent. "You can relax, Captain. You're among friends."

Watkins remained at attention, but his features softened a bit. When he spoke again his voice held a more conversational tone. "Thank you, sir."

"How many detonators to a case, Watkins?" This question came from a white-haired Treasury agent named O'Callaghan.

"Twelve."

There was a collective groan from those seated around the table.

"What else is missing?" Cole spoke for the first time since entering the conference room.

"There is nothing else missing from the installation. . . ." The captain's voice trailed off.

"Is there something else you want to tell us?" Cole pressed.

Watkins shifted uneasily in his seat. He moistened his lips with a dry tongue and said, "When we conducted the inventory, we discovered the anti-thermal canisters and the detonation devices missing. We carry out two types of inventories in cases where there is missing equipment. One is a sight-search, the other by computer.

"Our sight-search revealed the missing items I have already reported. The computer search showed that there were a number of things credited to our inventory that we never received."

"Such as?" Cole asked.

Watkins reached into his jacket pocket and extracted a folded computer printout. He unfolded the single sheet of paper and began reading from it. "One Starfire Military Assault rifle, one box of fragmentation grenades, one Britton and Mauser .440 sniper-rifle with infrared scope, and two disposable light anti-tank weapons."

"Jesus, Mary, and Joseph!" Schmidt jumped to his feet and stormed toward Watkins. "That's a goddamned arsenal!"

CHAPTER 22

APRIL 17, 1991
7:06 P.M.

Riseman and Cole left the superintendent's office and headed for the stairs, which would take them to detective division headquarters on the fifth floor. They walked along slowly, discussing the case in hushed tones.

"We'll let the Feds work their side of the street and

we'll work ours," Riseman said, as they entered the stairwell. "Carduci sold those weapons in Chicago. I'd be willing to bet my next paycheck that he sold them to the same buyer."

"A street gang, Chief? One of Abdul Malik's rivals?"

"Possibly, but Gang Crimes has too many ears on the smaller gang operations. On top of that, they couldn't afford to pay the freight unless Carduci was giving the stuff away. He doesn't strike me as the type to be charitable with the kind of high-priced hardware we're talking about."

They exited the stairwell onto the fifth-floor corridor.

"So we've got to have someone with enough money to make a potentially long stretch in a federal penitentiary worth Carduci's while. Maybe the Arcadio Mob?" Cole said.

"You know, I was thinking the same thing, but it doesn't fit. If the Rabbit's boys got their hot little hands on the stuff Captain Watkins was talking about, they wouldn't just use it to take out the Temple of Allah and a couple of cops that got in the way. By now we'd have bodies dropping from coast to coast."

They crossed the outer detective division office, where a few officers remained working late on cases. Cole paused as they passed his old cubicle. A pretty female sergeant wearing glasses occupied it now.

"Maybe we should give it some time, boss," Cole said, as they entered Riseman's office.

Riseman proceeded to a file cabinet in the corner from which he removed a bottle of cognac. "Purely for medicinal purposes," he said, as Cole retrieved paper cups from the watercooler.

Riseman filled both cups. Cole took one and emptied it. Riseman sipped his.

"I don't think we've got much time, Larry. This thing will pop wide open before we know it."

"I've got Bronson and Sherlock checking Carduci out back to the day he was born. I've got another team of detectives going through all the fancy watering holes in town that might attract a fast-track GI. We should come up with something, but it's going to take time."

He watched Cole empty the second cup in the same fashion as the first. It had been a long day for both of them.

"How are Lisa and Butch?" Larry "Butch" Cole Jr. was four.

Cole's head came up with a jerk. He looked as if he was about to say something, but thought better of it. He crushed the empty paper cup into a ball and flipped it into the wastebasket beside the chief's desk. "They're just fine."

No, they're not, Riseman thought. Lisa and Cole were having problems. He could tell by Cole's manner. But he was the chief of detectives, not a marriage counselor.

"That Lou Bronson's a good man," Riseman changed the subject.

"The best."

"But isn't that kid Sherlock a little strange?" Riseman said with a frown. "He caught me at the Christmas party last year and started telling me this joke about a man falling out of the Sears Tower. It was pretty funny, but when he found out who I was he took off like a scared rabbit."

Cole smiled. He recalled Sherlock spilling coffee on the hood of his car this morning. "He's learning, boss. Bronson'll make him one of the best in the department."

"I hope so. By the way, the first deputy wants to take you to the Press Club for lunch on Friday."

"You're kidding," Cole said with dismay. Schmidt certainly had no reputation as an egalitarian.

Riseman chuckled softly. "I thought it was a kick in the head, too, but he's serious."

"I don't have time for that, boss. With this case I'm working on—"

Riseman interrupted him. "Sure you do. You don't turn down an invitation from the First Deputy Superintendent of Police."

Cole's jaw muscles rippled. "I haven't got time to sit around having martini lunches with Captain Bluto."

Riseman shot Cole a hard look. Then his face split into a grin. "You heard about that nickname? Don't let him hear you say it." The chief of detectives leaned toward his commander and said, "You're not thinking straight, Larry. You don't buck a man with deputy superintendent's rank in this department. That's political suicide as far as your career goes. I've seen you come too far for that."

Cole nodded. He owed the man seated across the desk from him a great deal more than he could ever repay.

"Now you take some time off Friday afternoon and have lunch with the first deputy. That's an order."

"Is Schmidt picking up the tab?"

"Probably not, but you don't have to worry about it. A civilian will be paying the freight."

"A civilian?"

"Yeah," Riseman said. "A millionaire named Steven Zalkin."

CHAPTER 23

APRIL 17, 1991
11:14 P.M.

From the street, Steven Zalkin's warehouse was dark. Inside, the living area was pitch black. A silence hung over the expensive furnishings like a vacuum, as if all the air and life had been sucked from this place. Then, in the silent emptiness, there was a noise.

A click snapped through the silence like a small-caliber pistol shot. The antique door leading from the gym opened. A shaft of bright light flashed across the varnished floor. The shadow of a man was silhouetted in the light. He walked into the designer-accented space carrying a large-bore rifle equipped with an infrared sight.

Zalkin swung the Britton and Mauser .440 sniper-rifle over his shoulder. He was certain it was unloaded or he would never have been so careless in handling it.

As he crossed the studio, he turned on lights to illuminate his way. He went first to the safe and, after putting the rifle down on the varnished floor, he worked the combination. The door swung open on well-oiled hinges.

Inside there was a lot of cash. There were hundreds, fifties, twenties, and tens all arranged in neat stacks. Zalkin ignored the money. It was only there for emergencies and took up too much room. The next time he went to the bank he planned to get larger bills.

In slots above the money were three photo albums. He removed the top album. Relocking the safe, he carried the album and the sniper-rifle over to the kitchen counter.

The title *Louise and Friends* was stenciled in black across the inside cover. Turning to the first page, he examined the full-color reproduction of an oil portrait of a pretty, young blond woman.

Zalkin frowned. He'd never liked this picture. Like everything else he owned, it had cost a great deal. The artist had worked from a poor black-and-white snapshot and the rendering merely resembled the original subject. But he could live with that, because he had his memories. Memories that would suffice for the time being.

The next page held two official, full-face photographs. Both were in color. They had been taken fifteen years ago.

Zalkin looked into the faces of Larry Cole and Blackie Silvestri, as they had appeared in their Chicago Police Department personnel files in 1976. He didn't like these photos either, but for different reasons.

The album contained over one hundred pages. Newspaper articles, official reports stolen from police files, and reports from private investigators on the lives of the three people whose pictures were on the first two pages of the album were neatly pasted on both sides of each page. The pages were encased in plastic sleeves to protect the material. Zalkin had read each entry many times, but now the album took on a new meaning for him. Especially now.

He flipped through the album and selected an entry at random. It was a newspaper clipping. A front-page article from the *Chicago Times-Herald* edition of February 12, 1978:

COP IN DOUBLE SHOOTOUT WITH MOB

CHICAGO. TOWN HALL DISTRICT TACTICAL OFFICER LARRY COLE, 28, HAS BEEN A POLICEMAN FOR FIVE YEARS AND IS A VETERAN OF THE WAR ON CRIME WAGED ON OUR CITY STREETS. YESTERDAY HE CAME FACE-TO-FACE WITH THE VIOLENCE ON THOSE STREETS WHEN HE WAS INVOLVED IN TWO SEPARATE SHOOTINGS WITH REPUTED MEMBERS OF THE ARCADIO CRIME FAMILY.

There was a photograph of Cole with the article. It was the same as the one in the front of the album. Zalkin wondered if the cop still carried the .45 automatic he used to kill the Mafia button men with. He'd need it, Zalkin thought, and he'd need it very soon.

He possessed a great deal of information about Cole and Silvestri. The newspaper clippings, other than detailing the shoot-outs both cops had been in over the course of their careers, didn't have much. Even back then the information carried in the tabloids had questionable accuracy. There was also information about their promotions. Cole had five, Silvestri one. Again, those didn't tell much. But Zalkin had additional sources of information that told him much more.

He knew where each of the officers was born, how much each weighed at birth, and the names of their parents. He knew what grammar schools they'd attended and the names of all of their teachers. He knew the grades of each course they had taken throughout their high school years. He had copies of their military service records. He had copies of their police personnel files. He knew their scores on the pistol range and the contents of each of their twice-yearly performance evaluations from their immediate supervisors for the past twenty years.

But Zalkin had more than just statistics. He knew about their personal lives. He was aware that Blackie Silvestri had two children by his wife, Maria. Zalkin also knew that Maria had miscarried with their last child—a girl—and after that could have no more children. Zalkin knew how much money Blackie owed on his southwest-side home, how much he owed creditors, and how much he had in the bank.

There was not as much information available to Zalkin about Cole's private life. He did know that he was separated from his wife, Lisa, and that she and Cole's son, Larry Jr., were staying with Lisa's mother. Zalkin had the mother's address and telephone number.

He also knew that Cole had been a pretty good defensive back in high school and had gotten a scholarship to the University of Iowa. During his freshman year, however, he had gotten a young student pregnant and had been forced to return to Chicago where he joined the police department. He knew Cole's favorite football team was the Green Bay Packers, whom he rooted for even when they were losing.

Zalkin knew much, much more about Comdr. Larry Cole and Sgt. Cosimo "Blackie" Silvestri. His album contained dossiers on their lives as complete as could be compiled by any intelligence organization in the world. Zalkin knew their strengths and their weaknesses. To him, their lives were as interesting as stamps, coins, or butterflies would be to an obsessive hobbyist. Each bit and piece of information he gleaned about them was carefully collected, examined, and stored for future reference.

For future reference. Zalkin stopped reading and looked up into the shadows of the loft. Shadows reminded him of them. Because of them he had feared shadowy, dark places for years. Even now he felt the need to get up and turn on all the lights. But the psychologist had told him he had to face what he feared if he was ever going to conquer his phobias.

For future reference. So it was coming down to the last confrontation with something he feared.

Earlier that day Zalkin had telephoned Ray Schmidt and asked him back to lunch on Friday.

"Yeah, Steve, I can make it. Nice place, that Press Club. Pretty good food, too."

"Maybe you could get someone else from the department to come along," Zalkin said, guardedly.

"Like who?"

"I was watching the news and noticed that black detective commander—the one who was in charge at the Temple of Allah—looked pretty sharp."

"Cole?" Schmidt spat out the name.

"Yes, Ray. I'd really like to meet him."

"Oh, hell, Steve, there are plenty of other cops I could introduce you to. Forget about Cole."

But Zalkin had insisted. If he had the guts to face Cole

on Friday, then he could do the rest. Then they would pay. They would pay dearly.

He came to the end of the album. From the second page to the next to the last were completely taken up with the lives of Cole and Silvestri. One hundred and fifty pages worth. Only the first and last page of this first album were devoted to her.

On the last page of the album there was a newspaper clipping from *The Chicago Catholic* edition of July 15, 1987. It was a short, two-paragraph column with a photograph of two people. The item was contained in the paper's "Parish News" section.

SISTER MARY LOUISE JOINS STAFF AT
OUR LADY OF PEACE PARISH

SISTER MARY LOUISE STALLINGS OF THE SISTERS OF THE SACRED HEART WILL JOIN THE TEACHING STAFF AT OUR LADY OF PEACE SCHOOL. SISTER MARY LOUISE, WHO SPENT THE PAST FIVE YEARS STUDYING IN ROME, WILL TEACH THE UPPER GRADES.

WHEN ASKED, FATHER KEN SMITH, PASTOR OF OUR LADY OF PEACE, SAID THAT THE NUN WILL BE A WELCOME ADDITION TO THE DEPLETED TEACHING STAFF.

Zalkin studied the photograph of Father Ken Smith and Sister Mary Louise Stallings. They were standing in front of the church on a sunny day. They were smiling.

"First the cops," Zalkin said, breaking the silence of the cavernous building in which he lived alone, "then you, Sister. Then you."

CHAPTER 24

APRIL 17, 1991
11:30 P.M.

A thunderstorm formed northwest of the city and raced southeast toward the lake. Thunder and lightning echoed and flashed through the heavens before the rain came in great lancing sheets to shower across the city.

Sister Mary Louise had just gotten the last and youngest of the newly orphaned Price children to sleep when the rumblings began. The children were in a spare bedroom on the second floor of the rectory. There were many spare bedrooms in the rectory, as Father Ken lived here alone. Sister Mary Louise usually slept in the convent on the other side of the playground from the school. As she was the only nun, she was there alone in a desolate place; hence, she spent as little time in it as possible. However, to move into the rectory would have had the appearance of an impropriety neither she nor Father Ken wanted to bother to explain. But tonight was an exception. She was taking care of the three children, whose parents had been so brutally murdered that morning.

The oldest child was a girl of eight named Rebecca. Sister Mary Louise noticed instantly that she bore up well under the severity of her loss. The two remaining children were boys: Sean, aged five, and Randy, aged four. They were confused at not being permitted to go home. They knew something was wrong, but they didn't know what. The boys clung to their sister as a substitute for their missing parents. Sister Mary Louise had made tremendous headway in gaining their trust and respect during the few hours they had been with her.

They slept in a huge four-poster bed, which had once belonged to a monsignor. The three children looked like dolls arranged beneath the blankets. Randy slept on his side with his arms around Rebecca. Sean was more independent, sleeping on the other side of the bed with his back to them.

As a precaution, Sister Mary Louise had placed a rubber sheet over the mattress. She made them go to the bathroom before going to bed, as accidents were known to happen during the night.

She watched them for a moment, then moved quietly across the room to the bathroom. She turned on the light and left the door ajar in case one of the children woke up. Then she stripped off her habit and underclothing and stepped into the shower.

She was exhausted from the long hours of teaching and by the shock of what had happened on the boulevard that morning. They were some distance from the Temple of Allah, so they hadn't known what happened until Grady Johnson had told them. Sister Mary Louise did recall a slight tremor during the first period, which had shaken the classroom windows. She had figured it to be no more than a sonic boom. Now, she knew better.

She lathered herself with a bar of scented soap. She had brought an overnight bag from the convent in preparation for spending the night and being ready for a full day of school tomorrow. She didn't know what she would do with the children if Grady didn't return in the morning. But her faith was strong. God would provide.

She washed her hair and was rinsing it when she saw a shadow move on the other side of the shower curtain. Someone was standing at the entrance to the bathroom. She couldn't see much because the thick plastic curtain and the water made images hard to discern.

Her eyes went wide in fright. She ignored the suds running down into her face and backed against the shower wall. There was a frosted-glass window set in that wall, which was three stories above the ground. The window hadn't been opened in years, and she doubted whether she would be able to open it now. She considered breaking the glass, which would probably cut her badly, but she would never allow herself to be caught again and . . .

A lightning bolt struck nearby, sending a flash through the window. It was followed by a resounding clap of thunder. The lights in the old building flickered off, dimmed back on, and brightened to stay on.

She was so terrified she opened her mouth to scream, but no sound came out. The noise from the storm rumbled away, leaving a silence in the former monsignor's bathroom where Sister Mary Louise was trapped in the shower by an unknown intruder.

Then she heard a child crying.

Cautiously, she pulled the shower curtain back. Standing in the open bathroom door, clad in one of Father Ken's T-shirts, stood little Sean Price. He had been what she had seen moving through the curtain. She was so relieved that she laughed, but a frown erased her mirth. She realized that she was a naked nun with a little boy standing between her and her habit.

Don't be silly, she scolded herself. *He's not Martin Zykus.*

As soon as the thought entered her mind, fear chilled her bloodless. *Why did I think of him again?* That made it twice in the same day.

She pulled on a terry-cloth robe and wrapped a towel around her head. As she stepped out of the shower to help the child, Martin Zykus was forgotten.

2

"Never a dull moment."

—Larry Cole

CHAPTER 25

Martin Zykus sat in his rust-spattered '69 Chevy in the Burger King parking lot. The engine was running, causing a slight fog to build up in the car due to a defective muffler. Zykus cracked the driver's-side window and ignored the carbon monoxide as he ate a double-beef Whopper with cheese, a Whaler, and an order of french fries chased with a large Coke and a vanilla shake. He used one hand to jam food into his mouth and the other to stroke his erect penis through his pants.

At five feet, ten inches, Martin Zykus weighed a blubbery 235 pounds. His hair was combed back in greasy strands from his forehead and his face had acne scars still visible from his recently passed adolescence. In an attempt to look older than his twenty-one years, he was growing a mustache and goatee—no more than lonely strands of hair on his face at this point.

Music blared from his radio, which was turned to a local rock station. The objects of his erotic attention were seated in booths visible through the restaurant windows. There were three groups of females jabbering over soft drinks and hamburgers. As his fantasies of engaging in sexual acts with each one or with each group raged through his mind, he rubbed at his crotch more violently. Shoving food into his mouth, he paid little attention to the actual act of eating. His face was smeared with catsup tinted with the white of mayonnaise, and the front of his green cloth jacket was littered with crumbs, bits of lettuce, and a spreading ice-cream stain from the vanilla shake.

The groups began breaking up just as he finished the last of his Whaler. Two of them, made up of three teenaged girls each, climbed into cars in the parking lot and in moments had driven off into the night. The third party, consisting of two women, dawdled a moment inside before stepping into the lot. They stood together talking. Zykus became aware that except for him and them, the parking lot was deserted. The Burger King was also empty with the exception of the hired help, who were starting to clean up in preparation for the 9:00 P.M. closing time.

Balling up the Whaler wrapper, he threw it out the window and turned his total attention to the remaining females. One was short and dumpy with limp hair and a habit of punctuating her words with sweeping hand gestures. Although he couldn't hear what she was saying because of the distance between them, he figured her to be a squealer. Probably sounded like a pig in heat when she laughed. He hated squealers.

The other one was something else entirely.

She was tall. Maybe as tall as Zykus. She had long red hair that hung to her shoulders. Her face had an oval shape, although he couldn't see her features clearly. He imagined her to have freckles, no makeup, and green eyes. He reconsidered the eye color in favor of blue, but then settled on green again.

She was well built, with a prominent behind and nice legs stuffed into a pair of the tightest jeans he had ever seen on a woman. He wondered how she got them on. He couldn't tell what kind of tits she had because of the baggy high-school jacket she wore. Zykus noticed the jacket bore the school colors of one of those faggoty Catholic boys schools. The letter on the front of the jacket looked like it was for football. He hated football.

The short one walked to a Toyota, which was the last car in the lot besides his. She opened the door and turned back to her friend, who remained on the sidewalk in front of the Burger King. He turned the radio off and rolled his window down so he could hear what they were saying.

"C'mon, Rena. Let me drive you home." The dumpy one did have a squealy voice.

Rena. Zykus liked that name.

Rena's response was muffled and indistinct, but her posture said a decisive *no.*

Rena walked away from him across the parking lot. He was breathing hard as he put his car in gear and followed her.

The Burger King was on a main street sandwiched between a funeral home and a corner Shell gas station. Rena cut through the gas station onto a dimly lighted two-way street. Zykus followed, his muffler rumbling steadily as a foggy exhaust belched out behind him into the night.

It was a damp, chilly, late-fall evening with the temperature hovering at the freezing mark. Zykus shivered from a combination of the cold blowing into the car through his still-open window and the excitement coursing through him. He rolled up his window and flicked on the heater. A loud rattling noise came from the unit before it settled into a hum, as warm air blew through the car.

Rena walked a half block before turning and looking back over her shoulder. He couldn't see her face, but he could tell she was looking right at him. He wondered if she was curious about him? He wondered if she was becoming afraid of him?

He smiled. Acclerating, he drove past her. At the next intersection he made a right turn onto a side street, drove a quarter block into an alley running parallel to the street

Rena was on, and cut the lights. He jumped out and trotted back to the mouth of the alley. Carefully, he peered around the edge of a garage at the intersection. Rena was crossing the street on the same course she had taken since leaving the Burger King. Zykus ran back to his car and floored the accelerator. The balding, underinflated tires churned up rocks and dust as the battered Chevy hurtled down the alley. He planned to be waiting for her when she crossed the next intersection.

He turned out of the alley onto another side street. He rolled to a stop thirty feet from the intersection. He left the headlights off and waited.

The seconds ticked by and she failed to appear. No cars went by, nor was there any pedestrian traffic. More time passed.

"C'mon, Rena," he said. "Move your ass."

On cue, Rena walked into view and started across the street. Then she stopped.

She was backlit by a street lamp, her face cast in shadow. Her hair turned a deeper shade of red under the light and the silhouette of her body, which had excited him only moments before, suddenly appeared menacing.

"What the hell?" Zykus said as he stared back at her.

She turned to resume her path across the street, but then curled back to head straight for the Chevy. His breath caught in his throat as she walked over to his car and stood outside the driver's-side window staring down at him.

He couldn't meet her gaze. He had followed her in order to . . . in order to what? He really didn't know. Now she stood outside his car and he couldn't muster up the nerve to turn and just look at her.

She tapped on the window. He glanced sideways and said a strangled, "What?"

She tapped on the window again.

I ain't no fool, he thought. *I'm not rolling my window down for no crazy broad on a dark street.*

Rena opened Martin Zykus's unlocked car door.

He recoiled in terror and tried to crawl across the front seat to get away from her, but she reached down and grabbed a handful of his jacket.

"Let me go!"

"Listen, you fat creep bastard!" she screamed. "You keep following me and I'll kick your ass!"

Her entire head and upper body were inside the car now. The face he had thought to be that of a teenager belonged to a much older woman. A woman of at least forty, possibly older. And she was strong.

"Let me go!" he yelled again, but she pulled him back toward her with a strength he couldn't believe.

"Oh, big crybaby," she mocked him. "Likes to hide in the dark and scare little girls." She slapped him across the face with her open palm.

He screamed and tried to cover his face with his hands. She reached out with long, sharp nails to pinch the flesh of his thumb until she drew blood. He screamed again, as tears of pain and fear sprung into his eyes.

She clawed at his face, raking her nails across the backs of his hands. He managed to ward off the talons, but she quickly changed tactics by balling up her fist and punching him in the face.

The blow landed on his cheek. He felt the flesh go numb. He caught a glimpse of her at close range and was terrified by what he saw. Any pretense at prettiness had long since vanished from her features. On top of the meanness stamped there were the features of a harridan from hell, her eyes gone mad with fury. And he was sure she was trying to kill him.

She scratched, beat, and slapped with a relentless intensity, continuing to stand half in and half out of the car. Zykus's attempts to fight back were futile. His inability to defend himself drove her to punish him all the more.

He was bleeding from wounds on his face and hands,

but still she continued the assault, screaming as she did so, "You slimy, filthy bastard! I'll kill you! Following me down the street like I'm some kind of common street whore! I'll kill you! Do you hear me? I'll kill you!"

A terrible despair settled on Martin Zykus. He was helpless to stop her or to escape. She had him and she was doing with him as she pleased. He had managed to cover up his face, and a greater number of her blows were landing harmlessly on his head, shoulders, and arms. This enraged her and she abandoned her assault momentarily to attempt to pull his arms down with her hands. As she did so, her elbow hit the gear shift lever and the car began to roll.

She fought to crawl completely inside on top of him, but was having difficulty. Zykus felt her attack wane dramatically and in that instant saw his escape route. He stamped his foot down on the accelerator and the car leaped forward.

Rena's terrible presence suddenly vanished from the car, followed by a loud thump from the left rear quarter panel. The Chevy rocketed through a stop sign, across the vacant intersection and hit a mailbox on the opposite corner. The mailbox was knocked from its brackets and hurled against the brick wall of a corner house. The car came to rest with one wheel up on the sidewalk. The engine was running, as the exhaust beat a steady rhythm. The driver's-side door was open. Frantically, he swung around in his seat to see if the woman was pursuing him.

The street was empty.

A light went on in the house the mailbox had struck. Quickly, he slammed the door and drove recklessly back onto the street. He accelerated too fast, making the car fishtail wildly. He managed to bring it under control and make steady progress away from the scene of his humiliation.

"Goddamn!" he said, once he'd put a few blocks

between himself and the nightmare the woman had inflicted on him. "Goddamn!" he repeated, as he checked the scratches and bruises all over his hands. He adjusted the rearview mirror without slowing down and looked at his face. He was bleeding and bruises were beginning to show on his cheek and under one of his eyes.

A red light halted him. He trembled violently as he waited for the light to change. The terror, however, was dissipating rapidly, to be replaced by anger.

She had kicked his ass. A woman had kicked his ass. What would Dave say if he found out? He'd have to make up an excuse to explain the bruises and scratches. If he could have just gotten out of the car, he rationalized, he would have done the ass-kicking.

The light changed and he gunned the Chevy across the intersection. He made a right turn followed by another right. He was going back for her. He was going to kick her ass.

A few minutes later he arrived back at the street where his confrontation with Rena had taken place. There were people out now. A lot of people. A few minutes ago there had been no one there but him and that crazy woman.

He cruised by slowly, watching a small group hovering around the mailbox he had knocked over. There was a larger group on the other side of the street. He ignored the mailbox gawkers and studied the others.

There were between fifteen and twenty men, women, and even a few children standing in the shadows of the side street at about the same spot where Zykus had been parked when he had stalked Rena. There was something lying in the street. Now Zykus recalled the thump at the rear of his car when he had floored the accelerator and Rena had fallen out. Now he had a pretty good idea of what was lying on the street. He was speculating whether she was alive or dead when the first police car pulled up. Martin Zykus got the hell out of there.

CHAPTER 26

Nineteenth District tactical officers Blackie Silvestri and Hugh Cummings were on a stakeout at Klein's Jewelry Store on Lincoln Avenue. A stickup man had been hitting savings-and-loans, clothing stores, and doctor's and dentist's offices from Montrose to Fullerton since Halloween. The offender was white, six-foot-four, and very thin. On his jobs he wore a stocking mask and carried a six-inch Colt .45 Peacemaker. On November 10, an aggressive sales clerk in a men's clothing store had figured the gun to be a fake and decided to call the robber's bluff. Three days later, they buried the clerk.

Twenty-two people had seen the stickup man. Nineteen of them had been able to tell the police no more than that he carried a gun and wore a mask. But two witnesses had provided detailed descriptions of what could be seen through the mask. It came down to blond or reddish hair, and a hawk nose like Abraham Lincoln's.

So Blackie and Cummings were in a deserted second-floor office over a drugstore on Lincoln Avenue. Through the front windows of the office they had a perfect view of Klein's Jewelry Store. A pair of binoculars on a tripod were trained on the storefront where two sales clerks, the full-time jeweler, and Charles Klein himself were busy emptying display cases into the vault in the back.

The cops each took turns at the lookout post and Cummings was at that moment sitting on a milk crate staring through the eye pieces. Blackie sat on a folding chair against the opposite wall watching *Hawaii Five-O* on a small portable television. The volume was turned down so he could easily hear the speakers connected to the microphones concealed in the store. The owner and employees knew the mikes were there, which inhibited normal conversation. They spoke in tight, stilted phrases while the bored policemen listened.

In 1976, Blackie's hair was darker and thicker. He possessed a more slender waistline than would be the case in the future, but he was as much a cop now as he would ever be. Some speculated that he'd been born to be a cop.

Hugh Cummings looked more like a college professor than a cop. After being assigned to the tactical unit he had convinced their team supervisor, Sergeant Novak, to let him grow a beard. The facial hair—along with his horn-rimmed glasses and a propensity for wearing corduroy sports jackets with patched elbows—made him look very scholarly. In fact, Cummings did have a degree in criminal justice from the University of Illinois at Chicago campus. However, beneath his sports jacket he carried a nine-millimeter Browning automatic, which had been adapted to take a special twenty-round clip. He had killed three men during his twelve-year police career and had also cracked his share of skulls.

The speaker crackled. "I'm turning off the inside lights now, officers." It was the voice of Charles Klein, the jewelry-store owner. "We'll all be leaving through the front door."

The policeman watched as the store lights blinked off and the people filed out onto Lincoln Avenue. The jeweler was a short little man with a bald head; the female clerk was pretty, but too skinny for Blackie's tastes; the male clerk looked like an undertaker; and Charles Klein looked like a wealthy North Shore suburban businessman, which, in fact, he was.

"Well, that does it," Cummings said, as the last car pulled away from the store parking lot.

"Yeah. You want a cup of coffee before we hit the streets?"

"Save the coffee till later. I've been cooped up in this place too long. Makes me jumpy. Let's ride for a while."

"Suit yourself."

They packed the binoculars, the audio equipment, and the television in a metal case, which they secured with a padlock. Then they hit the streets.

It has been said that working a district tactical team is the best job that a street cop in Chicago could have. There were a lot of policemen in the Windy City who would disagree, but they would get their heaviest opposition from Silvestri and Cummings.

The two cops thrived on the action of the streets, to the point that they made their fellow officers look bad. They accounted for the most felony arrests, the most illegal-gun arrests, the most felony convictions, and the most overtime of any cops on the North Side of town. Their aggressiveness sometimes got them into trouble with their contemporaries, who referred to them by such uncomplimentary terms such as "hot dogs," "Dudley Do-rights," and "brownnosers." They ignored the snide comments and kept on doing their jobs.

"I heard Cue Ball Wright is expanding into drugs," Cummings said, as he pulled their unmarked Dodge police car from behind the stakeout location.

"Bullshit! He ain't got the balls," Blackie said.

"It's supposedly gospel according to my source. He's selling marijuana around Lake Shore High School and looking to get into cocaine."

Blackie lit a cigar and cracked his window. "Cue Ball's been a burglar since he was seven, like his Daddy before him. What does he know about dope?"

"What does he need, a college degree? That's why all the street punks are getting into it. A little brains and little strain for a big return."

"I guess you got a point. It's easier to sell a kilo of cocaine for a loser like Cue Ball than to be a good second-story man."

The police radio broadcast periodic calls while they talked. They were both tuned in for the hot call broadcast, as well as any call with the potential for producing a good arrest. So far the night had been slow. Then, as they were discussing strategies to stop the flow of illegal drugs into the city, Blackie caught a call with possibilities.

"Did you hear that?"

"No," Cummings said. "What was it?"

"A woman down. Could be a DOA."

"It's probably just a drunk."

"Let's take a look. We're not doing anything else."

"All right," Cummings said with a sigh. "What's the address?"

There were two marked police cars on the scene when they pulled up. The crowd had been forced back onto the curb and the body covered with a rubber sheet. The two tactical cops pinned their badges to their jackets and got out of the car.

A gray-haired, pinch-faced sergeant named Matthews was assisting the beat officer, who had drawn the initial call.

"How's it going, Matt?" Blackie said.

The sergeant was interviewing a woman with a head full of rollers and a housecoat so long it dragged the ground.

"Hiya, Blackie," Matthews said. "Things must be pretty slow for tactical to respond on a routine call like this."

"What've you got?" Cummings asked.

Matthews dismissed the woman, who refused to move

until the sergeant gave her an evil glare. When they were alone he said, "It's hard to tell at this point. Could've been a hit-and-run traffic accident, or maybe she was thrown from a car. Looks like her neck's broken."

"Mind if I take a look?" Cummings asked.

"Dead bodies are his thing, Matt," Blackie said. "Especially women."

"It's their cold flesh," Cummings said. "Reminds me of my ex-wife."

Cummings walked over to the rubber sheet and pulled it back. He removed a flashlight from his pocket and shined it on the corpse. The woman's long red hair was splayed across her face. The head was tilted at an unnatural angle from the body. There were no other injuries evident and he didn't want to move the body until the crime lab arrived to photograph it in the position in which it was found.

The patrolman assigned to the case walked up beside Cummings. "How do you think she got here?"

The tactical officer snapped off his flashlight and stood up. The patrolman was a young black man. He was slim and sported a thin mustache.

Cummings thought for a moment before answering. "Could have been killed elsewhere and dumped here. Might have been hit by a car. Her neck could have broken by a very strong man. The medical examiner will point us in the right direction, if he ever gets here."

"I think that what you said about the car is our best possibility, but there are a couple of things that I noticed which might tell us more."

"Like what?"

The officer went to the bottom of the sheet and lifted the edge to expose her feet. He shined his flashlight on her boots. "Look: There are scrape marks on her toes, but her knees haven't been touched. It looks to me like she was outside a car and was dragged a short distance before falling."

Cummings nodded. "That's a possibility."

"Now, take a look at this." He lowered the bottom of the sheet and picked up the top, exposing the corpse's upper body. "Take a look at her right hand."

Cummings could see bloodstains on the fingers and in the palm.

"I don't think that's her blood," the young cop said.

"You think she hurt her killer? That's a strong possibility. Oh, by the way, I'm Hugh Cummings."

"I know," the patrolman said, taking the offered hand. "A lot of guys talk about you and your partner. I'm Larry Cole."

Blackie and Matthews walked over. The woman in the long housecoat followed them.

"What've you got, Hugh?" Blackie asked.

Cummings told them Cole's theory.

Blackie studied the young policeman. No one Cole or Matthews had interviewed in the neighborhood had seen or heard anything except the noise the mailbox made when it was knocked over. The man whose house the mailbox had landed against found the woman lying in the street, but had seen no car driving away, nor anyone else on the street. It would follow that she could have been thrown from a moving car, breaking her neck in the process.

Blackie looked down the street and across the intersection at the overturned mailbox. He conjured up an image of a car speeding down the street, the woman's body thrown from it before the driver lost control and careened across the intersection into the mailbox. At this point it was all a mystery.

The medical examiner was a tall, gaunt man with thinning hair and eyes that protruded due to a thyroid condition. He spoke in sepulchral tones as he said, "I can't be sure without an autopsy, but she suffered a severe blow to the right side of her skull. The blow itself or her fall caused the broken neck. Because of the force necessary to do this kind of damage, I'd say she was thrown from a car."

The cops exchanged knowing glances.

"She fought with whoever killed her, because there's blood on her hands and what appear to be pieces of human flesh under her nails. I'll know more after we get her to the morgue."

The body was taken away by a squadrol and the crowd dissipated, except for the woman in curlers and a couple of die-hard cop-watchers.

Sergeant Matthews had searched the woman's pockets and come up with a set of keys on a Las Vegas Riviera Hotel keychain and a wallet with a few snapshots, an Illinois driver's license, twenty-two dollars, and a folded marriage license tucked into one of the plastic cases. The marriage license was for the union of Rena Ford to Maurice Hartley and issued on the 17th of July 1974.

"The address on her driver's license is only a couple of blocks from here," Sergeant Matthews said. "The dicks can go by there to notify her next of kin."

In unison Blackie and Cummings smiled. They loved to steal investigations from detectives, especially when none had so far put in an appearance at the scene.

"Why don't you let us do it, Sarge?" Cummings said. "We'll turn anything we find over to them when they show up."

"I bet," Matthews said. "All you guys want to do is steal the pinch from Homicide."

"Can't steal a homicide pinch, Matt," Blackie said. "They'll still get credit for it. We'll just be doing the work for them."

Cole listened to the exchange between the senior officers. "Do you think I could go along?"

"No way, Cole," Matthews said. "You finish up your paperwork and get back on patrol. These two glory boys can submit a supplementary report if they come up with anything."

Cole looked disappointed.

Blackie patted him on the shoulder. "If we come up with a pinch we'll put your name on the arrest report, kid."

CHAPTER 27

NOVEMBER 17, 1976
10:24 P.M.

Maurice "Mo" Hartley was worried. Rena had found his gun that afternoon and confronted him with it when he walked in the door. She'd also called the construction company he told her he worked for. They had never heard of a Maurice Hartley. So she put two and two together and figured he'd gone back to doing stickups. As usual, she was right.

Mo was tall, thin, had a hawk nose, and sandy red hair. His gun was a six-inch-barrel Colt .45 revolver he'd bought off a down-on-his-luck gambler before they left Vegas. The gun was Mo's insurance policy. Rena was his life.

In her day, Rena had been a Vegas show girl, a part-time lady mud wrestler, and the assistant manager of a Vegas gambling casino. She was fifty, but looked thirty. Mo met her after he did a stretch in San Quentin for a Los Angeles bank robbery. He was thirty-nine and looked sixty. She kept him from going back to prison. She had some money saved, so they left Vegas and moved to Chicago. They bought a house and settled down like any other married couple. That was two years ago.

Rena opened a beauty shop in a trendy area of the Near North Side and, like everything else she touched, it flourished. Mo tried to make it at a number of jobs, but nothing ever worked for long. During his first attempts after their marriage, Rena had been sympathetic and supportive. But then as he either quit or was fired from job after job, she began to look more skeptically at his reasons for being unable to hold steady employment.

As Mo saw it, he was just not cut out to be a follower or anybody's flunky. He was executive material. A boss. Why should he have to start off at the bottom? Why couldn't Rena help him start his own business?

She had grudgingly agreed to help him, but he had no idea of what type of business he wanted to go into. He considered a restaurant, then an ice-cream parlor, and finally decided on a bar. But Rena quickly vetoed the bar idea. The way she saw it, Mo drank too much as it was. His owning a bar would turn him, as she put it, "into a full-fledged drunk."

This hurt. It hurt him bad. Calling him a drunk gave him a perfect excuse to go out and get drunk. He woke up on the living room couch the next afternoon. Rena had gone to work, so he was alone in the house.

As darkness fell, the doorbell rang. It was a bunch of kids wearing masks and carrying paper bags. It was Halloween. He chased them away hoping that no more would come to the door to aggravate him, but his hopes were in vain.

In a way, as he saw it later, the trick-or-treaters turned out to be a good thing, because in the third group to ring the doorbell there was a kid wearing a stocking mask and carrying a toy pistol. After getting rid of them, Mo went to the basement, where he had hidden the .45 Peacemaker beneath some loose bricks behind the furnace. He cut up a pair of Rena's old pantyhose to fashion a mask. Then he went hunting.

In San Quentin he had learned a lot more about armed robbery than he had known before. So it was that he recognized on his first job in Chicago that he was violating three basic rules of the trade: 1) He didn't know the area well; 2) He didn't have a backup; and 3) He was on foot.

According to the lifers in Cellblock C at "Q," the odds of him being caught or killed before the job was completed were high. To tilt the odds a bit more in his favor he picked a small, one-clerk boutique.

Mo was in and out in less than a minute. He couldn't believe it when he got back to the house and found that the clerk had stuffed $350 into the paper bag bearing the boutique's logo. It wasn't a fortune, but it was a lot more than he had expected to get. He took this as a good omen and began planning his next job.

He didn't really think about it as he pulled seven more armed robberies, but he was forming a pattern with his crimes. A pattern that had Blackie Silvestri and Hugh Cummings waiting for him at Klein's Jewelry Store that very night. The reason he had not gone out was Rena.

Mo had always been a generous spender, as long as he had money to spend. The Lincoln Avenue Savings and Loan robbery had netted him over ten thousand dollars. The other jobs came to about three thousand total, so in his hiding place behind the furnace Mo had close to twelve grand in cash keeping the Colt Peacemaker company.

He knew Rena would become suspicious if he started spreading money around without having a visible source of income, so he told her a lie about getting a job with a construction company. Because he had big money, he decided to tell a big lie. He told her he was the assistant foreman making twenty dollars an hour. He also told her the boss had given him an advance, which was to cover the money he was already spreading around. He told her she couldn't contact him at work because they were always out on jobs.

He told her so many lies he could never keep them all straight. That was how he finally gave himself away.

After the discovery, they hadn't really had an argument. Mo had said little. Then Rena had grabbed the high school jacket she had bought at some rummage sale and ran out of the house.

He knew where she was going. Somehow, since they had moved to Chicago, Rena had gotten religion. She went to mass at St. Thaddeus Catholic Church every Sunday and had even become friendly with one of the nuns. Mo met the nun once when Rena invited her to dinner. Sister Frances Lucille was a short woman with a high-pitched voice. Made Mo sneer—until Rena gave him one of those looks that chilled him thoroughly. After that he had silently hated the nun.

So he figured Rena had gone to see the nun. This could become a problem. Rena wasn't the type to talk too freely about her private life. She had more than her share of dirty linen to keep out of the public eye. But Rena and the nun were tight. This could lead to anything happening.

He considered getting out of town fast. Twelve grand wouldn't go very far, but it was better than nothing. It would at least get him back to Vegas and serve as a bankroll until something better came along. The only thing he was concerned about was Rena.

Mo paced back and forth in the living room of their small bungalow. If Rena was coming back she would have been here by now. He finally made a decision.

Dashing to the basement, Mo reached behind the furnace and loosened the two bricks securing his hiding place. He grabbed the gun and the canvas bag filled with cash. He was walking up the basement steps when the doorbell rang. Mo Hartley froze.

The weight of the .45 was comforting. He eased up to the top step and peered around the edge of the door. He had a view through the kitchen, across the living room to the front door. There was a curtain across the small glass windows in the upper part of the door. He could see the shadowy shapes of two figures moving around outside on the front porch.

The bell rang again.

Maybe, he thought, *if I don't answer it they'll go away.* But the lights were on in the living room and kitchen.

Mo raised the .45 and scratched his pointed chin. He was going to have to answer the door one way or another. If it was the cops, then . . .

He turned out the kitchen light and then the living room lights. He cocked his ear close to the front door and listened. No sound came from the other side. He couldn't afford to peek through the curtains.

There came a heavy knocking on the door. Mo jumped and raised the .45 to shoulder level. He pointed it right at the closed front door.

"Yeah?" he called, as he began backing across the living room.

"Police! Open up. We want to talk to you."

Mo scowled. He never thought Rena would talk. But that didn't matter now. It was just between him and whoever was on the other side of that door. He fired three shots through the door.

When the lights went out in the house, Blackie and Hugh Cummings knew instantly that this was not going to be a routine job. Blackie pulled his .357 Magnum from the belt holster beneath his jacket and Cummings did likewise with his nine-millimeter Browning.

"Easy, partner," Blackie said, backing against the wall of the house running perpendicular to the door. "We don't know what we've got here."

Cummings crossed the porch and attempted to peer inside through the front windows, but the blinds were drawn. "I'm cool, Blackie. Watch the door."

"Get us some backup," Blackie hissed at his partner, who was carrying their portable radio.

Cummings banged on the front door again.

A man called from inside. "Yeah?"

"Police!" Cummings shouted. "Open up. We want to talk to you."

A long paused followed. A span of time during which everything slowed down for the two cops. The cool fall air seemed to warm slightly and the darkness of these final hours before midnight dissipated a bit. Then bullets from a heavy handgun punched holes in the front door.

Blackie retreated down the steps to the sidewalk. Cummings remained on the porch.

"Make the call, Hugh!" Blackie yelled, but Cummings ignored him. Instead of using the radio he raised the automatic and fired eight bullets from his extended twenty-round clip through the door. The bullets ripped the wooden frame to pieces and destroyed the locking mechanism. The last two rounds knocked the door open. It swung back into the darkened house. Through the opening Cummings saw the figure of a man backing across the living room. Without hesitating he let four more rounds go in his direction.

"Get down, Hugh!" Blackie shouted, but Cummings was already leaping through the door, firing more bullets as he did so.

"Hugh!"

The hollow roar of gunfire echoed through the house before stopping abruptly. Blackie could see the muzzle flashes reflected off the walls of the house like a crazy strobe-light show. At the point the shooting stopped, he could see neither his partner nor anyone else inside.

Cautiously, Blackie mounted the steps and flattened himself against the outside wall, where he had stood only seconds before the shooting had started. He looked around the edge of the door. He could see the furnishings and even make out some bullet holes in the far wall. But there were no bodies. He fought the urge to rush inside screaming, and instead forced his body into a crouch to provide a smaller target. With his gun raised in front of him, Blackie duck-walked into the house. Then he saw the shooter.

Mo Hartley was leaning against the far wall of the living room. Blood, shining black in the dim light, ran down his chest and stomach. He was still holding a gun, a long-barreled revolver. He looked at the policeman and spoke.

"I killed him."

Blackie kept moving forward, cutting the distance between him and the man with the gun. He looked quickly from side to side to see if there were any more strangers with guns in this house, as well as searching for his missing partner.

"I killed him," the man repeated, his voice coming out as a weak, gurgling rattle.

"Drop the gun now!" Blackie shouted.

The cop's voice startled the gunman. He began trembling and swayed unsteadily. His face split into a grin that held no mirth. Blood oozed from his lips and ran down his chin.

"I killed him and I'm gonna kill you."

The bleeding man started to raise the gun. Blackie fired once. The policeman's bullet caught his assailant in the face and hurled him back into the kitchen. Still alert for additional dangers, Blackie moved over quickly to check the body. The man was dead.

Blackie picked up the .45 Peacemaker and stuffed it in his belt. Then he began looking for his partner. It took him less than five seconds to locate Hugh Cummings.

He was lying over by the front window. He still held the Browning with the banana clip in his hand. He looked as if he were either asleep or just resting. His eyes were shut and his face had a contented, serene expression. Then Blackie noticed the wounds.

The most noticeable one was in the throat exposing the larynx all the way to the collarbone. The other was a massive chest wound that looked big enough for Blackie to put his fist into. He had been a cop long enough and seen enough bodies to know that Cummings was dead.

Blackie reached down and gently removed the walkie-talkie from his partner's jacket pocket. The radio was on but silent on this cold November night.

"Nineteen sixty-six," Blackie said their call numbers into the speaker.

"Go ahead, 1966," the dispatcher answered.

"I've got a police officer down with serious gunshot wounds and a possible deceased murder suspect at 2623 North Portside Avenue in the house. I need a supervisor, a backup unit, and an ambulance."

"Help is on the way, 1966. All cars stay off the frequency, 1966 has an emergency."

"Negative," Blackie said sadly. "The emergency is over." Unkeying the mike, he looked down at his dead partner. "There's no reason to hurry now."

CHAPTER 28

NOVEMBER 18, 1976
1:00 A.M.

John T. Ryan, the Chicago Police Department chief of detectives, entered the Nineteenth District police station at Addison and Halsted. With long, aggressive strides he crossed the lobby to the front desk. A white-haired sergeant, who had eyes that would have looked more natural on a toy doll, was talking to a short man with an elaborate handlebar mustache, a derby hat, and an overcoat two sizes too big.

"Sarge," Ryan said without preamble, "where's the commander's office?"

The sergeant glared and started to snap at the rude interruption, but something familiar about the newcomer made him hesitate and say, "It's upstairs. All the way in the back."

Ryan turned and without further comment headed for the stairs.

The second floor of the station had been recently remodeled with new floor tiles and partitions for the offices of the district commander and his staff. The cubicles and narrow corridor they formed through the center of the second floor were filled with police officers.

Some were standing or leaning against walls. Others were seated behind desks talking into telephones or pounding on typewriters. Some were in uniform, others were in plainclothes. Guns hung from shoulder holsters or were strapped to belts. There were blue-shirted patrolmen and white-shirted supervisors present, with every rank represented from the three stripes of a sergeant to the gold oak leaf of a commander. No one present outranked the chief of detectives.

When Ryan reached the top of the stairs a quiet murmur rumbled across the floor, heralding his arrival. As he walked toward the district commander's office, he was greeted with a chorus of "Hello, Chief," "Good evening, Chief," and "How's it going, boss?" He acknowledged each officer with a nod and twice stopped to speak personally with men he knew. At the door to the commander's office he was met by Comdr. Joseph Thomas O'Casey, who was nicknamed "the Leprechaun."

"Good evenin' to ya', Chief," O'Casey said with a thick Irish brogue.

Ryan nodded and walked past him into the office.

Ryan was six-foot-four, heavily built, and brutal-featured. O'Casey was five-foot-seven and weighed two hundred forty-two pounds. Ryan was known as one of the best—but most unorthodox—cops on the force. O'Casey was seen as a nice, but not too smart district police boss, whose greatest achievement, other than attaining his current rank, was playing Santa Claus in the annual Christmas parade down Michigan Avenue held the day after Thanksgiving.

O'Casey closed the door and turned to face the chief. Ryan towered over him. "I've got a dead tactical officer and an equally dead stickup man, Chief."

Ryan perched a haunch on the edge of O'Casey's desk and fired up a Camel. "Run it from the top for me, Joe. Let's put it together piece by piece."

When O'Casey finished, Ryan was on his third cigarette.

"So this Maurice Hartley kills his wife and leaves her lying in the street," Ryan said. "He goes home. Cummings and Silvestri go to check him out. He pops Cummings. Silvestri gets him. That's a neat rap. Too bad we had to lose a cop, though. I want to talk to Silvestri before I go. Is he up to it?"

"Blackie?" O'Casey's face brightened. "He's the best I got. A bit surly sometimes and has a tendency to overstep his bounds with the brass, but there's none better in Chicago." He pronounced it "Chicaga."

"Get him."

Ryan was lighting another cigarette when Blackie and his tactical team supervisor, Sgt. Wally Novak walked into the office.

"Which one is Silvestri?" Ryan asked.

Before O'Casey could answer, Blackie said, "I am."

"Who are you?" Ryan said, pointing at Novak.

"Sergeant Novak is Blackie's supervisor, Chief," O'Casey said.

"Out, Sergeant," Ryan said. "We need you, we'll call."

Novak fumbled with the knob until he got the door open and escaped into the corridor. When he was gone the chief of detectives studied the tactical cop. He recognized the type instantly. Tough, smart, a self-starter, needed little supervision, and could get the job done. Didn't care personally for rank and probably never took a promotional exam. Thought anyone above the rank of sergeant was a Class A asshole, which at times Ryan agreed with.

"You been given your criminal and administrative rights, Silvestri?"

O'Casey gasped. "But, Chief . . . !"

"Shut up, Joe. Let him answer."

"You come up here to bullshit me, Chief, or do you want to know how my partner died?"

"What did you say?"

Blackie smiled. "Okay, I didn't get my criminal or administrative rights. If you come up here to give them to me don't bother. I already know them and I'm especially aware of the part that says, 'You have the right to remain silent.' "

Ryan glared at Silvestri. Finally, the chief's face split into a grin. "Sit down, uh . . . what was that the commander called you? Blackie?"

Silvestri nodded and sat down in a chair in front of O'Casey's desk. Ryan offered him a cigarette, which he declined. Pulling a cigar from his pocket, Blackie looked at his district commander for permission before lighting it. Ryan noticed this, too. Dammit, this Blackie Silvestri was an arrogant prick, but Ryan had to admit that he liked him.

"Let's take it from the top, Blackie," Ryan said. "I want to hear it all."

Blackie told his story. Ryan was impressed not only by the detail, but also his powers of observation.

"Why do you think he killed his wife, Blackie?" O'Casey asked.

"There's a possibility he didn't," Blackie said. "She could have been killed by someone else."

"That doesn't make sense," O'Casey said.

"Hartley's the Lincoln Avenue stickup man, Boss," Blackie said. "That would be enough reason for him to open up on us. Cole figures that the dead woman fought with her attacker and left some marks on him. Hartley's pretty messed up, what with the bullets me and Hugh put in him, but an autopsy could tell us about the scratch marks."

"Who's Cole?" Ryan and O'Casey asked at the same time.

"The beat cop who got the call on Hartley's wife. Works patrol in Sergeant Matthew's sector. He noticed some things about the body that were pretty interesting. Me and Hugh planned to question the next of kin about them, but . . ."

For the first time since he entered the office, Blackie Silvestri displayed emotion over the loss of his partner. He tensed, and his eyes watered as his voice became choked by the turmoil raging inside him.

Ryan hurriedly said, "Why didn't you wait for the detectives to do the leg work?"

Fighting for control and winning. Blackie looked up at Ryan and shrugged.

"What about this Cole?" Ryan asked O'Casey.

The commander rubbed his fleshy chin. "I think he's a Negro officer. Nice, polite young fella. Writes a decent report. Keeps his nose clean."

"Sounds to me like he's doing some creative detecting," Ryan said. "Making conjectures at crime scenes is a job for trained investigators, not beat cops."

Blackie glared a silent *bullshit,* which the chief ignored.

"Okay, Blackie," Ryan said. "It was nice talking to you and I'm real sorry about your partner."

The cockiness and defiance Blackie had shown before deserted him now. Both Ryan and O'Casey could see he was hurting. But he wouldn't give in to the pain. He'd keep fighting it and maybe later, when he was alone behind closed doors with someone he loved and trusted, he'd allow the pain to take him. But not now. Not while he was around other cops.

Alone in the office with O'Casey, Ryan said, "I want you to talk to the beat cop and order him to leave out of his report any mention of the woman showing signs of having injured her attacker."

O'Casey frowned. "I don't understand, Chief."

"Don't you listen at staff meetings, Joe, or are you asleep all the damn time? We've got a woman murdered, a string of armed robberies, and a suspect we don't have to keep in jail or lug in front of a cop-hating judge and jury, because he is very conveniently dead. You clear up two weeks of crime and come out smelling like a rose. But if this black cop starts making mysteries out of simple cases, we'll all be up shit creek."

O'Casey's face turned a deeper shade of pink during Ryan's tongue-lashing. The embarrassing thing was that he did have a tendency to fall asleep during staff meetings. Ryan was right on some counts, but O'Casey still had problems with what he was saying.

"I'll go along with you about Hartley, but suppose someone else did kill the woman, Chief? Maybe there's enough evidence at the scene for us to find out who."

"I don't believe this," Ryan said, stomping around the office and stopping at a picture of O'Casey with Mayor Richard J. Daley. He spun around to face the district commander. "What are you doing, O'Casey, playing Sherlock Holmes? The broad is dead, her husband killed her and one of your men. He's a stickup man, for chrissakes! It fits!"

O'Casey stood with his crimson face pointed toward the floor. It had been a long time since he'd let anyone talk to him like this. He didn't like it, but realized there was nothing he could do about it.

Ryan headed for the door. "Take my advice, Joe. Do this my way. The easy way. Okay?" He let himself out.

"Pagan bastard!" O'Casey hissed into the emptiness of his office.

CHAPTER 29

NOVEMBER 18, 1976
8:24 A.M.

Martin Zykus arrived for work at Bill Michael's Restaurant and Bar. He was a busboy and only allowed to enter the restaurant through the alley door. He changed into his whites in the small locker room behind the freezer. He didn't start work until nine, but he usually came in early to have a snack with Dave Higgins, the short-order cook.

"What happened to you?" Higgins said when Zykus walked into the kitchen.

The cook was frying six eggs and nine strips of bacon on his grill, while keeping tabs on the orders clipped to the flywheel by the waitresses working the main restaurant.

"I got into a fight," Zykus said sullenly. He opened the door to the walk-in refrigerator and stepped inside. A moment later he came out carrying an Italian sausage link. He gave it to Higgins, who flipped it on the grill.

"Who were you fighting with?"

Zykus moved over to a dispenser and poured a glass of chocolate milk. "Just some guy."

He watched the milk swell up through the glass, making frothy little bubbles on the surface. The glass was nearly full when he became aware of Higgins standing behind him. Slowly, he put the glass down on the counter and turned around.

Higgins was half a foot shorter than Zykus and didn't weigh more than a hundred and forty pounds. He had sharp cheek bones and eyes with a decidedly reptilian cast. Higgins had learned to cook in the Navy and told Zykus that he'd been around the world and back. He had the tattoos and fight-scars all over his body to prove it.

He looked from Zykus's face down at his hands. After a moment he snorted and turned back to his grill. He said over his shoulder, "Some guy, my ass. A broad did that to you."

Zykus stood very still and concentrated on the tips of his scuffed work shoes.

"Why you come in here bullshittin' me, boy? 'Some guy.' Shit!"

Zykus couldn't look at him. He felt ashamed.

"What'd she do, scratch you up when you tried to take some pussy?" Higgins was shoving eggs and bacon onto plates along with hash brown potatoes and toast.

"I guess so."

"Speak up, boy!"

"I guess so," Zykus spoke louder.

Higgins scooped the Italian sausage off the grill and stuffed it into a piece of French bread. He wrapped the bread in a paper towel and handed it to Zykus.

"You better eat up and drink your milk. Your shift starts in a few minutes."

Zykus ate his sandwich and gulped milk. That way he didn't have to talk. He didn't have to explain.

The breakfast rush was over and Higgins stood at the back door smoking a cigarette. Zykus came by carrying a garbage pail to empty in the alley Dumpster.

"Take a break, boy," Higgins said. "No sense working yourself to death for these fucking Greeks."

Higgins's tone was friendly, which was a relief to the busboy. He had thought he would be mad at him for lying earlier. After dumping the garbage, he joined Higgins.

"So did you get it?" Higgins said, exhaling a cloud of smoke.

"Get what?"

"You dumb Polack son of a bitch, the pussy? Did you get the pussy from the broad who scratched you up?"

"No."

"You let a woman tear you up like that and you didn't get nothing for your trouble? What kind of man are you, anyway?"

Zykus looked from Higgins back inside the deserted kitchen. "I think she's dead."

The short-order cook stared hard at the fat busboy. "I told you I don't like you lying to me, didn't I?"

"I wouldn't lie about something like that."

The manager—a short, swarthy man with thick black hair—came into the kitchen, forcing them back to work.

They were changing in the locker room after work when Higgins said, "We're going to the Sheridan Inn. I want you to tell me all about last night."

"I've got to get my lottery ticket first."

"You idiot. You and a million other suckers plunk down your hard-earned dollars every day playing that stupid game. Okay, go get your numbers, but you come down to the Sheridan Inn right after. You hear me?"

"Yes, sir."

CHAPTER 30

The Sheridan Inn had seen better days, but still had a classy air about it. The restaurant served a fairly decent meal and the place was clean. The bar was a hang-out for the more serious drinkers in the neighborhood with beer and whiskey being the principal beverages consumed. Except for conversations between the patrons and the bartenders, there was no entertainment available other than a black-and-white television set.

Higgins was watching a situation comedy rerun when Zykus walked in. Higgins drank Seagram's Seven with Seven-Up. Zykus ordered the same.

"You need to cut your hair and do something about the way you dress," Higgins said. "I'm embarrassed to be seen with you."

"I'm sorry," Zykus said, running a hand through his greasy hair.

"And stop apologizing all the fucking time. Makes you look weak."

"I'm sorry."

Higgins snorted. "Okay, what happened to the broad last night?"

Zykus looked around to make sure he couldn't be overheard and then told him. When he finished, the cook

ordered them another round of drinks. After they were
served he said, "Jeez, boy, sounds like you was running
away from her. What's the matter with you? Don't you
know how to deal with a woman?"

Zykus stared into his glass. He felt hot tears of shame
sting his eyes. It wasn't so much the woman as the fact he
had somehow let Dave down.

"C'mon, Marty, develop some backbone. Didn't your
daddy ever teach you anything?"

Zykus's head snapped up and he stared at Higgins. "My
dad never liked me. Called me 'lard ass' all the time."

Higgins laughed. "Don't take offense, boy, but he was
right about your ass. But he was dead wrong not to teach
you how to handle women."

"What about the one last night?"

"To hell with her. She got what she deserved. Hope she
did break her neck. But don't worry about that now." He
reached down and slapped Zykus's forearm. "Uncle
Dave's gonna teach you how it's done. C'mon, let's go find
ourselves a broad."

CHAPTER 31

NOVEMBER 18, 1976
8:11 P.M.

They went up on Montrose Avenue, where one of the
worst slums in the city began. Here there were
Appalachian whites, blacks, and American Indians
jammed into a simmering melting pot that was always on

the brink of exploding. Here Dave Higgins took Martin
Zykus hunting for his first victim.

They stopped in a bar called the White Horse Tavern.
Because of the strong smell of stale bodies, spilled booze,
and urine assaulting their nostrils at the entrance, Zykus
stopped and refused to enter until Higgins grabbed him
and forcibly pulled him inside.

As they took seats at an oblong bar, Higgins whispered, "Just order beer and drink it straight out of the
bottle. No telling where the glasses in this dump have
been."

Zykus ordered, but would be damned if he'd ever drink
anything in this place no matter what kind of container it
came in.

There was a jukebox blaring country-and-western
music, and a few other lonely-looking patrons besides
them. A huge Indian with the same lank, greasy hair as
Zykus and a gut protruding in rolls of fat from beneath a
dirty knit shirt tried to make small talk with them, but
Higgins kept silent and Zykus followed his lead.

Back on the street Higgins said, "That Indian prick was
drunk. Probably looking to pick a fight. You steer clear of
guys like that. You hear me?"

"Yes, sir."

The third bar they hit was called Connie's. It was the
cleanest yet, but not by much. The thing that made it
attractive to them was the women inside.

They sat at the bar and ordered beer. Zykus kept his eyes
on his Schlitz bottle and waited for his mentor's instructions.

"What do you think?"

"About what?" Zykus answered.

"The women in here, boy! Goddammit, ain't you even
looking?"

Zykus looked around the room. There were a couple of
women sitting in a booth. He couldn't see them too well

because the lighting was bad. There were two other women. They were seated separately at the bar. Zykus developed an instant interest in the younger one. She was white, had long black hair hanging to the small of her back, and wore a pair of tight jeans.

"What about the one down there?"

Higgins looked up. "Don't mess with her. She's Henry's girl. He's the owner. Big hillbilly. Likes cutting people open for laughs. But the other one's got potential."

Zykus studied the other woman. She couldn't be a day under sixty. She had an obese body stuffed into a dirty two-piece suit, which was a size too small for her. The blond hair she had left had come out of a peroxide bottle and her face was pancaked with layers of makeup.

"C'mon, man. She's ugly," Zykus said.

Higgins bristled. "I ain't asking you to marry the slut, asshole. I want to teach you a thing or two about dealing with them. We'll start picking them for looks after you learn some of the basics."

"So what do we do now?"

A chilly smile shimmered over Higgins's face. "Nothing. We just drink our beer and wait."

Zykus was getting drunk. He was on his sixth beer since they'd entered Connie's and he wasn't used to drinking so much. Higgins matched him beer for beer, but was showing no ill effects.

"This broad is a lush," Higgins hissed, as he signaled the bartender for their seventh round. "She's gonna sit here and drink all night."

"But what are we—"

Higgins hushed him, as the aged bartender set two bottles of beer in front of them.

"What are we waiting for?" Zykus asked when the bartender walked away.

The peroxide blond slapped a bill on the bar and slurred

a slobbery, "Check me out, Charlie. It's time for me to blow this dump."

Higgins's chilly smile returned. "The time has arrived, sailor. The time has arrived."

They waited until she staggered out into the cold. Higgins said to Zykus, "Pay the bill and meet me outside."

Zykus began fumbling for cash as Higgins walked out.

"Over here, boy!" The cook was in the doorway of a closed variety shop next door to Connie's when Zykus came out.

Zykus slipped into the shadows beside his friend. "What now?"

"Let's see where she goes." Higgins was staring down the block at the blond, who was staggering along, making slow but steady progress toward the corner. Zykus shot a sideways glance at his friend. The skinny little man was breathing hard and there was a scary glint in his eyes. Zykus started to suggest that they call this off, but he knew Higgins would only get mad at him.

A quarter of a block away the woman turned the corner and disappeared from view.

"C'mon," Higgins said, bolting from the doorway and trotting down the street.

Zykus followed slowly, looking around to see if there was anyone watching them. The street was deserted.

He caught up to Higgins at the corner and together they walked up the street. They saw her instantly. She was twenty feet down the block, bending over a metal trash basket, vomiting up her guts.

"Would you look at this bitch?" Higgins said.

"We can't do nothing now, Dave. She'll be a mess."

Higgins's eyes flared. "She needs her ass whipped for being out here like this!"

Martin Zykus's fear of Higgins and what he was about to do made him tremble. "C'mon, Dave. We can . . ."

But Higgins was already walking toward her. Reluctantly, Zykus followed.

As they approached her she straightened up and stared at them with bloodshot, unfocused eyes.

Higgins struck her in the face with his fist. Her heavy body sagged back into the wastebasket, toppling it over. She came down on top of it and slid off onto the ground. Higgins kicked her twice. She lay on the ground, looking up at them without making a sound.

"Drunken bitch!" Higgins snarled with a fury that caused goosebumps to rise on Zykus's skin.

"C'mon, man. We gotta get out of here," Zykus said.

Higgins reached out and grabbed his arm. "We ain't going nowhere yet. Help me pull her into the alley."

Frantically, Zykus looked around. "Dave . . ."

"Shut up and help me, boy!"

Higgins yanked her into a sitting position and grabbed a handful of her coat collar. Zykus grabbed her arm and together they dragged her into the alley thirty feet away. She made no effort to resist and when Zykus caught sight of her face, in the illumination from a street lamp, her eyes were closed. The odor coming off her, even in the autumn cold, was a gut-wrenching mixture of booze, vomit, and unwashed flesh.

Flanking the alley on both sides were the backs of three-story apartment buildings. Darkened wooden staircases formed skeletal structures above them, making the darkness of the shadows beneath them impenetrable.

Higgins motioned to Zykus to pull her beneath a first-floor porch. He did so, but didn't stoop low enough and struck his head.

"Ow!"

"Shut up! You wanna bring the cops down on us?"

Zykus rubbed his head and strained his eyes to see what Higgins was doing to the woman in the shadows. As his vision became adjusted to the darkness he was able to make out their silhouettes. Then he could see the texture of their skin. There was the fleshy lower stomach, the thighs, and the triangle of pubic hair of the drunk woman's exposed lower body. As knowledge of what Higgins was doing dawned on Zykus, he opened his mouth to speak, but before he could make a sound he saw the fry cook's pants drop down to his ankles. Zykus mouth stayed open as he stared at Higgins's runty, cigar-shaped penis.

Martin Zykus had seen sex acts performed on the screens of porno movie theaters, but he had never seen two live people do it before. Now fascination overrode his fear, as he watched Higgins get down on his knees, force the woman's fleshy thighs open and mount her.

Ninety seconds later Higgins let out a soft cry, which held more pain than pleasure. Then he was off of the unconscious woman and yanking up his pants.

"Okay, boy," he whispered in the dark. "It's your turn. Sloppy seconds is better than nothing."

Zykus couldn't see himself trying to screw this stinking drunk in this cold alley. But watching Higgins do it had given him an erection.

"C'mon, boy," Dave said. "Get with it. She smells, but her snatch is real."

Zykus dropped his pants and shuffled forward until he stood over her. He lowered himself on top, feeling the flabby flesh of her torso give beneath his weight. He entered her, but didn't last much longer than Higgins had. The excitement, the cold, and the danger made his ejaculation quick. He was still throbbing inside of her when she stirred.

"Get off me!" she screamed.

"Get up!" Higgins said, urgently. "C'mon, we gotta split!"

"Rape!" she screamed. "Help! Rape!"

Zykus stumbled back away from her. His pants were trapped around his ankles. They had become entwined with his shorts. As he struggled to pull them up, the screaming woman began clawing at him. Images of Rena the night before flashed through his mind.

"Rape!" she screamed again.

She grabbed Zykus's leg with a rough palm and held him fast. He tried to pull away, but he had no leverage with his pants shackled around his ankles.

"Rape! The bastards raped me! Help!"

Zykus looked around for Higgins, but couldn't see him in the dark, confining space under the stairs. He couldn't believe Dave would desert him.

The woman sat up and began striking him across his bare legs with her open palm. He could see her pale skin and overly made-up face, and could smell the stench of booze on her.

Then Higgins appeared behind her. An object glinted in the available light, as he raised his right hand and swung downward at her head. There was the shattering of glass followed by a terrifying howl of pain from the woman. She released Zykus and fell back onto the concrete. Zykus yanked his pants up and leaped to his feet, once more banging his head on the overhead porch. This time he saw stars.

"We gotta go now, boy!" Higgins said.

Together they ran from the alley.

They sat in a tavern four blocks away. Zykus was trembling so violently that Higgins ordered him a double shot of bourbon to go with his beer. After swallowing the whiskey and fighting to keep it down, Zykus drank half his beer. He was starting to regain control when he noticed that Higgins's right hand was bleeding.

"That broad's skull was hard," the fry cook said. "Shattered that fucking beer bottle right in my hand."

Zykus looked at Higgins's ugly face, then at his hand, then back into his face.

"What are you staring at, boy?" Higgins looked ready for a fight.

Zykus raised his beer bottle in a salute. "To the man who got me the scroungiest, slimiest piece of ass I ever had in my life."

Higgins picked up his own bottle, but before toasting his young friend he said, "Well?"

Martin Zykus understood Higgins's question. He understood it exactly. He looked away for a moment before looking back at Higgins again and saying, "It was great. Absolutely fucking great!"

Dave Higgins grinned in triumphant agreement.

CHAPTER 32

NOVEMBER 24, 1976
1:55 P.M.

M r. Cole, your paper on the police forces of the Third Reich was interesting. Brutal, but still interesting."

The rest of the class snickered, as Professor Levinsky handed Cole's term paper back to him. The policeman opened the folder and looked at the grade written on the title page. *A.* A shiver of exhiliration ran through him. They said that Levinsky never gave As. Cole flipped through the twenty-five-page term paper. There were a few marks on it, where the professor had not approved of Cole's word usage, and two punctuation corrections. However, there was nothing else until the final page. There Levinsky had written in bright red ink: "You followed the assignment to the letter, Mr. Cole. You did not attempt to moralize what the Nazis did, nor did you make condemning editorial comments about the methods their police forces used. Your analysis of the police state they inflicted on the people who came under their control during World War II was cold-bloodedly efficient. You are a credit to your profession." It was signed "Aaron Levinsky."

The last sentence of the professor's analysis stung Cole. What did he mean by "a credit to your profession?" Cole considered asking him when class was over, if the cop had the time.

Levinsky, a white-haired, seventy-year-old academic with a cutting wit, gave the class a reading assignment to be completed over the upcoming Thanksgiving holiday before dismissing the class. Before Cole could make a move toward the front of the room to inquire about the comment on his term paper, two students were already at the professor's desk protesting their grades. Cole, the author of "Policing the Police State," collected his books and left the room.

The Roosevelt University campus was in downtown Chicago. Professor Aaron Levinsky's European history class met on the eighth floor of the south Michigan Avenue building. Cole was carrying nine hours in the undergraduate history degree program. He hoped to graduate in the next eighteen months. Going to school was all part of his plan for the future.

As he descended the stairs to the main floor, he found himself following a group of his younger fellow students from Levinsky's class. He knew a few of them by their last names, but for the most part they were strangers. It was not that Cole was antisocial—he simply didn't have the time to socialize with them after class.

"What'd you get?" a blond girl asked a black kid, who sported a bushy Afro.

"A *C*! Do you believe Levinsky game me a C? I'm on the Dean's list."

"Wait a minute," a long-haired white boy with thick glasses piped in. "He gave me a C, too. I've never been so humiliated."

"Well, I got a B," the girl said. "That's probably the highest grade in the class. After all, Levinsky never gives As."

Cole started to tell them about his grade, but stopped. What good would it do? He wasn't busting his ass working full-time and going to school on the side to compete with them. He had a plan. A plan that would see him promoted up through the ranks of the police department to become at least a lieutenant in ten years.

In the university lobby he left his classmates, who were still bickering over their grades. He exited onto Michigan Avenue and was startled at how the weather had changed so drastically in the past few days. A week ago, when he'd been assigned to the "woman down" call that had led to Tactical Officer Hugh Cummings's death, the temperature had hovered at the freezing mark. Now it was sixty degrees on a bright, sunny day in the Windy City.

Cole had parked his '74 Mustang convertible in the Grant Park underground garage while he was in school. After retrieving the midnight black car, he drove east into Grant Park and turned north on Lake Shore Drive. He was headed for the Nineteenth District station.

Besides history, Cole was taking a political science class and a contemporary American literature seminar. Other than the problems presented by Professor Levinsky, who enjoyed reinforcing his reputation as a prick by generally giving low grades, Cole found that the other courses were fairly easy. That is, if he kept up with the reading assignments and

turned in all his papers on time. Cole always tried to go by
the book with his schoolwork. He realized that, as a street
cop, there was always the danger that he would have to miss
a class because he had to go to court or work overtime. So
he stayed prepared.

It was 2:26 P.M. when he pulled into the parking lot of
the station at Addison and Halsted streets a couple of
blocks east of Wrigley Field. After locking his car, he
started for the station. He was smiling when he realized
that for the first time since early September, he wasn't carrying a book. The next day was Thanksgiving and Cole
didn't have another class until that following Tuesday. Six
days. It was almost like a vacation. Even if he did have to
work on the holiday, it would seem like a short tour of duty
for him because he wouldn't be on the go from nine in the
morning until well past midnight, which was generally the
case.

The Nineteenth District station house was quiet. As
Cole passed through the lobby on the way to the patrolmen's locker room, he noticed Sgt. Dick Beazley behind
the desk reading the *Racing Form* and Captain O'Neill,
Cole's evil-tempered watch commander, in his office pag-
ing through the *Times-Herald*. For just a moment, Cole
stopped and listened to the silence of the station. The
place was almost as quiet as a tomb. Not even the phones
were ringing.

Cole took that as a good omen for the weekend ahead. As
he continued to the locker room, he was smiling. Little did
he know that it was not going to be a good weekend for
him. Not a good weekend at all.

Capt. Homer O'Neill had been a policeman for thirty
years. As he had given up any hopes for further promotion,
he held abbreviated roll calls during which a minimal
amount of information was given out to the officers under
his command. However, today, at Commander O'Casey's

insistence, O'Neill was forced to cover a current crime pattern.

In a sarcastic voice he began, "Our esteemed Detective Division has saddled us with a severe crime problem, gentlemen." There were no female officers present at this roll call. "We've had four women raped on the north end of the district." O'Neill suppressed a grin. "The victims are between the ages of . . . now get this, guys . . . fifty-six and sixty-eight."

The roll call room erupted with laughter. Cole, who had handled three of the four cases, was one of the few who did not even smile.

"The only thing we've got on the offenders is that they're a couple of white males. Apparently, our victims' eyesight hasn't been too good."

There was more laughter from the officers in the room.

O'Neill was really enjoying himself now. "I think we've got a few cases here of wishful thinking on the part of the victims."

Howls and snickers from his audience punctuated this statement. Cole felt the back of his neck starting to get hot.

The captain's eyes were starting to tear when he looked up and saw Joseph Thomas O'Casey standing in the back of the room. The commander had come down the back stairs from his second-floor office. The captain didn't know how long the Leprechaun had been standing there.

"Good afternoon, Commander," O'Neill said as a warning to the men.

The thirty-odd cops in the room spun around to get a glimpse of their commander. Most immediately turned back to face front, as it was apparent that the usually easy-going, mild-mannered O'Casey was far from happy.

"I'd be expectin' that police officers assigned to this district would take vicious assaults on some of our more senior ladies a bit more seriously than what you were doing just now."

"We do take them seriously, Commander," O'Neill said. "We were just having a little Thanksgiving Eve laugh."

"Did you read the reports on those crimes, Captain?" O'Casey demanded.

O'Neill looked down at the surface of the podium he was standing behind. The "No, sir," he uttered was barely audible.

"Is Officer Cole present?" O'Casey asked.

Cole raised his hand.

"You took three of the reports on these assaults, didn't you?"

Cole stood up and said, "Yes, sir."

O'Neill glared at Cole. He didn't like the black cop. He was always running around trying to show everyone how smart he was. In the captain's book, this marked Cole as "uppity."

"Do you remember any of the details of these assaults?" O'Casey asked Cole.

Cole could feel more than one hostile stare cast in his direction as he replied, "Yes, Commander, I remember them."

"Then please tell Captain O'Neill and your colleagues in blue about how the victims they were having such a good time laughing about were so viciously assaulted."

Cole cleared his throat and began. "The first victim was a fifty-six-year-old white female. She was grabbed off the street, forced into an alley and raped by two men. She was intoxicated when it happened and one of the offenders stunned her with a punch to the face when it started, so she was unable to recall a great deal about them later. She really didn't know what was happening until it was all over. When she woke up and started struggling, one of them smashed an empty bottle over her head. It took thirty-seven stitches to close the cuts. That was last Thursday.

"The next one took place on Friday. Again, the victim was

a white female. She was sixty-two. She was found in an abandoned garage by a factory worker coming home from a late shift. The victim lived with relatives in a house a block from the scene. She had a history of mental problems and wandered off when her brother wasn't looking. She was not only raped but severely beaten. She's still in a coma."

The roll call room was as silent as a tomb now. Captain O'Neill's head was down and he was studying the wood pattern on the surface of the podium. Commander O'Casey's eyes never left the captain. The Leprechaun was wondering how long it would take him to get a new captain assigned from downtown and this one transferred to the busiest hellhole in the city.

"The last one I handled on Monday," Cole said. "She's the one they stabbed. Her name was Gloria Hill. She was sixty-eight and lived in the Sheridan Rest Home. She likes to slip off alone, even though it's against the home's rules. The head nurse said that Gloria liked to sneak a cigarette or two even though she has emphysema. They pulled her into a gangway. She was a frail lady, but she put up quite a fight."

Cole stopped. They all waited for him to continue. When he did, his voice was lower, more subdued. "One of them, 'the little puny one,' she called him, took a knife and stabbed her seven times. Kept calling her names while he worked. They ripped her dress and tore her underpants off, but they didn't succeed in raping her. She's the one that gave us the best description."

Cole turned to look at the captain, who was still studying the podium surface. "I understand that Gloria died last night."

"That's not in the pattern," O'Neill said. "Now it's murder."

"Maybe if we made fewer jokes and spent more time caring about this job we're doing we wouldn't need to wait for the detectives to tell us everything about what's happening out there on our streets?" O'Casey said. "Read the descriptions to us, Captain."

Somberly, O'Neill complied. "We've got two male whites, ages twenty-five to fifty, medium complexions, dark hair. Number one is short and thin. Number two is reportedly tall and heavyset. Half the guys on the street fit that description, Commander."

"Then we start stopping half the guys out there until we get lucky!" O'Casey's voice was sharp, adding to the tension in the squad room. "Innocent old ladies are being raped and brutally assaulted out there and not one of you is making any effort to do anything about it. Well, I want to see some action on this and I want to see it soon. Am I understood?"

Every blue uniform in the room jerked to attention and they all responded, "Yes, sir!"

CHAPTER 33

NOVEMBER 24, 1976
6:20 P.M.

Six, twelve, eighteen, twenty-four, and forty-six," Zykus said to the lottery-computer operator.

The operator looked up at him. She had thick glasses, which dwarfed her eyes, and thin lips under a pinched nose. In a bored tone, she said, "Shouldn't that last number be forty-two?"

Martin Zykus glared at her with an intensity that made

her turn pale. She lowered her eyes to her keyboard as he said, "Just put the numbers in like I told you." He started to call her a bitch, but there were too many people and too much light here. He realized he did his best work in the dark. This thought made him smile as he handed over the money and snatched his lottery tickets from the nosy clerk.

Stuffing the tickets into his wallet, he headed for the Sheridan Inn.

Higgins sat at the bar drinking a Seven and Seven. Zykus ordered a beer. He waited until the bartender had served him and moved away before saying, "What have we got on for tonight, Dave?"

"Don't you ever make any plans of your own, boy? Or do you expect me to do all your thinking for you from now on?"

Zykus blushed. Higgins was still mad about his performance with the last broad. Higgins had instructed him to grab the old woman and pull her into the gangway beneath a building under construction. Zykus went after her, grabbed her from behind, and started dragging her off the sidewalk. But before he could get total control of her, she had started fighting.

He did manage to get her into the gangway, but he was damned if he could handle her. Higgins came to his aid and together they forced her to the ground. They had started ripping her clothes off, when she reached up and grabbed Higgins's ear. He tried to twist away, but she held on tight and used her nails to dig into his flesh.

Zykus tried to help him, but she held on, screaming and cackling like a woman possessed. Zykus became really frightened and for the first time considered abandoning his partner right there. It was at this point that Higgins pulled the knife.

It was a Swiss Army knife with multiple blades. Blood was running down the side of Higgins's face when he started cutting her. In seconds, as Zykus looked on, there was blood all over the floor of the gangway.

She finally let Higgins go, but she never stopped making those eerie cackling noises. It was like she was a witch or something, Zykus thought, and he was glad that they hadn't screwed her.

"It's time you found your own pussy, boy," Higgins rasped.

The fry cook's ear was hurting. It was a bad cut, but because it was at the junction of ear and skull, not easily noticeable. He held his head rigidly erect, and when he spoke, turned his upper body toward Zykus. Other than that, to the casual observer, he didn't appear to be injured.

"I can do it, Dave," Zykus said with more confidence than he felt. "Just give me a chance. I'll find me one of those old broads and—"

"Enough of this worn out, drunk-tank shit. Time for you to go after something nice, young, and tender."

Zykus said nothing, but his bowels turned to ice.

"Finish your drink. We're going shopping."

CHAPTER 34

NOVEMBER 24, 1976
7:00 P.M.

Louise Stallings rode the el train that rattled south toward the Addison Street station. As the train skimmed over the rails, the overhead lights periodically flickered on and off, giving an eerie appearance to her fellow travelers in the half-full train. She looked around at them. No one looked back at her.

She had been living in Chicago for over a year and still couldn't get used to the cold suspicion exhibited by most Chicagoans. At home, back in Kellam, Iowa, everybody was friendly. Everyone spoke upon meeting on the street, and thought nothing of passing the time of day with a total stranger. Here you were lucky if your next-door neighbors even spoke to you.

Louise was an English major at Loyola and carried a full course load. Every day she took the train north and every evening back south again. She had friends on campus and dated occasionally. But she couldn't get into the lifestyles of some of her fellow classmates, who sought entertainment in excessive drinking, pot-smoking, and casual sex. Sometimes she thought there was something wrong with her, and she was often lonely. But she had been raised a certain way, and she didn't intend to change because she was living alone in the big city.

The train pulled into the station and she got off. Darkness had fallen and with it, the temperature. At noon she had eaten lunch on the lawn in front of the student chapel. Now it had gone from the mid-sixties of midafternoon into the low forties and was still dropping. Down on the street she turned east and began walking toward the lake.

Louise didn't dress like a college student, but instead like a young businesswoman. She wore masculine-tailored suits in somber colors and dark medium-heeled pumps to her classes and even out on dates. She carried a sturdy, black attaché case containing only the materials and books she needed for that day's classes. She didn't try to be severe, simply efficient. Being from a farming community she did own jeans, sweatshirts, and other casual clothing, but she only wore those items when cleaning up around the apartment or doing the laundry.

As she walked along, she remembered that tomorrow was Thanksgiving. The thought of spending the holiday alone depressed her, but she fought through it. She would call home early and wish her family a happy holiday. Then she would go to church like they always did back home. She would fix a regular Thanksgiving dinner. Maybe she'd be able to find a small turkey. If not, then a duckling, and if worse came to worse, she'd broil a chicken.

She started feeling better. It was too bad she didn't know anyone she could invite over to share the meal with her. But it was too late to invite anyone from school, and she had never been able to go into a bar or one of those discos to make herself available to be "picked up" by a strange man. Maybe she would meet someone tomorrow at church. St. Thaddeus was down on the other side of Diversey, but if she got up early enough and the weather was nice, it would be a good walk for her. The walk would also help her build up an appetite for all the food she planned to cook.

She was approaching Halsted Street when she glanced over at the Nineteenth District police station on the opposite corner. She'd walked past it many times in the last year. She was curious about the men and few women in uniform she saw going in and out of the building. Once, last summer, when she'd been walking past the station on her way to a Cubs game at Wrigley Field a few blocks away, she'd seen two policemen struggling with a handcuffed man.

The policemen weren't in uniform and to Louise they looked more like bums than law-enforcement officers. The handcuffed man was screaming, "You got nothing on me, Blackie! This is harassment! Fucking police harassment! This is police brutality!"

Louise had watched them from across the street, as they forced the man into the station and out of sight. She could still hear him screaming and cursing inside. Later, she was unable to enjoy the Cubs–Cardinals game she'd been looking forward to for a month. She kept wondering what the man had done to deserve that kind of treatment at the hands of the police. She considered making a formal complaint against the officers. One of them had been called "Blackie." Sounded more like a crook than a cop to her. But then they hadn't actually done anything to him—like beat him up with a blackjack, as she'd seen in a movie once. Maybe the prisoner was a bad person who deserved rough treatment? It would probably be better to adhere to the silent code of the urban dweller, Louise decided: "Don't get involved."

She crossed Halsted without giving the aging building a second glance. In another block she was at Broadway. The shadow the police station had thrown across her soul was gone.

The Treasure Chest supermarket was on Broadway. Louise considered the prices high, as they were in all the Chicago stores compared to what they were in Kellam, but the food was fresh and the store clean.

She pushed a cart through the fresh produce section and selected vegetables for a salad and side dishes. From the bread section she picked up a package of dinner rolls. She had enough fixings at home to make dressing, so she headed for the poultry counter to decide on the type of bird.

Louise was crossing the store in that direction when she felt a presence behind her, accompanied by a whiff of boozy breath. She kept moving without turning around and momentarily lost the feeling of someone standing close to her.

She glanced around her to see if she could spot anyone standing near her or watching. But the store was too crowded with too many different types of people to make such an identification easily. No one seemed to be paying her the slightest attention.

Suddenly, an uneasiness swept over her. She had never felt this way before in her life. But then she realized that she was a Stallings from good prairie stock, as her grandfather always said. The heebie-jeebies and things that go bump in the night never bothered her. At least, they weren't supposed to.

The turkeys were too large, but she found a nice plump capon. It was big, but she could use the remains for leftovers. She headed for the checkout counter.

The grocery bags weren't heavy, but with her attaché case and purse, they were awkward. She had a four-block walk to her apartment building. The streets were fairly busy, and as she walked along she felt a certain safety at being in a crowd even if they were all strangers. This was also a new experience for her, as she never thought about the congestion of city life except in a negative way.

Louise recognized that the uneasiness remained with her. Whatever had happened back there in the store lingered. She glanced around occasionally, but there was no danger she could detect on the street.

She turned off Broadway onto her street. It was as if a door had slammed behind her, leaving her alone in a dark room. The auto and foot traffic vanished. The street was dimly lit by lamps spaced at eighty-five-foot intervals. Tonight they all appeared to be on half-power, making shadows appear longer and darker.

She quickened her pace.

The sense of impending peril increased. She could feel something there. Something with a cold, slimy presence. Her insides quaked as she got up the nerve to look back the way she had come. Broadway looked miles away now, and between her and the thoroughfare were two figures coming in her direction. One was heavy, the other thin, but they walked at a leisurely pace. There was no danger there. Turning around, she looked for any other danger that could be hiding in the darkness up ahead.

As she got closer to the entrance to her building, she walked faster, almost breaking into a run, until one of the bags began slipping from her grasp. She braced it with a knee and regained her grip.

She hurried the last few steps to her entrance. In the vestibule she dropped one of the bags on the floor and fumbled with her keys to get the security door open. It took her two tries before she could get the door unlocked. Then, grabbing the grocery bag from the floor, she fled into the inner lobby.

There, her fear began to dissipate. Now she felt drained. She dragged herself across the lobby to the elevator and pressed the *"up"* button just as she heard a noise behind her.

She jerked around quickly to find two men standing in the outer lobby she had just passed through. The heavyset one was staring through the glass at her, while the smaller one concentrated on picking the security door lock with a knife.

Louise Stallings felt her breath lock in her throat, as she jammed the button frantically with the heel of her hand. Then she noticed that the indicator lights for both cars were on the fourth floor of this five-story building.

Clutching her bags to her bosom she ran for the stairs. As she started up she heard the security door click open behind her in the empty lobby. She reached the first landing and made it to the second floor. As she started up to the second landing she heard the sounds of feet on the stairs below. Her breath rasping in her throat, she ran as fast as she could.

Turning to ascend to the third-floor landing, she lost the grip on one of the bags and it, along with its contents, spilled onto the stairs. She dropped the other one and hung on to her attaché case and purse, as she continued to climb. She could clearly hear the sounds of her pursuers coming closer.

The fear and exertion of running up five flights of stairs left her badly winded by the time she reached the top floor. She rushed into the corridor from the stairwell and raced for her corner-apartment door. She had her keys clenched in the same hand with the handle of the attaché case. She was prepared to unlock the first of two locks as soon as she reached her door. She glanced back at the corridor and found it empty. She bent to unlock the door. She fumbled momentarily before inserting the key. She got it in and heard the click of the bolt snapping back. Then she went for the second lock. Before she could insert the key again, they grabbed her.

She screamed. The smaller man shoved a knife against her throat. "Shut up, bitch, or I'll cut your fucking throat."

His heavyset companion snatched the keys from her and found the right one for the remaining lock. The man with the knife pressed his body against her back, while holding the blunt edge of the knife against her flesh.

"Wait a minute," he said to his companion.

The heavyset one with the bad skin stopped. He turned to stare at them with wide-eyed fear. The one with the knife put his mouth against Louise's ear. "Who's inside, girlie?"

She started to say "No one," but quickly corrected, "My brother. He's in there. He's got a gun."

"Let's split," the acne-faced one said.

The man with the knife didn't move. She could smell him and the odor made her gag. There was the stench of liquor and grease on his body.

"You're lying. There's nobody in there. You'd have called to him instead of trying to open the door yourself."

She felt her hopes disintegrating.

The fat one waited for instructions.

"Open it," the knife-wielder said. "Let's go introduce ourselves to her brother."

After a moment's hesitation, the fat one opened the door. He let it swing into the darkened one-bedroom apartment. The man with the knife forced Louise Stallings inside.

CHAPTER 35

NOVEMBER 24, 1976
7:15 P.M.

All cars stand by," the dispatcher said into the mike. Then he turned to the policeman seated at the telephone position on the Zone Two console at 1121 South State Street. "What've you got, Charlie?"

"It could be a prank, Joe. The caller wouldn't give me a name. When I tried to get some particulars, the guy hung up." Charlie handed Joe a buff-colored card.

The dispatcher read it before depressing the transmitter pedal and seeing the red light illuminate on his console.

"Units on the City-wide and in the Nineteenth District we have a woman screaming at 733 West Barry Place. Unit to respond?"

"Nineteen Twenty-three. I'm going."

"That's your paper, Twenty-three."

"Nineteen Seventy. We'll take a ride on that."

The dispatcher smiled. The last voice was Blackie Silvestri's. He was riding with Sergeant Novak until he found a new partner. It was too bad about Hugh Cummings.

Three more units joined in, which the dispatcher

promptly acknowledged before listing them on the back of the assignment card.

"Nineteen Seventy. Have you got any more information on the call? Is it on the street or inside the building?" Blackie was forced to raise his voice to be heard over the wail of the siren.

"That's all we have, Seventy."

"Ten-four. We'll take a look."

Larry Cole accelerated the squad car through dense, pre-holiday, midevening traffic. His siren was set on the "wail" frequency and the Mars lights spun twin blue beacons around him. Driving in an emergency situation was always dangerous, and Cole stayed alert for the unexpected. Some drivers would pull over and yield to the emergency vehicle, as they were supposed to; others would simply stop and wait for the police car to go around them; and a small minority of drivers, either through stupidity or stubbornness, ignored the lights and siren altogether. This last type of driver could be dangerous to both themselves and the police.

Cole made it across Belmont and was accelerating toward the street the call was on when he saw an unmarked car, its alternating headlights flashing, coming fast from the south. Cole decelerated to let the tactical car make the turn first, then he followed close behind.

On the side street they killed their emergency equipment and glided toward the address given. In front they stopped bumper-to-bumper and got out.

Cole recognized Blackie Silvestri and Sergeant Novak in the unmarked unit. Blackie nodded to him as he started for the apartment building entrance. Novak followed.

Blackie stopped on the sidewalk and looked up at 733 West Barry Place. There were five stories with ten apartments per floor.

"We don't have much—" Cole began, but Blackie hushed him with an upraised palm.

Surprised, but curious, Cole shut his mouth and waited. Sergeant Novak stood mutely by.

Finally, Blackie said, "No woman screaming out here. Let's have a look inside."

They moved across the sidewalk to the entrance. Before going inside, Novak said, "Cole, get one of the responding units to cover the alley behind this place just in case we flush something."

"Yes, sir."

He made the call and joined them in the lobby seconds later. The buzzer unlocking the security door sounded continuously.

"We got a complainant?" Cole asked.

"No," Novak said with a frown. "Blackie rang all the bells."

Cole suppressed a grin as they entered the lobby.

Again, Blackie stopped and listened. The building was as silent as a tomb. He walked over to the stairwell door and opened it. Nothing.

"It's a phony, Blackie," Novak said, turning to leave. "Let's get back on patrol."

"Hold it, Sarge," Blackie said. "We should take a better look around. Maybe go up top and take a walk down the stairs. We could come up with something."

Novak appeared undecided.

"It'll take us five minutes," Blackie said.

"You think something's going on here?" Novak asked.

Blackie shrugged. "Just good basic police work, Sarge. We should exhaust all the possibilities before we take off."

Again Novak hesitated, but Cole could see that he was about to give in. Blackie just wanted to make it seem like it was the sergeant's idea.

"Okay, let's do it," Novak said. "Cole, you come with us. It's always best to have a uniform along in case we run into trouble."

"Yes, sir."

As they started for the stairs, their walkie-talkies crackled. "Nineteen Twenty-three or Nineteen Seventy, come in for the watch commander."

Cole responded. "This is Nineteen Twenty-three."

Captain O'Neill's voice came over the air. His tone was far from congenial. "Twenty-three, are you inside the building at 733 West Barry?"

"That's affirmative, Captain."

"I want you and any other officers on this call to meet me out in front of the building right now. Do you copy?"

"What's the matter with him?" Novak asked.

"He forgot to take his Asshole Control pills this morning," Blackie said.

O'Neill was waiting for them on the street. He was wearing a civilian coat over his uniform and his face was flushed. When they got closer they smelled the alcohol.

"What's up, Captain?" Novak said.

O'Neill was steady on his feet and his speech was clear; however, his eyes were bloodshot. "What've you got here?" While Novak patiently explained, Blackie and Cole stood by watching.

When Novak finished, O'Neill said, "You're wasting time. You got no complainant and no leads. Get back on patrol."

"But, Captain—" Cole started to protest.

"And I've had enough of your lip, mister!" O'Neill's face darkened. "You're probably looking for another old lady crying rape to write up. Well, you won't be doing it tonight, because I want you to write parking tickets on Broadway."

"That must be where the saloon he's been hanging out in is located," Blackie quipped.

"What did you say, Silvestri?" O'Neill swung aggressively toward Blackie, but Novak was already hustling him toward their unmarked car.

"He didn't say anything, Captain," Novak said over his shoulder. "We're leaving right now."

As they pulled away, O'Neill turned back to Cole. He appeared to have sobered slightly, which the young cop took as a bad sign.

"Did you understand my order, Cole?"

"Yes, sir. You want me to write parking tickets on my beat on Broadway."

"Oh no, my smart one," the captain grinned. "I want you to write tickets on Broadway for every illegally parked vehicle from Montrose to Fullerton."

"That's the entire length of the district, Captain," Cole protested.

"So you'd better get started."

The captain turned and walked back to the unmarked car he had arrived in. Before getting in, he turned around. "And Cole, I'll be checking to see how many tickets you write, so don't get lost. You can get a thirty-day suspension for disobeying a direct order from a superior officer."

Silently, Larry Cole watched the captain get in his car and drive away. He couldn't help but notice the grin of triumph on the captain's face.

CHAPTER 36

NOVEMBER 24, 1976
7:40 P.M.

What does it look like, boy?" Higgins said from the shadows by the door where he held the girl. "The pigs still out there?"

"Please, don't hurt me. I've got money—" Her voice

was cut off so abruptly that it frightened Zykus.

He moved quickly across the living room to Higgins's side. The fry cook had clamped a hand over the girl's mouth and his knife blade was pressed against her cheek. Her eyes had gone wide with fear.

"Don't cut her," Zykus said.

Higgins spun to face him. There was something in the fat boy's voice that had not been present before. "What did you say?"

Zykus could see the girl's face despite the darkness in the apartment. She was pale with terror and there was a mark on her cheek where Higgins's knife had been, but she wasn't bleeding.

"You said she was mine." The touch of anger and menace that had been there moments before had vanished.

Higgins's eyes bulged. "You ain't got no exclusives, ya damn fool! We've shared everything so far and we're gonna share this, too."

With that, the fry cook turned back to the girl and held the knife to her throat. However, this time the blade didn't touch her skin. "Bedroom?"

"Please . . . !" Tears began rolling down her face, as she looked past the smelly, evil man at Zykus.

"Shut up!" Higgins hissed.

Zykus felt a hollowness invade his being. He wanted to help her. To become her hero. To make her like him. But he was afraid of Dave.

Higgins grabbed her by the hair and twisted it viciously. She cried out.

"I said, where's the bedroom?"

Her eyes flowed liquid, as she looked away from the darkened entrance into the apartment shadows off to the right. Higgins began pushing her in that direction.

"Dave?"

Higgins stopped. Zykus couldn't see his face, but his

posture exuded tension. "Why don't you tell her where I live too, asshole?"

"I'm sorry," Zykus said.

By the time he looked up again Higgins and the girl had disappeared into the shadows. An instant later a door slammed. Martin Zykus waited.

"Boy?" Higgins called through the dark.

For twenty minutes Zykus had stood in the same spot in Louise Stallings's living room. He was afraid to turn on the light, he was afraid to go into the bedroom, and he was afraid for the girl. But as the fry cook's voice came to him through the dark, Zykus realized he was no longer afraid of Dave Higgins.

"What?"

"Don't use that tone to me, goddammit! What in the hell's wrong with you?"

Zykus advanced toward the sound of Higgins's voice. He could feel his fingers clenching into fists and his breathing coming in sharp rasps. There was a rage pounding through him that he had never felt before. He felt at that instant that he could indeed kill.

Higgins's skinny body shown faintly white against the darkness of the bedroom. He was naked. His skinny legs and wiry upper body surrounded the dark mound from which his small organ protruded. Zykus could see his face. He was grinning.

"It's good, boy. Best I ever had."

Zykus could see the girl lying on the single bed in the room. She was also naked. And she was lying very still.

"What did you do to her?"

Higgins tensed. The blade of his knife flashed dully in his hand. "I had to hit her to keep her quiet and make her cooperate."

Zykus caught the trembling in Higgins's voice. Dave was afraid of him.

"Get out," Zykus snapped. "It's my turn."

Higgins paused a moment. Again the knife blade flashed. "Sure thing, boy." He began dressing.

Zykus never moved. Never said a word.

Half-dressed, Higgins went to the bedroom door and said. "Don't be too long. We gotta split."

"You can leave without me if you want."

"I'll wait," Higgins said. "Just don't take too long."

When the door shut, Zykus walked over to the bed and looked down at the girl. She looked all right, except that the left side of her face was puffy. This was where Higgins had struck her.

He studied her body. The breasts weren't large, but they were well-formed. She had none of the veins and wrinkles of their other victims. Her arms were thin. No fat there. Her stomach was flat, with the small indentation of a belly button giving way to white flesh sloping to her pubic mound. Zykus's eyes widened when he noticed that she was a natural blond.

Her legs were muscular. Both thighs and calves were shapely. To Zykus, she was perfect. Like those photographs of models he'd seen in girly magazines. But this one was naked and alive right here in front of him.

He looked at her face. Her eyes were open and she was staring up at him with the same terror she had shown in the living room.

Realizing her nudity, she folded her arms across her breasts and curled her knees up on the bed. "Please don't let him hurt me again."

He felt a wave of anger at Higgins sweep over him. "How did he hurt you?"

"He . . ." she had trouble forming the words. "He hit me with something . . . here. . . ." She touched her fingers to the discoloration on her cheek. She winced in pain and tears started to flow again.

Martin Zykus knelt down beside the bed and placed his hand on top of her head. He ran his fingers through her hair, feeling the softness of her blond curls. He looked into her face. She looked back at him, a silent plea in her eyes. He leaned down and placed a soft kiss on her lips. She remained rigidly still. Then, as Dave Higgins had done before him, Martin Zykus raped Louise Stallings.

"Let's go," Zykus said. "We been here too long as it is."

"You giving orders now?" Higgins said. "You been talking shit every since we grabbed this broad."

"Fuck it," Zykus said, going to the front door and slinging it open. "Stay if you want to."

Quickly, Higgins followed him out.

Out on the street they turned back toward Broadway. They walked along in silence for a while before Higgins said, "What's wrong with you, Marty? You're acting goofy."

For Zykus this one had been different from the others. They had sex in a bed. A clean bed. She was warm, soft, and smelled good. Previously, he had only done it in bed with prostitutes, and twice he had contracted venereal diseases. The woman in the apartment had been something new and very wonderful to Martin Zykus. The only thing that had ruined it was Higgins being there.

"I asked you a question, boy."

They turned onto Broadway. Zykus wondered how he'd ever get a chance to see her again. He'd like to just talk to her; be her friend. Maybe in time . . .

"Just keep walking natural," Higgins said.

Zykus turned to look at him. He hadn't the slightest idea what Higgins was talking about. Then he saw the cop standing on the street a few feet away. Zykus stopped.

The cop had been writing a parking ticket. Now he

looked up and right at Martin Zykus standing thirty feet away. Their eyes locked, and in that instant Zykus was certain that the cop knew what they'd just done back in that apartment. Zykus turned and ran.

CHAPTER 37

NOVEMBER 24, 1976
8:05 P.M.

Blackie Silvestri and Sgt. Wally Novak were having dinner at Geno's hot-dog stand on Racine. Blackie ordered two garden dogs with mustard, onions, relish, peppers, tomatoes, cucumbers, and pickles. The sergeant had a single chili dog, minus the onions. Blackie took a sharp bite that erased half the sandwich. Novak wondered what the tactical cop's bite-radius was.

"You been thinking about who you might want for your new partner?" Novak asked. "The Leprechaun says it's up to you."

Blackie chewed, swallowed, and took a sip of root beer before answering. "I been looking at Larry Cole."

Novak nodded. "Not a bad choice. Not a bad choice at all. He does the job. But I heard he's going to school."

"What do you have to be, Wally? Stupid to work tact?"

"I didn't mean that, it's just—"

"Nineteen Twenty-three, emergency!" Cole's voice sounded over the walkie-talkie clipped to Blackie's belt. They both stopped eating and listened.

Cole was breathing hard, but his words were clear. "I'm in pursuit of a white male, twenty-one to twenty-five years, heavy build, medium height . . ." Cole paused to take in a breath. ". . . running westbound on Lund Avenue from Broadway."

The dispatcher's voice came over the air. "What's your suspect wanted for, Twenty-three?"

There came no response.

Blackie dropped the remains of his garden dog back onto the paper it came wrapped in. "Let's go, Wally. The kid's headed this way."

Their squad car was parked in front of Geno's. Blackie jumped behind the wheel, gunned the engine to life, and peeled rubber as they rocketed away from the curb. At the first intersection he took a hard right. They were traveling east toward the area where Cole was chasing his suspect.

"What's he wanted for, Larry?" Blackie said to the silent radio.

The dispatcher came on the air again. "What is your location, Twenty-three? Please advise."

There was a flash of static. Then, ". . . we're approaching Halsted. . . . Still . . . on . . . Lund."

"We're close, Blackie!" Novak banged on the dashboard with his palm. They were less than two blocks from Halsted.

They saw Cole and the fugitive at the same time. The policeman had caught his man and had him down on the ground. Cole was trying to cuff his wrists, but the suspect was struggling.

Blackie jumped out of the car and crossed to them. The suspect had an arm free and was using it for leverage to throw Cole off. The suspect was fat, but his bulk gave him strength. He didn't see Blackie until the tactical cop stepped on his exposed fingers.

"Owww!" The howl split the night air. A small crowd was gathering on Halsted to stare at the policemen fighting with the fat man.

Cole looked up at Blackie with obvious relief. He was still breathing hard from the chase and the suspect putting up such fierce opposition.

Blackie helped him snap handcuffs on both wrists and stand him up.

"What's he wanted for?" Blackie asked.

"Suspicion. I was writing parking tickets on Broadway when him and a little guy came around the corner off of Barry. This one did a double take on me and went into his Jesse Owens imitation."

Blackie looked at the suspect. He was surprised that a fat boy like this had been able to hump it for nearly a half-mile and outrun a slim, long-legged sprinter type like Cole. Then, the devil could have been chasing him.

"So what's the story, pal?" Blackie said, grabbing him by the back of his jacket. "Why are you running from the police on a lovely night like this?"

"I want a lawyer!" the suspect bellowed. He was still breathing hard and sweating from the exertion of the chase. "You can't question me without a lawyer."

Novak joined them and said, "I gave a slow down on the assist call, but we'd better take this into the station."

The crowd of spectators was growing larger. It was always best to get off the street before some curious, unknowing citizen started yelling "police brutality," "off the pigs," or some other civic-minded phrase.

They piled into the unmarked police car with the prisoner and headed back toward Cole's car.

CHAPTER 38

NOVEMBER 24, 1976
9:25 P.M.

Capt. Homer O'Neill wasn't drunk, but he wasn't quite sober, either. He wasn't necessarily an alcoholic, at least in his own estimation. He only drank when he was thrown off balance by something unexpected. The Leprechaun had managed to send him to the bottle today.

He had thought the time was past that he could have any feelings for this whore of an organization called the Chicago Police Department, but he was wrong. The Leprechaun had embarrassed him in front of his men. However, the real reason he had gone to the bottle today was shame.

He had been a good cop once. A cop who worked long hours, back in a time when a policeman made as much as a ditchdigger and was considered on the same social plane. When every cop in town had his hand out for a bribe, and there was nothing a cop wouldn't do for a price—including murder.

He remembered an old-timer telling him a story years ago. At the time, he had been a rookie, filled with wonder at the terrible excitement and accompanying danger of the streets. He was passing through a stage in which the gleam was still on his shiny, six-pointed, pie-plate star.

They were walking a beat on Clark Street on a warm

June evening in 1950. The old-timer had been on the beat for twenty-two years. He had a rolling gait like a sailor walking across the deck of a ship. But he could move fast, and O'Neill had seen him level a two-hundred-pound steelworker with one punch to the solar plexus. He was showing the rookie the ropes and as he did so, he told story after story about the "auld daze."

"February 14, 1929. 2122 North Clark Street. Ten A.M. It was cold like only Chicago winters can make it. The garage was a hangout for Bugs Moran's bootleggin' gang. Six of Moran's boys and a dentist, who liked hanging around the gangsters, were inside waiting for Moran.

"Outside, a flivver pulls up in front. Black Cadillac with 'Police' in white on the side. Didn't have many cars back then. Hell, don't have many now."

As the old-timer walked along, he began swinging his baton by the leather strap wrapped around his wrist. The first time O'Neill had tried this, he'd bloodied his own nose. So now he just let the nightstick hang down at his side.

"Four men got out of the flivver. Two of 'em wearing the uniforms of Chicago Police officers. It was said later that the others looked like a couple of bull dicks from downtown. The two uniforms go inside, while the guys dressed like dicks wait in the street. It's Prohibition, right before the Depression. Everybody was into something they shouldn't have been, so nobody paid no attention to what was going on. They stood in the cold, one cradling a Thompson .45-caliber submachine gun with a fifty-round drum, and the other a shotgun.

"Inside, the uniforms shout 'raid' and line the Moran gang up against the brick wall of the garage for a frisk. There might've been some back talk from Moran's boys, but they all did as they were told. Back then, if you gave a cop any lip he could drop you in your tracks without a howdayado.

"So everything's under control, when the two from outside enter the garage. They level their guns on the gang, and *tat-tat-tat-tat*." The old-timer raised his baton and pointed it like a gun. "Bullets and shotgun blasts tore 'em to pieces. After the two in the suits done the damage, one of the uniforms goes around and shoots each of the survivors through the head with a thirty-eight.

"There was this one guy who was slumped over a chair with his ass sticking up in the air. Our uniformed assassin put a bullet right in the crack of his behind. Tore out the seat of his pants. 'Course, he didn't care at that point."

A couple of teenaged girls walked past them and the old-timer stopped to get an eyeful of their legs under short skirts. Then he resumed.

"So the killers take off and the city has the St. Valentine's Day Massacre. Capone engineered the whole thing from down in Florida. Some say he went too far. Too much public outcry. Brought the Feds down on him. On top of that, he didn't get Moran. And there was a survivor of the shoot-out."

O'Neill, who was destined to be a police captain someday, stopped and stared at the old-timer.

"Yeah. He was never mentioned because he didn't last long. Must have had ten bullets in him. They took him to the hospital and some eager detective tried to get a statement out of him. Asked, 'Who shot ya, kid?' Well, you got to figure this guy's just been turned into a sieve by a bunch of guys he thinks are cops. So he looks up into the dick's face and tells him, 'Go fuck yourself, cop! I ain't no fink.' Then he dies."

The two cops laughed. For a while they walked along in silence, scanning the street for wrongdoers and touching their batons to their caps to passersby.

"Did they ever find out?" O'Neill asked.

"Ever find out what?"

"Whether it was cops or not?"

The old-timer smiled. "Maybe it was, then maybe it wasn't."

Bringing himself back to 1976 in the Nineteenth District police station, as his tour of duty wound to its conclusion on the day before Thanksgiving, Homer O'Neill opened the bottom drawer of his desk and removed a pint bottle of Crown Royal. He took a healthy pull directly from the bottle. The whiskey made him grimace. Then a drunken smile split his face. He said out loud, "Maybe it was, then maybe it wasn't."

He had seen a lot of things go down in Chicago since that day back in 1950. He'd seen money change hands, politicians influence promotions, and bad guys allowed to openly thumb their noses at the police. He'd been a good cop once. He took a hit of whiskey to salute himself. Made his share of arrests. Another hit. He'd just never learned to play the game like the Leprechaun or that prick Ryan, who was now the chief of detectives.

He started to raise the bottle again and stopped. "Enough of that now," he said, replacing the top and returning the bottle to the drawer.

He stood up to go into the washroom in the watch commander's office. He lost his balance and had to put out a hand against the desk to keep from falling. He righted himself and made it to the sink.

He splashed cold water on his face and neck. His uniform shirt got wet, but what the hell. His tour was nearly over anyway.

There was a knock at the door to his office. He reached for a towel and began drying his face, as the door opened. It was Sgt. Wally Novak.

"Could I speak to you a minute, Cap?" Novak's voice held the proper degree of contrition at having disturbed the captain at this late hour of his tour.

"C'mon in." O'Neill's words were slurred. He walked slowly over to his desk, flopped down in his chair, and waited for the sergeant to get to the point.

As the watch commander had not indicated otherwise, Novak remained standing.

"We'd like permission to photo and print a guy without charges, boss."

O'Neill sighed. The whiskey was making his head swim. "You know the Leprechaun frowns on prints and photos without a charge. You got a reason?"

"He's dirty, but he's keeping his mouth shut. Took a duck on Larry Cole over on Broadway and . . ."

Novak stopped when he saw the captain's face turn cold and hard, making the rosy glow of booze dissipate to the point of nonexistence. "Are you okay, Captain?" Novak asked.

O'Neill jerked open his center desk drawer and snatched up a cellophane-wrapped peppermint candy. He dropped the paper in his wastebasket, popped the candy in his mouth, and stood up. "Where are you holding this man?"

"Up in the tactical office," Novak said, becoming wary now. Usually, a request for prints and photos was routine despite O'Casey. However, the captain was reacting in a far from routine manner.

"Let's go."

Novak followed the captain out of the watch commander's office, across the first floor lobby, into the deserted squad room, and up the back steps. It was a slow night, so there were few policemen around, but everyone they passed noticed that O'Neill was half in the bag and on the warpath, which wasn't a good sign.

On the second floor the captain walked directly to the tactical office door, threw it open, and stormed inside.

The prisoner sat on a bench against the far wall. His head was lowered with his long hair obscuring his features. His left wrist was handcuffed to a metal ring embedded in the wall. When the captain walked in, he didn't look up.

There were three desks in the narrow room. Each of

them had paper and haphazard files stacked on their sur-
faces. Royal manual typewriters on individual stands were
available to be rolled into position beside each desk. Larry
Cole sat with his back to the door typing up an arrest slip.
He didn't see O'Neill come in. Blackie Silvestri sat at the
desk facing the door. When he saw the captain, he sneered.

"What's going on here?" O'Neill demanded.

Cole spun around and looked up at his watch commander. He realized in the instant he saw the drunken man's
face that the fat boy could confess to assassinating the
Pope and the arrest would still be criticized.

Cole explained the events leading up to the arrest. He
made sure to emphasize that he was dutifully writing parking tickets when he first set eyes on Zykus.

While Cole was still talking, O'Neill reached over and
snatched the arrest-report formset from the typewriter. He
studied it as Cole finished his story and waited in silence
for the verdict. It was not long in coming.

"Martin Stephen Zykus," O'Neill said. "No prior
arrests."

"That's according to the name check," Blackie said. "He
could be using an alias."

The prisoner did not look up or move.

O'Neill walked over to Zykus. "Mr. Zykus, are you
injured?"

Blackie and Cole exchanged infuriated glances. Novak
motioned with a downturned palm for them to take it easy.

Zykus didn't respond.

"Mr. Zykus," O'Neill's voice was purringly conciliatory,
"did any of these officers injure you?"

"Why don't you give him a written invitation to beef,
Captain?" Blackie said.

"Shut up, Silvestri," O'Neill snapped without taking his
eyes off Zykus. "I gave you a pass earlier tonight. You
won't get another one."

"Mr. Zykus," the captain pressed. "I'm attempting to

find out if these men violated procedure and your civil rights when they arrested you."

Zykus's head slowly came up and he looked warily at the captain. Then he looked at Blackie and Cole. "Yeah," he finally said, timidly. "They beat me up. The colored one knocked me down and the other one stepped on my hand. See?"

O'Neill looked at Zykus's hand. The fingers were encrusted with dirt, but there was no sign of injury.

"Would you be willing to give me a signed statement concerning what you just told me?"

Since his capture, Martin Zykus had withdrawn into a shell. He figured that sooner or later these cops were going to put two and two together and connect him with that apartment on Barry. But now this captain was coming on like it was the cops that were in the trick bag. His retarded self-confidence soared.

Zykus looked mockingly at Cole and Silvestri as he said, "Yeah, I'll sign a statement. I'll sign anything you want as long as you let me out of here."

A cruel smile cracked O'Neill's bloated face. He turned back to Sergeant Novak. "I want you to prepare a statement of charges against Silvestri and Cole charging them with conduct unbecoming a police officer, failure to follow proper arrest procedure, and neglect of duty."

"But, Captain—" Novak whined.

"That's a direct order, Sergeant! Now you do what I say and I'll mitigate the supervisory culpability. You screw around one more second and those charges will include you."

"Captain," Cole stood up. "This was my arrest. If you've got a bone to pick then it should be with me."

O'Neill didn't acknowledge Cole, but said to Novak, "Add failure to follow a direct order and insubordination to the charges against Cole."

Novak stood dumbfounded, unable to fathom what was going on here.

O'Neill opened the office door and stopped, turned around, and said to Novak, "Bring the prisoner down to my office—and I'm holding you personally responsible for his safety."

With that he was gone.

Zykus didn't know what going on, but he looked defiantly at the three policemen and said, "I guess you guys are in trouble."

The three cops stared back at the prisoner with hostile silence.

CHAPTER 39

NOVEMBER 24, 1976
10:00 P.M.

Comdr. Joseph Thomas O'Casey and his wife Mary Beth O'Casey looked so much alike they could have easily passed for brother and sister. They were also alike in temperament and had the same basic likes and dislikes. They had been born less than twenty miles apart in County Mayo, Ireland, and had come to the United States in the same year. When they first met, at a St. Patrick's Day dance, they initially thought they were cousins. Later, they would be very glad that they weren't related.

The only substantial difference between the Leprechaun and the elfin Mary Beth was their birth dates. Mary Beth's was in late January and the Leprechaun's, although in the same year, was in July. Their only child, Mary Frances

O'Casey, was a believer in astrology and was sure that this minor difference in her parents' existence was what kept them from driving themselves and her completely crazy.

Now, Mary Frances, aged twenty-seven and still single, sat slouched in an armchair in the living room. She was reading a Robert Ludlum novel, while her parents stood in the center of the room going through an annual pre–Thanksgiving Day ritual.

The Leprechaun stood on a milk crate that was exhumed from the attic once a year, while Mary Beth, who was the same height as her husband, fussed about him, making alterations and repairs to his Santa Claus costume.

Mary Frances placed the book down on her lap and watched her parents for a few minutes. The Leprechaun was fully outfitted as Santa Claus, down to his white beard and patent leather boots. Every year, she noticed, he put on a few more pounds, making it unnecessary to use as much padding around the middle as had been the case in previous years. On Friday morning O'Casey would climb aboard the Santa Claus float and lead the Christmas parade down Michigan Avenue. He had been doing this as long as Mary Frances could remember.

The daughter returned to her book. She recalled that when she had been a child, her father had dressed up like this just for her every Christmas morning. Then it had been the most exciting thing that had ever happened to her. Now, as she felt herself teetering on the brink of middle-age and life as a spinster, she thought this playacting at his age ridiculous.

"You'll be needing a new costume in a year or two, Joseph," Mary Beth said, as she studied the worn seat of his red trousers.

"Nonsense." The Leprechaun studied the suit in the living-room mirror over the couch. "It's got many a good year left in it."

The telephone rang. Not one member of the O'Casey

clan moved to answer it. Mary Beth noticed a piece of loose thread in the seam of the Leprechaun's coat. Admonishing her husband to stand still she reached for it. Stepping up on her tiptoes, she snagged the errant fiber in her teeth and bit it off.

The phone continued to ring. As one, the parents of Mary Frances O'Casey shot their offspring a demanding glare. The two sets of blue eyes flared together, as they had done so often in the past. Although she didn't jump to do their bidding, she moved fast enough to catch it before the next ring.

"Sometimes that girl . . ." Mary Beth said, examining her husband's Santa suit for more loose threads and worn spots.

"Needs a husband," O'Casey said, assuming his best Saint Nick pose with belly thrust forward and thumbs in his belt. He was about to give out with a decent, "Ho, ho, ho," when Mary Frances called, "Dad, it's the station."

The Leprechaun's face changed from jovial to grim, while his wife's eyes widened with concern. He climbed down off the milk crate and crossed the living room to take the kitchen extension from his daughter. As he came up to her she said, "It's somebody named Blackie Silvester."

The Leprechaun hesitated before taking the phone. He knew that Blackie's proper surname was Silvestri, but that wasn't what stopped him. Patrolmen didn't call district commanders at home, even if they were superstars like Blackie.

"O'Casey here." There was an edge in his voice transmitting his annoyance.

He listened in silence for a long time. As he did so his face turned pink and then began darkening toward a red that easily matched his costume.

Finally, he said, "I'll be right down. You just tell the young officer to stay calm. You hold onto that prisoner, Blackie. I'll fix everything." The Leprechaun paused to listen and then exploded, "What do you mean, he let him go?!"

The wife and daughter of Joseph Thomas O'Casey had never seen him so angry. It at once terrified and fascinated them.

"Just sit tight," O'Casey said. "And keep that smart mouth of yours shut. I'll be there in ten minutes."

The Leprechaun slammed the phone back on its cradle with such force that plates in the kitchen cabinet rattled.

"What is it, Joseph?" Mary Beth said with concern.

"I got to go to the station and straighten out a mess."

"You can't go like that, Dad," Mary Frances said, pointing a finger at her father's costume.

The Leprechaun looked down at his red and white suit, but was too angry to consider changing. He lived only a few minutes from the Nineteenth District by car. He looked at his daughter and said, "Get your coat on, Mary Frances. You're driving me."

"But, Dad . . ."

"Don't argue with me, girl. This is police business. Now move!"

Mary Beth O'Casey made the sign of the cross as her daughter went to get her coat.

Captain O'Neill snatched up the receiver and was dialing the number of the Office of Professional Standards when the door to his office opened and Santa Claus walked in. For a long moment the captain stared at the rotund man in the red suit. Then his nerves overloaded and he began to laugh.

As Comdr. Joseph Thomas O'Casey looked on, Captain O'Neill's laugh escalated from a chuckle to a howl and finally to full-throated hysteria. The Leprechaun stepped inside and closed the door behind him.

CHAPTER 40

NOVEMBER 24, 1976
10:23 P.M.

Martin Zykus's luck was changing for the better. He could feel it. First the pretty blond, and then the cops picking him up and letting him go. Both were proof that things were beginning to turn around for him. He only wished there was someplace open where he could buy a lottery ticket now.

After getting out of jail he headed for the Sheridan Inn. He wanted to see what had happened to Dave. As he walked along the empty streets, he was becoming angry. Dave Higgins came on so tough, yet he hadn't lifted a finger to help Zykus after the cop started chasing him.

Suddenly, Zykus came to the realization that he no longer liked Dave Higgins. In fact, he found that he actually hated Higgins. He thought back to all the times when Higgins had either cursed him or called him "boy." Then he thought about the girl. Dave had hurt her. The skinny bastard had hurt her. Zykus ground his teeth together and began clenching and unclenching his fists.

He cut through a gangway and came out across the street from the flophouse on Irving Park Road where Higgins rented a room. As he was about to step out of the shadows, he saw the fry cook come out of the hotel. Zykus backed up against the brick wall of the gangway and watched. Higgins was carrying a canvas bag and wearing the funny-looking pinstripe suit he always called his "dress-up duds." The fry cook's hair was slicked back and he looked like a freshly laundered skid-row bum as he shuffled west.

Zykus checked the street in both directions, which Higgins had taught him to do when they were stalking women. Then he followed.

Zykus thought that it was funny that for a man so good at following other people, Higgins walked along without even once glancing back over his shoulder. The fry cook was in a hurry, which was evident by his rapid pace. They were halfway there when Zykus realized where the fry cook was going. The busboy allowed a bit more distance to come between them. He was glad he did so because without warning Higgins stopped and took a long look back the way he had come. Zykus ducked out of sight behind a parked car before Higgins spied him. When the cook resumed his journey, Zykus was still behind him.

Higgins entered the el station on Sheridan Road off of Irving Park. Zykus made it to the entrance just as he started up the stairs. There was no attendant in the booth at this hour, as fares were paid on the train. Zykus waited a moment, and then entered the station.

The trains ran at half-hour intervals after ten o'clock. When they had approached the station, a train had rumbled overhead traveling south. Zykus was certain that was the direction Higgins would be taking. South. South to the Loop and the Greyhound Bus Station located there. Higgins had told Zykus his plan after he stabbed the woman who had ripped his ear.

"I ain't letting no cop put me back in prison, boy. I ain't got much in the way of things. No bank account, no property, no family. Better that way. I pack my bag, put on my dress-up duds, and I'm gone."

The night had turned damp and cold. Higgins had his

hands thrust in his pockets and the collar of his cheap suit up around his neck. He bounced from foot to foot on the vacant platform. He was looking north in the direction the southbound train would be coming when Zykus stepped up beside him.

"How ya doing, Dave?"

Higgins almost leaped off the platform onto the tracks, he was so badly frightened. His wrinkled, washed-out complexion went deathly pale, making his eyes seem to sink back in his skull as he stared at Zykus. His mouth opened, but no sound came out.

Zykus looked around the platform. Both sides were dimly lit and empty. The street below was visible, but where they stood was above an alley. The sky was overcast, and the low clouds held the promise of snow. It was just him and Higgins now.

"You scared the shit out of me, boy," Higgins gasped. "I thought that cop nabbed you for sure."

"He did catch me, Dave," Zykus said matter-of-factly. "He even took me in. But they didn't have nothing on me, so they let me go."

"Bullshit! You're lying!"

Zykus's head snapped around. His eyes bore into Higgins. "You calling me a liar after all we been through, partner?"

Higgins looked unsure of himself. "It's just that cops ain't usually so charitable. I figured they'd hold you for a spell. Maybe sweat you into telling about me."

"Is that why you're ducking out of town? I guess that way you'd be safe in California or Jersey, while I was left here to take the rap."

Higgins began moving his right hand around inside his pocket. "What kind of shit are you talking now, boy? I never run out on nobody in my life."

Higgins was slipping the Swiss Army knife out of his

pocket when Zykus grabbed him. The fry cook was fast and scared, but Zykus had become a different street animal in the last few hours. A street animal who could sense his former partner's weakness.

Using his bulk and greater strength, Zykus grabbed the hand still holding the knife and held it fast. He grabbed Higgins by the throat with the other hand and forced him across the platform railing. Before Higgins could make a move to defend himself, Zykus had him over the top of the railing, dangling above the alley fifty feet below.

"Put . . . me . . . down . . . fool!" Higgins lashed out and struck Zykus in the head with his fist. The fat boy held him fast above the alley floor.

"Help!" Higgins screamed. "Help me!"

Zykus let him go and he fell into the darkness below. He hit something hard and a resounding crash echoed up from the alley. Then there was silence.

Zykus looked around at the still-empty platform. He ran a hand through his lank hair, combing it back off his face, picked up Higgins's bag, and headed for the stairs. He found Higgins's body wedged in between the station wall and an overflowing garbage Dumpster. Higgins's eyes stared sightlessly up at Martin Zykus. Blood oozed from his mouth and ears. His legs were twisted beneath him like those of a discarded rag doll.

Zykus clawed the corpse out of the narrow space and tore through his pockets. Higgins had a couple hundred dollars in cash, an unopened package of Salems, a gold pocket watch, and a wallet with his ID inside. Zykus pried open the fingers and took the Swiss Army knife. It was fairly new. He pocketed it. Taking Higgins's bag, he turned to leave the alley—when something occurred to him. He walked back to the body. Drawing back the steel-toed boot on his left foot, he kicked Dave Higgins in the face four times. Under the unprotected attack, the dead man's features were mashed and shattered into an unrecognizable pulp.

Zykus stood over him and examined his handiwork. "That was for my girl," he said to the corpse.

Then he turned and left the alley.

CHAPTER 41

NOVEMBER 24, 1976
10:42 P.M.

Blackie, Cole, and Sergeant Novak were ordered to report to Commander O'Casey's office. When they entered, the Leprechaun was seated behind his desk, wearing his Santa Claus suit minus the cap. However, his fake flowing white beard and mustache were in place. He glared at the three officers. None of them returned his gaze and Cole was close to drawing blood from biting his bottom lip to keep from laughing.

But Santa Claus had never looked so grim.

"Commander, I'd just like to . . ." Novak began.

"Shut up!" O'Casey roared in uncharacteristic fashion.

All of them tensed and Cole was able to release his lip. From the look on the commander's face, it would be a long time before he laughed again.

O'Casey remained silent. He swung his chair around and looked at the photograph of himself with Mayor Richard J. Daley hanging on the wall. He stared at it for a long time. Then he swiveled the chair back to face his men.

"There will be no formal charges placed against any of you for anything that happened tonight."

Blackie smiled, which was a mistake.

"You wipe that smile off your mug, Silvestri, or I'll make you sorry you ever heard of the Nineteenth District or the blessed Chicago Police Department!"

Blackie's face went obediently blank.

The Leprechaun paused for effect before continuing. "There's going to be talk around the station about this. Your comrades in blue will want to know what happened between you and the watch commander. Now, for your information, the captain hasn't been feeling well. He left a few minutes ago with a touch of the flu." O'Casey paused to make sure this sunk in. "Any conversations you had with him tonight were purely in line with routine police business."

O'Casey dropped his voice an octave. "I want to hear nothing from anybody about the captain's condition. We had a talk and he's getting some help, but he doesn't need any tongues wagging behind his back. Do I make myself clear?"

They nodded.

"Then I suggest you hit the streets and see if you can keep this night from being a total waste of time for all of us."

They turned to leave. At the door Blackie hesitated and turned back to say something to the commander. But when he saw the look on the Leprechaun's face, he continued out into the corridor. Blackie could talk to him about the assignment of his new partner later.

There was less than half an hour left on the tour, but Cole didn't feel like hanging around the station. He had been through so much during the past eight hours it was difficult for him to put it all in perspective. After they left the commander's office, Sergeant Novak had told him that Blackie wanted Cole as his new partner. Life on a roller coaster, Cole thought. That's what he liked about being a cop; never a dull moment.

He cruised down Broadway and then swung west on Diversey. He kept replaying the events of the tour over and over in his mind. Each time Martin Zykus came back as an unsolved mystery.

It suddenly struck Cole that Zykus had run from him not far from the address where they'd had the "woman screaming" call. Now that O'Neill was out of the way, Cole considered taking a closer look at the apartment building on Barry.

"Nineteen Twenty-three," the dispatcher's voice came over the air.

Cole answered.

"On your way into the station, take a look at a man down in the alley behind the Sheridan–Irving el station. The caller wouldn't give his name. If you get tied up, I'll send a midnight car to relieve you."

"Nineteen Twenty-three, 10-99," Cole responded. He turned the police car in the direction of the call.

He found the "man down" without any difficulty, and it was quite obvious that he was dead. The face was a bloody mess that would make later identification difficult. Without touching anything, Cole backed out of the alley and raised his walkie-talkie to his lips. He hesitated a moment before depressing the transmit button. His earlier thoughts came back to him. *Never a dull moment.*

"Nineteen Twenty-three. I've got a D.O.A., possible homicide victim behind the CTA station at Sheridan and Irving Park. Would you make the notifications for me and send a supervisor over here?"

Down in the radio room at Eleventh and State streets the dispatcher acknowledged, "Ten-Four, Twenty-three." Then he took a buff-colored dispatch card and wrote "possible homicide victim" across the top. This was the first piece of information regarding another violent crime in the Windy City on the night before Thanksgiving, 1976.

3

"Do you remember Martin Zykus?"

—Larry Cole

CHAPTER 42

Sgt. Blackie Silvestri stood at the podium in the Area One squad room. Ten pairs of detectives sat at desks in front of him. Lou Bronson and Manny Sherlock were two of those present.

"We've borrowed four guys from the third watch and, if necessary, we'll get some additional help from downtown. It's Bronson's and Sherlock's case, but the entire department's on alert because of the heavyweight hardware the military's missing. We're still keeping this under wraps, so don't go shooting off your mouths about it.

"You guys know what to do," Blackie concluded. "Cover the ground until you flush something. Somewhere there's a lead on this thing. It's up to us to find it. Let's get to it."

Coffee cups were picked up, suit jackets donned, and briefcases snapped shut as the detectives headed for the outer office. Blackie moved along with them, noticing a strange silence and a lack of the good-natured kidding among them that usually followed roll call. He glanced at a face or two and noticed that even the hardest, most veteran cop looked frightened. Blackie really couldn't blame them.

The commander's door was open and Blackie crossed to

it. Looking inside, he found Larry Cole going through the previous day's reports.

"You're in early, boss," Blackie called through the door, as he poured Cole a cup of coffee from a pot beside his desk.

"Woke up early and decided to come in and tackle some of this paperwork."

Blackie carried the coffee—black with sugar—into the office and set it down on the desk blotter. Cole looked up at him and the sergeant marveled at the change his former partner had undergone since last night. Whereas yesterday he had looked tired and worried, now he appeared alert and rested.

"Excuse my asking, Commander, but you ain't on pep pills are you?"

Cole laughed. "No. Why would you ask me something like that?"

Blackie shrugged. "I don't know. It's just that you look like a new man. Like you got laid or something."

Cole looked thoughtfully at Blackie for a moment and then said, "You know, that might not be a bad idea, but I'm not on pills. I feel great and we've got a lot of work to do."

"Yes, sir," Blackie said, taking the seat across from his boss.

CHAPTER 43

APRIL 18, 1991
8:47 A.M.

Bronson and Sherlock signed their squad car out and headed for the parking lot. As they pulled onto Fifty-first Street, Manny said, "I figured you'd want to head for Astrolab right away."

Bronson was reading a message that he'd found in his mailbox. "We've got time for that later. Last night Watkins agreed to restrict everyone who knew Carduci to the base, so they're not going anywhere. Head up to Our Lady of Peace on Washington Park Boulevard. I've got to talk to someone."

When they pulled up in front of the church a few minutes later, Manny asked, "You want me to wait in the car?"

"Why?" Bronson said.

"I thought this might be something personal."

"Probably, but you can come along. It will give you a chance to meet Father Ken."

"Oh, that's okay. I'll stay in the car."

"No, it's not okay. I want you to meet my pastor. Now c'mon, Manny."

As they started up the stairs, Bronson looked questioningly at his partner. "What's the matter with you?"

"It's this religion stuff. Gives me the creeps."

Bronson stopped. "You an atheist?"

"No," Manny said. "I just was never involved with any church."

"Then you're an agnostic?"

Manny Sherlock shoved his hands into his pants pockets and said sheepishly, "I don't even know what that is, Lou. All I'm saying is that I never had anything to do with churches. So far they've left me alone and I've done the same with them."

Bronson stepped forward and took Manny by the arm. "C'mon, Father Ken really needs to talk to you."

Reluctantly, Manny followed Bronson into the church. They stood at the back. Manny watched curiously as Bronson dipped his right hand in the holy water font and crossed himself. The fifty-odd people inside were filing up to Communion. Bronson left Manny with the admonition, "Don't move," and joined the communicants.

A short time later Bronson returned and knelt in a rear pew. Manny watched him for a moment, and then took a better look at his surroundings.

Manny figured he had been inside a church before. In fact, he was certain he had. He just couldn't remember when. He had come from a normal American family, he guessed. His father had been a professional stage magician and his mother a dancing instructor at the Arthur Murray dance studio downtown. He had two older sisters. One had married a musician and moved to California, and the other had married a cop. The cop was a sergeant in the Eighth District and was responsible for getting Manny on the force. God and religion had never been an issue in his life. He hoped he could keep it that way, despite Lou Bronson.

However, he did have to admit one thing. This church was one of the most beautiful places he had ever been inside.

Bronson finished praying and rejoined Sherlock. "Mass

is almost over. We'll wait for Father Ken by the sacristy door."

They walked along the side of the church and behind the school. It was a few minutes before nine, and boys in sky blue shirts, dark trousers, and black ties, along with girls in dark blue skirts and white blouses, were filing into the school building. Occasionally, the cops got a look of hostility from one of the older kids, but there were no derogatory remarks made. Sherlock was impressed by the order, dignity, and quiet demeanor the children possessed.

"Detective Bronson," Father Ken called, as he stepped from the church. Accompanying the black priest were Sister Mary Louise Stallings and the three orphaned Price children.

"How are you, Father?" Bronson said, taking the priest's hand. "And how've you been, Sister?"

"I'm fine, Mr. Bronson, but I didn't know you were a policeman," she said with surprise.

"I don't go around making an issue of it. By the way, this is my partner, Manny Sherlock. Father Ken Smith and Sister Mary Louise."

Self-consciously, Manny shook hands with them.

"I got your message, Father," Bronson said. "I figured we'd stop by now, because we've got a full day ahead."

"If you're too busy, I won't trouble you," the priest said.

"Father, you promised," Sister Mary Louise said.

"Okay, Sister, I'll ask him. Detective Bronson, would you step over here for a moment and I'll explain the situation to you."

"Sure thing," Bronson said. "Oh, by the way, Sister, Manny's an agnostic, but salvageable. Maybe you could talk him into taking instructions."

Since she'd come out of the church with the children, Sister Mary Louise had seemed drawn and tense. Now her face lit up, as she studied the potential convert.

As Bronson and Father Ken walked away, she smiled at

the tall policeman. "Are you really an agnostic, Detective Sherlock?"

He still didn't know what an agnostic was. He told her this.

"Labels really don't matter when you're talking about faith, Manny," she said. "You don't mind if I call you Manny?"

"Nah, go ahead," Sherlock said, once more jamming his hands into his pants pockets and looking over his shoulder at Bronson and the priest, who were still talking.

Rebecca and Randy Price began playing a game of skipping on one foot between the cracks in the sidewalk beside the church. Sister Mary Louise kept an eye on them while she continued to work on the gangly policeman. Sean Price, however, remained by her side, staunchly refusing to move. The child stared up at Manny Sherlock.

"That's one of the problems we have in this world, Manny," she continued. "There are too many labels. They even have labels for policemen. Negative ones at that."

"I guess so," Sherlock said, not really understanding where she was going with this.

Sean Price began tugging at Sister Mary Louise's habit.

"One of the reasons we as human beings put so many labels on things is because we need to categorize them in order to make them easier to understand."

Manny's eyes drifted toward Bronson and the priest. They were still talking and looked like they'd be at it for a while. *Please, Lou,* Sherlock's brain screamed, while his face remained outwardly passive.

"But understanding doesn't come that easily. We use labels like 'Catholic,' 'Baptist,' 'Jewish,' 'agnostic,' and the like to explain away entire concepts of God's relationships with his creations." She stopped and smiled at Manny. Sean Price had become so insistent and was yanking on her habit with such force that she was starting to lose her balance.

"Excuse me, Manny." She looked down at the little boy. "Why don't you go play with your sister and brother, Sean?"

With wide-eyed innocence Sean pointed up at the detective. "Is he a policeman?"

Manny took this as a greatly desired reprieve. "Yes, I am, little boy." He squatted down, which put him still a head taller than the child. "Haven't you ever seen a policeman before?"

Sean nodded. "I saw a whole lot of policeman yesterday. They was over by that bad temple place on the boulevard after my mommy and daddy went away."

Manny noticed the nun tense. Quickly, she said, "I know some policemen too, Sean."

Sean ignored her, but Manny looked up. Curiously, he asked, "Yeah, like who?"

"Larry Cole and Blackie Silvestri."

Sherlock stood straight up, forgetting about the little boy. "You know the commander and Sergeant Silvestri?!"

Smiling, Sister Mary Louise realized she had the skinny detective's full attention now. "Yes, we're old friends. I guess you know them, too."

I know them, Manny thought, *but do they know me?*

At that point Bronson and Father Ken returned.

"I'll check this guy out for you, Father," Bronson was saying. "If I turn up anything, I'll let you know. We'd better get going, Manny. It's a long ride out to Astrolab."

"Sure thing, Lou," Manny said, still staring at the nun.

"Take it easy, Father," Bronson said. "Have a nice day, Sister." Seeing that Manny still hadn't moved, he added, "Detective Sherlock, are you coming?"

Manny snapped back to his senses. "Yeah, uh, I'm coming. Nice meeting you folks." He backed away, giving a weak wave to Sean Price. The child waved back.

Father Ken and Sister Mary Louise watched them go.

"Did you know the nun knows the boss and Blackie?" Manny said.

Bronson shrugged. "So?"

"Don't you think that's odd?"

"No. But it might tell us they're not agnostics."

"Yeah," Manny said, unlocking the squad car door. "You may be right."

"I usually am."

As they drove away from Our Lady of Peace, Bronson opened his notebook and looked at the name Father Ken had asked him to check out. Steven Zalkin.

CHAPTER 44

APRIL 18, 1991
9:30 A.M.

Rosalie "Rosie" O'Grady entered the *Times-Herald* building on Michigan Avenue. In the lobby she stopped at the concession stand and purchased two rolls of peppermint Certs for her boss. She then headed for the elevators.

Rosie O'Grady was sixty-three years old and had been with the *Times-Herald* for forty-one years. She had been a copy girl, crime reporter, and gossip columnist. She had never moved up to positions such as feature writer or staff reporter simply because she couldn't write and had never taken the time to learn. That is not to say that she was illiterate, but rather that her prose style was dull and she had never mastered proper English usage. In a Rosie O'Grady story, punctuation and capitalization did not exist.

But Rosie had managed to hang on in a Chicago newspaper business fraught with price wars, hostile corporate takeovers, and reporters holding on to their jobs from paycheck to paycheck. This was because she had two things going for her: She knew the ins and outs of the newspaper business like few others, and she was patently vicious.

During her forty-one-year career, Rosie had slept with more than her share of politicians, cops, reporters, and general-category others in order to get a story. When she reached her mid-thirties, two things happened to her at once. She began putting on excessive weight, which—like her writing—she never tried to do anything about, and she began losing her hair, which she couldn't do anything about. After purchasing a plethora of expensive wigs in different colors, but still awash in layers of fat, she attempted to keep up her amorous liaisons in order to scoop the opposition. However, when invitations to join her in the boudoir were met first with skeptical smirks and finally hysterical laughter, she decided to change tactics.

In her middle years, Rosie became an information gatherer, or, more basically, a gossip. But she did her work on a citywide scale with such skill that she secretly became a source for rival-newspaper gossip-columnists until the *Times-Herald* editorial board found out about it. The board considered asking for her resignation, but at that point, like J. Edgar Hoover of the FBI, Rosie had so much in her files on each of them that they were afraid to let her loose on the city.

They tried giving her a column of her own, with a smart young journalism intern to do the writing for her. By this time Rosie had turned fifty with a vengeance and was making life miserable for her third of five husbands and her intern. Before Rosie turned fifty-seven, she was working on her fourth husband and fifth intern. By the time she turned sixty, her last husband had run screaming from their North Lake Shore Drive condo with only the clothes on his back, never to be seen again, and her tenth intern had quit. Also, as she approached senior-citizen status, her column had become a major liability for the *Times-Herald.*

Generally, gossip columns contain good gossip, bad gossip, and to some extent, nasty, unsubstantiated rumor. Rosie's column, which was being ghostwritten by her eleventh and twelfth journalism interns—replacements for which were becoming increasingly hard to find—contained none of the first, little of the second, and a great deal of the last.

In her Christmas Day column of 1989, Rosie questioned the mayor's sexual preferences, accused a federal judge of taking bribes, romantically linked a nationally prominent African-American religious figure with a white female movie star of questionable virtue, and accused the Chicago Police Department of covering up wrongdoing in the suicide-by-hanging of a mentally deranged prisoner. Separate investigations conducted by the *Times-Herald* and other city papers revealed that each story was false. Libel suits followed.

At this point the editorial board decided that Rosie had to go; however, not by way of the pink slip. She still possessed a wealth of information about her superiors and coworkers on the *Times-Herald.* The managing editor, a practical man who had been in the business as long as Rosie and was addicted to cocaine—which Rosie was aware of—had always been taught, "If given a lemon, make lemonade."

As the New Year of 1990 rolled around, the two biggest problems facing the *Times-Herald* were Rosalie O'Grady and Frank Delahanty, who was writing better than ever and drinking like the world would end on February 1. So in a moment of tremendous insight, which a management-seminar instructor once called, "A blinding flash of the obvious," the editor decided to combine both problems into one. So he made Rosie O'Grady Frank Delahanty's research assistant, but kept her at the same rate of pay she had earned as a gossip columnist.

The editor figured they would mutually self-destruct in six months. A year and a half later, they were still together and, in fact, doing well. Delahanty was as big a drunk as ever and Rosie had never been bitchier, but like the Odd Couple, they complemented each other. Far from being happy with the development, the editor waited for disaster to strike. It did so on the morning of April 18, 1991.

Rosie stepped off the elevator into the twenty-seventh floor corridor, where the *Times-Herald* executive offices and offices of the senior columnists were located. She generally dressed her overweight frame in dark, shapeless clothing, and wore orthopedic shoes to ease her bunions. Today's wig was bright red and elaborately styled into a Greek-goddess ponytail. As she clomped down the marble-floored corridor a number of secretaries, reporters, and a couple of *Times-Herald* senior editors passed her. A few spoke, but Rosie did not return their greetings. Like her boss Delahanty, she didn't speak to the hired help or menials.

The double wooden doors were halfway down the corridor. The number four was on the south door. This was to prevent the casual—or even intended—visitor from knowing whose suite this belonged to. Using her key, Rosie unlocked the door and went inside. The minute she stepped across the threshold, she knew Frank had had one of those nights. The place smelled like a saloon.

The suite was big, containing a reception room, private offices for her and Delahanty, and a bathroom with shower. Delahanty lived in a Lake Shore Drive apartment not far from her own, but since his second wife had left him, he had taken to staying overnight in the office more and more. Especially because he was drinking more and more.

To accommodate the paper's star columnist, Rosie had a couch installed that pulled out into a bed. There was always an extra change of clothing for the columnist in his office and she kept various hangover remedies here. Also, because Delahanty insisted on it, there was a fully stocked bar, which she had instructions to keep perpetually replenished.

Once, when she'd been remiss in her bartending duties and had allowed the celebrated columnist to run out of vermouth for his daily gallon of martinis, she had been the subject of a column. He had mildly rebuked her, which from Frank Delahanty was like having your bare flesh scrubbed with a steel brush. But she got over it, because she found that she loved Delahanty.

That was not to say that she was "in love" with him. She had been in love with three of her five husbands. That is, at least for the first six months of the marriages. She loved Frank because, despite her own inability to write, she admired good prose, and Delahanty was the finest stylist working for any newspaper in the country—at least, in her estimation.

She had also adopted a particular fondness for the way he ruthlessly destroyed the opposition in print. How he wrote it like he saw it instead of like it was. How he could employ his wit to castigate anyone, big or small, black or white, mighty or poor. How he could make a shrine out of that poor black church on the South Side or make fools out of an untouchable institution like Alcoholics Anonymous.

At times Rosie O'Grady fantasized what her journalism career would have been like had she possessed a gift like Frank's. Then she would have been a tabloid terror, the likes of which the gossip columns of the world had never seen.

So she took care of the columnist. She poured his drinks, cooked his meals on the office hot plate, nursed his hangovers, and made sure that he stayed on schedule with his columns. That was six columns a week, forty-two weeks a year, running anywhere from seven hundred to one thousand words each. About two hundred thousand words a

year. And Delahanty did them all while Rosie stood by
watching, proud to play a part in the perpetuation of this
journalistic legend.

Now the legend was lying on the floor snoring. His suit
jacket had been balled up to use as a pillow on the couch,
but during the night the esteemed *Times-Herald* columnist
had rolled off onto the floor, where he now slept. There
was a chance he wouldn't be too sick to write tomorrow's
and Sunday's columns, which had to be in to editorial by
three o'clock that afternoon.

But first things first.

Rosie grabbed her charge and pulled him into a sitting
position on the floor. He smelled like the devil. He
groaned, but his bloodshot eyes fluttered open and he
looked evilly at her.

"What the fu . . . !" He tried to lie back down, but she
wouldn't let him.

She hefted him onto the couch with surprising ease. Any
woman who had survived five bad marriages had to be
strong. Now, Delahanty was awake and looking like he'd
rather be dead.

"I need an eye-opener, Rosie," he growled.

"Coming up, boss." Even though she was far senior to
the columnist in the newspaper business, she still called
him "boss."

She crossed to the bar and began mixing a Bloody Mary
in a blender. She knew Delahanty liked it roaring hot, so
she didn't skimp on the Tabasco. Pressing the mix button
she turned to gaze at the stinking, sorry-looking man
whose words millions of people read every day.

"You didn't come back from lunch yesterday." It was a
statement, which left Delahanty with room to either
respond or ignore.

"I went to the Press Club." He didn't say anything else
until she handed him a Bloody Mary. She had stuck half a
celery stalk inside the mixture, which was the only food

Delahanty had been near, other than martini olives, for the past sixteen hours.

He removed the celery and dropped it on the cocktail table. While he gulped his drink, Rosie picked up the celery and wiped the wet spot it had made with her handkerchief.

He downed half the liquid in one long swallow. When he came up for air he didn't look any better. Only more flushed.

"I went to the Press Club for lunch."

"You said that, Frank." She thumped back across the room and picked up the blender, which still had another serving left in it. She returned and refilled his glass.

He glared at her as she poured. "I wrote Friday's column. It's in my frigging notebook."

Good luck, Rosie thought, as she picked up his wrinkled, mashed suit jacket from the couch and searched the pockets. She found his wallet first and checked the cash and credit cards. Cash—seventy-eight dollars, credit cards all accounted for. She found his keys and an empty matchbook on which "Sandy 963-0415" was written.

"You might want this later," she said, handing him the matchbook cover.

He stared at it. She knew he probably didn't have the slightest idea who Sandy was or where he'd gotten the matchbook from.

Finally, she found the notebook. She flipped it open and braced herself. If he was past the twelfth martini when he started writing, neither Rosie nor Delahanty would be able to read a word. To her relief, she could tell he was around martini five or six, which wouldn't qualify him for the good penmanship award, but meant that the page was at least readable. That is, most of it.

Rosie read a few paragraphs and was enthralled by the narrative. She could tell this was Delahanty at his best. She walked over and sat down in one of the easy chairs. She never took her eyes off his scribbling.

"Is this Steven Zalkin for real?" she asked.

Delahanty shrugged and now sipped at his Bloody Mary. The Tabasco and vodka were making him sweat. "That's what I want you to check out today before we send the column down. Sounds as phony as hell to me."

"You've got the cops here, too. Schmidt, Baldwin, and Riseman. I wonder who was watching the store?"

"That's my point." Delahanty struggled to his feet. Once upright, he stood rigidly still. She merely glanced at him. His head was probably throbbing. She had a couple of Tylenol that could mute that. Then he would need a shower and some real food. Soft scrambled eggs, toast, grits, bacon, coffee, and orange juice. No booze until sundown, she hoped. She'd order from the restaurant on the first floor while he was showering. Then they had Sunday's column to worry about.

"You're really cutting the brass buttons off these cops and their Cops for Education campaign."

"Their what?" Delahanty was heading across the reception area where no one was ever received and where he sometimes spent the night.

"Cops for Education campaign," she repeated. "You mention it three times."

He paused a moment and then said a half-mumbled, "Yeah."

This Steven Zalkin was going to wish he'd never approached Frank Delahanty's table at the Press Club.

She picked up his suit jacket and crossed the office. She noticed there was a cigarette burn in the lapel. The suit had cost a thousand dollars from a tailor on the Magnificent Mile of Michigan Avenue. Now it was ready for the trash. She would never consider giving it to charity. She wouldn't let Frank know about it though. When he was drunk and did things like this, finding out about it later depressed him. She was there to make sure he didn't get depressed. She would order a new suit in the same style and material.

It would go on his expense account, which the paper never questioned.

Rosie was certain that she was the best editorial assistant in history. Undoubtedly, she was the highest paid.

She heard the shower going as she entered Delahanty's office. It was as neat as a pin because he hadn't been here in a while. She moved over to his computer terminal and opened his notebook. She decided to do a little editing—Frank would never know about it.

Rosie was reaching for the keyboard when she noticed the message light flashing on Delahanty's answering machine. It was probably easier to obtain the home telephone number of the Governor of the State of Illinois than to obtain Frank Delahanty's private number. Since he and his wife had split up, the number had been changed. The only ones who had it were the paper's managing editor and Rosie O'Grady.

She pressed the play button on the answering machine and waited. There was a beep and then the message began.

At first Rosie thought it was a woman with a cold speaking. Then she realized that what she was hearing was a computerized voice transmission. The sound itself was mechanical and eerie, which only enhanced the effect of the words.

"Francis Xavier Delahanty, between the time you hear this message and midnight of the evening of the eighteenth of April, I intend to burn you alive. You may go to the police with my blessing, but it won't help. Use the time you have left wisely."

CHAPTER 45

The yellow taxi cab pulled to the curb two blocks from Steven Zalkin's building, and Brian Littlejohn got out. Littlejohn was a monstrously muscular man wearing a short-sleeved knit shirt over a fifty-eight-inch chest. He squeezed a roll of bills out of his jeans pocket and paid the fare. The driver was a small Lebanese who had never seen a human being this large before, even though bodybuilding was a sport in his country.

After paying the cabbie, Littlejohn turned and began walking west. He was white, in his mid-thirties, and bald, with wispy fringes of hair combed haphazardly over his ears. He had good features, which under other circumstances would have earned him the label *nice-looking*—if not *handsome*. There was, however, something furtive and suspicious about the eyes. A look so raw and primitive as to be on the edge of violence. People gave him a wide berth as he passed, but it wasn't only because of his eyes.

Few humans who had ever lived on this earth had ever achieved the muscular development and definition of Brian Littlejohn. Every muscle from chin to ankle was supremely developed into a size and vascularity that was truly astonishing. He was a sculptured monument, a man who had developed the body God gave him to awesome proportions.

Fellow bodybuilders were amazed by his perfection. In the mid- and late seventies, he had won a number of bodybuilding contests, sharing stages and the pages of muscle magazines with such greats as Arnold Schwarzenegger, Franco Columbu, Robbie Robinson, Bill Grant, and Sergio Oliva. He was on his way to stardom—and even considered an acting career like Arnold's—when the International Federation of Body Builders announced a ban on steroid use and instituted urine testing prior to events. This edict put Littlejohn on the sidelines, because although he had worked hard to develop his body, he was a heavy steroid user.

So it was that Brian Littlejohn dropped out of competition, but still trained from six to ten hours a day. He still took regular steroid injections, which had led to his hair loss, total absence of sex drive, kidney damage, and developing coronary problems. But he didn't plan to stop using the drug—instead, he got into the business end of steroid sales.

Now, in his left hand, Littlejohn carried an attaché case. It would have taken his death or severe incapacitation to get the case away from him.

He reached the door to the three-story, redbrick building and looked around to see if any of the passersby had noticed him. In fact, everyone he had passed in the last two blocks had noticed him, and had even stared openly after he had gone by. A few remembered him from pre-steroid-ban competition days. The rest had simply never seen anyone like him. He might as well have been standing out on the street dressed as Bozo the Clown for all the good his careful approach to Zalkin's building had done. He pressed the bell and waited.

When the security door snapped open, Littlejohn proceeded inside and climbed the single flight of stairs to an iron door. Littlejohn stopped and idly flexed the muscles of his arms and chest, making them ripple like waves under a breeze at sea. He felt strong enough to rip the door off its hinges, and he probably could have given it a decent try.

But after the short stair climb, his breathing had become slightly labored and his heart was beating discernibly faster. Brian Littlejohn did no aerobic exercise in the gym, and the steroids were rapidly destroying his heart.

There was a clanging of bolts being undone, and then the door slid back to reveal a smiling Steven Zalkin. "How's it going, Brian?"

Littlejohn sat down on the sofa, which sighed under his weight. His jaw jutted from a twenty-inch neck as he looked up to study his host, who was his best-paying client.

"Can I get you something to drink?"

"What you got?"

The voice that came out of that massive body was high-pitched, almost girlish. Zalkin smiled and said, "Papaya or coconut juice."

"Good," Littlejohn said. "Let me have a glass of the coconut."

Zalkin went to get the drink while Littlejohn picked up his attaché case, placed it on the cocktail table, and opened it. There were six syringes inside, along with a bottle of alcohol and cotton balls for administering the injections. The syringes had been marked and filled with the proper steroid injection for each of Littlejohn's customers. Four were for athletes: a pro football player, a basketball player on a North Shore college team that was in contention for the NCAA finals, and two bodybuilders, who were intent on looking like gods despite the IFBB ban. The last two were for Zalkin.

Littlejohn placed the syringes for his rich customer down on the cocktail table. He figured that, after taking this double whammy, Zalkin should be able to leap tall buildings with a single bound.

Zalkin came back into the room carrying a glass containing a cloudy liquid. Before taking it Littlejohn asked, "This come out of a can?"

"No," Zalkin replied. "I watched the health-food store

juice-bar attendant extract it myself. It costs, my friend, so enjoy."

Littlejohn took the glass and gulped it down. When it was empty he set the glass on the table, flexed his dinner-plate-sized pectoral muscles, expelled a belch, and said, "Take your clothes off. I want to take a look at you."

Automatically, Zalkin complied, stripping down to a pair of black briefs and stepping obediently in front of Littlejohn. The bodybuilder struggled up from the couch and walked around Zalkin. He studied his physique with a trained eye.

"You been working out?" Littlejohn asked.

"Five days a week for at least two hours a day." Zalkin had affixed his gaze on a point where the ceiling and wall met.

Littlejohn nodded with some degree of approval over the millionaire's build. He was nowhere near competition size or definition, but he was passable. Good muscle balance over-all, and some degree of vascularity. Littlejohn frowned when he saw there should have been more muscle and less fat.

Littlejohn soaked a cotton ball from the bottle of alco-hol, picked up a syringe, and stepped behind Zalkin. He flipped down the elastic of the black briefs, exposing the two mounds of gluteus muscle. With a seasoned eye Littlejohn noticed that Zalkin had unusually large glutes, which made giving the injection easier. He noticed Zalkin flinch as he rubbed alcohol on one of his cheeks. Littlejohn quickly followed by plunging the needle beneath the skin. In less than ten seconds it was over.

As Zalkin adjusted his briefs and began climbing back into his clothes, Littlejohn returned the empty syringe and used cotton ball to his case. He left the second full syringe lying on the cocktail table. "You need to refrigerate that until you get ready to use it. You got good size for a man under two hundred pounds, but you're putting on too much fat. You're not watching your diet."

Zalkin's face was tight with strain. The shot had hurt. He buttoned his shirt and walked over to his desk. On the blotter there was a sealed envelope. There was no name or address on the envelope. Inside was the agreed-upon sum for Littlejohn's product and services.

"I thought the exercise and the injections would be enough," he said, handing the envelope to Littlejohn.

"Not if you eat a lot of shit, it's not. When are you going to take the next injection?"

Zalkin thought for a moment. "Tomorrow at about midday. Maybe early evening."

"That's too soon. I wouldn't take them like that even if I was training for the Mr. Olympia contest."

"But you won't be training for Mr. Olympia or any other contest for a while now, will you, Brian?"

The bodybuilder glared back at Zalkin for a moment before turning to pick up his briefcase. He stuffed the envelope in his pocket and headed for the door saying, "You have a nice day, Mr. Zalkin. Hope you break that second needle off in your ass."

Zalkin laughed as Littlejohn let himself out.

CHAPTER 46

Zalkin crossed the Chicago River bridge and ran past the Merchandise Mart. He was headed back to his building after his daily five-mile run. He checked his watch. A little more than six minutes per mile. That was too slow. He quickened his pace.

He could feel the effects of the steroid injection. He could feel its power surging through his muscles with each step. He held his arms up like a boxer in training. Occasionally he even flipped a jab into the air in front of him. Despite the coolness of the clear spring day, he was dressed only in shorts, jogging shoes, and sweat socks. His muscular chest was bare and he noticed more than one glance cast his way by admiring females he passed. But he only had eyes for one woman, and in a little while she would be his.

Zalkin was heading in a north-northwesternly direction back toward his building. His thoughts were random as he made his way along, barely feeling the exertion of his run. He had a great deal to do in the next thirty-six hours. Then it would all be over.

He was so absorbed in his thoughts that he ran off the sidewalk and into the middle of the street—in front of an oncoming truck. The driver slammed on the brakes, but much too late to avoid hitting him. The grill in front of the right headlight made contact with the runner's side and right arm with enough force to hurl him ten feet through the air. No sooner did Zalkin hit the pavement than he rolled over and bounded to his feet.

In twenty-five years behind the wheel as a professional, the truck driver had never struck a pedestrian before. In fact, he had never been responsible for causing an accident, although he'd been in a few. In scant seconds he went through a plethora of emotions. First there was terror, which gave way to fear, and finally anger when he saw the shirtless jogger jump to his feet like a jack-in-the-box. He came out of the truck with a roar.

"What the fuck is wrong with you, man?" the truck driver bellowed as he approached the runner. "You trying to get your ass killed?"

Zalkin glared at him. The truck driver was heavy, but most of his weight had collected in the shape of a medicine ball around his waist. He looked at least fifty, maybe older. People called such men "hard hats." Drank beer by the case and took their shirts off at December Bears games.

A small crowd had gathered on the sidewalk.

"You yuppies go jogging around in your little shorts, while honest people got to do a day's work just to make ends meet. For chrissakes, man, will you watch where the hell you're going from now on?"

The driver turned to walk back to his truck when the jogger made his move. Rushing up behind the driver, he threw a punch which detonated with tremendous fury above the kidneys. Screaming in pain, the driver dropped to his knees. Zalkin stepped around him, grabbing the back of his neck as he did so. He tilted the driver's head forward and slammed his knee into the exposed face. He watched the man's eyes roll back in his head.

Zalkin snatched him to his feet and rammed him face-first into the truck's grill.

Blood spattered as the driver bounced away from the metal-on-flesh impact to collapse on the street. A woman in the crowd screamed. Zalkin began pulling him to his feet for an encore when he heard a shout.

"Freeze! Let him go right now!"

Zalkin's head snapped around. A female police officer in uniform stood beside the open truck door, pointing a four-inch-barrel .38 at him. He noticed that the gun trembled slightly; her eyes, however, never left his. Zalkin dropped the bleeding truck driver. His steroid-fueled fury still raged inside him. He took a step toward her.

She stood her ground and cocked the weapon. "I'm only going to say this once, asshole. What you just did was attempted murder. That is, if he's still alive. So you take another step and I'll blow your ass right out of those Nikes."

Zalkin listened, considered his situation, and slowly raised his hands. As the policewoman stepped around him to begin snapping handcuffs on his wrists, he heard a familiar voice echo through his head, *"You fucked up, boy."*

It startled Zalkin, but perhaps it shouldn't have: It came to him frequently when he was under stress. The voice was that of the long-dead Dave Higgins.

"You're under arrest," the policewoman said, leading him away to her patrol car. She began reading him his rights.

CHAPTER 47

Chief Riseman was seated in the superintendent's office when First Deputy Schmidt entered. Schmidt took the remaining chair in front of the desk and waited.

"This message was on Frank Delahanty's answering machine this morning." The superintendent activated a tape-player on his desk. They listened.

When it finished, Riseman said, "It could be a prank. Delahanty pisses off a lot of people with that column of his."

"According to his assistant," the superintendent took the slip his secretary had written the name on and squinted at it, ". . . this Rosalie O'Grady, the number's unlisted and hard to get."

Schmidt snorted. "If you ask me, we'd be doing this town a favor by letting whoever made that call fry Delahanty and that Rosie O'Grady."

The superintendent stared a silent rebuke at his first deputy as Riseman said, "We could offer Delahanty protection. Set up a detail for a day or so until this thing blows over. That would make it hard for him to give us any negative press."

"I agree," the superintendent said before Schmidt could

put his foot in his mouth again. "But I don't want you using detectives, Bill. That's why you're here, Ray. I want you to assign a couple of good tactical officers to Delahanty until this is all over."

"What are they supposed to do, boss, follow him from saloon to saloon?"

The superintendent was having a bad morning. This Temple of Allah thing, along with a host of do-gooders coming out of the woodwork with charges that the department had had a hand in the explosion that killed Abdul Ali Malik and his followers, was making his ulcer act up. On top of that, he'd have to bury Kessler and Brick on Monday—a job he didn't relish. Now his first deputy was acting stupid, as usual.

"I don't give a damn what they do with him, Ray,·as long as he keeps breathing," the superintendent snapped. "Now, you pick two good men who are levelheaded and know how to keep their mouths shut, and send them over to the *Times-Herald*. They're to stick with Delahanty until I say different. Have you got that?"

"I got it, boss."

"Then, if you have nothing else, you can go," the superintendent said. "I want to talk to Bill alone."

Schmidt's face reddened as he left the office. He had been dismissed like a rookie. It hurt, and he walked back to his office feeling the sting of his embarrassment festering into anger.

Lt. Patrick Roberts was waiting for Schmidt. "We got a call from the Eighteenth District, sir."

"I don't have time for this shit now." Schmidt stormed past him.

Roberts followed. "It concerns your friend Steven Zalkin."

Schmidt stopped. "What about him?"

"He's been arrested for battery."

"What?"

Roberts looked down at his steno pad, although he had memorized the information written there. "He beat up a truck driver. It must have been pretty bad because the driver's in the hospital."

"Get me the Eighteenth District commander on the horn." Schmidt stomped behind his desk and stopped. "No. Forget that. Tell my driver to pick me up in front. I'm going up there."

CHAPTER 48

APRIL 18, 1991
11:22 A.M.

Lou Bronson and Manny Sherlock were on their way back into Chicago from Indiana. While Sherlock drove, Bronson looked over the notes he'd made at Astrolab.

"Carduci played his cards real close to the vest, Manny. Made no friends and few acquaintances, while keeping pretty much to himself. When he got a three-day pass he spent it alone. Nobody knew the places he hung out except that Corporal Winters."

"I thought it was kind of strange that she was the only one who ever bumped into Carduci in Chicago."

"Yeah," Bronson said. "And she said she saw him three times at this Club Cosmos on Superior. Doesn't sound right to me."

"You think she's lying, Lou?"

"Probably. She overplayed the ironpants female-professional-soldier bit. Tomorrow I'm going to have Watkins bring her into the Area. A change of scene will do a world of good for her disposition."

"You think she knows who iced Carduci?"

Bronson nodded. "She knows, but she probably doesn't know that she knows. Take the One hundred fifteenth Street exit. I want to make a couple of telephone calls from Area Two."

The Area Two police center was more modern than Area One and twice as large. They parked their car in the lot behind the station and entered through a back door. A heavyset sergeant with a menacing scowl manned the huge station desk in the lobby. Bronson flashed his ID and asked to use the phones.

"To call your girlfriend or your bookie?" The sergeant's scowl did not change.

"Strictly official business, Sarge," Bronson said.

"Too bad," the sergeant said. "Be the first time today anyone has used them for anything having to do with police work. Help yourselves."

Bronson and Sherlock exchanged wary looks as they proceeded to the far end of the desk, out of earshot of the sergeant.

"I want you to call the License Unit and find out who owns the Club Cosmos," Bronson said. "We can give him a call and find out when would be the best time to talk to his staff. I'm going to look into something else."

"For the priest, right?" Manny grinned.

Bronson nodded.

For the next twenty minutes the two detectives stood side by side, engaged in separate conversations. Sherlock hung up first and leaned against the desk casually, waiting for his partner to finish.

Finally, Bronson hung up. He wore a puzzled frown as

he scanned the notes he'd made during the telephone conversation.

"How does a guy just show up at the First National Bank and plunk down twenty million dollars in cash?" Bronson said.

"Easy, if he's got it," Sherlock quipped.

"But there's nothing on him prior to that. According to the bank's records, all the references he gave are dead. He just came out of nowhere with a truckload of money."

"Who are you talking about?"

"The guy Father Ken asked me to check on this morning. Wants to give the church a half a million dollars. His name's Steven Zalkin."

Sherlock's eyebrows shot up as he stared at this partner.

"What's wrong, Manny?"

"I called the License Unit."

"And?"

"The Club Cosmos is owned by Steven Zalkin."

CHAPTER 49

APRIL 18, 1991
NOON

The first deputy superintendent stormed into the Eighteenth District police station like the Marines taking the beach at Iwo Jima. The Near North Side district was one of the busiest in the city and had a branch of the Circuit Court of Cook County in the same building. As the lunch hour approached, the desk area was congested with people making inquiries or conducting court business. Schmidt waded through this mass of humanity, shoving, elbowing, and bullying his way to the gate behind the desk. A sign across the gate read AUTHORIZED PERSONNEL ONLY.

There were four desk officers and a sergeant working behind the desk. All but one officer, who was seated at a computer workstation facing the gate, failed to notice Schmidt enter. Before the officer could warn the others, the first deputy had crossed the desk area and stormed into the watch commander's office. It was only when the door slammed behind him that the others looked around.

"Who the hell was that?" the sergeant asked.

"Trouble," the officer at the computer workstation commented.

Lt. Michael Holland was the watch commander. At the age of thirty-one, he was one of the youngest lieutenants on the force. He also considered himself one of the most attractive. Single and available to any woman who came his way, Holland was particularly fond of young female police officers. At this moment he was personally interviewing Officer Eileen Glover regarding the circumstances surrounding her arrest of Steven Zalkin.

It was not normal procedure for the watch commander to interview police officers after routine arrests. However, Lieutenant Holland had had his eye on Officer Glover for some time. Now, as she recited the circumstances leading up to the arrest, he focused his gray eyes on her and tried to appear as concerned and caring as he could. He believed that women of the nineties admired sensitivity in a man, and he virtually reeked with it—that is, until First Deputy Superintendent Schmidt barged through his office door.

When Holland looked up from where he was hunched over his desk—with his face less than eighteen inches from

Officer Glover's—and saw Schmidt, his studio tan vanished and his eyes widened in shock. He jumped to attention and tried to speak, but words failed him. Glover, who only had two years on the CPD and had never been in the military, did not stand.

"I want to talk to you about someone you're holding, Lieutenant," Schmidt said with a scowl. "His name's Steven Zalkin."

Glover now stood and faced Schmidt. She had been in sales before joining the department and had a basically outgoing personality. She extended her hand and said, "Police Officer Glover, sir. I arrested Zalkin."

Schmidt stared at her for an instant, unable to fathom what she was doing with her hand. Then he spun back to Holland. "I want to see the arrest report and find out what the hell's going on here."

Glover dropped her hand and frowned. "What's going on here, sir, is that Zalkin tried to beat a man to death after a traffic accident."

"I want to speak to you about this alone, Lieutenant."

Refusing to drop his future intentions toward Glover, Holland said an apologetic, "Would you give us a minute to discuss this, Eileen?"

Schmidt looked on in disbelief.

In something of a snit, Glover snatched her cap off Holland's desk and stormed out.

Holland stood wilting under Schmidt's glare. "You got a lot to learn about supervision, Lieutenant."

"Yes, sir."

Steven Zalkin sat on a bench in a narrow cell. The walls were of steel and painted a battleship gray. There was a toilet and stainless-steel sink installed on one wall. The only entrance was through a sliding iron-barred door, which was part of the bars that ran from the floor to the ceiling to make up the entire wall.

Zalkin was alone and cold. He still had on nothing but his shorts, sweat socks, and running shoes. The jailer, a balding man with thick eyebrows, had offered him a disposable paper shirt. At the time Zalkin was too angry with the cops to take it. Now the body heat generated during his steroid-enhanced run had dissipated. On top of that, the hostile atmosphere of his surroundings was chilling.

He got to make one telephone call. He had considered a lawyer, but then a lawyer wouldn't do him any good at this point. He needed to get out of here with all charges dropped. This had happened to him before. He needed some juice on this one, so he called Ray Schmidt. To his dismay, Schmidt was out of the office. Then the jailer had taken his fingerprints.

Now he sat in the narrow cell, staring at the graffiti etched into the walls by past inmates. One particular etching drew his attention. "Life sucks!" It made Zalkin chuckle, because it was so true.

He heard footsteps approaching the cell. Idly, he looked up. Ray Schmidt stood outside, looking in on him. The jailer was with him.

"Well, it looks like you've gotten yourself into a fine mess," Schmidt said.

"It looks that way," Zalkin responded, deadpan.

"Open it," Schmidt said to the jailer.

"You can leave us," Schmidt said to the policeman. The first deputy stepped into the cell and left the door ajar.

The jailer looked at Schmidt's holstered revolver and started to say something. Guns in lock-ups were against regulations. But Schmidt's reputation preceded him, so the jailer kept his mouth shut and walked away.

Schmidt sat down on the bench across from Zalkin. "What happened, Steve?"

The millionaire shrugged. "I was out jogging. This guy

hit me with a truck. He gets out and comes after me. We tussle and the next thing I know I'm in here."

"The truck driver's in the hospital."

Zalkin tensed. "I don't understand you people! I get run down by a guy driving a fucking truck, who attacks me. I defend myself and because he ends up in ·the hospital instead of me, I get arrested. Sounds like a case of lopsided justice to me."

"Take it easy," Schmidt said. "Are you hurt?"

Zalkin remembered being in a situation like this once before, and being bailed out. He decided to play this one better than the last time. "You know you're the first policeman who's asked me that, Ray. I gave you guys a million dollars, and for my trouble I end up in the can."

"C'mon."

They walked to the front of the cell block.

"Give me this man's arrest slip," Schmidt said.

The jailer handed over the formset, but he kept the fingerprint cards and Polaroid photos. He didn't want to have to do them over if the arrest did stick, which had happened to him before. He shuffled Zalkin's prints and pictures in with some other papers on his desk.

Schmidt stepped to the cell block entrance and ordered the jailer to open up. He came forward with the keys, but picked up the custody log, which was attached to a clipboard. Schmidt saw this and stared at him.

"I need you to sign the prisoner out, boss."

"Sign him out for me. You know who I am."

"I'm sorry, First Deputy, but it's against regulations. You take him out, you gotta sign the sheet."

Schmidt whirled on him. For a long minute the jailer patiently endured his relentless stare. Then Schmidt snatched the clipboard and·scrawled his name across the line indicating that he was removing the prisoner from the cell block. He left the "Reason" box blank.

Taking the clipboard back, the jailer unlocked the heavy cell-block door and allowed Schmidt and Zalkin to leave. As he relocked the door, he called a cheerful, "You all have a nice day."

CHAPTER 50

APRIL 18, 1991
1:01 P.M.

"Two for lunch, gentlemen?" The female maître d' met Bronson and Sherlock at the entrance to Club Cosmos.

They flashed their identification.

She was a very cool lady. Her hair was perfectly done, her makeup flawless, and her expression as neutral as Switzerland. She was dressed in a well-tailored but masculine-cut business suit, which did not hide her femininity. When she saw the badges, not one crack appeared in her mask.

"We'd like to talk to the manager about one of your patrons," Bronson said.

"I'm the manager." A chilly smile altered her features ever so slightly. She extended her hand to each of them in turn. "Lauren Holmes."

She escorted them across the restaurant to a staircase and then up to the second floor. A balcony ran around the upper level of the club affording a view of the diners below. She walked to one of the tables. When they were seated, her slick front melted a bit. "It's a good thing you came during lunch. After six this place becomes a madhouse."

They took a look around. The interior was all glass and chrome with a buffet table running the width of the dance floor at the center of the lower level. The detectives had considered having lunch here until they saw the twelve-dollar freight for the buffet, which looked to have little more on it than sandwiches, soups, and salads. Of course, this was the Near North Side and was supposed to cost more.

"Tell me," Sherlock said, "why do they call this place Club Cosmos?"

Lauren smiled. "At night there's a dome hidden behind that far wall that swings over the skylight. On it we project an image of the Chicago night sky. It's quite an effect. Very popular with the yuppie set."

"Must have cost a lot," Bronson said.

"A fortune. But then everything in here costs. So, what can I do for you gentlemen?"

Sherlock took a photo of SFC Bryce Carduci from his pocket. He placed it on the table in front of her.

"Have you ever seen him before?"

"He's been in. Quite a few times, in fact. Has a girlfriend. I think her name is Debbie."

Bronson and Sherlock exchanged glances.

"Who did he associate with when he was here?" Bronson asked. "I mean, did he run with any particular crowd?"

"No. He and the girl kind of kept to themselves. I think he"—she tapped his army photo—"had a roving eye for the ladies. The girl didn't like it. One night they had a fight and she threw a drink in his face. He slapped her, but the boss stepped in and stopped them before things could get out of hand."

"Would the boss be—" Sherlock began, but Bronson cut him off.

"The boss?"

"C'mon, you guys are up to something," Lauren said. "I can tell."

"Why would you say that, Ms. Holmes?" Bronson said.

"You ever heard of Lieutenant Edgar 'Doc' Holmes?" she asked him.

Bronson's brow curled. "He was the commanding officer of the citywide Burglary Unit back in the sixties. Everybody knew Doc."

Lauren smiled. "He was my uncle. Used to rock me to sleep telling cops-and-robbers stories."

"How is old Doc, anyway?" Bronson asked.

"He died of cancer two years ago."

"Sorry to hear that," Bronson said, sincerely.

"Me too," Sherlock echoed.

"So, since I'm almost a member of the family, you want to tell me why you're so interested in Mr. Zalkin?"

"What do you think of him, Lauren?" Bronson said.

"He pays well, but he's a creep," she said. "What do you want to know?"

Bronson smiled. "Well, why don't you start at the beginning and go from there."

"Okay. I answered an ad in the *Times-Herald* last November. It offered a good salary for experienced restaurant and lounge managerial people. I've got the experience so Zalkin hired me. The place wasn't even open yet, but he had it furnished and just about ready. He was in a hurry to hire staff, because he wanted to open the Wednesday before Thanksgiving."

"Why?" Sherlock asked.

"I really never found out, but we did open on time. Your soldier showed up a little after New Year's. His girlfriend started coming with him shortly after that. After the night they had the fight, the soldier never came around again. But he called to talk to Zalkin."

"How do you know it was him?" Bronson asked.

"I recognized his voice and once he left a message with me. Just the first name, Bryce, but it was easy to remember. He called a lot."

The eyes of both detectives flared with interest. "Go on," they said as one. And she did.

CHAPTER 51

Schmidt's car pulled up in front of Zalkin's building. As the first deputy's driver sat with his eyes cast stonily forward, Schmidt twisted around to look at Zalkin, who was seated in the back. "I expect you to go to court on the truck driver, Steve."

"Sure thing, Ray," Zalkin said. "And thanks for everything."

"We still on for lunch at the Press Club tomorrow?"

Zalkin was crossing the sidewalk to the entrance. He stopped, turned, and said, "Sure thing. You, me, and Commander Cole."

Schmidt waved as the driver pulled from the curb and headed for headquarters.

Zalkin removed the key from the pocket of his jogging shorts and let himself in. Once inside, with the door locked securely behind him, he let out a howl of triumph. He danced around wildly, still yelling, as he released the pent-up emotion that had been stored inside of him.

"You stupid sons of bitches," he howled. "I've always been smarter than any of you!"

He stripped off his running shorts and sat down on the couch to untie his shoes. As he did so, the bruise on his buttocks from the steroid shot stung. He thought about the full syringe in the refrigerator. He considered taking the injection now and calling Littlejohn later to have him bring another one tomorrow. However, he quickly rejected this option. The first injection had gotten him into trouble with the truck driver.

Moments later Zalkin stood under the shower. He chuckled every time he thought about the way Schmidt had bullied that Lieutenant Holland into not only releasing him, but also charging the hospitalized truck driver with reckless driving.

Stepping out of the shower, he began toweling himself dry. The day had not been a complete waste because, while Holland had been preparing his release papers, two tactical cops had reported to Schmidt in the watch commander's office. Zalkin had monitored the exchange.

They were both in plainclothes and male. One was a squat Asian with black hair that continuously fell into his face. The other was a thin Caucasian who had a hairline receding rapidly from a sharp widow's peak. Schmidt thought they were making a bad joke when they introduced themselves as Charles and Chan.

"Okay, you guys are detailed to Frank Delahanty starting as soon as you can hustle your asses over to the *Times-Herald* building and pick him up."

They nodded, although it was evident from their expressions they didn't relish the assignment.

"He's been threatened by some nut says he's going to burn the asshole alive. Now it could be bullshit, but it's up to you guys to make sure Delahanty keeps on breathing."

In his building Zalkin laughed. After dressing he headed for the kitchen. He'd missed lunch and was famished.

Swinging open the refrigerator and looking inside he began singing, "Oh, it's gonna be a hot time in the old town tonight."

The doorbell rang.

A frown crossed the millionaire's features. He seldom received callers other than the invited.

He closed the refrigerator and walked into the living-room area. He picked up the remote control from his desk and activated the television set. He pressed a button, which transmitted a picture of the street in front of the entrance. Two men—one black, the other white—were standing on the street.

Zalkin made them instantly as cops.

He pressed the speaker button. "Yes?"

"Mr. Zalkin, my name is Detective Manny Sherlock and this is my partner, Detective Lou Bronson. We're from Area One Violent Crimes. We'd like to ask you a few questions."

"Ask me questions about what?"

"Sergeant Bryce Carduci of the U.S. Army."

Zalkin's jaw muscles tensed. Then he pressed the release button and said over the intercom, "Come in."

CHAPTER 52

Mr. Zalkin, you are the licensed owner of Club Cosmos," Sherlock said.

Zalkin stared icily across at the skinny detective. He looked from him to Bronson, as he answered, "That wasn't a question. You are saying something you apparently already know as fact."

"Yes, sir," Sherlock said. "It is a fact. We've checked."

It was a needle aimed at either placing Zalkin on the defensive or getting a rise out of him. When it did neither, Sherlock went on.

"There was a customer who came into your place frequently. A Bryce Carduci."

Zalkin's eyes casually swung from Sherlock back to Bronson. The black detective wasn't even looking in his direction. Instead he was examining the furnishings arranged around the large room. He didn't appear to be interested in their conversation at all.

Zalkin looked back at Sherlock. "Have you ever been inside the club, Detective . . . ?"

"Sherlock. We were there earlier today."

"You should come to the club at night. Then you would understand how difficult it would be for me to answer a question like that."

"Why is that?" Sherlock asked.

As Zalkin began his answer, Bronson stood up. He stretched and walked around the chair with his back turned to his partner and their host.

"The Club Cosmos is one of the most successful night spots in Chicago. For that I am grateful. Every evening of the week, from about five o'clock on, the place is packed to capacity. At times, especially on weekends, I've had to turn paying customers away. Our maximum is a little over six hundred. I never exceed that number, because it's against the city code."

Bronson began moving slowly away from the office area. He was looking around with the casual, unstudied interest of a visitor to a museum exhibit. Zalkin's eyes followed him.

"Then you have never heard of Bryce Carduci?" Sherlock said.

Zalkin smiled. "I'm not very good at names, Detective Sherlock. Maybe if you told me a bit more about this man I could sort him out in my cluttered memory a bit easier."

Bronson had reached the bookcase against the far wall of the loft. With hands clutched behind his back, he scanned the titles of the books and magazines stacked there.

Sherlock handed Zalkin Carduci's photograph. Casually, he studied it before looking up to see Bronson still standing at the bookcase. "I recognize him. Came in the club quite frequently a few months ago."

Bronson picked up a magazine. Sherlock took the picture back. "Could you tell me what you remember about him?"

Zalkin stared at Bronson. "That depends on what you want to know. Say, where are my manners? I didn't offer you fellows any refreshments. What about a soda or maybe a beer?"

"We're on duty, Mr. Zalkin," Bronson said, replacing the

magazine. "But a Coke would be nice." He remained at the bookcase.

"I don't have Coke. What about fruit-flavored seltzer?" Zalkin stood up.

"Sounds good to me," Bronson said.

"No thanks," Sherlock said. "Gives me gas."

Zalkin hesitated for a moment before turning and walking into the kitchen area. He disappeared from view. He opened the refrigerator and removed a bottle of grape seltzer. He turned to a cabinet to get a glass when he discovered that Sherlock had followed him.

Sherlock held his notebook in hand and was studying it. He blocked Zalkin's path. "Sergeant Carduci was killed a couple of days ago. His body was found in an alley about a mile from here. We're trying to trace his activities on the day of his death."

Zalkin twisted off the bottle cap of the seltzer and poured the liquid into the glass. "And?"

"I beg your pardon?" Sherlock said.

Zalkin faced him. "And what has all this got to do with me?"

"Well, since he used to come to your place, we thought you might have seen him."

"I haven't seen the man in months." Zalkin stepped forward, but Sherlock didn't move. "Excuse me." Zalkin spoke with a flat lack of emotion, but there was definite menace there.

Obediently, Sherlock stepped aside. Bronson was back in the chair in front of Zalkin's desk. Zalkin handed the detective the glass of seltzer. He then looked over at the bookcase before returning to his seat.

"Did you know any of Sergeant Carduci's associates? People who might be able to give us a lead as to what happened to him?" Sherlock asked.

Zalkin responded with a curt "no."

Bronson drained off his glass of seltzer.

Sherlock snapped his notebook shut. "You have anything else for Mr. Zalkin, Lou?"

Bronson shook his head.

"Well, we'd like to thank you for your time, Mr. Zalkin."

As he escorted them to the door, Zalkin relaxed. "Where did you fellows say you work again?"

"Area One Detectives," Sherlock said.

"Commander Cole's your boss, isn't he?"

"Yes, sir," Sherlock responded.

"I'm having lunch with him and First Deputy Schmidt tomorrow. I'll tell them that I met you two."

Zalkin opened the door and Sherlock stepped out first. Bronson started to follow, but stopped at the threshold. "I heard you gave a lot of money to the Cops for Education campaign."

Zalkin grinned. "I gave you guys a million dollars. I really support what you're doing in this town. I wish it could have been more."

"That was very generous of you," Bronson said. "We need more people like you out in the community. We could really do something about crime then."

"Thank you, Detective Bronson. That's a compliment."

"You're a real philanthropist, Mr. Zalkin," Bronson added.

"I do what I can."

"Father Ken Smith at Our Lady of Peace is looking forward to getting the half million you're going to give him for the youth center. Him and Sister Mary Louise Stallings can really use that money."

Zalkin stared back at the detective with a curious apprehension. Bronson stepped into the hall and said over his shoulder, "Nice talking to you."

Slowly, Zalkin closed the door.

* * *

As they drove away from the building Sherlock said, "So? What do you think?"

Bronson stared sightlessly out at the passing traffic. He didn't respond immediately.

Sherlock knew his partner well enough to wait. Bronson would tell him when he was ready.

Ten minutes later they were backed up in traffic on the Dan Ryan Expressway when Bronson finally spoke.

"That building was once a tool-and-die factory. Specialized in manufacturing precision equipment for industry."

"When did you find that out?"

"I called the Building Department while you were making goo-goo eyes at Lauren Holmes."

"Oh."

"Nice girl. Did you get her phone number?"

Sherlock grinned. "Yep."

"Good boy. Our friend back there bought the company lock, stock, and barrel back in July of 1989. Sold off a lot of the equipment to a place called Chauncey Industrial Works out in South Chicago. They wanted it all, but he kept some of it."

"How do you know that?"

"I called them while you were—"

"Yeah, making goo-goo eyes."

"You'll make a good detective yet, Manny. The manager at Chauncey's was real helpful. He's going to send us a list of the stuff they really wanted. Stuff you can use to manufacture precision machine parts."

"Like for guns?"

"Exactly like for guns."

"So what does that tell us, Lou?"

"By itself, nothing. But he's got a lot more room in that place than what we saw just now. More than half a city block on that first floor and a full basement with loading dock and garage."

"Maybe he's running some type of business out of there. He seems to have his fingers in a lot of pies."

"Good, Manny. You keep playing devil's advocate. But I don't think he's producing anything for the commercial market. I'd say he's using it for storage."

"Storage for what?"

Bronson smiled.

Sherlock made the connection. "We'll never get a search warrant on what we've got so far. The judge will laugh us out of court."

"You're right. So let's forget the building for a moment and concentrate on our man. What did you think of him?"

"He's hiding something, but then, who isn't?" The traffic thinned and Manny accelerated south.

"He has an interesting collection of reading material in that bookcase. Most of it is paperback garbage. But he's also into bodybuilding and military manuals. He's got one there that looked fairly new. The cover was ripped off where the 'Classified' stamp would have been. It was a technical manual containing the nomenclature for assembling and servicing a weapon. It wasn't on Watkins's inventory, but then maybe he's branched out to making his own stuff."

Sherlock shook his head. "He doesn't look like the mechanical type to me, Lou."

"Maybe he's not, but it's possible he could have had Carduci make it before he died."

"Okay, I'm playing devil's advocate again. Say Zalkin is our man and has all that stuff Carduci stole. What else would he need?"

Bronson sighed. "The manual was for the assembly, care, and maintenance of a six-point-two-pound flame-thrower."

They pulled into the parking lot behind Area One. "I've got another question for you."

"Go ahead," Bronson said. "I've still got a lot of questions on this thing myself."

"What does he want with your pastor?"

Bronson shook his head slowly from side to side. "I don't know, Manny. I really don't know."

CHAPTER 53

APRIL 18, 1991
4:45 P.M.

The conference was held in Commander Cole's office. Present were Cole—the Violent Crimes commanding officer—Lt. Doug Conrad, Sgt. Blackie Silvestri, Detective Lou Bronson, and Detective Manny Sherlock. The issue under discussion was what, if anything, they were going to do about Steven Zalkin.

Bronson, with assistance from Sherlock, had just finished the report of their investigation, which had led them to Zalkin. He told his bosses everything, including the involvement of Father Ken and Our Lady of Peace Church, up to a point. Conrad and Blackie had interrupted periodically with questions about one phase of the investigation or another. Cole said nothing.

Blackie had been watching his friend all day for any signs of the tension he had shown the day before. There was seemingly nothing amiss, other than the pressure of a complicated, hot case. But now Cole's silence had Blackie worried.

"Zalkin sounds like our man, but I don't know," Blackie said, guardedly.

"The only thing we do have is that he's rich and likes to give away money," Conrad said. "Rich guys always act a little strange anyway."

"He knew Carduci," Blackie said.

The lieutenant smirked. "From what I'm hearing, a lot of people knew the dead GI. Zalkin just happens to be the most prominent." Doug Conrad was a cop cut in the mold popularized by Mickey Spillane: heavy fists, lantern jaw, and a total intolerance for bullshit.

"So far," Blackie said, "this is the only real lead we've got. The question is, do we follow it alone or keep on looking?" He looked at the commander.

Throughout the discussion, Cole had sat with his hands resting on the desk blotter. He had listened to everything that had been said. Now the ball was in his court. They didn't have enough to go downtown with, so it was his decision.

Zalkin sounded right, but just a little too right. Cole had seen cases blown before when detectives had jumped the gun on the first lead and followed it into a blind alley, while other investigative trails went cold. This was not to say that he questioned Bronson's and Sherlock's judgment. In his estimation, they were very good. But they'd need a lot more before they could move on Zalkin.

"Where do you want to go from here, Lou?" Cole asked.

Bronson reached for a cigarette before remembering the commander didn't allow smoking in his office. He dropped his hand back to his case file, moistened his lips, and said, "We still need to talk to Corporal Winters. I called Astrolab and talked to Captain Watkins. I was going to have him bring her in here tonight, but after we left this morning he lifted the restrictions on his people. She left the installation about three o'clock. She's not due back until midnight."

"As I see it, that's all we can do until tomorrow," Cole said. "In the morning we'll take a look at what the others have turned up and decide where we go from here. At least we have made some progress."

They took this as a signal the meeting was over. They began filing out, but Bronson lingered. "Can I see you a minute, Commander?"

"Sure, Lou."

Bronson resumed his seat. He waited until the door was closed behind the others before he said, "Zalkin told me he's having lunch with you and the first deputy tomorrow."

Cole nodded. This item had been excluded from Bronson's report. Cole knew enough about the detective to be fairly certain that he wasn't prying; however, he waited for him to continue.

Bronson was nervous as he did. "I guess you know him and since he gave us all that money for the education campaign, me and Manny bird-dogging him could be an embarrassment for you and the department."

"I've never met him," Cole said.

Bronson appeared surprised, but didn't comment.

Cole noticed the reaction. "Is there something wrong?"

Automatically, Bronson again reached for a cigarette and again stopped. Seeing his distress, Cole opened the bottom drawer of his desk. He removed a small glass ashtray and handed it to Bronson.

"It's for Sergeant Silvestri," Cole said with a grin. "When he starts going into burning-rope withdrawal, I let him take a few puffs."

"Thanks, boss." Bronson lit the cigarette. This would make it easier for him to talk.

"I mentioned that Zalkin is giving a half-million dollars to Our Lady of Peace parish."

Cole nodded.

"Well, the reason I found that out is because Father Ken's my pastor. He called this morning and asked me to check out Zalkin for him. Unofficially, of course. The reason Father Ken wanted me to check Zalkin out was because of Sister Mary Louise Stallings."

Cole's eyes narrowed. "Louise Stallings?"

Bronson could tell he'd hit a nerve. "She told Manny that she knew you and Sergeant Silvestri."

Cole looked away. That had been a long time ago. He totaled up the years in his mind: at least fifteen, maybe sixteen.

"Father Ken was a little reluctant to even ask me to do it," Bronson said. "But Sister Mary Louise insisted. Said it had something to do with Zalkin's last name beginning with the letter *Z*."

Zykus, Cole remembered. *Martin Zykus.*

"Boss, what I'm trying to say is that there are a lot of coincidences about this case. Carduci, Our Lady of Peace, Club Cosmos, and Zalkin. Somehow I can't help but think all of this is tied together."

Cole looked back at Bronson. "Is there anything else?"

The detective stubbed out his half-smoked cigarette in Cole's ashtray. "When we were leaving Zalkin's place, he mentioned that you were having lunch with him and the first deputy tomorrow."

"You said that before, Lou."

"But I got the impression from the way he talked that he knew you. It was the way he said your name. But then you said you don't know him, so I guess it's just an old dick's imagination acting up." With that, Bronson turned to leave.

He had reached the door when Cole called to him. "Lou?"

Bronson turned.

"Thanks."

"Yes, sir. Anytime." Bronson let himself out.

CHAPTER 54

Frank Delahanty was having problems. The foremost of these was that he hadn't had a drink all day and he was starting to get the shakes. On top of this, the managing editor had killed his "Steven Zalkin and Part-Time Cops" column, because he didn't want to get the cops mad at the *Times-Herald* right now. Instead, the paper was going to run a "Best of Delahanty" column, which was usually done only when he was too drunk to make a deadline. Delahanty had raised hell, but then he wasn't able to generate his usual level of fury because he was out of martini fuel. So, pale and shaken, he had stomped back to his office, seething with anger and craving a drink in the worst way.

To his dismay he found that Rosie, in her usual meddling, incompetent fashion, had dumped every drop of booze in the office down the toilet. He could have killed her and would have had he not been confronted with two *Times-Herald* security guards and a couple of plainclothes cops, who said they were there to protect him.

"Protect me from fucking what?!" he screamed at Rosie as he stormed around his private office. "Some fucking crank caller threatens me and all you idiots go off the deep end!"

Rosie stood in front of the door, as if her presence there

could stop him from going out and having a drink if he wanted one.

"Can I get you some coffee?" Her tone was sharp.

"No. I don't want any goddamned coffee!" He felt his insides quaking and, despite the eight Tylenols he'd taken during the day, he still felt sick. The only thing that could cure this sickness was a drink. In fact, a lot of drinks.

"Well, you're not getting any booze and you're going to stay right here until this thing is over and I mean that." She folded her arms across her chest and stood with legs splayed in a gesture of such supreme defiance it further infuriated him.

"Look, you stupid old broad, if you don't get out of my way I'm going to knock the crap out of you." He took a menacing step toward her.

She didn't move.

"You do that and I'll have those cops put your drunk ass in jail. There I know you'll be safe."

"You're out of your mind! This whole damned place has gone crazy."

"You're the one that's crazy, bucko, if you think you're going to get out of here before six o'clock."

"To hell with it." Delahanty charged her. Let them put him in jail. He wasn't going to stand by while she pushed him around. Who did she think she was, anyway? Just an over-the-hill slut the paper felt sorry for.

He started for her, intending to throw her bodily out of his way, go through the door, and take his chances with the cops outside. He was reaching for her when she hit him in the face. Her fist caught him flush on the nose and knocked him to the floor. Stunned, he lay on his back looking up at her. She stood over him in a boxer's stance, ready to give him more.

"Listen, you booze-sodden idiot, you're not going any-where except to a hospital and you won't get there until after six o'clock. Do you understand me?"

There was a heavy knock on the office door. One of the cops called, "Is everything okay in there?"

"Everything's fine," Rosie responded. "You boys just go back to doing your job and let me do mine."

Delahanty struggled up into a sitting position on the floor. His nose was bleeding and little black specks danced in front of his eyes. He couldn't believe that this was happening to him.

"You hit me," he managed to mumble with blood dripping down into his mouth.

"C'mon, get up, Frank." She reached down and yanked him to his feet. "You'll hurt for a while, but at least you'll still be alive tomorrow."

He stood unsteadily and she had to support him. She walked him behind the desk and shoved him into a chair. "Now, be a good boy and I won't have to hit you again."

She dabbed the blood off his face with her handkerchief. The cloth smelled faintly of the booze she had wiped up in the office earlier. It was the only liquor he was going to be near for a while.

CHAPTER 55

APRIL 18, 1991
5:45 P.M.

Cole completed his Confidential Investigative Summary report, which would be delivered to Chief Riseman in the morning. There was little of any importance contained in the page-and-a-half he had typed on his computer. He had left out any reference to Bronson's and Sherlock's investigation of Zalkin. That he would have to sort out for himself.

He leaned back in his chair and contemplated the evening that stretched before him. He considered calling Lisa, but as he did, doubts clouded his mind. She'd hung up on him yesterday, saying she needed more time to sort out the problems she had with their marriage. He felt that with each passing day his marriage was slipping away, and he felt powerless to stop it.

There was a knock on his office door, followed by Blackie coming inside. "Pick up line two, boss. Someone wants to talk to you."

"Who?"

Blackie gave him a patient smile.

A thrill went through Cole. Could it be Lisa? He picked up the receiver, punched the button over line two, and said a slightly breathless "Hello?"

"How are you, Larry?" It was Maria Silvestri, Blackie's wife.

Masking his disappointment, he said, "I'm fine, Maria. How have you been?"

Blackie remained standing at the office door, while Cole listened to Maria talk about the Silvestri children and the basement they'd had remodeled during the winter.

"You haven't been over to see us since the holidays," she was saying. "I'm fixing lasagna tonight. Why don't you come home with Blackie?"

There was no mention of Lisa. That meant that Blackie had talked about Cole's problems to Maria. For an instant this angered the commander. It seemed that all of a sudden a lot of people were interested in his personal life. First, there had been Lou Bronson; now, Blackie. But then, Blackie was not just somebody who worked for him, and Maria was also very special. Maybe he needed an evening with them. A chance to talk about his situation and how he could take steps to do something about it before it was too late.

He looked up at Blackie as he said into the phone, "Blackie's here with me now. What time do you want us to come?"

"It's about six," she said. "Why don't you come now? You men spend too much time at that place anyway."

"I'll be there, but Blackie has to work late." Cole laughed when his ex-partner's jaw dropped in surprise. Maria laughed with him. "Okay, we're on the way, but please—only one helping of lasagna tonight. I'm trying to watch my weight."

After hanging up he said, "Now why do you suppose she invited me tonight?"

"Don't ask me," Blackie said. "You run it here, she runs it there. All I do is what I'm told."

"Okay," Cole said. "Let's go."

CHAPTER 56

APRIL 18, 1991
6:01 P.M.

Delahanty checked his watch before looking cautiously at Rosie, who stood guard at his office door. She looked meaner than he'd ever seen her before. So he had called her a few names. He always did dumb shit like that when he was drunk. She was supposed to understand. To take care of him, not beat him up.

He touched his fingers to his nose and winced.

"It's not broken, Frank," she called across the office. "Just a little swollen."

He tried to give her a dirty look, but it failed. With each passing second he was approaching a full-blown, terrifically hungover sobriety. Accompanying this state was a frightening depression. Once, when he was still with his first wife and working on his second book about Chicago politics, he had sworn off the sauce for a month. It had almost driven him and his wife crazy. She had advised him to seek professional counseling to help him get through this critical period. That, he had refused to do.

He'd been around newsmen and newspapers all his life. The best always drank. It enhanced the creative process—at least, in Delahanty's estimation. He remembered Sven Erickson, who had been his mentor over at the old *Daily News* thirty years before. Now the Swede had been a drinker! Used to say, "A reporter who can't down a fifth of booze, bring in a five-hundred-word story before the bulldog edition deadline, and walk out the door on his own two hind legs will never make it in this business."

Delahanty had lived by this creed every since, although he never paused to critically examine Erickson's words. He did recall that, at the time he'd said them, they'd both been blind drunk.

He was afraid. Afraid that if he stopped drinking, the well of words he scrawled effortlessly across the pages of his notebooks to be read by millions would dry up. He'd seen this happen to reporters before.

Sol Bukowski had been the best in town over at the *Tribune.* He drank. Delahanty didn't know how much he drank, because he'd never liked Bukowski or the *Tribune.* But there had been stories going around about Bukowski passing out at one party or another, puking up his guts in his editor's office, and blowing the plate-glass window out of his South Shore home with a double-barreled shotgun. Each of these incidents had occurred while Bukowski was drunk. He was becoming the joke of the Chicago newspaper industry when he went on the wagon. Less than six months later, he killed himself. This frightened Delahanty. He could see the same thing happening to him.

So he figured he needed the booze not only to keep writing, but to stay alive. The bottle was his life preserver in a sea of shit. All he wanted to do was write and drink. One couldn't happen without the other. Now he felt himself sinking. He had to get away from Rosie and go someplace to fortify himself before the fragile fabric of his miserable existence came completely undone.

He mustered what nerve he could and said, "Rosie, it's after six."

"I know that!"

"I've got . . ." He choked on his words. He still had his pride. He'd die before he'd beg.

"You've got to go home." There was no room for compromise or negotiation in her voice. "And those cops are going with you. I talked to a captain in the superintendent's office and they're going to be with you until midnight. Then another team will take their place."

He stood up abruptly. "How long has this got to go on?"

Her features softened, but her words did not. "Haven't you been paying any attention to what's been going on in this town, Frank? Strange things have been happening, like that gang hangout being blown up and those two cops getting killed."

"What has any of that got to do with me?"

"There's talk that the police are holding back something. It's all very mysterious, and then you got that call."

Sweat was collecting on his forehead, and his hands trembled. "You're not making any sense. You're just trying to persecute me with this bullshit."

"No, Frank," she said with compassion. "I'm just trying to keep you alive."

"Okay, I'll go with the cops. Just let me out of here."

She considered this for a moment. "I should go with you, so you won't pull any of that patented Delahanty bullshit on them, but then it is your life and they're not going to let you out of their sight."

He headed for the door. She stepped aside to let him pass. He was reaching for the knob when she said, "Frank, please be careful. Do what the cops say. This could be more serious than you think. I've got a bad feeling."

Delahanty opened the door. In the outer office the two

plainclothes cops and two security guards stood up. Delahanty's confidence increased. "Rosie, just leave me alone."

He crossed the office with decisive strides, calling to the tactical cops, "Let's go, boys."

They scrambled out after him.

CHAPTER 57

APRIL 18, 1991
6:31 P.M.

Blackie drove his aging Chevy Blazer west on the Stevenson Expressway toward the Pulaski Road exit. He had his window halfway down and a burning cigar clenched in his teeth. Larry Cole sat in the passenger seat. Cole had the seat in the recline position. His eyes were closed and he hadn't said a word since they had pulled out of the station parking lot.

They were rolling up the exit ramp when Cole spoke. "Do you remember Martin Zykus?"

"I remember him," Blackie's tone was flat. "The guy that beat the system. Almost."

"Yeah, almost."

They rode in silence for a time.

"So what about him?" Blackie asked. They were cruising south on Pulaski. The rush-hour traffic had thinned, and Blackie was making most of the lights because he drove like he was going on an in-progress call.

"Who?"

"Zykus," Blackie repeated. "What about him?"

Cole spoke with a drowsy slur. "Nothing. Just something Bronson said earlier made me think of Zykus. We never heard anything about him after that night."

They pulled up in front of Blackie's house. Cutting the engine, Blackie got out. "I thought we weren't going to talk about that again."

Cole sat up and rubbed his palms across his face. "You know, I could sleep for a week."

They were walking up to the front door when Blackie said, "You didn't answer me."

"You said we weren't supposed to talk about it."

Blackie inserted his key in the front door lock, but hesitated before opening the door. "Okay, you got me. What about Martin Zykus?"

"Nothing," Cole said. "It's just that Bronson mentioned something that reminded me of him."

"And what we did?"

"We did what we had to do, Blackie. At least we didn't kill that fat bastard."

"You sound almost sorry we didn't."

Cole stared at his old friend. "That would have been murder. We're cops, not killers."

Maria Silvestri opened the door. "I thought I heard voices out here. What are you two doing, still talking shop?"

"Hi, Maria," Cole said, stepping inside and kissing her on the cheek. "You look great."

Blackie stepped around them and said, "It's aerobic classes at the health club three days a week. Getting so now, when we go out, people ask if she's my daughter."

"Why don't you go with her sometime?" Cole said. "You could stand to lose a pound or two."

"Don't have the time. My boss works me too hard."

"Complaints, complaints," Cole said with a grin.

"Cosimo," Maria said, using the first name her husband detested. "Show Larry the basement."

"He knows where the basement is," Blackie said. "You go on down, kid, and I'll get us some beer from the kitchen."

Maria and Blackie left him standing in the living room alone as they walked, or more accurately ran, to the kitchen.

He stood there for a moment, shrugged, and headed for the basement. The lights were on. At the bottom of the steps he found a brand-new recreation room with floor-to-ceiling wood paneling, indirect ceiling lighting, a pool table, bar, stools, and a refrigerator in one corner.

Cole stood stock still. The breath rushed from his lungs. Two things drew his attention and riveted him to the spot. A minor item was that the sliding-glass-door cooler was filled with beer, making Blackie's excuse of having to go to the kitchen and get them beer an obvious fabrication. The other was that his wife, Lisa, was here. She had been sitting on a stool at the far end of the bar. Now she stood up and faced him.

They were on opposite sides of the room, each afraid to take a step toward the other. The moment was frozen in time because they had been apart for so long.

She moved first. She was a tall woman with a beautiful figure. She was dressed in jeans and a sleeveless blouse, which were as elegant on her as a Paris-original gown.

She came to him. She stood before him having to look up only a fraction, because she was nearly as tall as he was. A tear escaped the corner of one eye. As it rolled down her cheek Cole's heart lurched and he drew her into his arms.

She rested her head on his chest. "Baby, I'm sorry."

He touched her chin and tilted her face up to his. He could smell the warm sweetness of her breath and the feel of her body made him agonizingly aware of how much he had missed her.

"I love you, Lisa."

"I love you, too."

Their lips met.

At the top of the stairs, eavesdropping politely, stood Maria and Blackie. Gently, Blackie closed the door and said to his wife, "Baby, you're the greatest."

CHAPTER 58

APRIL 18, 1991
6:45 P.M.

Collin Charles and Henry Chan had never seen anyone drink like Frank Delahanty. After they left the *Times-Herald* building, Delahanty had directed them to drive to Murphy's Bar on lower Wacker. The cops had argued against this and lost. The only concession they had managed to obtain from the abrasive columnist was that they would sit at a table, as opposed to standing at the bar, which Delahanty preferred. To their further dismay, everyone in the crowded bar knew Delahanty. He continuously bought rounds of drinks for the house, making him and them the objects of unrelenting scrutiny.

The cops were not drinking, which initially annoyed Delahanty. But he was doing enough for all of them many times over. Charles was a teetotaler and Chan drank sparingly when he was off duty. Because they were at the table and there were no waitresses, Delahanty ordered a carafe of bourbon and a pitcher of beer, which he began to consume with concentrated abandon. The bourbon went into a cocktail glass without ice or chaser. The beer into a stein. The bartender also provided Delahanty with three packs of Benson and Hedges Gold cigarettes, which he chain-smoked while he drank. Neither Charles nor Chan smoked.

Charles and Chan were street cops, not bodyguards. They knew how to make a drug bust, street-stop of an armed suspect, or tell that a guy was wrong just by the way he acted or talked. Bodyguards were trained to do different things. Charles and Chan realized their shortcomings. However, this was an assignment, just like any other shit detail cops were sometimes given. They would do their best to keep Delahanty alive, drunk or sober.

But then, the assignment hadn't turned out to be as bad as they thought it would. When they first got to Murphy's—before Delahanty had consumed his first pitcher of beer and a third of the bourbon-carafe—the journalist had been morosely silent. Then, as a flushed glow of inebriation settled over him, he became talkative, and then uproariously funny. The columnist was a natural-born storyteller—maybe even a brilliant liar, but he always had a punchline. Pretty soon they were in stitches, despite the distasteful nature of the duty they had drawn.

Delahanty took a pull of bourbon, swallowed it with a grimace, and picked up his beer stein. "So we get this new editor. Guy named Murdock. Prick spoke with a very, very British accent. From fucking England. The owners of that rag I work for figured he'd give the joint some class. Didn't give a rat's ass that the bastard wouldn't know a good story if it bit him in the ass. First name's James. James Murdock. Not 'Jim,' but 'James.' He liked to say it like Connery used to say 'Bond. James Bond.' Asshole thought he was real smooth."

Charles and Chan were listening, looking around only occasionally at the tide of booze-swilling humanity beginning to thin out around them as the evening progressed.

"This one time," Delahanty said, "he called a staff meeting. Mandatory for everyone—no exceptions. So I go, but I'm stiff. Was out on a toot the night before with a broad very well-placed in a certain mayoral administration a few years back. If I told you who she was and what we did that night you'd fall outta them goddamned chairs, but then that's another story."

Delahanty lit another Benson and Hedges from the butt of the last, swallowed bourbon and beer before continuing.

"So anyway, I go to the meeting and I'm plastered. Haven't been home to shower or shave and I smell like I doused myself with hundred-proof aftershave."

The cops noticed that Delahanty was open and honest about his drinking. Even made a point of emphasizing how drunk he'd been during one episode or another. It was as if he was proud he was a lush.

"I come in late to the meeting and there's only one seat left in the room, which is right up next to Murdock-James-Murdock. He said, 'So veddy good of you to join us, Mr. Delahanty. Won't you sit down?'

"Well, I was so bad I could've fucking fallen down, but I'm a good little soldier in the *Times-Herald* army, dedicated to doing my duty of keeping this town informed, as long as the asshole on the street keeps plunking down his quarter per copy."

"It's thirty-five cents," Chan said.

"What?" Delahanty turned the most bloodshot eyes Chan had ever seen in his direction.

"It's thirty-five cents for a *Times-Herald* now."

"No shit," Delahanty said with open amazement. "No matter. I never read the *Times-Herald* anyway. Nothing but garbage. I want the news, I watch TV. Faster that way."

The two cops exchanged curious glances. They didn't know if this was a put-on. Somehow, they didn't feel that it was.

"So anyway," Delahanty said, after a booze and smoke

pause, "I sit down, and Murdock wrinkles his nose like he's smelled a skunk. And he is glacially distressed. I mean, it's like I blew a fart in Westminster Abbey or some such shit.

"The meeting gets going again, but I'm not paying any attention. Some journalism-school M.A. is going on at the other end of the table about responsibility, integrity, and a lot of other garbage that nobody, including and especially me, is paying the least attention to. So I'm trying to make a good show of sitting up straight and looking appropriately concerned without dozing off, when Mr. Murdock-James-Murdock leans over and whispers to me, 'Mr. Delahanty, have you been drinking?'

"I'm not really in the mood for this, so I say, 'You're damned straight! Anybody forced to come to one of these stupid meetings should get drunk first!' "

Delahanty laughed uproariously, while Charles and Chan smiled politely.

The columnist drank more booze and lit another cigarette before saying, "Don't worry, boys, it gets better.

"So, Murdock-James-Murdock throws me out of the meeting. Talks about suspending me, which is okay because I've got a ten-year contract with options. The prick don't have to print me, but he sure-as-shit has to pay me. The lawyers explain it to him. The word goes out he's after me. I send back word, 'Good luck, asshole.' "

Charles and Chan grinned. Despite themselves, they liked this guy. They only wondered how long it would take him to reach his limit. They noticed that, as the brown contents of the carafe dwindled along with the dregs of the second pitcher of beer, his words were becoming less distinct, but not by much. He was also working on his second pack of cigarettes and coughing more frequently. It would be more efficient, they figured, if he used a gun to kill himself rather than the poison he was force-feeding his lungs and kidneys.

"So, it's Christmas." Delahanty was breathing heavier

with just a slight wheeze. "Everybody's exchanging gifts. I'm keeping a low profile, staying out of Murdock-James-Murdock's way, but I haven't forgotten the prick. I figure that someday he's got one coming and I'm the asshole going to give it to him.

"Now this guy likes hats! I mean hats! English bowlers, stovepipes, fedoras. He's very cerebral from the outside, because he ain't got nothing inside. So that gives me a clue.

"I check around and find out he's in the market for a little piece of headgear called a deerstalker. Same type of hat Sherlock Holmes always wore. So I figure a way to do a number on Murdock-James-Murdock.

"I have a guy I know on the *London Times* go to one of those big-time, hoity-toity gentleman's shops in England and buy me three of these deerstalkers as presents for my editor."

Charles and Chan looked quizzically at the reporter.

"Hang on guys, it's coming. I send my assistant, Rosie," self-consciously Delahanty touched the tip of his still sore nose, "to find out what size and color Murdock-James-Murdock likes. I have the hats shipped over on the Concorde. Cost me a fortune. Then, at the *Times-Herald* Christmas party, I humbly present the one in his size to my esteemed editor."

"The one in his size?" Charles asked.

"Yeah, I bought two others," Delahanty said, smugly. "One an eighth-of-a-size larger and one an eighth-of-a-size smaller. Before I make the presentation, I take them to a tailor I know here in Chicago and make sure all three hats look identical. He won't know the difference by simply inspecting them."

Charles was confused, but Chan was starting to get the drift.

"So at the party, Murdock-James-Murdock raves about the hat. Runs around wearing it and telling everybody he got it from me. Figures I knuckled under to him. He didn't give me anything at the party, but a couple of days later I got a gold cigarette lighter from him. I've still got it."

Delahanty paused for effect and booze.

"After the New Year I put my plan into effect. I'd been screwing the chick Murdock-James-Murdock selected for his personal secretary. Nice body, but not a brain in her head. Plus, a couple of hundred dollars bought her silence and a bit of collusion.

"Whenever Murdock-James-Murdock wore the deerstalker to work, she'd give me a call. Then she'd let me know when he was out of the office at some meeting or such and I'd slip down and switch hats.

"One time I'd give him the size smaller, another time the size larger, and every once in a while slip his size in for good measure."

The cops stared at him in amazement.

"Diabolical," Chan whispered.

"Fiendish," Charles echoed.

"But certifiably brilliant, boys," Delahanty said. "And you should have seen it. One day he's walking around with the damn hat perched on top his head like a fucking egg. The next, it's down on his ears. Then again, it fits perfectly. And he can't figure out what's going on. His secretary lets me know when he's about to leave the building, so I break my neck to get down to the lobby every night and check him out. You had to see it to believe it. He was going out of his fucking mind!"

The cops were in stitches and already trying to figure out how they could run a game like this on First Deputy Schmidt.

"Did he ever catch on?" Charles asked, wiping tears from his eyes.

"No, the bastard got fired first. Left with the right size, too. Figures the expanding and shrinking hat had something to do with the *Times-Herald*. Guess he'll never know."

"Mr. Delahanty," Chan said.

"Call me Frank."

"Okay, Frank. I read your column all the time. You're really brilliant. How do you come up with all that stuff?"

Delahanty studied his bourbon glass. "Trade secret."

"What journalism school did you go to?" Charles asked.

"School? I didn't learn to write in any school. I learned it by doing it. I never even finished high school. I flunked English twice. Formal education is bullshit, if you ask me. Never teaches you what you need to know, just what they want you to know."

The cops didn't know whether to agree or disagree.

"Gotta pee," Delahanty said, standing up unsteadily.

They stood with him.

"Aw, c'mon, guys. I can take a leak by myself."

"We've got to go with you, Frank," Charles said.

Delahanty started to argue and then said, "To hell with it."

In the washroom they flanked him at the urinals. He swayed back and forth as he gushed liquid into the bowl. "This is bullshit," he said. "You guys should be out catching crooks instead of watching me get plastered."

"It's our job, Frank," Chan said.

"We were gonna ask," Charles said carefully, "how much longer you plan to stay here?"

"Why?" Delahanty finished and zipped his pants.

"Because we get off at twelve and our relief is supposed to take over at your apartment."

Delahanty stood in the center of the washroom floor and looked blankly from them to his watch. He couldn't read the dial.

"What time is it anyway?" he slurred.

"Twenty minutes to eleven," Chan said.

"Okay, let's go."

CHAPTER 59

APRIL 18, 1991
10:50 P.M.

They stepped out onto the street in front of Murphy's. The squad car was parked in a no-parking zone down the block. With Delahanty walking between them, Tactical Officers Charles and Chan headed for the car. They were more intent on watching the columnist than the deserted street around them. A black van was parked directly across from the squad car. As they approached the end of the block, the cops heard a car door slam.

"Do you believe this shit?" Chan said, snatching the buff-colored parking ticket from the windshield.

"Who wrote it?" an equally peeved Charles asked from the curb, where he stood with a swaying, totally oblivious Frank Delahanty.

"That fucking Pankowski, who else? That silly bastard would write his own mother a ticket if they gave driver's licenses to things that walked on four legs."

Delahanty thought that was funny. He began to laugh. Charles started to laugh with him, and Chan would have joined in if he hadn't died at that instant.

Henry Chan was standing with his back to the street. The high-powered rifle slug slammed into the base of his skull and tore through his neck to exit under his chin. The dynamics of the explosive round caused his head to be

ripped from his body and flung vertically into the air. It
flew upward for twenty feet before beginning the descent
to the ground. It landed on the hood of the police car and
bounced twice before rolling off. Like a puppet whose
strings have been cut, his body collapsed.

Charles instinctively turned toward Delahanty. He was
not thinking, but reacting. He would later say that he was
diving to protect the columnist. He was actually doing no
more than attempting to save his own life.

The turn saved Collin Charles's life, but not his health.
The second round fired by the sniper caught him in the
shoulder, severing his right arm and slamming into his
chest. The bullet's velocity diminished when it struck his
rib cage, which deflected it into his breastbone. The steel-
jacketed missile, carrying bits of bone, blood, and tissue,
exited his chest. He was hurled across the sidewalk to land
against the wall of Murphy's Bar.

Now Frank Delahanty stood alone.

Terror fought through the liquor anesthetic, but his
reflexes were frozen. He looked at Chan's head, lying on
the street in front of the police car, and Charles's body on
the sidewalk. Delahanty turned to run from them and
Murphy's, but there was nothing in that direction except
the dark emptiness of lower Wacker Drive. Then he turned
to run back into the bar. His brain screamed, *Get out of the
line of fire!*

Delahanty was moving, but not fast enough. The sniper
could take him at any second. However, there had been no
more rounds fired. He tried to step over Charles's prone
body and tripped. The columnist fell hard on the pavement. He crawled a few feet and stopped. There was
someone standing a few feet away. Slowly, Delahanty
looked up.

The man was wearing a motorcycle helmet and dressed
in a black jumpsuit with multiple pockets. He was carrying
a tube-shaped device, which was connected to his waist by

a hose. The image of a painting Delahanty had once seen in Paris came back to him. It was a depiction of the dark angel Satan. Now Satan stood before him on lower Wacker Drive.

The voice that came to Delahanty was the same as the one used to leave the message on his answering machine. " 'A man who hunts women in the night is vermin.' "

"What?" Delahanty's voice came out a squeak. The words were familiar, but his booze-damaged, terror-filled brain could not recall where he'd heard them.

" 'Such things should be exterminated. Eliminated. Incinerated.' Do you remember who wrote that, Frank?"

"No. No! I don't! What do you want?"

Satan paused. Then, " 'The law should not protect Martin Zykus.' "

"Zykus?" Delahanty whispered.

Flames leaped from the tube Satan carried and enveloped the columnist. Frank Delahanty screamed as his soul plunged into hell.

CHAPTER 60

APRIL 18, 1991
11:25 P.M.

Lisa Cole slipped out of bed and walked nude to the bathroom. She relieved herself, aware of the tenderness of her vaginal walls and nipples. She and Larry had never made love like this before. After they had arrived home from the Silvestris's a little before nine, they had engaged in sex so primitively violent it was frightening. She had ripped the buttons off his shirt and he had torn one of her bra straps.

They had done it on the carpet, right inside the living room door. They had not taken the trouble to disrobe, except for those items of clothing covering loins, breasts, and behinds. He had hurt her with the intensity of his longing, plunging into her repeatedly until she felt his organ spasm and the warmth of his semen jet inside her to mix with her own juices. At that instant she had climaxed, biting his shoulder hard enough to make him cry out. The teeth marks they found there later made them laugh.

The next time they did it right. They stripped, showered together, towel-dried each other's bodies, and went to bed. This time was slower, gentler, more loving. Absent was the animal lust of before. Both times the sex had been good, but uniquely different. The primitive rutting on the floor had been an appetizer. In bed was the main course they enjoyed with exquisite slowness.

After the second time, they talked. They whispered in the darkness—not for fear of being overheard, but to prolong the sense of intimacy. They did not discuss problems. Working out their differences was a job this period of supreme pleasure would not permit. Perhaps after this night together, they would not need words. Indeed, Lisa thought, perhaps love *could* conquer all.

She returned to the bedroom and looked down at her sleeping husband. She loved him so much that it choked her. Maria had made her understand that it didn't matter if your husband was a cop, the president, or a bum lying in the gutter. What mattered was your love for him. There was never any doubt in her mind that she loved him and that he loved her. She would never let anyone or anything stand in the way of that love again.

She was about to climb back into the bed when the beeping started. Larry's pager was on her nightstand. It was turned low and didn't wake him, although he shifted on his side. She reached down and shut it off. There was only one number for him to call when the little black box went off. Lisa had watched him make that call many times before. He would say little as he listened, his body tensing and the muscles of his face going rigid. Then he would go out into the night, leaving her. On many such occasions it had been for hours—once, for two days. Not tonight, she vowed, shutting it off.

She lay on her back for long minutes in the silent darkness. The steamy heat of their spent passion hung in the air. Gently she touched his back. He was sleeping soundly and did not move. She remembered how tired and thin he looked when she saw him at Blackie's house. God, she had felt like a bitch for doing that to him. She pondered briefly what would have happened if Maria had not called her. Would she have allowed this estrangement to continue until there was nothing left of their relationship?

Again, guilt tore at her. What was she doing now? They wanted him. It was his job. She had known what he was when she married him. In fact, she was proud of him. *A cop, the president, or a bum lying in the gutter.* They'd had their night of passion. Now he was needed elsewhere. He would go, but he would also return to her when it was over.

"Larry?" she called to him. She had to repeat it twice before he awoke.

Bleary-eyed, he turned over and smiled at her. He kissed her with an urgency that foretold his intentions. She was about to surrender to it when she realized that too much time had elapsed since the pager's irksome summons.

"Your beeper just went off. You've got to call in."

His passion melted as he rolled away from her. The familiar tension was on his face as he reached for the bedside phone. *Damn, being a cop's wife can be hard,* she thought. But she knew now that she was in it for the duration.

CHAPTER 61

APRIL 18, 1991
11:45 P.M.

The black van was parked inside the enclosed loading dock, which led off the alley behind Steven Zalkin's building. It had served the killer well on his two missions of vengence, but he couldn't afford to use it again. Its burned-out hulk would be discovered in a vacant lot near the Cabrini–Green housing project before dawn.

In Zalkin's workroom, a scanner broadcast transmissions on the frequency being used by the police investigating the murders in front of Murphy's Bar on lower Wacker. After an initial flurry of activity, the channel had gone eerily quiet. Zalkin smiled. They were keeping a lid on it as best they could, but this wouldn't work for long. Delahanty was too prominent, and there had been a witness.

Zalkin unstrapped the compact flamethrower from his back. It was a sixteen-inch tube attached to a tank the size of an automobile fire extinguisher. Carduci had assembled it for him using an instruction manual. That night—the last of the larcenous soldier's life—he had drunk beer while he worked. Zalkin had noticed that he kept dropping tools and cursing while he struggled to complete the task. When they gave the weapon a short test fire out on the loading dock, it had performed remarkably well. A burst of concentrated flame had erupted from the barrel to scorch a brick wall thirty feet away.

Zalkin had done the test-firing. Carduci stood by with a special chemical extinguisher to douse any remaining fire. The flamethrower's igniter was volatile enough to ignite solid brick if the brick were exposed to the heat long enough.

In those predawn hours of Wednesday, the seventeenth of April, Zalkin had considered incinerating the GI as a complete test of the flamethrower's effectiveness. But he had not wanted to use any more of the special igniter fluid than necessary. This he had saved for Frank Delahanty. A bullet from the Magnum had worked just as efficiently on Carduci.

He examined the flamethrower. All of its tubes and mechanisms looked in good working order; it had not, however, performed up to expectation.

After trapping Delahanty on the street, Zalkin had planned to torch not only him, but also the two cops and their squad car. He activated the computerized voice box in his helmet and watched with tremendous enjoyment as Delahanty's horror turned to knowledge when he recognized the name "Zykus." Then Zalkin had pulled the trigger.

The bright stream had efficiently enveloped Delahanty and turned him into a bonfire. Then the flamethrower died.

"Hey!" A big man in a white apron was standing in the entrance to Murphy's.

Zalkin spun toward him and pulled the trigger of the flamethrower. A gurgling noise escaped from the nozzle, but no flame came out. The big guy sized up the situation quickly enough and rushed back inside the bar.

Now, back in his lair, Zalkin studied the flamethrower. Maybe he could repair it. He looked for the manual

Carduci had used as a guide for the assembly. The killer couldn't find it. He stopped and focused back on Wednesday morning. In his mind's eye, he saw Carduci working at the table. The soldier had plunked down an empty beer can and said, "Hey, Steve, how about another cold one?"

Zalkin walked up beside Carduci, noticing the TOP SECRET stamp on the manual's cover. He had called it to Carduci's attention.

"That don't mean shit. Everything is 'top secret' at Astrolab. That queer scientist and knothead captain think their locks, cameras, and top secret stamps keep everything secure. Hell, that just makes it easier for me to steal." Carduci snatched up the book, ripped the cover off, and dropped it on the floor. Zalkin burned the cover in a metal wastebasket before returning to the table where the soldier was working. He picked up the manual.

"You can burn that, too," Carduci said. "I didn't really need it anyway. I could assemble this baby in the dark."

Carrying the manual, Zalkin left the workroom and . . . then?

Zalkin retraced the steps he had taken on Wednesday. In the living area he turned on the lights and stopped. He remembered going to the refrigerator and removing a can of beer for Carduci. But he no longer had the manual in his hand when he headed back for the workroom.

It came back to him. He recalled placing it in the bookcase before he went to get the beer. Zalkin had lived for many years in cramped spaces, so he had a tendency to keep things in their proper places.

He walked over to the bookcase and found the manual lying faceup on top of a stack of *Hustler* and *Penthouse* magazines. He frowned. Zalkin distinctly remembered placing it facedown. He hadn't been near the bookshelf since that night and no one else . . .

Detective Bronson had been rummaging around there

earlier. Why hadn't Zalkin simply told Bronson to sit down and mind his own business? But Zalkin hadn't figured there was anything to hide at the time. That was a bad mistake. A very bad mistake.

CHAPTER 62

APRIL 19, 1991
MIDNIGHT

Cole was forced to park two blocks from Murphy's Bar. The circus was in progress. There were not as many spectators out at this time of night, but there were enough. However, the players in the main attraction were in evidence and doing their bit to make this spectacle of urban street-violence a success. Parked in the center ring was the Mobile Command Vehicle. First Deputy Superintendent Ray Schmidt had arrived.

Cole walked toward the MCV. The night was chilly with a threat of rain in the air. Cole flipped the collar of his trench coat up. He was sleepy, and would rather have been at home in bed with his wife. The thought of Lisa waiting for him made Cole smile.

Minicam crews and print reporters were gathered outside the door of the white motor home. They shouted questions at every cop entering or leaving.

"Where's Schmidt?"

"Who was killed here?"

"When is someone going to make some kind of statement about this?"

Cole reached the edge of the media throng, hoping against hope that he could slip through without being recognized. He was about to make his move when a heavy hand clamped down on his shoulder. He spun around to face Comdr. Peter Stanley, his opposite number in Area Six Detectives.

Stanley was a humorless man who sported a prickly crew cut over a wire-thin body emaciated by marathon runs. "Chief Riseman's in the bar, Cole. He wants to talk to us right now."

Grateful for the reprieve, Cole followed Stanley into Murphy's. The bar had been divided in two by a barrier tape. On the side opposite the door, three teams of Area Six detectives were interviewing two dozen witnesses who had been in the bar when Delahanty was there with his two bodyguards. On the other side, seated alone at a table watching the detectives work, sat William Riseman. A steaming Pyrex coffeepot and stack of Styrofoam cups rested on the table in front of him.

Cole and Stanley pulled up chairs at Riseman's table and sat down.

"Somebody used a flamethrower on Frank Delahanty earlier tonight," Riseman said without emotion. "There were two cops bodyguarding him at the time. They were both shot. One's dead; the other's in critical condition at St. Anne's Hospital. Delahanty was burned down to nothing but a pile of ash and scorched bone."

"Christ!" Cole said, unable to control himself. Another cop dead. He reached for the coffeepot and poured. He sipped the hot, bitter liquid, hoping it would remove the chill he'd caught. It didn't.

"I know this isn't your beat, Larry," Riseman said in deference to Stanley, "but one of our eyewitnesses said that the killer used military hardware on Delahanty and the tact people."

Cole sat very still. Stanley looked from Riseman to Cole, but remained silent. If Cole wanted this case, he could have it.

A uniformed lieutenant with the face of a bassett hound came into the bar and hurried over to the table.

"Excuse me, Chief," the lieutenant said with distressed breathlessness. "The first deputy sent me to get Comdr. Cole. He wants him in the MCV on the double."

Riseman smiled at Cole. "Let's not keep the first deputy waiting, Larry."

"Why me?" Cole got to his feet and followed the lieutenant from the bar.

Schmidt was beginning a press conference under the MCV's exterior Chicago Police Department logo. He was in full uniform and spoke in measured tones, which were almost funereal. "Police Officer Henry Chan was pronounced DOA at St. Anne's Hospital. Police Officer Collin Charles is in critical condition and currently in surgery at St. Anne's. They were both shot from ambush by an as-yet-unknown sniper."

A voice rose from the circle of light surrounding Schmidt. "We understand the officers were assigned to tactical patrol in the Eighteenth District. What were they working on when they were shot?"

Schmidt stared sightlessly into the barrage of lights. "They were on a bodyguard detail."

"Who were they . . . ?" came a chorus of voices from the throng. A male voice rose above the rest to complete the question, "Who were they bodyguarding?"

"The principal was *Chicago Times-Herald* columnist Frank Delahanty. Mr. Delahanty was also killed in the attack."

The media went wild. Questions began flying with such abandon that all Schmidt heard was an undecipherable babble. Walter Moseby, the CPD's Director of News Affairs, had arrived shortly after Schmidt began. Moseby was standing beside Cole when the press riot erupted. Cole heard him say, "Holy shit!" before wading through the throng to forcibly pull Schmidt inside the MCV. Cole noticed that the first deputy went docilely with the smaller man. Schmidt was obviously relieved to escape the barrage of questions quickly turning into accusations of incompetence.

The reporters surged forward en masse to attempt to fight their way past the sergeant and two patrolmen standing guard at the side door of the MCV. Caught in the rush, Cole flashed his identification at the sergeant and slipped behind them into the converted motor home. Before a heavyset black man carrying a minicam on his shoulder could follow him inside, Cole slammed the door.

The commotion outside was clearly audible. Cole looked around to find a handful of uniformed officers standing in the dining area. The first deputy sat at a table looking visibly shaken after his encounter with the press. Moseby stood over him.

"Why didn't you wait for me?" Moseby's voice held a flatly critical ring. "We didn't have to give the press the details yet. The superintendent told me to make an assessment of the situation and then call him before issuing a statement."

"What difference would that have made?" Schmidt's voice was unusually subdued.

Moseby rolled his eyes. He had been trained as a professional journalist, not as a cop. His job was public relations for an organization the public and the press was seldom sympathetic to. It would be difficult to keep the department from getting a black eye on this one, but he could have done better than Schmidt.

"If we gave them a prepared statement instead of shooting from the hip, giving the story our way, they'd have to at least print it," Moseby argued. "Later they could make their allegations of incompetence and maybe worse, but we'd have told our side first. Now anything we say will look like a cover-up."

Schmidt slammed his fist down on the table with such force the entire van shook. "Goddammit, I don't care what those vultures think! I've got a dead cop and another one who might not live through the night. The body count of dead cops this week is three, Mr. News Director, or aren't you counting anything but press releases?"

Moseby didn't shrink from Schmidt's wrath. He worked for the superintendent, not the first deputy. "The boss wanted this handled differently." The words came out as a warning.

"I'm the boss here tonight, Moseby," Schmidt said.

The news director nodded and turned to leave. "I'll tell the superintendent you said that."

"Do whatever the fuck you want," Schmidt said to Moseby's back.

Cole started to follow Moseby out, but Schmidt stopped him. "I want to talk to you, Cole. The rest of you, out."

When they were alone, Schmidt motioned Cole to take the seat across from him.

"Assholes," the first deputy said vehemently. "They're all assholes. They're only worried about Delahanty. What about the dead cop? The son of a bitch who did this blew his head right off his shoulders! What kind of animal . . . ?"

Cole watched Schmidt's eyes water. His voice cracked. Cole looked away, masking his embarrassment at witnessing the first deputy's display of emotion. After a moment Cole looked back at Schmidt to find him rubbing his hands across his face. His voice was hoarse but nearly back to normal as he said, "Riseman talk to you?"

"Yes, sir," Cole responded. "He wants me and Pete Stanley to coordinate our investigations. We think there's a link between what happened here and the Temple of Allah incident. We're going to—"

Schmidt frowned. "I'm not talking about that stuff stolen from Astrolab. I mean, did he talk to you about having lunch with me and Steve Zalkin at the Press Club tomorrow?"

"He mentioned it."

"Good." Schmidt stood up, extending one of his bear paws to Cole. "See you at noon."

CHAPTER 63

APRIL 19, 1991
12:46 A.M.

Sister Mary Louise Stallings couldn't sleep. She was exhausted, but her brain was too alive with thought to allow her to sleep. She was alone in the convent. That morning Grady Johnson had picked up the Price children for placement in a temporary foster home until a permanent place for them could be found. Sean Price cried when they parted, but she promised to come visit him as soon as she could. She intended to keep that promise.

Her room was on the second floor. It had once been the quarters of the Mother Superior of the order that had serviced Our Lady of Peace parish during the Washington Park Boulevard area's affluent years. Back then, up to twenty nuns had been housed there at one time. Now she was alone.

The room was simply furnished but twice as large as the other cell-like cubicles. There was a walk-in closet, a chest of drawers, a bookcase, a desk, and a small shrine to Our Lady of Peace in one corner. There was a queen-size bed over which a large wooden crucifix was displayed and a leather easy chair big enough for Sister Mary Louise to sleep in—which she often did after dozing off while reading.

Now she sat in the chair with a book on her lap. She had been reading since nine o'clock in the hopes that this simple mental exercise would fatigue her brain sufficiently to send her into oblivion. However, as one A.M. approached, she was still at it.

She stood up and crossed to the bookcase. She picked up a new book. She hadn't planned to start it tonight, but it didn't look like she was going to sleep tonight either.

She was turning from the bookcase with the novel in hand when she heard a dull thud behind her. She spun around quickly with her heart leaping into her throat. The noise had come from the bookcase.

Her first thought was rats. The boulevard area was infested with them, and although Father Ken had an exterminator in last March, it was possible that a new breed of poison-resistant rodent had invaded the convent. She listened carefully, but could hear none of the muted scratching noises the furry little intruders made when they were foraging for food. The bookcase was silent.

A metallic object shone dully from the back of the shelf. "Oh, Mother of Our Lord!" She reached inside and removed the snub-nosed .38 pistol. She had forgotten about it. How long had it been here? She could almost remember the exact date. January fifth. The day Shirley, the student with the razor-cut forehead in her seventh-grade history class, had given it to her.

It was after school on a bitterly cold day. Shirley had lingered after the others had left the classroom.

"Did you want to see me, Shirley?" the nun asked.

Shirley had looked around with frightened eyes at the empty classroom. Certain that they were alone, the girl came forward and whispered, "You got to help me, Sister Mary. My brother Andy's gonna kill someone."

Sister Mary Louise had masked her horror and asked with concern, "How do you know?"

"It's all he talks about. There's this boy they call Little Man. He's trying to get in with the Brotherhood. Says everybody in our project building got to pay protection or he's gonna make trouble."

Ordinarily, the nun would have made Shirley speak proper English, but this was not the time for grammar correction. She let Shirley get her story out.

"Little Man threatened my mama. Andy heard about it and went somewhere and got a gun. Says he gonna off Little Man."

"Have you called the police?"

Shirley snarled. "We ain't gonna have nothing to do with no pigs, Sister. It's because of them that my daddy's in jail."

"But I can't help you without the police, Shirley."

"Yeah, you can, Sister." Shirley reached in her bookbag and removed the gun. "I stole it. If Andy don't have it, he can't kill Little Man."

"I can't—" Sister Mary Louise began, but Shirley thrust the weapon into her hands.

"You got to help me, Sister. I ain't got nobody else."

The nun had reached her level of tolerance. "You don't *have* anyone else."

Obediently, Shirley corrected her English, and Sister Mary Louise took the gun.

She considered mentioning it to Father Ken, but he'd had enough on his mind at the time. On top of that, she felt a certain responsibility to her student. So she had carried the gun with her to the convent and hidden it behind the book-case.

Now she held it in her hand. She knew enough about guns from the ones her father owned in Iowa to know that the one Shirley had given her was loaded. She had even fired rifles on the farm to kill small pesty varmints that destroyed crops. But this instrument she held had only been created to do one thing: kill human beings.

After a moment, she put it back on the shelf and concealed it once more behind the books. She would someday have to do something about it. But not tonight.

Sister Mary Louise returned to the chair and opened the new book to the first chapter.

4

"Martin Zykus is a real live menace to society."

—Blackie Silvestri

CHAPTER 64

Louise Stallings crouched in a chair in her West Barry Place apartment and stared at the living-room wall. She had been there through most of the night, afraid to move after the two men who had raped her left. She was aware that the sun was up, but she kept the blinds shut tight against the encroachment of daylight. The apartment was comfortably warm, but she felt chilled to her marrow and didn't know if she'd ever be warm again.

The previous night after the front door slammed behind the rapists, Louise had leaped from the bed, run to the door, thrown the dead bolt lock, and fastened the chain. She stumbled through the dark to the telephone. The dial tone whined back at her. She started to dial 911. Then she stopped.

She was naked and felt dirty. She remembered a movie she had seen once on television. It was one of those docudramas that told the story from the raped woman's perspective. Louise recalled that the police in the TV show had not let the victim bathe until they had taken some type of vaginal smear sample. In the movie a stern-faced, unsympathetic nurse had stood over the victim. The nurse had lowered the glass slide between the victim's legs. Louise would never let anyone do that to her for any reason.

She hung up the telephone.

Her skin crawled from their touch. One side of her face burned where the unshaven cheek of the first one had scraped her when he . . . The memory of it made her tremble. Clutching her stomach, she rushed into the bathroom. She vomited. She bent over the toilet bowl and heaved until her face and throat ached. She turned on the shower full blast and stood beneath the stinging spray scrubbing her body until her skin glowed red from the irritation. Even then, she remained there, hoping that the water would somehow cleanse the defilement from her soul.

Finally, she stepped out of the shower. She reached for a towel behind the bathroom door and caught a glimpse of her reflection in the mirror. What she saw there startled her. Her eyes were surrounded by dark shadows and sunken back into her skull. She could see the slight puffiness at the place over her right temple where she had been struck. With her hair plastered down, she looked like the ghost of a drowning victim who had come back to haunt the living. At that instant, she wished that she were indeed dead.

Then the tears came. At first they were merely whimpers, but as the horror of the depravity inflicted upon her was relived, she began sobbing hysterically. Naked, she collapsed on the bathroom floor and curled her body into a fetal position. There she remained for a long time, even after the crying had stopped and the cold porcelain surrounding her had chilled her bloodless.

Finally, with an effort, she forced herself up. She staggered into the bedroom. Her mind locked on what had occurred here. She could still see them. First the little man, then the other one. She could see herself lying beneath each of them. She felt her stomach wrench violently. She fled into the living room.

She snatched an afghan from a chair and wrapped it around her. Then she took up her vigil in front of the blank wall.

Now, as daylight seeped through the blinds, Louise remained at her post. She was hungry, but knew that she couldn't eat. Her eyes burned from lack of sleep, but she was afraid to sleep. She tried to formulate a course of action, but none would come. If she stayed here just a little longer, a part of her brain rationalized, maybe this nightmare would go away.

Her telephone ringing made her jump. It was on the desk, within arm's reach of her chair. All she had to do was pick it up. Instead, she recoiled back into her chair with a whimper. She clutched the afghan tighter around her.

It rang again.

She stared at it, as if an act of her will would make the ringing cease. She couldn't talk to anyone now.

It rang again.

Terror fought to control her. Her teeth ground together, as her empty stomach churned. Why would anyone be calling her now?

It rang again.

Her hand trembled, as she reached out and pulled the receiver from its cradle.

Her voice came out a harsh rasp. "Hello?"

"I got her, Ma," her older brother's voice boomed across the line. "Hello, Louie! What're you doing, still asleep? It's Thanksgiving morning, girl. Out here among the cornfields, we've been up for hours."

"Hello, Louise." It was her mother. "Happy Thanksgiving, honey."

The memory flashed back to her. It was two years ago.

"But why Chicago, Louise?" her mother said from across the dining-room table, with that look on her face that was part pleading, part pain, and all control-seeking.

"Because that's where Loyola is, Mother." Louise had always been a respectful child, even though she was now almost twenty and most of her friends from school were married.

Her brother Mike stood up and walked to the front window. He was the only Stallings boy left. The other two, Claude and Christopher, had been killed in Vietnam. "Chicago's dangerous, Louie."

God, how she hated that name!

"I can take care of myself," she said.

Her words came back to her as she said into the phone, "Happy Thanksgiving, Mother."

"You sound like you've got a cold," her mother said. "Have you been dressing right and taking your vitamins?"

"Yes, Mother," Louise said, trembling with the effort to keep her voice normal. She would never let them know she had failed. Never let them drag her back under their control.

"So, how's school?" Michael was on the extension. "They put you on scholastic probation yet?"

She hated him for that remark. She had always gotten better grades than he. She had always been braver than he, too. After Claude and Chris were killed at a place called Khe Sanh, Michael didn't have to go to the war. But Louise had tried to join, even though she'd been too young. She wanted revenge for her brothers' deaths.

"I'm doing quite well," she said, attempting to lighten her voice as best she could.

For the next half hour they went on and on. Mother talked about her high school girlfriends still living in Kellam, while Mike talked about her old boyfriends. The girls were all having babies, while the boys were giving the babies and working the farms. Louise took it all, making the appropriate noises and keeping herself rigidly under control.

"Now, Louise," her mother said. "You be sure and go to church. You know your father always wanted the family to go together on Thanksgiving. It's not a holy day, but . . ."

It was as always. Mother talked about Father, and then started crying. But now Louise also felt a lump form in her throat. She had dearly loved her father and wished that he were alive now. She could talk to him about what had happened last night. Trust him with her secret.

She managed a cheerful goodbye before hanging up. Then she cried. She sank back into the chair with the afghan still wrapped around her and sobbed. She did not become hysterical or shriek, but allowed the emotion to take her completely. But she was not crying for her father and brothers, whom God had taken. She cried for a little patch of dirt off Route Six in Kellam, Iowa, where she had spent the happiest days of her life but could never return to. Her life, for better or worse, was out here in the world now. Out here beyond the cornfields and friendly farmers. She stopped crying.

Louise Stallings stood up, shed the afghan, straightened her back, and walked into the bedroom. She began to dress. She just had time to make the ten-o'clock mass at St. Thaddeus Catholic Church.

CHAPTER 65

NOVEMBER 25, 1976
NOON

Larry Cole considered his options. He could either celebrate or ignore Thanksgiving. He was in his efficiency apartment watching the Chicago Bears play the Detroit Lions on television. It was over two hours before he had to leave for work, and he didn't feel like lying around in front of the tube all that time.

He had worked out with weights when he awoke at 8:30. Then he had fried a couple of eggs and downed a half-quart of orange juice. Now, as midday passed, he contemplated the day before him. He was less than enthusiastic over his prospects.

Perhaps the one thing he hated most at this stage of his life was downtime. He attempted to fill every waking hour of every day with meaningful activity. If he wasn't working he was going to school, studying, or exercising to keep in shape for the rigors of police work. He also spent a great deal of time reading police manuals and general orders in preparation for the next promotional exams. He survived on four to six hours of sleep a night and he actually preferred the sixteen-hour days he put in when he had classes. When such days were over, he felt fulfilled. Atonement came with this fulfillment.

There was some reading he could do for his contemporary literature class, but he felt he had to get out of the apartment. But where would he go? It was too early to head for the station.

It had snowed the night before, and low clouds hung over the city. Most of the two inches of white stuff had turned to slush. The temperature hovered a couple of degrees above freezing. Dressed in jeans, turtleneck, and Navy pea coat, Cole walked to his car and brushed the snow off the hood and windshield. It was as he began working on the rear window of the Mustang that he remembered that St. Thaddeus Catholic Church had invited all Nineteenth District cops to have Thanksgiving dinner in their school hall.

Originally, he had rejected going, as he figured nobody but a bunch of old ladies and local street people would show up. But now he didn't have anything else to do. He wouldn't have to show up in uniform, which was probably better.

He'd draw less attention like this. With the turtleneck on, nobody would notice his .45 automatic stuck in his belt.

The traffic on Lake Shore was sparse. The cars he passed generally held families of four, and in one case he counted eight heads in a station wagon. He was the only one out traveling alone. Sometimes he liked it like this. This was not one of those times.

He'd come out of Mount Carmel High School on the South Side of Chicago as one of the most highly touted defensive backs in the state. He'd never played one down of offense. Liked the contact and uncertainty of playing a good defensive game. On defense, it was the other guy's move: after he made it, Cole made his—a disadvantage Cole had always managed to turn to an advantage.

He had excellent speed, good size, and could hit like a linebacker. Had intimidated more than his share of receivers into dropping passes before he even touched them. Was All-Catholic League in Chicago, and was a runner-up for All-State honors. They recruited him from the Ivy League to the Pacific Eight Conference. He decided on the University of Iowa.

Cole exited at Fullerton and drove west. A few minutes later he could see the spires of St. Thaddeus. He parked across from the school hall and remained in the car. Maybe this wasn't such a good idea.

Iowa City. Home of the Hawkeyes. Right in the middle of a cornfield. But all college towns have their good points, and Iowa City was no exception. He was a highly touted football player, who could help the Hawkeyes in their quest for a Rose Bowl bid in the next couple of years. Everybody liked football players. Especially young coeds.

* * *

He locked the car and crossed to the school hall entrance. The aroma of roasted turkey hit him the instant he walked through the door.

A moon-faced priest with a tolerant smile greeted him. "God bless you, young man."

Cole felt awkward. "Thank you, Father. Uh, I'm from the Nineteenth District." He flashed his badge.

The priest's eyes widened. "Oh, has there been some problem, Officer?"

They always react this way, Cole thought. He explained to the priest that he was simply there at the parish's invitation for Thanksgiving dinner.

The priest was so relieved that he gushed, "I'm Father Tom Conley. We're so glad you could join us. You're our first policeman."

The priest led Cole into the hall where a row of serving tables was arranged along one wall. On the tables, starting from the near side, were heated serving trays containing sliced turkey, turkey parts, mashed potatoes, giblet gravy, squash, dressing, cranberry sauce, and green peas. On a separate table were trays for dinner rolls, along with slices of pumpkin and apple pie.

There was no one in the serving line, and few people were in evidence at the tables arranged around the hall. Noticing the policeman's inspection, Father Tom said, "We're expecting more diners after three o'clock. Please help yourself."

Cole was about to do just that when he noticed Gerry Harper asleep at one of the tables on the other side of the hall.

"How long has he been here, Father?"

A properly distressed frown pierced Father Conley's pious front. "I'm afraid for quite some time now. He fell asleep before he could even eat. We tried to wake him, but . . ."

Cole knew Gerry Harper as a regular in the Nineteenth District drunk tank. He was a wino, who panhandled enough to get his daily ration of White Port and then curled up to go to sleep wherever he found himself. Cole had rousted him a dozen times, sent him to the detox center more than once, and had housed him for trespassing and disorderly twice. Each time Gerry had been too drunk to care what the cop did.

"Would you like me to wake him up for you?" Cole asked.

"You won't hurt him, will you?" Father Conley said with alarm.

Cole smiled. "He won't feel a thing, Father."

Gerry Harper had developed a ripe, unwashed fragrance. A full tray of food rested on the table in front of him, and by some miracle his unshaven, dirty face had not landed in the mashed potatoes and giblet gravy when he passed out.

The policeman leaned over him and said softly, "Gerry, wake up."

A few heads turned in their direction. Father Conley, looking terribly uncomfortable, stood a few feet behind Cole.

Cole placed his hand gently on the sleeping drunk's shoulder. He would make sure to wash his hands thoroughly when this was over. He shook Gerry, but the man was as inert as a slug.

Cole moved his hand off the shoulder of the filthy, two-sizes-too-big overcoat onto the yellowing flesh of the neck. Cole turned to look at Father Conley, as his fingers sought the mastoid process located at the juncture of Gerry's ear and jaw. Cole smiled at the priest before lowering his head closer to the sleeping bum's head. At that instant Cole jammed his thumb into the gland. Gerry Harper came groggily awake.

"C'mon, Gerry," Cole said, helping the drunk to his feet. "Time to get some air."

The wino's bloodshot eyes took in the cop. "Cole!

What the fuck are you doing here? I heard you was supposed to be on tact with Blackie, not rousting drunks no more."

The policeman was dumbfounded. How a lowlife like Gerry Harper had learned about his pending assignment was a mystery. However, his smell and language made it imperative that Cole dispose of him as quickly as possible.

Gerry went along without protest. Outside the school hall, Cole slipped a five dollar bill into his coat pocket and said, "Happy Thanksgiving, Gerry."

The wino waved and shuffled off down the street.

Back in the school hall the priest was waiting for him. "You handled that very well, Officer. We were getting concerned about him. We really didn't know what to do."

Cole smiled. It was just another dirty job that cops did routinely. "Is there someplace where I could wash my hands?"

Father Conley led Cole to a washroom not far from the hall, where Cole washed the smell and germs of Gerry Harper off his hands. When he returned, a place had been prepared for him at one of the tables. He protested when Father Conley told him someone would bring his food. The protest did no good.

CHAPTER 66

NOVEMBER 25, 1976
12:35 P.M.

Louise Stallings had gone to mass that morning. After the service she remained in the church, praying. For the first time since the horror she had experienced the previous night, she felt some degree of spiritual relief.

The lights were extinguished and the sacristy became so still she could almost hear the silence. At that point, time ceased to exist for her.

"Excuse me." The woman's voice startled Louise. She spun around and looked up at a short nun, who was looking down at her with concern. "You've been kneeling here so long I became concerned."

Louise started to stand, but found that her knees had gone numb. She gave out a short cry and sat down heavily in the pew. She massaged her legs to get the blood circulating through them again.

"I've had that happen to me before too," the nun said, smiling. She whispered, but her voice squeaked in a cartoon-mouse tone when she spoke. "Usually makes for a mighty powerful prayer."

Louise managed to stand. "I didn't mean to stay so long. I guess I got carried away." She turned to leave.

"You're alone?" the nun asked with concern.

She started to deny it, but couldn't bring herself to tell a lie in this House of God. Louise nodded.

"Where's your family?"

"I'm from Kellam, Iowa. I talked to them before I came to church."

"That settles it: You'll have dinner with us."

So Louise Stallings found herself in the school hall when the black police officer removed the derelict for Father Conley. She had been sitting with Sister Frances Lucille, the nun who had found her in the church. She had eaten and was beginning to dread the thought of going back to her apartment when the brief excitement occurred. Louise had been impressed with the way the officer had handled the poor man. She remembered the time she had seen the policemen struggling with the prisoner outside the police station on Addison. This had been handled much better.

While the policeman was washing his hands, Father Conley rushed over to Sister Frances Lucille. "I want you to serve the officer's food to him. I'll sit him here with you and your guest." He gave Louise a friendly smile. "That way he won't feel isolated."

The nun got up to supervise preparation of the policeman's meal. When he returned to the hall, Father Conley escorted him to Louise's table. He sat down directly across from her.

"Hi," he said with a smile.

"Hi." She felt infuriatingly self-conscious. What did she expect him to do, take out a blackjack and hit her? She actually couldn't tell if he had a blackjack beneath his turtleneck sweater.

"This is a nice parish you have."

"Thank you." This really wasn't her parish, but she didn't know what else to say.

She wondered how he could be expected to eat all the food they brought for him, but he gave it an impressive try.

Louise and the nun had already eaten, but they had pie and coffee to keep him company. Sister Frances Lucille provided most of the conversation.

She talked about books about cops, movies with cops in them, the Swiss Guards in the Vatican, and state, county, and municipal law enforcement. During most of her monologue the policeman ate, while appearing politely attentive. Louise understood his reaction. Sister Frances Lucille had a gift for virtually nonstop gab. She was the type who could ask you ten questions, answer them all herself, and later boast what a brilliant conversationalist you were.

The nun turned her attention to Louise. "So how do you like Chicago so far? It must be a lot different than living in Iowa."

She was starting to give the stock answer that the city of Chicago had a larger population than the entire state of Iowa, when the policeman asked, "What part of Iowa are you from?"

"Kellam," she replied. "It's about a hundred miles southwest of Cedar Rapids."

"I lived in Iowa City for a while," he said.

Since coming to Chicago, Louise Stallings had yet to meet one person either from or who had ever set foot in Iowa. She warmed to the policeman. "Were you at the university?"

He nodded. She noticed a slight apprehension about him. She read it accurately as his having experienced something unpleasant in her home state. At once she regretted this, while wondering what could have happened to him in a simple little college town like Iowa City.

He finished his meal. "Well, I hate to eat and run, but I've got to go to work."

"You'll be going north, won't you, Officer Cole?" the nun asked.

He nodded.

"Could I ask you to give Louise a lift to her apartment on the way? She lives on West Barry."

"I wouldn't want to inconvenience him," Louise protested; however, she was hoping that she wouldn't have to travel the streets alone.

Cole glanced at his watch. "It's no inconvenience. It's right on the way."

CHAPTER 67

NOVEMBER 25, 1976
2:13 P.M.

Why didn't you go to school in Iowa?" Cole asked as they pulled away from St. Thaddeus.

"I wanted to go to Loyola," Louise said.

He shrugged. He guessed that it was her secret. He had enough secrets of his own without worrying about hers.

"So how long were you at the University of Iowa?" she said.

"A little less than a year."

"Why did you leave?"

"I got a girl pregnant," he blurted out before he realized what he was saying.

He glanced at her. She was staring out at the passing traffic. There was no indication that she had taken any offense at his sharp tone. He regretted having used it and having told her about his private life.

However, he found himself explaining, "She was sixteen. Got into college early. Was always hanging out with the cheerleaders. One thing led to another, and . . ."

"I don't see why you had to leave school. Students get pregnant on campuses all the time."

"The girl's father was a big-shot lawyer in Cedar Rapids. He raised a lot of hell. I was lucky I didn't end up in jail. When the shouting stopped, my scholarship had been revoked."

"What about the girl?"

"What about her? I told you her father was well connected. Nothing happened to her."

"I mean did she have the baby?"

"Of course not. What would she . . ." He stopped. In the five years that had passed since he left Iowa, he had never tried to get in touch with her. He didn't know whether she had had the baby or not.

He looked at the woman beside him. She stared back. There was not so much condemnation as questioning in her gaze. She turned back to face front.

"They told me never to try to see her again." It even sounded lame to him. "What else could I do?"

"West Barry's the next street, Officer Cole."

He made the turn onto her block.

Pulling to a stop, he frowned. He had been there the previous night.

"Were you at home last night?" he asked.

She went rigid.

"Hey, what's wrong?" he said. "You look like somebody just stepped on your grave."

She reached for the door handle, but before opening it she turned back to face him. "What was the girl's name?"

"Vickie."

"You should find out if she had the baby. It could make a difference later in your life." With that, she got out.

Cole watched her cross to the building entrance. He waited until she disappeared from view before putting the car in gear and cruising toward Broadway. He was thinking over what she had said about Vickie in Cedar Rapids when he saw the rusted-out Chevy belching exhaust fumes. It was parked a few doors from Louise Stalling's apartment building. There was someone behind the wheel, which would have been enough for Cole to issue a citation for excessive exhaust fumes. But he wasn't on duty yet.

He was driving past the offending Chevy when he caught a glimpse of the driver's face. It was Martin Zykus.

Cole drove to the corner and stopped. That fat creep in the rust bucket hadn't seen him. He wondered what Zykus was doing there. Cole made a right turn and cruised down Broadway. Traffic was light, and there were plenty of parking places on both sides of the usually crowded street.

He glanced at his watch. 2:27. He just had time to get to the station, change, and make the three-o'clock roll call. He gunned the engine, but just as quickly hit the brakes and pulled to the curb. Before he had given it much thought, he had locked the car and was trotting down the block back toward West Barry.

He spied a phone booth inside a drug store. He called the station.

"Nineteenth District, Sergeant Beazley."

"Sarge, this is Larry Cole assigned to Beat 1923."

"Yeah, Cole, we've been trying to get in touch with you. You've been assigned to the tactical unit. You're to report in at five."

"Great!" Cole said, jumping up in the booth and almost hitting his head on the roof.

"I don't know how great it is because the only two guys working tact tonight are you and Blackie Silvestri. Everybody else is off."

"Thanks, Sarge," Cole said, hanging up. He was already working on his first case.

CHAPTER 68

Martin Zykus got out of his car and walked back to her building. He had been thinking about her all night. He had to see her again. He remembered that last night she didn't scream, shout, or fight him. She had even asked him to keep Dave from hurting her again. Well, he had done that. Maybe that would be a good way to get the conversation going between them.

He rejected a frontal approach. Despite what Dave had instructed him to do, he didn't necessarily want to bully the woman. At least, not too much. He'd have to figure a way to do it more subtly. To ease up to her, so to speak. But he didn't know her name. He figured that would be easy enough to find out.

A notice taped to the downstairs door gave him an idea. He entered the lobby and after checking the bell for apartment 508 and seeing the name "L. Stallings" there, he pressed the manager's bell.

A slurred voice cracked over the intercom. "Whaddaya want?"

"I'd like to inquire about the apartment you have for rent," Zykus said.

"What?"

The busboy repeated his request.

"For crying out loud, it's Thanksgiving Day."

"And a Happy Thanksgiving to you, sir," Zykus said. "I only want to take a quick look. Then I'll be gone."

Zykus held his breath.

"Okay, c'mon." This was punctuated by a buzzer sounding, releasing the security door.

The manager's apartment was on the main floor next to the elevators. The man who opened the door was wearing a dirty T-shirt and carrying a beer can. He looked more like a janitor than the manager.

He was husky, but aging badly. He looked Zykus up and down with open skepticism. "The rent here starts at two hundred fifty dollars a month, pal."

Zykus smiled at him. "I'm sure my mother and I can afford it, sir. She gets my dad's pension check."

"Pension from what?"

He thought quickly. "He spent thirty years with the Chicago Police Department."

The manager's manner changed instantly. "No shit. Your pa was a cop, huh?"

Zykus locked the smile on his face. He'd have to play it very carefully now. "Sure was."

"My pappy did twenty-seven years out of the Stanton Avenue Station. 'Course, that was before World War II."

He paused for Zykus to make a comment. The busboy was composing a lie he hoped wouldn't have too many holes in it when a high-pitched female voice called from inside the apartment, "Joe, who is it?"

"Just a guy wants to see the vacant apartment, Betty."

"On Thanksgiving? Are you crazy? Nobody goes apartment-hunting on Thanksgiving."

The manager stepped out into the hall with Zykus and shut the door behind him. He was barefoot and the cold floor tiles made him bounce from foot to foot. "Look, that's my old lady. She's pissed cause I got to go see the kids from my first marriage in a little while. Why don't you do us both a favor and go take a look at the apartment yourself." He fished around in his pocket and came up with two keys on a dirty leather keychain. "It's apartment 205. Take a look and bring those back."

Zykus took the keys. "These for 205?"

"No." The manager looked up and down the hall. "They're my passkeys. Front and back door locks."

Zykus played it. "You trust me with these?"

"Sure," the manager eyed him conspiratorialy. "You're a cop's kid, ain't ya? Ain't shit up there to steal anyway."

CHAPTER 69

NOVEMBER 25, 1976
2:34 P.M.

Louise Stallings turned on every light in her apartment. She turned on her stereo and the television. Without paying attention to either, she began industriously straightening up the living room. This didn't take much effort, as she usually kept the place very tidy. After replacing the afghan she'd wrapped herself in through the night, she started for the bedroom. She stopped.

"Not yet, Louie," she said, in a fair imitation of her brother's voice.

Louise walked over to the kitchen, thinking she would cook Thanksgiving dinner even though she had already eaten at St. Thaddeus. She wasn't the least bit hungry, but the labor would do her good. Take her mind off of last night.

She was no virgin, but before last night there had only been one man in her life. That had been more of an adolescent mistake of curiosity than anything else, and she had vowed that the next time would be for love.

This brought her back to her original problem, which had been with her long before last night. It was why she had to get away from her family and Kellam, Iowa. Why she was out here in the cold, perilous world, going it alone. She was waiting. What she was actually waiting for she wasn't quite sure, but in her heart she was certain she would know it when it came.

She opened her cabinet to remove seasoning for the capon she had bought at the Treasure Chest when the events of last night rushed back at her. She'd dropped the groceries on the stairs when they were chasing her. Maybe they was still there.

She let herself out of the apartment carefully, checking the hall outside through the peephole and making sure the bolt mechanism was secure on the top lock. The fifth-floor corridor was deserted. Ignoring the images that kept leaping from her subconscious, she walked to the stairwell and descended.

Between the second and third-floor landings she found the bags and spilled groceries. Some of it was salvageable, but the perishables would have to be thrown away. One bag had a tear in it, but she was able to get most of the food back inside.

She was starting back up the stairs when a horrible thought occurred to her. *Suppose I'm pregnant!* A wave of nausea swept over her, and she had to brace herself against the cold stone wall of the dimly lit stairwell.

"Oh, Mother of God, please, no," she whispered.

She would have to go to a doctor tomorrow. But how could she explain what had happened? If she told him the truth, the police would be summoned. When the police found out, then somehow she knew they'd find out back in Kellam.

"No!" The sharpness of her own voice startled her. She had made a decision last night, and for better or worse, she'd stick with it. Climbing the steps, she remembered one of the last things her father had ever said to her.

He was dying of cancer and she'd been sitting by his bedside all night. Once, at about four A.M., he awoke to find her there.

"Baby, you've got to go to bed. You'll be too tired to go to school tomorrow."

His usually strong, booming voice was weakened to a croak. It tore her heart open when she heard it.

"I'm okay, Daddy," she told him. "I'll make it to school all right."

Knowing that she would made him smile, close his eyes again, and say, "You were always the stubborn one in the family, Louise. Once you make up your mind the man ain't been born who can change it."

He died the next day.

The memory brought a tear to her eye, which she brushed away with the heel of her hand as she climbed back to the fifth floor. She had made up her mind and she would stick to her decision. She stepped out into the corridor and stopped dead. A man was bending over the lock of her apartment door. His back was to her, but he looked like . . . She gasped.

Martin Zykus spun around. He forgot the passkey and began walking toward her. "Hey," he called to her with a grin. "I just wanted to talk to you."

She began backing into the stairwell as he approached.

"Hey, wait a minute. Let's not go through this chase-shit again."

For the second time, she dropped her groceries and fled into the stairwell. Martin Zykus pursued.

It was the recurrence of a nightmare. *This can't be happening to me,* her mind screamed: *He couldn't have come back here!*

Going down was much easier than coming up had been last night, but the terror had not diminished. She screamed.

She could hear him pounding down the steps behind her. She cursed the medium-heeled pumps she had worn to church, but there was no time to stop and take them off. At the third-floor landing she made the turn for the next flight and tripped. She began losing her balance as she stumbled down the steps. She was about to fall when Larry Cole, coming up from below, reached out and caught her.

Zykus was a flight above when he heard her stumble. She let out a soft cry and then there was only silence. He guessed that she had fallen and rushed on. He saw her and the colored guy at the same time. She cringed behind him.

Zykus slowed his pace and trotted down the remaining flight. There was something familiar about the black guy, but Zykus couldn't place it. The stairs weren't very well lighted.

"What're you running for? I told you all I wanted to do was talk."

"Leave me alone!" She was now almost completely hidden behind the newcomer's shoulders.

Zykus reached out his hand to pull her from behind the black man. "Don't do that," the man said quietly.

Zykus became wary. Even the voice sounded familiar. "Hey, man, this has got nothing to do with you so butt out, okay?"

The black man never took his eyes off Zykus, as he said, "Do you know this guy, Louise?"

"No!" There was terror in her voice.

"Oh, to hell with this." Zykus reached for her again. The black man hit him.

The blow caught Zykus flush in the chest and knocked him back against the stairs. He tried to get up, but a punch to the stomach knocked the air out of him. The woman screamed, "Stop!" The black man yanked Zykus to his feet and shoved him face first into the wall.

"Don't you remember me, Marty?" the voice behind him said, as his arms were twisted up behind his back and handcuffs snapped on his wrists. "Took a walk on me last night, but I got your fat ass now. You're under arrest."

Louise was sobbing as Cole snatched Zykus down the stairs. She followed them.

CHAPTER 70

NOVEMBER 25, 1976
4:15 P.M.

Thanksgiving was the one holiday of the year that Blackie Silvestri didn't spend with his family. This was by agreement with his wife, Maria. It was a compromise that kept their marriage together and kept him from killing any of her relatives.

He was dressing in their bedroom on the second floor of the South Side bungalow. He strapped on the Bianchi shoulder holster containing his .357 Magnum Python. Next, he slipped a .38-caliber Colt nickel-plated Detective Special into a belt holster, which he positioned opposite the shoulder holster. Three speed-loaders containing eighteen rounds also went onto his belt. In his back pocket went a blackjack. In the small of his back he positioned a set of Smith & Wesson handcuffs. Into his left front pocket, along with his car keys, went cash, spare change, and a six-inch switchblade. He strapped an ankle holster to his left leg. A .25-caliber Browning semiautomatic pistol went into the holster.

Carefully, Blackie checked to make sure he hadn't forgotten anything. The weight felt right, so he figured he was okay. The final items were his star, ID card, driver's license, cigarette lighter, and package of Parodi cigars. Now he was ready to face the bad guys.

He put on a leather, fur-lined jacket—which covered the items of mayhem he had stashed around his body—and checked his image in the mirror behind the bedroom door. He looked like a Mafia hit man. The irony of it made him grin. If things had been a little different, he might have been just that.

There was a knock at the bedroom door. Blackie turned to find his ten-year-old son Bobby standing there. "Hi, Dad. Could I have a dollar?"

"For what?"

"When we get to the old neighborhood me and Maureen want to go to Constantine's candy store. Get some of that candy used to cost a penny when you and Ma were kids."

Blackie glared at his child. If it were Maureen, this would have been a smart remark. However, Bobby was only saying what he thought was true. Then, as Blackie thought about it, he realized that it was true. He gave his son a dollar.

"Thanks, Dad."

"Sure," Blackie said, checking his appearance in the mirror once more. "But Constantine's probably won't be open on Thanksgiving."

"They were last year," Bobby said. "Mr. Arcadio made them open up and give all us kids candy."

Blackie's head snapped around. Maria hadn't told him about that. Paul "the Rabbit" Arcadio was the reigning Mafia boss of the Chicago mob. Arcadio came from the same neighborhood on the West Side as Blackie and Maria. The Silvestris made it a habit never to talk about Maria's visits to the old neighborhood. Every Thanksgiving she took the kids and went to see her relatives—that is, every year since Blackie had thrown Carmine Giordano, an Arcadio button man, through the window of Mama Mancini's pizzeria back on Thanksgiving Day, 1969.

Downstairs, he found his wife putting the finishing touches on her outfit. It wasn't black, but it was dark. *Jeez,* Blackie started to say, *you don't have to look like you're going to a funeral.* But that's the way most of the women in the old neighborhood would be dressed, so Maria did it out of respect. Blackie still didn't like it. Because she was going to Mama Mancini's house for Thanksgiving didn't mean she had to dress like she just got off the boat. *It's 1976!* he wanted to scream at her, but it wouldn't do any good. She had her own ideas about tradition and respect. Trying to change her now would just be a waste of time.

His thirteen-year-old daughter, Maureen, sat on the living room sofa flipping through *Vogue* magazine. She was dressed in a pink knit dress, which showed off every curve of her young body. He could just see the looks she'd be getting from Frankie Arcadio, the Rabbit's creep nephew, and some of the other low-life scum that would be at the dinner.

"What time are you leaving, babe?" He studied his wife for any signs of tension.

"Uncle Pete's picking us up at five." She turned and looked at him.

Oh, she's pissed all right, but she knows it's not my fault. I'm a cop, and half the people attending the dinner at Mama Mancini's tonight will be on the other side of the law. There would probably be a few cops, too. Good cops, who wouldn't take shit off of any Arcadio wiseguy. But none of them had the temper or reputation of Blackie Silvestri.

"I told you it'd be okay if you took the car," he said. "I could take a cab to the station and get a lift home tonight."

"No, Blackie," she said sharply. "We've already made our arrangements. I'll make sure to bring some food home for you."

She called him "Blackie." That wasn't a good sign. Maybe she was mad at him. Well, there wasn't a hell of a lot he could do about that right now. He was going to work.

He gave her a peck on the cheek, his daughter a hug, and his son a firm handshake. Then he was gone. He started his Ford station wagon and hesitated a moment before pulling away from the house. He felt empty inside, as if something vital was missing from his anatomy. He recognized this as a good feeling. This would keep him mindful of just how much the three people in that house meant to him. He'd make it up to them on Christmas, New Year's, anniversaries, and birthdays. They were the best things that had ever happened to him, and he'd never forget it.

It was getting dark. He flicked on the lights and a few minutes later was racing down the expressway. It was going to be a busy night: Holidays—especially ones that encouraged family togetherness—always were. Then all the old grievances and hatreds came out over the turkeys and hams. A few belts of booze thrown in for good measure, and you had the relatives turning the joint upside down. Then somebody would call the cops.

It generally wasn't too difficult to stop a family fight on

a holiday, if you were careful. All you had to do was corral the combatants who didn't live in the house where the melee was taking place, and expel them. That is, if you didn't have one of the battlers with a meat cleaver in his skull or a carving knife planted in his breastbone.

Blackie had seen it all. Cuttings, stabbings, turkey legs used as clubs, dinner fixings dripping from the walls after an adult food fight. The worst he'd ever had to deal with was a wrongly interpreted statement made ten years before by a now-dead uncle. A fight ensued, resulting in a six-year-old girl being shot to death by her father. The father had been shooting at his brother-in-law. Senseless violence—all in the name of family togetherness and giving thanks to the Maker.

Blackie sneered.

It wasn't that he was adverse to the concept of family or the practice of giving thanks. It was just that he didn't like his family not being with him when they should be.

He found that he was traveling at well over eighty miles an hour. With a heavy sigh, he slowed down and stuffed a cigar in the corner of his mouth. Before he had it going, he had chewed the tip ragged.

Blackie had come out of the old Italian neighborhood on the West Side as tough a street punk as they made. His dad worked in the South Chicago steel mills, and none of his family members had ever been in prison or involved with the mob. In his youth he had leaned toward a life of crime until he'd seen the machine-gunned body of a small-time hoodlum named "Wire" Scalise lying on the sidewalk on Taylor Street. A short time later, Blackie became a cop.

He was breaking in a new partner tonight. When Wally Novak and the rest of the tactical team had requested the night off, an arrangement was made to borrow Cole from uniform duty. Cole was going to be the new guy, but it would be a long time before Blackie forgot Hugh Cummings.

He found Cole in the tactical office. The young cop was appropriately dressed and it looked like he'd already made a pinch, which was a good sign. Then Blackie recognized Martin Zykus from the night before. When Blackie saw the look on Cole's face, he knew there was something wrong.

"Could I talk to you outside?" Cole said.

Blackie could see that Zykus was once more handcuffed to the tactical office wall. Also, like last night, he had his head down. Blackie followed Cole out into the hall.

"Do you remember him?" Cole said.

Blackie nodded. "O'Neill cut him loose."

Cole let out a sigh that seemed to drain his spirit. "I arrested him again this afternoon, and now my victim refuses to sign complaints."

Blackie's eyebrows went up. "That could be a problem, kid. A real problem."

CHAPTER 71

NOVEMBER 25, 1976
5:07 P.M.

This was the worst experience of Louise Stallings's life. For the tenth time in the past thirty minutes, she pinched herself to make sure she wasn't dreaming. The flesh in the webbing of her left hand was becoming sore from this. She had been waiting about twenty minutes when Cole had returned.

"Okay, Louise," he said with a breathlessness revealing

barely controlled excitement. "I've got the detectives and a state's attorney on the way in. We need to talk about what Zykus did to you last night."

Her head came up with a jerk as she stared with wide-eyed shock back at him. "How do you know about last night?"

"When I got our boy upstairs, he started bellowing about how he didn't do anything to you last night. About how it was some other guy. I figured—" Cole stopped when Louise lowered her head.

The shame spread through her like a disease. She couldn't see how anything as horrible as this could be happening to her.

"Look, Louise," he said softly, "if you want, I can get a policewoman to talk to you about it."

"No," she said, refusing to look at him.

"Well, I've got to know what happened. What he did last night and what happened this afternoon."

"He didn't do anything."

"I don't understand." Cole leaned forward, attempting to get a better look at her face.

"He didn't do anything to me last night." Her voice was so tight with strain she could barely get the words out. "I've never seen him before today."

"That's not true!" Cole kept his voice low, but the impact of what he said hit her hard. "He did something to you last night. Maybe raped you. Him and another guy. I've been able to put that much together just from the blubbering he's been doing upstairs."

"You didn't hit him again, did you?" she asked with alarm.

His features hardened into a cynical mask. "What's with you? Is that punk your boyfriend or something? Is that what this is all about?"

"He's not my boyfriend," she whispered.

"So what's going on? Why are you trying to protect

him? It can't be because you like him. You were scared to death when he was chasing you."

With a great effort she composed herself. "I appreciate everything you've done. I honestly do. But nothing happened last night and he didn't do anything to me today."

"Then why were you running from him?"

"Can I go now?" she said, standing up. "I have nothing else to tell you."

He stood with her. "You know, I thought I was helping you. Now it looks like I'm the one in trouble."

"How could you be in trouble?"

"Last night I was writing tickets on Broadway when I see Zykus and another man come around the corner off your block. I was in uniform. Your pal upstairs took one look at me and took off running. I caught him and brought him in. Later, I was forced to release him for lack of evidence. Now today, I see him casing your building and following you inside. Next thing, he's chasing you. I bring him in again, and it looks like he's going to walk again."

"I don't see how that would get you in any trouble."

He stared hard at her. "He's already making noises about me harassing him. Oh, I could hit him with a disorderly conduct charge or some other such garbage, but that would only make it worse. I need a victim. Somebody he's done something to. Somebody with enough concern for herself and this sick society we live in to come forward and help me put that human slime away. Instead, since I've got no complainant, I'm the one behind the eight ball."

"I'm sorry," she said sincerely.

"Are you afraid of him? Is that why you won't tell me what happened to you?" Cole said.

She stared at the floor. "I told you nothing happened. Can I go now?"

"The detectives and the state's attorney will want to talk

to you. You'd better stick around. Maybe at the rate we're going, you'll be able to testify at my trial."

"Don't say that," she said, but he was gone.

Fighting the impulse to just walk out and put all of this behind her, she returned to her seat on the bench. That had been over an hour ago.

No matter what she did, she kept becoming more ensnared in this thing. Then a jolting thought struck her. She could tell Cole the truth. Tell him what happened last night, and again in the hall outside her apartment. Ask him to help her. To protect her.

A short time later she was called into a narrow, barren room and questioned by an owlish state's attorney and two totally unsympathetic detectives. Before they had opened their mouths, she had decided to tell them nothing. They made her feel like a criminal, and by the time she returned to the bench she understood why the criminal justice system in America was in such a shambles.

More time passed.

She was again mustering up the nerve to walk out when a man who looked vaguely familiar approached her.

"Excuse me, Miss Stallings," he said, sitting down beside her. "My name's Blackie Silvestri. I'm Larry Cole's partner."

The scene outside the station last summer, when she had seen this man and another policeman struggling with a prisoner, came back to her. She inched away from him to the far end of the bench.

"I'm not going to hurt you," he said. "And I'm not going to try and talk you into signing complaints against Martin Zykus. I guess that's been tried and didn't work. As far as I'm concerned, your mind's made up."

She stared at him. He looked tough and had an intimidating presence. But there was also something honest and maybe even a little tender beneath that brutal front. Despite the incident last summer, she found that she liked him.

"Cole's a young officer," Blackie was saying. "Has his entire career in front of him. Before it's over, a lot of good pinches will get away from him. It happens."

"Pinches?"

"Yeah," Blackie said. "It's slang around here for arrests. Busts. Collars. They all mean the same thing. Translated: putting bad guys in jail. When we can."

Guilt began settling in on her again.

"But that's not why I came down here to talk to you. See that doorway over there?"

The place he indicated was where Cole and Martin Zykus had disappeared when they first entered the station. Louise nodded.

"In a minute or so, the guy who was chasing you is going to come out of there and walk over and talk to that sergeant."

She followed his nod to a man in uniform standing behind the station desk.

"Then the sergeant is going to pick up one of those telephones and call downtown to the Office of Professional Standards. He's going to be getting a complaint against Larry Cole, which will at best put him through some changes and at worst . . ." Blackie's voice trailed off. He shrugged.

"At worst, what?" Louise asked, but he never got a chance to answer, as Martin Zykus walked through the doorway and sauntered over to the sergeant.

She could detect his arrogance even at this distance across the room. He had won. He had beaten her, and he had beaten the man who had tried to help her. Now he was going to try to hurt Cole.

"All you have to do is tell me the truth about him, Miss Stallings," Blackie was saying, but she wasn't listening.

She stood up and walked across the station lobby toward Martin Zykus.

CHAPTER 72

Zykus was about to begin telling his story to the desk sergeant when he heard a familiar voice behind him. He spun around to find Louise Stallings standing a few feet away.

"What's that you said, babe?" He hadn't quite caught her words with his back turned.

"I want to talk to you."

He noticed that her voice trembled and she wouldn't look directly at him. Zykus figured the complaint against the cop could wait. He'd take care of her first.

"Let's go outside," he said with a grin.

"No," she said tightly. "We'll talk over there." She indicated an area in the lobby next to a pay telephone. They would not be alone, but no one would be able to hear them.

"I'd like it more private," he said, "but you're calling the shots now."

Her cheeks colored as she walked across the lobby. Zykus caught a whiff of Blackie Silvestri's cigar. He turned to see the cop standing at the building entrance. He was casually studying Zykus. The busboy didn't like the way this was shaping up.

She stopped and faced him. Her entire body went rigid.

"Were you going to make a complaint against Officer Cole for arresting you?"

He laughed. "I am going to make a complaint against Cole. That nigger hit me. Then a little while ago, he pushed me around for nothing. I'm not going to take that."

"Don't call him that!" she said through clenched teeth. "He's a better human being than you'll ever be."

"What's the matter, Louise? You a nigger-lover or something? I thought you had more class than that."

She began to tremble and tears welled in her eyes. "If you say anything about Cole to that sergeant or anybody else I'm going to press charges against you for what you did to me last night and what you tried to do today."

His grin dissolved to a weak smile. He reached out a hand to touch her shoulder. She jerked away. "Hey, take it easy. There's no reason to get all bent out of shape. The only problem with what you're saying here is why you haven't told them before? Maybe it wasn't so bad after all, huh, Louise? At least the part between you and me."

She glared at him with red-rimmed eyes. "You petty low-life bastard!" With an effort, she kept her voice below a scream. "How dare you say something like that to me!"

Out of the corner of his eye, Zykus was aware of Silvestri by the door. This, along with the way she was acting, made him very uncomfortable. "Take it easy, baby. No need to get the cops all excited again."

"Let me tell you something, Mister Martin Zykus! I'm going to give you five seconds to get out of this building or I'll start screaming rape loud enough to bring every cop within five miles down on you."

He managed a weak laugh. "Hey, c'mon now. Let's stop playing games. You could have done that a long time ago. They probably won't even believe you now."

With her fists clenched tightly at her sides, she began counting, "One . . . two . . ."

"Louise, I just wanted to—"

"Three . . . four . . ."

"Okay," he looked around nervously. "I'm going. I'm going."

Martin Zykus walked quickly across the lobby of the Nineteenth District station. Silvestri opened the door for him, puffed a cloud of smoke in his face and said, "Happy Thanksgiving, asshole."

CHAPTER 73

NOVEMBER 25, 1976
6:50 P.M.

They pulled up in front of Louise's apartment building on West Barry. Cole got out of the unmarked yellow Dodge police car. Blackie was driving. Cole escorted Louise Stallings into the building. They didn't talk.

In her apartment door they found the manager's passkeys sticking out of the bottom lock. She recognized them and told him what they were.

"How do you suppose Zykus got hold of them?" the policeman said, stepping forward and removing the keys from the lock.

"I don't know." She refused to move.

Cole took her keys and opened the door. He checked the apartment. Finding it empty and secure, he returned to where she was still standing out in the hall.

"I'll give these back to the manager," he said, dangling

the passkeys in his hand. "That top lock should keep anyone out."

She nodded.

He was turning to leave when she said, "Officer Cole,
thank you for everything."

He hesitated a moment, then without turning around,
called over his shoulder, "Yeah."

Blackie was lighting a fresh cigar when Cole got back in
the car.

"Would you believe that drunk manager gave Zykus the
building passkeys?" Cole rolled the window down to ven-
tilate the smoke despite the evening chill.

"How do you know he gave them to Zykus?"

"The description fits. He told the manager he was a
retired cop's son."

"No crime in that," Blackie said as they rolled toward
the lake. "You're going to have to let this thing go, Larry. It
won't be the last one you lose because a complainant won't
sign."

"There's more to it than that," Cole defended. "I got a
feeling about this guy. He's dirty in more ways than one."

"Are you psychic?" Blackie shot Cole a less-than-
approving look.

"You know what I mean. I got a hunch about him."

"Let me give you a little friendly advice, kid. I been on
the job better than seventeen years, and every year the
number of hunches I get doubles. I got a hunch my paper
boy's running smack, I got a hunch the butcher's a child
molester, and every time I see a guy in a parked car I get a
hunch he's casing a joint for a burglary. Being a cop makes
you think that way."

"So you think I'm nuts," Cole said defensively.

"No, but you've got to combine your hunches with some
evidence. A hunch by itself don't mean shit. Will only get
your ass in trouble, which you barely avoided tonight. Get
something on the guy. Except for our girl back there, who

ain't talking, you don't have beans on Zykus except he's an ugly, fat fuck who is obnoxious but hasn't broken any law that we know of. At least, not yet."

"You're right," Cole said thoughtfully. "But I bet if we checked him out—"

At that moment the radio crackled to life. "Cars in the Nineteenth District and units on citywide, we have a man with a gun firing shots on the street at 1536 West Wrightwood. Unit to respond."

"They're playing our song," Blackie said, flipping on the siren and emergency lights.

As Cole acknowledged the call, he shoved Martin Zykus to the back of his mind. However, he hadn't forgotten him. He hadn't forgotten him at all.

CHAPTER 74

NOVEMBER 25, 1976
7:15 P.M.

After leaving the Nineteenth District station, Zykus hit a few bars before ending up at the Sheridan Inn. He was surprised to find the place crowded. There were only a couple of seats at the bar and the adjoining restaurant was doing a brisk business.

Zykus ordered a beer. There were two bartenders working, and he asked the one who waited on him why it was so crowded.

The bartender turned out to be the owner. He was heavyset with a bushy head of salt-and-pepper hair. He took one look at Martin Zykus's appearance and took an instant dislike to him. "It's a four-day weekend for a lot of working stiffs. It'll be like this through Saturday or as long as their money holds up." With that, the bartender turned and went off to wait on another customer.

Zykus didn't like the tone the guy had used. The owner had looked at him as if he wasn't good enough to come into this dump.

There was a large mirror behind the bar with the words "Sheridan Inn" written across it in frosted script. Zykus remembered the full-time bartender telling Dave about how much the mirror had cost. It had to be ordered and specially made. Zykus looked down at his Budweiser bottle and then back at the mirror. He could see his reflection just below the *H* in "Sheridan." A decent toss, and he could plant the bottle smack in the middle of the mirror. He could be out the door before the glass settled.

He took a look around the bar before making his move. He noticed there were at least three, maybe four people there that knew him from Bill Michael's restaurant. Even if he did manage to bust the mirror and get away clean, the cops would beat an easy path to his door.

Thinking about cops brought Cole and Silvestri back to mind. Boy, did he want to get even with them. He would have gotten Cole in trouble if Louise hadn't interfered. She would have to learn that things must be done his way.

He finished his beer and ordered another. The owner took his time before thumping the bottle down and snatching up Zykus's dollar. When he returned, he slapped the quarter change down on the bar top with his open palm. He walked away without giving Zykus a second glance.

Smashing the mirror was out, but then Dave had taught him that there were other ways to skin a cat. Using his thumbnail, Zykus began stripping the paper label off his beer bottle as a vent for his frustration while he thought.

The Sheridan Inn's garbage went into a metal Dumpster in the alley. Setting a fire in that wouldn't do much good. But a half-gallon of gasoline spread around the service entrance could do a lot of damage before the smoke eaters in this town got there to douse the flames.

He was considering a plan to return in the wee small hours of the morning to accomplish the deed when a sweet perfume enveloped him, followed by a hand caressing his shoulder.

Zykus turned around and looked into the blubbery face of a man with a grotesquely wide mouth.

"And what is a handsome lad like you doing drinking by yourself on a holiday evening?" He yelled to the bartender, "Innkeeper, give this young man another drink on me." As he spoke, he bumped Zykus with a hip and began massaging his shoulder with a slow rhythm.

The owner looked in their direction and then resumed the discussion he was having with another patron at the other end of the bar.

Zykus squirmed on his stool to ease the pressure of the hip pressed against his leg.

"My name's Randy—and you're Morty, right?"

"My name is Marty," Zykus said, standing up, which made Randy step back and drop the hand from his shoulder.

Randy wasn't tall, but he outweighed Zykus. The bus-boy figured he topped the scales at a good two-eighty. He was over fifty with thinning hair. He dressed in a pink shirt, white pants, and out-of-season white shoes. Zykus also noticed that he wore a lot of jewelry. The stuff looked real, but Zykus didn't know anything about diamonds.

"Well, hello, Marty." Randy extended a pudgy, moist palm before turning and yelling to the owner, "Could we please get some service?"

"Keep your shirt on," the owner yelled back, without making any move in their direction.

"It's not my shirt I'm worried about," Randy said. "It's

my pants I'm trying to get out of." He paused a moment to
gauge Zykus's reaction. When there was none, he mumbled, "But the night is still young."

Finally, the owner stood in front of them. He didn't ask
for their order.

"Give my friend another beer and I'll have another
Scotch on the rocks," Randy said.

The owner let them have a sarcastic smirk before turning
to get their drinks. Zykus was really pissed at him now;
however, another idea was taking shape in his mind. An
idea directly connected to Randy.

"You're a very handsome man, Marty," Randy lied after
they had been served. "And you look strong." He pinched
Zykus's biceps. "Why are you out alone on Thanksgiving?
No family or friends? Perhaps, no girlfriends?"

Zykus didn't answer him about a girlfriend, although
Louise Stallings flashed through his mind.

"Could I ask you a personal question?" Randy said.

Zykus merely stared at him.

Randy dropped his voice to a whisper. "Are you gay?"

Zykus didn't answer him.

Randy's lips came so close to Zykus's ear the busboy
could feel the pressure of his words when he spoke. "We
could go someplace and become friends."

Zykus pushed him away. "Just leave me alone, man!"
The busboy headed for the door. At the entrance he looked
back to see the owner, backed up by the regular bartender,
approaching Randy.

"I told you not to come on to no more of my customers!"

Zykus walked out.

Zykus stood in the doorway of a barber shop a quarter
block down and across the street from the Sheridan Inn. He
didn't think it would be long before Randy came out. He
had been waiting less than five minutes when he caught a
glimpse of the pink-and-white ensemble. Randy was

pulling a beige cashmere overcoat on. There was a matching cashmere cap on his head.

He muttered something Zykus was too far away to hear and began walking south. The busboy flattened himself against the locked glass door of the barber shop, using every ounce of shadow available.

Across the street, Randy passed without seeing him.

Zykus waited a moment before sticking his head out of the doorway and checking the front of the Sheridan Inn. No one else came out. Then he followed Randy.

CHAPTER 75

NOVEMBER 29, 1976
3:10 P.M.

It was a cold sunny Monday with unlimited visibility under blue skies and temperatures in the mid-twenties. It was the first of two days off for Nineteenth District tactical officer Larry Cole.

In the morning he had done some library research for his history class, and in the early afternoon had the Mustang serviced at a Firestone Auto Center in the district. Then, after a stop at the Far East Garden Chinese Restaurant on Clark—where cops got half price—he headed for the station.

He carried a shopping bag into the Review Office on the second floor. Officer Pete Burke waited expectantly for him.

"Whatever it is," Burke said, swinging his three-hundred-pound bulk around in a loudly protesting swivel chair, "it smells delicious."

Cole put the shopping bag down and began removing white cardboard cartons filled with steaming food. "We've got spareribs, shrimp fried rice, pepper steak, and chicken wings."

Burke's eyebrows went up. "No egg rolls?"

Cole removed the final carton from the bag. "And egg rolls."

Burke rolled his chair to a small refrigerator in the corner of the office and removed two sixteen-ounce bottles of Pepsi. He opened them and handed one to Cole. Then they dug in.

The Review Office was a narrow room, made narrower by a row of filing cabinets against one wall and two desks with multilayered trays on the opposite wall. The lone window afforded a view of Addison Street and beneath the window an ancient radiator hissed steam, keeping the room just a shade warmer than what could be considered comfortable.

The function of Review was to collect, distribute, and store all case reports submitted by Nineteenth District officers. There were two police officers assigned to do this job: Pete Burke on afternoons, and John Shaughnessy on days. As Burke was considered the easier of the pair to get along with, Cole had approached him with a proposition.

Burke bit into a chicken wing and sighed, "Now how do you suppose they get this particular flavor? It's different. It's got a tangy sweetness that drives me wild."

"Probably the batter," Cole said, cleaning the meat from a sparerib.

Burke was sixty-one and seriously considering retirement. He was rumored to be a relative of the Leprechaun, and had been in Review for the six years O'Casey had been the commander. He was five-foot-nine, and his excessive weight caused elevated blood pressure. Except for this, he was otherwise healthy. Nevertheless, his wife had him on a diet, which made him rather susceptible to food bribes from curious young tactical officers.

Burke finished the chicken wing and began ladling pepper steak and rice onto a paper plate. "You're a gentleman and a scholar, Larry. A gentleman and a scholar."

Cole watched Burke savor the food for a moment and then said, "Did you have a chance to take a look at the reports for me?"

Burke shoved a forkful of steak and rice into his mouth, chewed, then reached into one of the trays on his desk. From it he removed a clipped stack of papers. He handed them to Cole.

Burke swallowed and explained, "That's everything involving a man fitting the general description you gave me for the last two months. I even typed an analysis for you, which has been made well worthwhile by this sumptuous feast."

"Thanks a lot, Pete." Cole began scanning the reports.

On Friday, before his tour of duty with Blackie began, Cole had approached Burke with his proposition. Check the case reports in the past two months for unknown offenders fitting the description of Martin Zykus. In return, Cole offered to buy carryout lunch from the Far East Garden as compensation. The review officer had instantly agreed.

There wasn't much in the reports, and most of what there was Cole already knew. Primarily, there were the assaults on the elderly women that Cole had personally investigated in the past two weeks. In each case, the offenders were listed as two white males, one heavyset, the other small and thin. The age ranges on the heavyset man and the hair length could fit Martin Zykus. But then, the three victims Cole had handled had not been in any condition to positively identify any offender on the nights of the crimes, so it was doubtful they'd be able to identify one now. So much for that.

There were a few reports with heavyset offenders described. There was a burglary a three-hundred-twenty-five-pound male had committed by entering and exiting the back door of a first-floor apartment. Cole smiled when he read that the burglar was caught after he jumped a chain-link fence and ran a block with the cops in pursuit. The next report concerned a two-hundred-fifty-pound man who had pulled into a gas station on Diversey, filled up his car, and taken off without paying. The last one was a two-hundred-sixty-five-pound guy who had knifed his girl-friend. He was identified by name in the report and still wanted.

Burke swallowed and said, "Those rapes you talked about were all on the north end of the district. I pulled all the unknown-offender crimes in the general area. There's only a couple of any note: a guy got tossed off the Sheridan el platform last Wednesday night, and a man got mugged on Thanksgiving night two blocks north of Wrigley Field."

Burke took a healthy bite out of an egg roll, chewed, and then chased it with Pepsi. "I read your rape reports and noticed that one of your victims got stabbed to death and another got her skull creased with a beer bottle. We haven't had a lot of violent crimes in the district since summer. Now, all of a sudden, they're coming out of our ears. Throw in Cummings getting killed, Blackie killing the guy who did it, and the Rena Hartley murder, it's driving the Leprechaun crazy."

He took another bite of his egg roll. It took him awhile before he could talk again.

"So I look at your Sheridan el homicide. Guy's face was kicked in."

"I know," Cole said. "I was the first car on the scene. The dispatcher gave the paper to a midnight car. Somebody really did a job on the victim."

Burke finished off the egg roll and wiped his hands with a paper napkin. "I spend a lot of time with all this paperwork." He waved his hand at the file cabinets. "After looking at report after report after report, you begin to notice stuff."

"Stuff like what?"

Gingerly, Burke reached forward and pulled a typewritten report out of another tray. He used his thumb and little finger to keep sweet-and-sour sauce off the paper.

After Cole took the report, Burke reached for another egg roll.

"That's the detectives' report on your boy in the alley. Not much there, is it?"

"Not really."

"Look at his height and weight."

Cole did. Five feet, four inches tall; one hundred forty pounds.

"He's the same basic size as one of the offenders in the rapes, but . . ." Cole said.

Burke stripped the meat off a chicken bone with the efficiency of a school of piranhas in a feeding frenzy. Swallowing noisily, he said, "Look at the report of the mugging."

As Cole looked through it, Burke explained, "There was a witness. An old lady in the window of a second-floor apartment on Grace Street. Been taught to observe offenders. Gave a pretty thorough description for a woman of seventy-six sitting a quarter of a block from the incident."

But Cole wasn't listening to Burke anymore. He was absorbed in the description: male, white, twenty to twenty-five years, five-foot-ten to six feet tall, 225 to 250 pounds, wearing a dark windbreaker, blue jeans, and dirty white gym shoes. When Cole had released Zykus on Thanksgiving night, he had been dressed the same as the described offender.

Burke noticed the tactical cop's excitement. "I'd take it easy on this if I was you, Larry."

"Why?"

"Because it will never stand up in court. One of those overeducated glory boys from the state's attorney's office will shoot the description down in thirty seconds."

"I don't understand," Cole said with a frown.

"She's seventy-six years old, lad. Maybe you and me will be lucky to make it in this life that long with our faculties in the shape hers are in, but she won't be looked at as any prize on a witness stand. Call it age prejudice if you want, but any half-assed public defender will shoot her down no matter how accurate the description."

Cole's shoulders sagged. "What about the victim?"

Burke finished his chicken wing and dropped the bones in the shopping bag. "There you might have something, although you won't find it in the report. The guy's got a bit of a reputation in the bars around Wrigley Field. He's basically harmless, but I checked our victim file and found he's been beaten up four times in the last two years. Each time was right in the neighborhood.

"Okay, this Mr. Randolph Klein, our victim, cruises the bars in the neighborhood looking for a pickup. This guy's a copy editor at the *Times-Herald* and lives in a building on Waveland Avenue. I figure the way he looks," Burke patted his own girth for emphasis, "he won't find many willing takers for his advances unless there's some monetary incentive involved. Our boy's never been busted, so it's likely he's not going up to little boys in gin mills saying, 'I'll give you twenty if you let me blow you.' "

Cole laughed.

"So I figure he flashes a roll to get the party interested. The problem is," Burke examined what was left of the food, "flashing the roll makes him an easy target for a strong-arm man.

"So what have we got? Number one: a guy dead under the el tracks, fitting the general description of one of your rape offenders. No witnesses, no suspects. Number two: We have this guy Randolph Klein who was mugged and a good description of an offender—which we can't use—fitting the ID of your second offender. A little bit of imagination thrown in and you could have one of your boys icing the other over some dispute among thieves, if you get my drift."

Cole nodded. "We also have the guy who mugged Klein smashing a bottle over his head from behind, which was also what happened to the first rape victim."

"Give that man a silver dollar!" Burke said, finally settling on the last egg roll. "So now your boy is working solo. I suggest you see where our *Times-Herald* copy editor was and who he was with before he got the bottle smashed over his head and his billfold and jewelry taken. Then you might have something you can take to the state's attorney."

"Good," Cole said, snatching up a chicken wing. "Very good."

CHAPTER 76

NOVEMBER 29, 1976
4:15 P.M.

Cole found the address for Randolph Klein on Waveland. The building was a well-tended two-flat in the shadow of the Wrigley Field scoreboard. He parked his Mustang and climbed the stone steps to the front door.

There were two mailboxes over the bells. Both bore the name "Klein." He selected one at random, pushed it, and waited.

A thin woman with frightened eyes appeared behind the glass door of the vestibule. Cole held up his badge and ID card for her inspection. She studied them for a long time before opening the door.

"I'd like to talk to Mr. Randolph Klein," he said.

"Some detectives were already here," she said, with an edge in her voice. "They didn't seem very interested in what happened to him."

Cole smiled. "I'm interested."

Ten minutes later he left with the address of the Sheridan Inn.

CHAPTER 77

NOVEMBER 29, 1976
4:45 P.M.

Martin Zykus's car belched exhaust fumes into the air. He was parked across the street from the Division Street bar where he and the fence had agreed to meet. He had been waiting for thirty minutes.

A black man carrying an attaché case came out of the bar. He wore a full-length black leather coat over a pinstriped black suit, white shirt, and silver silk tie. To Zykus he would have looked like any other businessman, except for the wide-brimmed black hat trimmed with a bright red eagle feather he wore. The hat made him look like a pimp.

He knocked on Zykus's window. "You the dude looking to sell some merchandise?"

Zykus stared warily at him. "Yeah."

"Open the other door."

As the black man trotted around the car, Zykus considered driving away. But he didn't want to hang onto the stolen jewelry any longer. He unlocked the door.

The fence introduced himself as Slick Rick Johnson. In the future, he would adopt the alias Abdul Ali Malik. Zykus told him his first name. After making a few appropriately insulting comments about the Chevy, Slick Rick got down to business.

Zykus showed him the rings, the watch, and the money clip he had taken on Thanksgiving night. The fence opened the attaché case, which made Zykus tense. Johnson removed a small flashlight, which he used to examine the jewelry. He studied the mounted stones without making a sound. Then he took the watch.

"This is a Pulsar," Johnson said. "Nice, but digitals are getting to be a dime a dozen. The rings are okay, but nothing to write home about. The money clip is junk. I'll give you a C-note for the whole lot."

Zykus's eyes widened. "A guy I know told me the ring with the little blue stones is worth four, maybe five hundred dollars."

Slick Rick snarled, "That's across the counter at Tiffany's, white boy! You want to go in for an appraisal? Maybe see if they'll buy the shit off you at face value? Yeah, you can show them some identification with the initials R. K."

"R. K.?" Zykus said, confused.

"Yeah, the initials on the back of the watch. 'F. D. to R. K.—Merry Christmas, '75.' You do know who F. D. is, don't you?"

Zykus knew he was licked. It wasn't so bad—at least his victim had had two hundred and twenty dollars on him. "Okay, give me the hundred."

Slick Rick Johnson smiled and pulled a roll from inside the attaché case. This time, in the brief instant Johnson had the case open, Zykus spied two handguns inside. His mouth went dry.

Johnson peeled two fifties off the roll and handed them to Zykus. He dropped the jewelry into the case, which gave the busboy another glimpse of the guns.

Curiosity overrode the busboy's fear. "Those for sale?"

The fence snapped the case shut. "You looking to buy a good piece, a cheap piece, or a clean piece?"

"What's the difference?"

The fence snickered. " 'Good' means it'll work when you fire it. 'Cheap' means it might work or it might blow up in your hand. 'Clean' means nobody can ever trace it back to you."

"How do I get a good one?"

"You got a record?"

"No."

"Then it's easy. You're free, white, and twenty-one. Get yourself an Illinois Firearms Ownership identification card and go to a gun shop. They'll sell you a nice gun and it'll do the job."

"How much for a clean piece?"

"You ain't been around long have you, Marty? Cost you twice as much as retail will in a store. Can even get you one on order, if you'd like."

Slick Rick started to get out of the car.

"Would you know where I could get hold of some lock picks?"

The fence got back inside and slammed the door. "You looking to get into burglary, Marty? You don't seem the type."

"I just need to unlock one door. It has one of those dead-bolt locks on it."

"Just one door?" Slick Johnson opened his case and removed a small leather pouch. "I got just the thing for you, pal."

CHAPTER 78

NOVEMBER 29, 1976
5:20 P.M.

Every day of the long weekend, Louise Stallings's nightmare receded a bit more. Thanksgiving night and the following Friday had been the worst days. She had stayed in the apartment, jumping at every sound—once, screaming when the telephone rang. It had been a wrong number.

She had slept little, but early Saturday morning, as she huddled in front of a late broadcast of *Casablanca,* she dozed off. When she awoke it was midmorning, and the coyote was chasing the roadrunner on the screen.

Following the rest, her confidence increased enough for her to leave the apartment and have breakfast at a restaurant on Broadway. She watched everything around her with apprehension, but no Martin Zykus appeared.

Leaving the restaurant, she considered going back to

the apartment, but she had been cooped up there for too long. It was a cold day, with snow flurries blowing out of an overcast sky. She wandered down Broadway, considering her options, before deciding on the place she had actually known she was going: St. Thaddeus Catholic Church.

She didn't know what she was going to do when she got there or even if it would be open. She realized with a depressingly heavy heart that she had no place else to go.

The church was locked, but the school hall was open. There she found Sister Frances Lucille supervising a group of teenagers, who were getting the room ready for a dance. Without too much coaxing, Louise joined in and helped.

The dance started at six, and by that time she had become so indispensable to the nun that she worked right through, serving hot dogs and soft drinks to the kids. At midnight, Father Conley drove her home. She couldn't bring herself to ask him to walk her to the apartment door, and she experienced some anxious moments before she got inside. She slept soundly in her own bed for the first time since—it—had happened.

On Sunday she went to the eleven-o'clock mass and then had lunch with Sister Frances Lucille and Father Conley in the rectory. She spent the day with them. That night, Father Conley again drove her home. This time she was not half as leery of the dark as she had been the night before.

She was preparing for the next day's classes that night when the idea came to her. Instantly, she rejected it. After showering and washing her hair, she poured herself a glass of milk, checked the locks on her front door, and went to bed.

Louise Stallings had a dream that night. A dream about God, church, and her responsibilities in this world. Her alarm clock going off at seven A.M. snatched her from the dream. She came awake slowly, and moved through the first thirty minutes of her day in a fog.

She was on the train en route to Loyola when the impact

of the dream collided with her thoughts, desires, and emotions. Lightning didn't flash, nor did a celestial choir sing, but at that instant Louise Stallings of Kellam, Iowa, decided to become a nun.

That night, she caught the train south, and at Addison rejected walking east to Broadway in favor of catching the Addison Street bus. It was a cold evening, turning colder. She remembered how warm it had been the night before Thanksgiving. Chicago weather changed faster than anyplace she'd ever been, and she still had problems getting used to it.

At Broadway she exited the bus and considered joining a queue waiting for the southbound Broadway bus. Finally, she scolded herself for being overly cautious. West Barry was only a few blocks south, so wrapping her scarf tightly around her neck, she started walking.

She had traveled a block and a half when she saw the familiar black Mustang parked at the curb in front of an Italian restaurant. The St. Jude medal hanging from the rearview mirror made her certain this was Larry Cole's car.

Louise wondered if he was still angry with her. She regretted what had happened, but only his job had been involved. It was her life and reputation. She started to walk past when she heard his voice.

"Louise."

He stood in the door of the restaurant. She turned and walked over to him.

"How are you, Officer Cole?" She extended her hand.

"Make it Larry, okay? I wanted to apologize to you about the other night."

"There's really nothing for either of us to apologize for. It's just something . . . that happened." She looked away.

"Look, I'm having dinner inside alone. Why don't you join me?"

Louise hesitated. She wanted to get home and call Sister Frances Lucille.

"At least have a drink. It will prove that you forgive me."

"Just one drink then."

She followed him inside.

Cole was just finishing a plate of linguini with clam sauce when Louise sat down. She wasn't hungry, so when the waitress came she ordered a glass of wine.

After a few moments of idle chitchat, Louise looked at him and said, "Could I ask you something?"

"Go ahead," he said, shoving the last forkful of linguini into his mouth.

"Why are you so obsessed with Martin Zykus?"

"That's an easy one to answer. Because he's a bad guy, Louise. A low-life, no-good, wrong-doing criminal. And, in case you haven't noticed lately, I'm a cop. Putting him away is my job."

"But it just seems . . ."

"It just seems what?"

"It just seems that even if you do arrest him, it really won't do any good. You hear everyday about the courts letting guilty people go and people in prison being released early. I don't know, it just doesn't seem worth it all."

"Let me tell you a little something. I know Marty did something to you, which is probably a felony. Then you count a street mugging on Thanksgiving night, that's another felony. Four elderly women were attacked in this area in the last couple of weeks. One of them was killed. That makes six felonies. Then a little guy got thrown off an el platform on Thanksgiving Eve and had his face kicked in for good measure. I really can't pin this last one on our boy, but let's just say I've got a feeling that he's involved. So to be fair, we'll make it an even six felonies with perpetrators fitting Martin Zykus's description. That gives me enough reason to keep after him until I nail him with a nice long prison sentence."

"You think he killed two people?" Her voice was hoarse with fear.

"Oh, it's not something I can prove, but there were two offenders in three of the four attacks I mentioned. A heavy-set younger man and a smaller, older, thin man. It's nothing more than a guess, but I think Zykus killed and stomped his partner on Thanksgiving Eve after I caught him coming off your street and was forced to let him go the first time."

Cole noticed that Louise had gone pale.

"Are you ready to go?" he asked.

She nodded.

"So, I'll keep looking. I've got another day off tomorrow and I have school in the morning. On Wednesday night, I'll be back with Blackie. Between the two of us, we'll nail Martin Zykus. He's not going to stay lucky forever."

She made no further comment until they pulled up in front of her apartment building.

"Good night, Larry," she said, getting out of the car.

"Be careful, Louise."

CHAPTER 79

NOVEMBER 29, 1976
7:10 P.M.

Louise was frightened into a state very close to emotional shock. There were a few people going into the building at the same time and three of them rode up in the elevator as far as the fourth floor. She exited into her corridor alone.

She rushed to unlock her bottom and top locks. The

inside of her apartment appeared secure and warm. She left her purse and attaché case by the door and proceeded to turn on every light in the apartment. As she passed back through the living room, she fastened the front door chain. Still, she didn't feel safe.

She crossed to the front window and looked down at the street below. She could see very little at this height except the tops of a few trees, the upper floors of the buildings across the street, and the roofs of a few parked cars below. There was a great deal of darkness and shadow out there. Perhaps too much.

The phone ringing made her jump. She hesitated a moment before composing herself and crossing to answer it.

"Louise, this is Sister Frances Lucille from St. Thaddeus."

"Sister, how are you?" She had tried to call the nun earlier. She also remembered why she wanted to talk to her.

"I just called to see how you were doing."

Louise Stallings forgot her fear as she sat down at her desk and began talking to the nun.

However, outside her apartment, despite appearances to the contrary, all was not the way she had left it that morning. She was not capable of recognizing the problem. Perhaps even Larry Cole would have had difficulty seeing it. But Blackie Silvestri would have noticed instantly that the facings on the locks securing her apartment door bore minute scratches. Minute scratches made by clumsily applied lock picks, used unsuccessfully.

CHAPTER 80

Martin Zykus lived in the garden-level apartment of a converted coach house, south of Belmont just west of Racine. The wood-frame building had suffered twenty years of neglect. The roof leaked, the stairs leading to the apartment above Zykus's were in danger of imminent collapse, and roaches used the kitchen floor as a parade ground. But to Zykus, it was home.

There was little furniture in the two rooms he occupied, and the place was never cleaned. Dirty clothing, empty beer cans, and food containers littered every square foot of the living room area. In the midst of this debris, Zykus had set up a folding card table and chair. There he had sat, working through most of the night on locks he had purchased from a junkyard. As the sun came up and his red-rimmed eyes fumed with strain and fatigue, he felt he was becoming more proficient at handling the lock picks, but he realized it was still taking him too long to work the tumblers.

He had Dave's pocket watch open on the table. He would wait until the second hand hit twelve, then he'd begin. The picks were delicate instruments, the lock openings narrow, and Zykus was clumsy. However, through the night he had made progress to the point where it now took him less than three minutes to unlock the Yale bolt mechanism he had been practicing on. He realized that this was still too slow.

Last night, just after dark, he had gone to Louise's apartment building after parking his car on Broadway. The lights in her apartment were off and he couldn't detect any movement behind the windows. The leather pouch housing the lock picks felt hot beneath his touch, as he massaged them in his pocket. He examined the street carefully for cops and, certain that none were present, made his move.

He went in with a group of six tenants returning from work at the end of the day. There were four women and two men, with only a couple in the group appearing to know each other. They crowded into the narrow outer lobby, checking mailboxes and ignoring each other and him. A woman opened the security door and Zykus flowed in with the rest.

Zykus became alarmed when he saw the drunken building manager he had conned the passkeys off of on Thanksgiving. He was halfheartedly sweeping the first-floor hallway with a broom that looked to have been made around the turn of the century.

"Hey, Joe, why don't you do that on three sometimes?" one of the male tenants yelled at him.

"Don't tell me how to do my job, buddy."

With his back to Joe and the other tenants, Zykus walked quickly into the stairwell. After climbing a flight he stopped and listened. No one followed him.

He stayed in the stairwell outside the fifth-floor corridor for a long time. He watched as four tenants, all female, got off the elevator and went to their apartments. An elderly woman entered the apartment next door to Louise. He noticed that when she opened the door she spoke to someone or something. It could have been a dog or a cat, but he couldn't be sure.

When the corridor had been clear for a full fifteen minutes, he cautiously exited the stairwell and approached the door to 508. The only practice he had had with the lock picks was on his glove-compartment door. He was able to open it as fast as Slick Rick Johnson. Zykus was confident, but the Yale bolt lock on Louise's door was much sturdier than an old car lock.

He manipulated the picks around in the upper and lower locks until sweat dripped from his forehead down into his eyes. Not once did he feel a tumbler move or get any other indication that he was making progress. Finally, the noise of a door opening at the far end of the corridor forced him to abandon his task. He returned to the first floor and left the building through the rear service entrance.

"Goddamn!" Zykus raged, as he pounded the wheel of his car with his open palm. He just wasn't good enough. Yet.

So he had purchased the locks from a junkyard, and practiced with them throughout the night. The first time it had taken him nearly thirty minutes to open the dead bolt. Slowly, he progressed down to ten minutes, then to five, and now to less than three.

Wearily he dropped the picks and lock mechanism back on the table surface. Would he have three minutes to stand around out in that hall playing with Louise's locks? He ran his hands over his face and through his hair. His fingers were sore from manipulating the locks. He'd chance it. She was worth the trouble and on top of that, he owed her. He owed her a lot.

He was supposed to be at work at nine, but he was too tired. Plus, he'd have to save his energy for later. Louise Stallings would be receiving a visitor tonight.

He crossed the apartment and flopped down on the double box-spring mattress he used as a bed. The sheets were soiled gray and held a fetid odor, which Zykus had gotten used to. He was dozing almost as soon as his head touched the pillow.

CHAPTER 81

NOVEMBER 30, 1976
7:52 P.M.

It's not the easiest life, Louise," Sister Frances Lucille said. "At times you'll feel lonely and isolated. Like no one really understands you."

"I don't think I'll ever be alone again, Sister," Louise said with a smile. "It might sound lame, but I'm certain God will be with me."

They were sitting in Father Conley's study. The priest had remained silent up to this point, preferring to let Sister Frances Lucille do most of the talking.

"God is with all of us every moment of each day of our lives," Sister Frances Lucille said. "But before you make this decision, it is so very important for you to be certain. You seem to have come to this rather quickly. Are you sure it isn't the result of something that recently happened to you?"

"No," Louise said abruptly, before bringing herself under control. "This has been coming for a long time. I just needed the clarity of my life here in Chicago to bring it all together. I'm old enough to know what I want, Sister."

"I'm not saying that you're not, but this is a big step."

Finally, Father Conley spoke. "I think Louise has made up her mind, Sister. Now things are between her and God."

Sister Frances Lucille got up, went over to Louise's chair and embraced her.

Louise felt her excitement building as she rode in a taxi back to her apartment. It was as if she were in the process of being reborn. The future ahead was now clear.

She paid the driver and started for the entrance to her apartment building when the old fears returned. Before she had reached the door, the cab had pulled away. She thought she heard a noise on the street behind her and spun around. There was nothing there.

She entered the lobby and nervously fumbled with her keys while keeping an eye on the outside door. Her fears eased a bit once she was on the elevator. Riding up, she realized that the entire building had become a sinister place for her. The lease on her apartment wasn't up until April, but she would be enrolling in the novitiate program in January. Perhaps by then she could find a way to break the lease, so that it wouldn't be a lingering responsibility as she began her new life.

The fifth-floor corridor was deserted. She couldn't remember the last time that she had seen one of her neighbors either coming in or going out. The only people she had seen here recently were Larry Cole and, of course, Martin Zykus.

When she finally got inside her apartment, she found her heart pounding furiously. She stood with her back against the door until her breathing returned to normal.

She realized that she would have to pull herself together and put her fears behind her.

Resolutely, she walked to the kitchen and opened the refrigerator. She would have to do something about dinner. Broiling a steak or frying chops was out at this time of the night. On top of that, she was tired, and had a full day tomorrow with another meeting with Sister Frances Lucille, Father Conley, and a representative from the mother house in the evening.

In the refrigerator she found ham, cheese, lettuce, and mayonnaise. She checked her bread box and found half a loaf of pumpernickel. She had a can of tomato soup in the cupboard and plenty of milk. She decided to make what she and her brothers used to refer to as a "lunch supper" back in Iowa.

She wondered how her family would take her decision to go into the convent. Of course, they wouldn't know about it until it was already an accomplished fact. It was her life now, to lead as she saw fit.

She stripped off her suit and blouse and decided to take a shower before fixing her supper. She walked into the bathroom, clad only in her brassiere and pantyhose. She checked to make sure her robe was hanging behind the bathroom door. She turned on the water and sat on the edge of the tub to test the temperature with her hand. She remembered a question that Sister Frances Lucille had asked her earlier.

"What name will you take in the convent?"

She thought about it for a moment. "I want to keep my own name. My father gave it to me." She looked around Father Conley's study and spied a statue of the Blessed Virgin. "What about Sister Mary Louise?"

"Beautiful," they said as one.

"Sister Mary Louise Stallings," Louise said aloud into the emptiness of her bathroom. She smiled. "I like it."

The water was hot enough and she pulled the shower knob. As steam began billowing around her, she stripped off her underclothing and stepped into the tub.

She let the water run over her head and face. She could feel the knots of tension easing in her shoulders and back.

God, she thought to herself, *I'll have to learn to put the past behind me.*

She felt a brief chill, which she thought was caused by her negative thoughts. Picking up a bar of soap, she began lathering a washcloth.

The shadow appeared on the other side of the curtain long before Louise saw it. When she did, all she could do was stare at it with a fear that immobilized her entire body.

Then, Martin Zykus yanked the curtain back and snatched her from the shower.

CHAPTER 82

DECEMBER 1, 1976
7:40 A.M.

The *Chicago Times-Herald*'s early morning edition for December 1, 1976 carried Frank Delahanty's column on the mugging of Randolph Klein. The column bore the title STREETS UNSAFE, BUT COPS GO HO-HO-HO!

Comdr. Joseph Thomas O'Casey was sitting down to breakfast when he glanced at page one and flipped to page two to check the weather. Delahanty's column was on page three. Mary Beth was fixing the Leprechaun's favorite breakfast—corned beef hash with eggs over-easy. Generally, the Leprechaun didn't read the abrasive columnist, but something about the title of the story drew his attention. Especially since he had been the Santa Claus in the Christmas parade held that past Friday.

Mary Beth was stirring the corned beef hash in a skillet

when she heard her husband swear, "Son of a fucking bitch!"

Shocked at hearing him use such language, she spun around. He was staring at the paper with a look that truly frightened her. "What is it, Joe?"

He slammed the paper down on the kitchen table, causing his coffee to splash onto the tablecloth. "It's that—" He fought to keep the profanity out of his speech. "It's that Frank Delahanty. He's trying to crucify me."

"Calm down," she said, turning off the flame under the food and taking the seat across from her husband. She picked up the paper and began reading.

Delahanty began by stating that Comdr. Joseph Thomas O'Casey of the Nineteenth District was the yearly Santa Claus in the Christmas parade down Michigan Avenue. He wrote at some length that O'Casey performed this chore without pay and would also attend the children's party in the basement of St. Patrick's orphanage on Halsted after each parade. Then Delahanty mentioned the adult party. This was the first thing that bothered Mary Beth about the column.

She looked across at her husband. "You and the men are entitled to a little fun after all you do for charity."

"Read on," he said, glumly.

The party was a little bash the Holy Name Fathers threw for Santa Claus and his helpers after the parade and the orphans' party. The adult version, which was a stag affair, had been known to go on into the wee small hours of the morning. This last time Joe hadn't gotten home until three, and he'd been plastered. But Mary Beth hadn't been concerned about this, as he only did it once a year. Then she read the part about the "helpers."

Delahanty made it sound a great deal worse than it really was. Seven men, who worked for Joe, played the roles of Santa's helpers and rode on the North Pole float. Their primary job was to throw handfuls of wrapped Christmas candies to children along the parade route. However, there were an additional 150 police officers assigned to traffic control in connection with the parade. Delahanty referred to them as "more of Santa's little helpers."

The column went on. "So, while the Chicago Police Department plays Santa Claus for the Michigan Avenue Businessmen's Association on the biggest shopping day of the year, you and I, the average taxpayers, who have to work the day after Thanksgiving to pay for Comdr. O'Casey and his 157 helpers, must walk the streets unprotected.

"On Thanksgiving night, after O'Casey had given his tactical team the night off in preparation for their party over in the basement of old St. Pat's, Mr. Randolph Klein, a citizen of our fair city, was walking home after visiting with friends. Only a block from the house he has lived in all of his life, he was attacked by an unknown assailant. Mr. Klein's watch, rings, and billfold were taken after the mugger hit him with a beer bottle, which left cuts requiring forty stitches to close. This happened while Comdr. O'Casey and his 157 helpers in blue were resting up for the parade and their little bash with the good priests at St. Pat's the next day."

Mary Beth's mouth dropped open, as in Delahanty's conclusion he called for O'Casey's demotion and withdrawal from the Christmas parade. The columnist had made Randolph Klein's robbery the Leprechaun's personal responsibility.

"Oh, Joe," was all she could say. The police department and playing Santa Claus once a year were the biggest things in Joe O'Casey's life.

"Yeah, 'Oh,' " the Leprechaun responded.

CHAPTER 83

DECEMBER 1, 1976
3:07 P.M.

It was snowing when Cole parked his Mustang in front of the station. He didn't have to be at work until five, but he wanted to check a couple of additional details with Pete Burke in Review.

He was crossing the station lobby when Sergeant Beazley called him. Cole walked over to the desk. Beazley motioned him to an area over by a window overlooking Addison. This took them out of earshot of most of the station traffic.

"The Leprechaun's been looking for you."

"Me?" Cole said with a frown.

"Yeah, and he's on the warpath."

Cole felt a lump of anxious fear form a knot in his gut. "Have I done something wrong?"

"You see the paper today?"

"Yeah. I read the *Tribune* this morning before I went to class."

"What about the *Times-Herald*?"

"Never read it, Sarge. Nothing in it except maybe that guy Delahanty's column."

Beazley dropped his voice. "Whatever you do, don't let the Leprechaun hear you say that."

"Why?"

"You know a guy named Randolph Klein?"

"Yeah. He got robbed on Thanksgiving night over on Sheffield. I think I know who did it."

"You do?" The sergeant's face twisted in a curious scowl. "Well, you'd better hope you can prove it, because you might be saving O'Casey's career."

"What's going on, Sarge?" Cole asked. "I don't understand any of this."

Beazley walked back behind the desk and removed a copy of a newspaper clipping from the center drawer. He handed it to Cole. When he finished reading it, Cole stared at the sergeant.

"The Leprechaun's already been downtown to see the Chief of Patrol earlier today, and when he came back he looked fit to be embalmed. About thirty minutes ago his office called and told us to call you at home and have you come in early. I'll bet you dollars to doughnuts it has something to do with Delahanty's column."

This was the worst day of Joseph Thomas O'Casey's thirty-five-year police career. He couldn't understand how one vicious reporter with some kind of axe to grind could destroy all that it had taken him a lifetime to build.

That morning, when he had been summoned downtown, the chief had been polite, sympathetic, and extremely guarded.

"Yes, the superintendent has seen it, Joe."

"No. I don't know what he thinks about it, Joe."

"Were you really drunk at the St. Patrick's party, Joe?"

"Did you really use seven of your tactical officers as elves, Joe?"

"Helpers," O'Casey said into the emptiness of his office on the second floor of the Nineteenth District station. "They were helpers."

The one bright spot in the day had come from Mary Beth's second cousin, Pete Burke, who was the

Leprechaun's afternoon Review officer. He had come in at about two o'clock offering condolences, as if someone had died. With little self assurance, O'Casey had told him that he wasn't dead. Yet.

It was as Burke was leaving the commander's office that he turned and said, "I don't know if this will do you any good, boss, but that new tactical cop Larry Cole was looking into the Randolph Klein robbery just the other day. I think he might have come up with something."

"So why didn't you tell me that before?" the Leprechaun exploded, before screaming for his secretary to get Cole on the phone ASAP. No, he wasn't dead yet.

But as the minutes passed, O'Casey's gloom returned. What could a still-wet-behind-the-ears young cop like Cole have that could save him from the likes of Frank Delahanty? Oh, he knew the department wouldn't bow to any pressure from the Fourth Estate to remove him from his command immediately, but it would certainly come. He spun around in his chair to look up at the photograph he had had taken with Himself, the honorable Richard J. Daley, Mayor of Chicago. It would go nicely in his den after he vacated this office, O'Casey thought.

A knock on the office door roused him momentarily from his dark revery.

"Come."

Larry Cole walked in.

CHAPTER 84

The tactical team was gathered around Sergeant Novak's desk when Blackie walked in. He got a couple of suspicious glances, which told him that something was up. He took a seat behind the desk across from Novak and waited.

He was lighting a cigar when Novak finally spoke to him. "You and Cole been doing some freelancing, Blackie?"

Blackie had come on the department with Wally Novak and generally knew him to be a pretty decent guy. The problem Novak had was that he spent too much time trying to be liked by the men. Every once in a while this made him look stupid and weak. Like he didn't know what he was doing. Blackie thought about this a minute and decided that, in most cases, Wally Novak didn't know what he was doing.

"How's that, Sarge?" Blackie said, leaning back in the chair and blowing smoke rings into the stale atmosphere of the cramped office. The six other plainclothes cops stared at him.

"It seems your partner spent some time on his day off trying to run down whoever mugged the guy Frank

Delahanty wrote about in his column this morning. What
was his name, Randolph Klein?"

Blackie blew more smoke at the ceiling.

"Some people are saying," a thin cop named Roy
Martinez said, "that your new partner might have leaked
that story to Delahanty to make a name for himself."

"Yeah," a bald cop named Atkins chimed in. "Cole's in
with the Leprechaun right now. Probably he's telling
O'Casey how he can save his ass."

Blackie let their comments wash over him. He didn't
know if Larry had any connection with the story in the
paper, but if he was on the trail of whoever robbed
Randolph Klein, then Blackie was certain that Martin
Zykus was involved. Cole was obsessed with the guy and
now, because of what some cheap-shot newspaperman had
written, he was going to be in dutch with the team. That
wasn't good. It wasn't good at all.

Finally, Blackie took the cigar from his mouth, examined its glowing tip, and said, "Why don't you guys take it
easy until Cole has a chance to speak for himself?"

This backed them off a bit, but not by much. Blackie
recognized the collective emotion they were generating.
He figured it would be the same as a lynch mob.

The room lapsed into an uneasy silence. Blackie stuck
his cigar back in his mouth and leaned forward to check
the message spindle. There were no messages for him, but
there was one for Cole: "Officer Larry Cole, please call
Sister Frances Lucille at Louise Stallings's apartment. 474-
8965. Urgent!"

Blackie didn't know what that was all about, but he'd
make sure to give the note to his partner when he reported
for duty.

Cole felt the tension when he walked into the tactical
office, but he didn't have time to dwell on it. He was glad
that Blackie was there along with Sergeant Novak.

Cole hadn't been formally introduced to the rest of the team and he regretted that he didn't have the time now to go around and introduce himself to each one of them. But the commander's orders were to act with dispatch when going after Martin Zykus.

"Excuse me, Sarge," Cole said to Novak, "could I talk to you and Blackie alone?"

"What's the matter, Cole?" a voice he didn't recognize said from behind him. "You got something to say too good for the likes of your fellow officers?"

"So that's Cole," another voice said. "I thought it was the fucking janitor."

Cole turned around and was greeted by six hostile stares. Then Novak said, "If you have something to say to me, Cole, then you can say it right here."

Cole realized that something was very wrong, but he couldn't figure out what. He glanced at Blackie and was relieved when his partner gave him a sympathetic nod.

Cole proceeded to tell Novak about his orders from the Leprechaun to pick up Martin Zykus as a suspect in the robbery of Randolph Klein. When he finished someone quipped, "Will that get your name in the paper, too, Cole?"

He didn't respond or turn around.

"Well, if you've got orders from the commander, I guess there's not a lot I can do about it," Novak said, "but as soon as you get through with your little private investigation, you and I are going to sit down so I can explain to you how this tactical team is going to be run."

Cole was confused and even a bit angry. All he had tried to do was the best job that he could. He hadn't taken what he had to the Leprechaun—O'Casey had asked for it. Now Novak was trying to put him on the carpet like he'd done something wrong.

He felt his anger beginning to build when Blackie stood up and said, "If we're gonna run up on this asshole Zykus before midnight, kid, we'd better get cracking."

The eyes of the others followed them as they left the office.

"What in the hell's going on, Blackie?" Cole said as they started down the stairs.

"Jealousy and confusion, Larry, and in large quantities. Most of those dumb fucks up there don't even know what's going on, but they follow each other around like elephants in a circus." Blackie paused a tick and then added, "And the biggest dummy of them all is that stupid-assed Wally Novak."

They were crossing the lobby to pick up their portable radio and sign out an unmarked car when Blackie remembered the message he'd taken off the spindle.

Taking it Cole said, "Why would this Sister Frances Lucille want me to call her at Louise Stallings's apartment?"

"Got me, kid. Maybe you'd better give her a ring and find out what's cooking," Blackie said. "I'll get the radio."

A few minutes later, Blackie walked over to the desk area where Cole was just hanging up the telephone. When the older cop saw his partner's face, he knew that something serious had happened. Blackie had seen the look Cole had before. He could only characterize it as Cole having death in his eyes.

"Zykus somehow got into Louise's apartment last night and raped her. According to the nun, who's there with her now, he beat her up pretty bad. Louise won't go to the hospital, so Sister Frances Lucille wants us to come over to see if we can convince her."

"Let's go," Blackie said, heading for the door.

CHAPTER 85

DECEMBER 1, 1976
5:56 P.M.

Martin Zykus's right hand was tender from slapping Louise, and she had bitten his left wrist. For that, he had used his belt on her. He had even knocked her unconsious. When she came to, he had been in the saddle. She started screaming, but he shut her up with a backhand blow to the face. Then he'd made a night of it.

He'd never been so horny in his life. He just couldn't get enough of her, and it seemed that the more she cried and begged, the more he wanted her. He began dozing about dawn, but he didn't want her flipping out on him while he slept. She knew who was the boss now, but as Dave had taught him, he'd have to keep his foot in her ass to make sure she didn't stray.

"I'm going now," he said after he dressed. "I'll be back tonight. Now if you don't want another ass-whipping, I suggest you clean up and be ready to fix me some dinner. You don't have to worry about going out. I'll bring some frozen hamburger patties and stuff back with me. Oh, and Louise, no cops this time."

She didn't answer him. She was cowering against the headboard, wrapped in a sheet. He walked around the bed and, grabbing her hair, snatched her face up where he could see it. He was surprised she was so bruised up.

"I said no cops, bitch! Now you answer me when I talk to you!"

Her voice came out a hoarse croak. "No . . . cops. . . ."

He'd left feeling better than he'd ever felt in his entire life. He went back to his place and sacked out.

When he awoke, it was snowing heavily. He ate a can of sardines with some crackers, showered, and even washed his hair. He put on summer-weight slacks, which were the only clean pair of pants he owned, and a white shirt. When he checked himself in the mirror, he thought he looked pretty good.

Donning his hooded coat and the steel-toed boots he'd worn on that last night with Dave, Zykus headed for the street. He didn't like snow. It screwed everything up. The tires on his car were bald and the engine didn't turn over too fast when it was cold and damp. He decided to leave the Chevy and stomped through the ever-increasing drifts up to Belmont.

He caught an eastbound bus and got off at Broadway. He turned south when he remembered he had promised to bring hamburgers for Louise to cook.

He found a small meat market open with prices he thought too high for the fat ground beef the bald-headed, red-faced butcher shoved on the scale, but he paid. Next, he had to find someplace that sold buns, mustard, and stuff.

The drugstore was a block from the meat market. It had a small food section, where Zykus got what he needed. They also sold instant lottery tickets at the checkout counter. He purchased two tickets along with the food.

The lottery game was based on the same principle as a slot machine. Three bars netted the player a five-hundred-dollar prize and descending prizes for any other combination of threes. The first ticket had two bells and an orange. A loser.

A tall, middle-aged woman, who reminded Zykus of his fifth-grade teacher, was forced to step around him in order to get out of the store. She mumbled something he didn't catch as she passed him. He figured that it wasn't a compliment. He quickly forgot her and went back to his last ticket.

It would later seem to Martin Zykus that a number of things happened at once as he began scraping the coating off the symbols. The drugstore seemed to get warmer and brighter. The noise from people going in and out and the store's cash register clanging became muted to a whisper. He felt that, for those few brief seconds, he had become isolated from the rest of the universe. He would one day have this feeling again.

He used the edge of a dime to reveal the symbols. The coating came off in dusty curls, which clung to his fingers and floated down on top of his boots. The first symbol was a bar. Alone it meant nothing. He moved on to the second. His breathing became more labored, as he saw that it, too, was a bar.

He looked around the store. No one was paying him any attention. He turned back to the ticket.

Slowly, centimeter by centimeter, he uncovered the last symbol. When he saw it, his pulse rate accelerated as he abruptly rejoined the world. Now the noise and lighting of the store became amplified and harsh. Customers jostled him as they hurried in and out. It was as if he'd become trapped in one of those old-time silent movies where everything was speeded up. But it didn't matter, because Martin Zykus had a five-hundred-dollar instant lottery ticket in his hand.

He stood there for a moment or two, getting his head together. They wouldn't have enough cash to redeem the ticket here. For this amount he'd have to go downtown. It was after six, so the offices there would be closed. All he'd have to do was put the ticket in a safe place and go get his money tomorrow. He would have to tell Louise.

He secured the ticket in his wallet next to his driver's license and rushed from the store. The white stuff was turning to slush rapidly, but no longer bothered him as he made his way south toward West Barry.

On her block, he was making plans to take Louise out to dinner. He didn't want to spend the money until he got his ticket cashed, but he could always pay her back later. Dinner would be a way for him to make peace with her after cuffing her around the way he had last night.

The red lights caught his attention first. Through the falling snow and darkness he was unable to tell if it was a fire truck or an ambulance. Then, as he got closer, he saw that it was an ambulance. A hundred and fifty feet from the entrance to Louise Stallings's apartment building, Zykus froze.

The ambulance attendants were coming out of the building with one of those stretchers on wheels between them. There was a body wrapped in blankets on the stretcher. This didn't attract Zykus's attention as much as did the three people who walked out with the attendants. Zykus had seen the woman the night he had followed Rena Hartley from the Burger King. He remembered that she had a squeaky voice. Cole and Silvestri were with her.

For an instant, his anger at Louise flared—he had specifically told her, no cops! It was merely incidental to him that she was probably the one on the stretcher. *She'll need a fucking stretcher,* he thought, *when I get through with her!*

But his main problem at this point was not Louise, but the two cops. They were helping to lift the stretcher into the ambulance and hadn't seen him, but he couldn't expect that situation to last much longer.

Zykus backed into the shadows of a building and inched

his way along its face until he reached a gangway. He had just slipped into the dark passage leading to the alley when Blackie turned around and looked at the exact spot where Zykus had been standing.

CHAPTER 86

DECEMBER 1, 1976
6:42 P.M.

O pen your eyes, Louise." It was a whispered entreaty rather than a demand, but somehow she felt compelled to obey.

She forced her eyes open.

Initially, the overhead lights in the curtain-enclosed cubicle blinded her. Then her eyes adjusted. A woman stood over her. A woman dressed in a nun's habit.

"Now, listen to me," the nun said. "You're going to be fine. You just have a couple of bruises and a scratch or two. They'll heal."

Louise tried to speak, but her mouth and throat were too dry. The nun picked up a cup of water from the bedside table and held her head so she could drink. When she could finally speak she said, "Why?"

"I don't understand."

"Why did this happen to me?" There was a great deal of bitterness in her tone.

The nun smiled. "The best healers are the ones that know pain. You are part of God's plan."

"God's plan! Was it God's plan for that maniac to rape and beat me? Was it God's plan to have me humiliated like this? Don't talk to me about God's plan!"

She tried to snatch her hand away, but the nun held it firm. "You're tired and you're hurt. But God hasn't forgotten you."

The dam burst inside Louise. The tears came in great, gut-wrenching sobs. She reached out for the nun and was embraced. The nun held Louise like a child while she cried.

"Why, why, why?" she sobbed.

"It will be all right, Louise. I promise you, it will be all right."

"She's asleep," the doctor said. "She's simply lying there, sound asleep. All of her vital signs are good and she appears to have come through the trauma without complications."

"I thought you said she had a concussion?" Blackie said. He had never had a great deal of faith in doctors.

"She does," the very proper female surgeon said, "but her condition is stable now. Everything has concluded for the best."

" 'Concluded for the best,' " Blackie repeated under his breath as he turned away from her.

"When can we talk to her?" Cole said.

"I still want to run some tests, but I think we can chance waking her up."

Cole stepped forward and took Louise's hand. The sleeping woman immediately tightened her grip at the same time she opened her eyes. She looked curiously at each of them. They in turn looked back at her, relieved that she was still alive.

"How do you feel?" the doctor said.

"I'm hurting," she said in a weak voice, "but I'll live."

"Louise," Cole said. "Me and Blackie need to talk to you."

"It's about Martin Zykus," she said looked directly at him.

He nodded.

"He beat me up and raped me last night," she said in a firm voice. "He and another man raped me the night before Thanksgiving."

"Will you sign complaints against him?" Blackie asked with a skeptical frown.

"I won't only sign, but I want to testify at his trial," she said. "The world needs to know what kind of sick animal he is."

Cole and Blackie exchanged nods "Doctor," Blackie said. "Take care of our patient. We've got work to do."

"Larry," Louise called before they could escape beyond the curtained barrier. "You and Blackie be careful. He's dangerous."

"So are we," Cole said. Then they were gone.

"Doctor," Louise said, "where is the nun who was here before?"

The doctor was reading Louise's chart and looked up to study her curiously. "I don't understand what you mean."

"There was a nun here a few minutes ago. She held my hand. We talked before I dozed off. I'd just like to thank her."

"I'm sorry, Louise," the doctor said. "But no one's been in here with you except me and those two policemen."

"Of course there was," Louise said with a nervous laugh. "She had on a blue habit and she . . . Well, this is a hospital. Couldn't the nun be on your staff?"

"This is American Hospital. We're nondenominational. There are no nuns working here."

Louise stared back at her for a long time.

CHAPTER 87

Zykus wasn't going back to his apartment or to pick up his car. With Cole and Silvestri after him, his best bet would be to get out of town as quickly as possible. He still had a hundred and thirty dollars in cash and the instant lottery ticket, but he wouldn't be able to cash in the ticket until tomorrow. By then, it could be too late.

He kept to the side streets after escaping through the West Barry Place gangway. First he headed west, then doubled-back east. He was traveling in circles. He stopped under a streetlight on Halsted to collect his thoughts.

The snow was letting up, but it was starting to get cold. He'd have to get off the street soon. But he needed money. He would have to cash in the lottery ticket.

He remembered Slick Rick Johnson, the Division Street fence. He could be the answer to his problem. Zykus caught the next southbound bus.

By the time Zykus walked the three blocks from Halsted to the Division Street bar, he was frozen. For the first time he noticed the sign out front which read THE LAZY ACE. After a brief hesitation, he opened the door and went inside.

The place was about half full, with people seated in the

booths along the walls and on stools around the circular mirror-and-chrome bar. All of the patrons were black, but none appeared to be paying him the slightest attention. The place was comfortably warm, which Zykus welcomed. He took a seat at the bar and flipped his hood back. He began massaging his hands to restore circulation when Slick Rick Johnson slid onto the stool beside him.

"You slummin', white folk, or you want to do some more business with the Slickster?"

The barmaid, a black woman with short hair and the most voluptuous body Zykus had ever seen, came over to wait on them.

"A split of Mumm's for me, Zenobia, and whatever my friend wants," Johnson said.

Zykus ordered a straight brandy, hoping it would help him warm up.

When they were alone, Johnson lit a cigarette and, blowing smoke through his nostrils, said, "So what's happening?"

"I've got to get out of town fast and I need some money."

"I sure as shit hope you ain't talking about a loan, because I don't do that," Johnson said angrily.

Zykus looked around before pulling out his wallet and removing the instant lottery ticket. Before he could hand it over, Zenobia returned with their drinks. He waited until she'd served them and walked away.

"I need some cash for this tonight," Zykus said.

Johnson examined the ticket. "What in the hell is this?"

"An instant lottery ticket. It's worth five hundred dollars. You can cash it in tomorrow."

"You that hot you can't hang around another day?"

"Let's say I got a real serious problem with two Nineteenth District tactical cops."

"So what do you want me to do?"

"I need dough to catch the first Greyhound bus going out of here," Zykus said, after taking a quick pull of his brandy. "That ticket's worth five hundred bucks."

Johnson shook his head. "I ain't got five hundred on me now."

"Aw, c'mon, man! You had a wad that could choke a rhino the other night."

Johnson looked hard at Zykus. "Keep your voice down, Marty. We cool. Maybe we can strike some kind of deal."

"What do you mean?"

"This ain't something I got to take a chance on that got ripped off in a heist. This is legit. Anybody holding it walks into the State Lottery office downtown, plunks down that ticket, and gets the five hundred bucks. Right?"

"That's right." Zykus drained off the last of his drink and motioned for Zenobia to bring him another.

"I mean, I still got to charge you for the service, but that's only good business."

Zykus stiffened. He remembered how he'd gotten ripped off on the jewelry. "How much?"

Johnson sipped his champagne. "Take it easy, Marty. We still tight. Say you give me ten percent. That's fifty bucks. That's only fair."

"Okay, give me the four-fifty."

"Haven't got it," Johnson said. "All I got on me is two-fifty."

"What about the rest?!"

Johnson looked around the bar and then said to his guest, "You want to tell every motherfucker in here what we're doing? Just be cool."

"I need money, man," Zykus said, having difficulty keeping his voice down. "If I don't get out of town tonight, I'm in deep shit."

"Okay, listen," Johnson said, leaning close to the busboy and whispering. "I can give you two-fifty now. That's enough to get you a bus ticket to someplace else. You get somewhere you can hold up, you give me a call and I send the balance to you by Western Union. When the heat is off, you can come back to Chicago and we'll do some more business together."

"That won't work," Zykus said, picking up his lottery ticket from the bar.

"You don't trust me or something, white boy?"

"It's not that," Zykus lied. "I just don't want anybody to know where I'm going. Once I'm out of this town, I'm not coming back. But there is a way we might be able to do business."

"How's that?"

"You give me the two-fifty like you said, and one of those guns you carry around in your briefcase."

Johnson's eyes locked with the busboy's. "Those are expensive."

"C'mon, Slick," Zykus said with a careful smile. "You got something you can let me have for the two-fifty profit you'll be making."

"Maybe," Johnson said. "Just maybe."

They did the deal in the men's room. Slick Rick handed Zykus two hundreds and a fifty, which came out of an inside pocket. Then the fence opened the briefcase. He used his body to keep Zykus from seeing what was inside. When he closed it, he held a small, nickel-plated automatic in his hand.

Zykus examined it closely. At first, it looked to be no more than one of those cheap cigarette lighters shaped like a pistol. But this one was indeed real.

"You're getting a real bargain, Marty," Johnson said. "This is a .25-caliber Browning automatic. Six rounds in the magazine, one in the chamber. It's a precision piece made in Belgium. All the cops are carrying the Browning nine-millimeter now. This one's the nine's little brother."

Zykus handled the gun clumsily.

Slick Rick took it from him, ejected the clip and round in the chamber, and showed him how the safety catch worked. He removed the bullets from the clip, reinserted the empty clip into the handle, and pulled the slide. The gun gave a soft click when he pulled the trigger. The noise made Zykus jump.

"You load the rounds in the clip like this," Johnson said, demonstrating. "When the clip is in the gun, you pull the slide back, which chambers a round. Then you're ready to rock and roll. You can carry this baby right in your pocket, but I'd keep the safety on unless you want to blow your dick off."

Zykus stood in the Lazy Ace's bathroom hefting the small weapon. "It doesn't seem like it's worth two hundred dollars."

"It's a collector's item," Johnson said, turning to the sink to wash the gun oil off his hands. "You'll probably get a lot more for it someday."

Zykus stared at Slick Rick Johnson's back and considered giving the weapon a test fire right here, but at that moment a man in a red suit entered the washroom.

"What's happenin', Slick?"

"Nothing to it, J. D."

Zykus slipped the gun in his pocket.

Slick Rick Johnson watched Martin Zykus walk out into the cold of Division Street before he returned to his seat at the bar.

"Hey, Z," he called to the barmaid, "give me the phone."

She placed a telephone with a long extension cord on the bar in front of him. Slick Rick winked at her as he dialed the City of Chicago municipal government administation number.

"Would you give me the Nineteenth police district please?" he said to the operator. His ghetto drawl had vanished.

He busied himself refilling his champagne glass and lighting a cigarette while he waited. Finally, "Good evening, Sergeant Beazley. Look, I'm a concerned citizen and I understand a couple of your tactical people are looking for a young white fellow named Marty."

While he listened, Slick Rick examined the gold Pulsar watch on his wrist, which he had bought off of Zykus.

"Zykus, you say. Well, I'm not sure of the last name but he's about five-foot-ten, heavyset, and dresses like a skid-row reject. Well, he's running and right now is on the way to the Greyhound bus station downtown. Oh, I don't know that, sir, but I'd get somebody down there now if I was you. No, I don't want to give my name. Bye."

Slick Rick hung up and took a moment to enjoy his champagne and cigarette. Then he removed a notebook from his pocket and flicked it open to a page on which he had written a telephone number. He recited it out loud as he dialed: "Two two two, one, three three three."

"Mr. Delahanty? Yeah, I recognized your voice. I've seen you on TV a couple of times. You're a real smooth dude.

"The word's around on the street that you're interested in the guy who robbed this Randolph Klein you wrote about in your column this morning."

Johnson pressed a button, and the time was illuminated on the Pulsar's dial.

"Well, I know who he is. Yeah, it's Zykus. Marty Zykus. I don't know how to spell it, but the cops from that station you mentioned in the column are real anxious to get their hands on him.

"No, Mr. Delahanty, he's not black. He's as white as you are."

Then Slick Rick made arrangements to collect Delahanty's reward.

CHAPTER 88

DECEMBER 1, 1976
9:25 P.M.

Martin Zykus's boots were wet and his toes were going numb from the cold. He made his way east from Halsted Street toward the Greyhound bus station on Randolph. The streets of downtown Chicago were virtually deserted on this winter night, and between the high-rise buildings he could see for blocks in any direction he looked. That made it easy for him to spot the marked police cars silently prowling the streets. It also made it easier for them to see him.

Every other block a squad car either passed him or drove down the north-south, one-way cross streets. As he walked under the Wells Street elevated tracks, a marked unit approached slowly from the opposite direction and pulled to the curb fifty feet in front of him. The glare of the Bismarck Hotel's marquee off the windshield made it impossible for him to see inside the car, so he couldn't tell if they were watching him. The only thing he could do was keep his head down and keep walking toward them. He clutched the small Browning automatic tightly in his fist.

As he passed the car, he glanced sideways to find the driver writing on a pad of paper attached to a clipboard. Neither he, nor the cop in the passenger seat, paid Zykus the slightest attention.

He kept going across LaSalle Street, where he could see the bus station a block away. The end was in sight, but he stayed alert for cops.

Zykus walked on the south side of the street. On the north side, stretching from LaSalle to Clark, sat the vacant, windowed hulk of the once-prominent Sherman House hotel. The building was now slated for demolition, but vandals had pulled away some of the boards securing the ground-floor entrance and storefronts. He paid the building little attention as he crossed Clark and entered the warmth of the bus depot.

"Hey, man, you got some change?" An old derelict panhandled inside the entrance.

Zykus brushed past him and took the escalator down to the main terminal area. An arrival/departure board was set up against the east wall. Zykus stood under it, sniffling and rubbing his cold hands, as he searched for a possible destination.

Dave had always had two alternative destinations, but Zykus didn't have time for that now. He checked the departure time. The earliest was the 9:55 P.M. leaving for Detroit. He'd never been to Detroit, but he'd heard it was a lot like Chicago.

He headed for the window and purchased a twenty-two-dollar ticket, one way to the Motor City. The window attendant told him to report to the departure gate in fifteen minutes.

He was too nervous to sit down, so he wandered through the terminal. The smell of cooking popcorn and frying onions made his stomach growl. The grill was in a shop off the main concourse. Inside, Zykus ordered two burgers with everything on them, a large grape drink, and a bag of buttered popcorn. After paying he went back to the main concourse, found a seat on a plastic bench, and began to eat.

The first hamburger went down so fast he barely tasted

it. He was starting the second when he remembered that Louise was supposed to fix him hamburgers for dinner at her place tonight. A deep frown creased his features as he thought about how she had put the cops on him.

He was still thinking about cops and chewing on his hamburger when he saw Blackie Silvestri walking slowly along the upper level. Zykus sat stock-still as he watched the menacing cop scan the lower concourse. He hadn't yet looked in Zykus's direction.

The busboy lowered his head and flipped up his hood. He dropped the remains of his hamburger on the bench beside him and stood up. He turned his back to Silvestri and began walking slowly toward the bus-departure entrance. He was passing the bottom of the north escalator when he looked up. Cole stood on the balcony above, staring directly down at him.

"Hold it, Zykus!"

Martin Zykus ran.

CHAPTER 89

DECEMBER 1, 1976
9:45 P.M.

Zykus was making it easy for him, Cole thought as he bounded down the up escalator. He genuinely hoped that the fast busboy would put up the kind of resistance he'd tried last Wednesday night. Cole felt the steel shell of his Kelite flashlight hanging from a ring beneath his field jacket. It was made for heads like Marty's.

At the bottom of the escalator Cole stopped and yelled, "Blackie, he spotted me!" Without waiting for a response, Cole took off after Zykus.

The traffic in the terminal was sparse at this time on a weeknight, and Cole had no trouble keeping Zykus in sight as they ran through the baggage pickup area and out the door leading to the boarding area. Just inside the boarding area, he lost sight of Zykus and was forced to stop. Cole owed the fat boy for Louise, but he wasn't going to charge after him recklessly and get a bullet for his trouble.

Cole snatched his .45 Colt Commander automatic from the shoulder holster beneath his jacket and chambered a round. The sharp snap of the bullet sliding home sent a thrill through him. At that instant Cole realized that, if Martin Zykus gave him even the slightest reason, he would indeed kill him.

He glanced around the edge of the boarding area entrance to find a number of startled passengers and a couple of uniformed bus drivers staring down the row of perpendicularly parked buses. Holding his gun up at the port arms position, Cole trotted over to the first driver he saw and flashed his badge. "Which way did the fat guy in the black hooded jacket go?"

"Up the ramp to the street, officer," a driver said with a heavy Southern drawl. "But watch it, 'cause he's got a gun."

"Did you see it?"

The driver nodded his head so violently his Greyhound cap wobbled on his head. "I saw it."

"Larry, wait!" Blackie ran toward them from the concourse.

"He's got a gun," Cole informed his partner.

Blackie looked from Cole to the still-nodding driver.

Then he pulled his Magnum. "I called for backup and described us for responding units. Now your boy Martin Zykus decides how we bring him in: dead or alive. Let's go."

Together they ran up the ramp.

CHAPTER 90

DECEMBER 1, 1976
9:52 P.M.

Zykus pulled the gun when he saw Cole. He'd had it with the black cop dogging him. It was time, Zykus decided, for him to "kill a nigger," as Dave had told him one night. According to Dave, where he came from, killing a black was a sign of virility for a white man. Zykus wanted to become a member of that club.

The gun helped him get through the stragglers coming off the arriving buses. They scattered quickly, some ducking behind buses and one guy dropping face down on the ground. Zykus halted and looked back. He caught a quick glimpse of Cole trotting down the line of buses. He didn't see Silvestri. He noticed the gun in the black cop's hand. Even from this distance it looked to be three, maybe four times bigger than his. Terrified, he fled up the ramp onto Lake Street.

He looked first toward the lights of State Street two blocks to the east, but rejected going that way because there would probably be more cops hanging around the theaters and restaurants there. Instead, he turned back to Clark Street. Running in his heavy shoes was difficult, and he fell hard when he tried to turn the corner. Looking over his shoulder, he saw Cole and Silvestri come out of the driveway entrance to the bus station a quarter of a block away. He scrambled back to his feet and crossed Clark, heading for the abandoned Sherman House hotel.

When he reached the far curb, he heard Cole shout, "Stop right there, Zykus!"

He turned and, without aiming, fired a shot from the .25 in the direction the shout had come from. The recoil of the little gun startled him and he dropped it into the snow. He had no time to look for it as he stumbled behind a parked car and fell again. A loud report echoed from the street as a bullet whined over his head to smash into the wall of the hotel.

Zykus crawled through the snow to the wall of the building. There he stopped, expecting Cole and Silvestri to come for him at any second. Then, he was certain, he'd be dead.

He inched along the wall away from where he expected them to approach. His back hit something that gave under his weight. Turning, he found a boarded-up window of what had once been a Sherman House mall shop. One of the boards had been kicked in to open like a trapdoor. It opened enough for Zykus to slip through into the darkened interior. He climbed inside.

CHAPTER 91

When they reached the top of the ramp, Cole saw Zykus fall to the ground. The cop raised his .45, but before he could fire the busboy had scrambled out of sight.

"This way, Blackie!" Cole ran for the corner, barely aware that he had left his partner trailing behind.

Flattening himself against the wall of the bus station, Cole peered around the edge of the building across Clark Street. He could see Zykus running at an angle toward the Sherman House. Cole stepped around the edge of the building and raised his gun to shoulder level.

"Watch it, Larry!"

He heard Blackie behind him as he leveled the front and rear sights of his gun on the middle of the busboy's back. "Stop right there, Zykus!"

Cole would later remember seeing the glint off the housing of Zykus's gun just an instant before the flash of the discharge. Cole would also remember that Zykus never turned to aim, but fired wildly.

Larry Cole was seventy-five feet away from Martin Zykus when the bullet from the .25 was fired. The chances of an expert marksman hitting a target at that distance with such a small weapon would be phenomenal. All that could be hoped for would be a lucky shot. Zykus was lucky, but so was Larry Cole.

The small-caliber bullet zipped through the cold December air to singe the hair above Cole's right ear and sear the flesh open just enough to break the skin. The high-velocity buzzing of the bullet caused a sharp ringing in Cole's ear. Clutching at the wound, he dropped to one knee in the snow.

When Blackie saw his partner go down, he knew he'd been shot. He was twenty feet behind Cole, but was able to see Zykus as he reached the far curb. Blackie took quick aim and fired.

He saw brick fragments splatter off the face of the building, but knew he hadn't hit the rapist. Crouching to provide a smaller target, Blackie checked Cole.

Cole's automatic dangled impotently from his left hand, while his right hand clutched the side of his head. A thin trickle of blood escaped from beneath his palm to roll down across his cheek.

"How bad is it, Larry?" Blackie's words and heavy breathing formed dense vapor-clouds in the air.

Cole turned frightened eyes up to stare at Blackie, but he didn't speak.

"Let me see it." Blackie reached out and pulled Cole's hand away from the wound. Cole resisted, but Blackie forced him. Blackie kept glancing across Clark Street at the last place he had seen Zykus. There was no movement over there.

Cole's wound stretched for two and a half inches across the side of his head. It was shallow, but bleeding heavily.

"It's just a scratch," Blackie said, applying his handkerchief to the wound.

Cole attempted to laugh, but only a trembling croak came out. "You sound like a cowboy in one of those stupid Westerns."

Blackie managed a smile. "Okay, you stay here, kid. I'm going to bag that fat bastard." He got to his feet and pulled his Detective Special to supplement the Magnum.

"No!" Cole also got to his feet. "I've got to go with you. It was me Zykus tried to kill."

Blackie stared at his partner. In the instant their eyes met, they knew they couldn't let Martin Zykus walk away from this. Together they started across the street.

When they reached the far side, a marked police car came screaming down Clark Street toward them. Blackie flagged it down.

"We've got an armed suspect wanted for rape who just took a shot at my partner."

The two cops inside the squad car stared in silent shock from Blackie to Cole, who was prowling the sidewalk in front of the boarded-up mall shops of the Sherman House. They noticed that the black cop had a white handkerchief—which was quickly turning red—in one hand and a .45 automatic in the other.

Blackie snapped them back to their senses by giving them a detailed description of Martin Zykus. Before he could finish, more police cars came screaming up Clark. A tall black man in a sergeant's uniform jumped out of the lead car and approached.

"Blackie!" Cole called from the spot where he had found the loose board over the window to the mall shop.

Ignoring the sergeant, Blackie rushed to his partner's side.

Cole pointed to the fresh footprints in the snow and the disturbed dust on the windowsill as further clues to Zykus's whereabouts. "He went in here," Cole explained. Then he looked up at the building's facade. "This place has got to have a hundred ways to get in and out."

"Who are you guys?" the sergeant who had followed Blackie demanded.

Blackie flashed his badge and ID card, "Silvestri and

Cole, Nineteenth District tactical team. We're chasing a fugitive wanted for rape, robbery, and possibly murder."

"What happened to you?" the sergeant asked Cole.

"The guy we are chasing shot me." Cole removed the handkerchief from the wound. The bleeding had slowed.

"You should be on your way to a hospital," the sergeant said, testily.

"I'm not going anywhere until we get Zykus, Sarge," Cole said, tossing the bloody handkerchief into the snow.

"Look, boss," Blackie said before an argument could begin, "our man's inside. We're going in after him. All we need from your people is to surround the perimeter to keep him from getting out."

The sergeant shook his head. "I can't authorize you going in there. We'll call the canine unit for a search."

"We can't wait that long," Cole said. "This place takes up almost a full city block. There's got to be hundreds of places Zykus can hide or even make his escape from. We've got to go in now before he can get his shit together."

The sergeant's jaw muscles rippled. "Nobody's going in there and that's a direct order!"

Cole pulled his multicell Kelite, while Blackie took a four-cell flashlight from his coat pocket. As Cole pushed the board in and stepped into the derelict Sherman House, Blackie said to the sergeant, "Sarge, make sure your people know we're the good guys." Then he followed his partner inside.

CHAPTER 92

The darkness was so intense that Martin Zykus was literally unable to see his hand in front of his face. After climbing inside the Sherman House, he moved a few feet into the frigid blackness and then stopped to listen for sounds of pursuit. For a long minute there was nothing. Then he heard the sirens.

He inched further into the darkness, holding his hand out in front of him to keep from running into anything. His blindness was oddly comforting, as here in the dark he was hidden from his pursuers.

"Blackie!" The now damnably familiar voice of Larry Cole seemed to come from right behind Zykus. The busboy jumped at the sound, lost his balance, and went down hard. He hit his knee on something sharp and it was all he could do to keep from crying out. Then a sliver of light appeared behind him. By its illumination, Zykus was able momentarily to see where he was.

It had once been a store with display cases and shelves arranged around an aisle that ran to an entrance into the hotel lobby beyond. The shelves were now empty and the glass in the display cases was gone. Also, there were no doors at the lobby entrance.

Then the crack of light vanished, plunging Zykus into darkness again. But he knew where he was.

There were voices from the street. He heard Cole's again, followed by Silvestri's, and then another's. Zykus couldn't hear what they were saying, but he was certain of one thing: they would be coming in soon.

Fixing the deserted shop's lobby entrance in his mind, he struggled to his feet. The pain in his knee was intense, but subsided as he limped through the darkness. He had reached the entrance and taken a step into the lobby when the crack of light split the darkness again. Cole and Silvestri entered the abandoned hotel after Martin Zykus.

Martin Zykus's eyes began adjusting slowly to the darkness, but there was so little available light that he could make out nothing at first but a few variations of shadow. He constantly bumped into walls or tripped over discarded items on the floor, but he stayed on his feet and kept moving. Moving away from his pursuers.

He was aware of them following him, and their flashlight beams frequently pierced the darkness behind him. But they were moving slowly. Cautiously. He figured they still thought he had the gun. He cursed himself for dropping it outside. If he had it now, things would be much different in this little game of cat-and-mouse they were playing.

The floor was suddenly no longer there, and Zykus just managed to stop before falling. He felt over the edge with his foot until he touched something solid. He had reached a flight of steps. Turning sideways, he made his way down six steps until he hit level flooring. Again, he stopped.

The place was very cold and extremely damp. But now he felt a subtle difference in the air around him. Then, something happened to the darkness. It dissipated a bit, to the point where the vague shadows began to look more three-dimensional.

He stood still and closed his eyes for a moment. Opening them enabled him to see just a fraction better than he had been able to before. The shapes surrounding him formed enough of a pattern for him to make out that he was inside the entrance to a very large room.

He looked up into the shadows above him but could see nothing. Then he heard noises originating from someplace high overhead. He could barely hear them, but he guessed what their origin was. The sound was caused by flapping wings, and Zykus knew that pigeons didn't fly in the dark. His face split into a grin which no human eye would ever see. There were bats up there in the dark. A lot of bats.

A beam of light swung across the corridor behind him. Zykus spun toward it with a snarl of primeval anger mixed with fear. There was a flurry of wings flapping, which were punctuated by high-pitched chirps. He felt the air vibrate centimeters above his head. A bat swooped over him. This was followed by another and still another, each passing within inches of Martin Zykus.

He went into a crouch and raised his forearms up to protect the sides of his head. However, the flying animals never touched him. The flashlight beam in the corridor began swinging closer. He looked away from it back into the ballroom. The area had again gone inky black. Zykus blinked his eyes, coming to the realization that the light was damaging his ability to see in the dark. Then he noticed something else. The bats had gone quiet again.

His mind spun back over the past few seconds. He had made a noise, which had brought a few of the bats buzzing down around his head. He didn't know anything about these terrifying nocturnal creatures, but he figured that he had somehow disturbed them in their lair and they had come down to check him out.

The beams began moving directly toward him, but he refused to look at them.

Zykus wondered what would happen if something really disturbed the bats. Got them really pissed off.

As the lights penetrated the entrance to the ballroom, Martin Zykus scurried off into the shadows.

CHAPTER 93

DECEMBER 1, 1976
10:11 P.M.

Blackie's flashlight was old and the batteries had been in it a long time. The beam it cast into the cavernous emptiness of the old hotel was swallowed up by the darkness after only a few feet. This forced him to stick close to Cole, whose multicell unit lit up each room they passed through like a ceiling light bulb going on. However, this was not necessarily an advantage.

"Zykus will be able to spot us long before we see him," Blackie whispered into the silent cold.

"I know." Cole's voice was dead steady, but Blackie could detect the stress there.

"How big is this place?" Blackie realized that he was making unnecessary small talk. This was not the time for idle chitchat, which told him he wasn't concentrating. He knew himself well enough to know that this was an indication that he was afraid.

"It's big," Cole said quietly, as his breath came in quick, harsh rasps.

"What was that?" Blackie swung his Magnum in the direction from which the noise had come.

Cole stopped. "It sounded like a bark or maybe a growl."

"Well, it doesn't matter," Blackie said through clenched teeth. "Two legs or four, if it moves wrong, it's dead."

They were in a wide corridor with a high ceiling. The floor had been stripped down to a cement surface. A still-intact sign above a gilt-edged arrow read, GRAND BALL-ROOM. The sound they had heard had come from inside the ballroom.

"Shall we dance?" Blackie quipped.

Cole didn't answer.

"What is that smell?" Blackie said, as they walked down the steps into the ballroom.

Cole gagged and swung his light across the floor. It was slick with a wet, slippery mass of feces that covered every square foot of space.

"Where did all this—" Blackie stopped, "—all this shit come from?"

Cole swung his beam upward. The mass of inverted, hanging bats covered the ceiling.

"Let's get out of here, Larry," Blackie said, starting to back toward the ballroom entrance.

Without prompting or comment, Cole turned to follow him.

They never saw the rock that flew through the air from the far side of the ballroom. It crashed into the center of the dormant bat cluster, knocking a number from their inverted perches to slam into others. The disturbance turned into a frenzy as the bats left the ceiling and swooped down in one sightless cloud of flying vermin. Their frantic chirps combined into what sounded like the scream of a beast gone mad.

Cole and Blackie were trapped in their midst.

CHAPTER 94

After throwing the rock at the bat-infested ceiling of the grand ballroom, Zykus moved rapidly down a corridor running perpendicular to the balcony that had served as his perch for the attack. He was unable to run, but his ability to see in the dark was becoming extraordinary, enabling him to move at a fast walk while keeping his fingertips against one wall to guide him.

With a growing excitement, he had watched Cole and Silvestri enter the ballroom cautiously. He heard Silvestri complain about the smell. Zykus had stood stock-still until they reached a point far enough inside. Then he had hurled the rock.

He hesitated a moment to watch the bats descend from above like a black cloud. Then he made his way down the corridor. A couple of his blind, winged companions followed him. They fluttered their wings harmlessly over his head and then were gone.

The corridor came out into a hall nearly as big as the ballroom. Marble columns stretched from the floor to the ceiling above a wide staircase that descended back to the main floor. Zykus was able to make out the remains of a few furnishings, which indicated that this had once been the hotel lobby.

He followed the staircase down and crossed to the main entrance. Wooden boards hung off one of the entrance doors. Zykus was able to slip through it into an outer lobby. Instantly, the air became at once fresher and colder.

Martin Zykus had never been in the Sherman House when it was open, so he had no way of knowing what was beyond the wall of boards he faced in the dark. He attempted to get his bearings from his entry point on Clark Street to where he was now in relation to the ballroom. He found this impossible. He was faced with prying one of the boards away to look outside.

He searched for a seam. It took a full five minutes before he found one he could force. From the feel of the wood, it was apparent that the boards had been recently installed. The rough texture of the surface drove splinters into his hands, making him cry out. As the echo died away, he thought he heard an answering sound. He waited a second, but there was only silence. The board finally fell to the floor with a crash inside the hotel. Zykus was exposed to the outside air.

He blinked as the combined illumination from the street and the Mars-light of a police car engulfed him. Now that his eyes had become accustomed to the dark, the effect was blinding. He put his left arm up in front of his face and retreated back into the hotel. A voice amplified over a patrol-car loudspeaker shouted, "Hold it right there, mister!"

But Zykus had already disappeared back into the dark.

CHAPTER 95

DECEMBER 1, 1976
10:15 P.M.

The worst that Blackie and Cole had to fear from the bats was that the small flying creatures would cause one of them to hurt himself. The flapping of hundreds of small wings in the blackness of the abandoned hotel ballroom forced them to scurry back into the corridor they had entered from. The accurate echolocation process the animals used to navigate in the dark kept them from accidentally blundering into the cops, who were flailing their arms in the air to ward off nonexistent attacks.

As the main body of the bat cluster flew back toward the perches on the ballroom ceiling, Blackie and Cole leaned against the corridor wall and trembled.

"What the hell were they?" Cole gasped, as he fought to catch his breath without vomiting.

"Bats," Blackie said. "Something got them riled up."

"Do you think it was Zykus?"

Blackie checked his flashlight. It was dead. "Who else? That's another one we owe the bastard. How's your light?"

Cole was amazed that he still held it. The beam was strong. "It's working."

"Okay, we're going to have to stick close together from here on out. He's in here and we're going to get him. I promise you that."

Blackie's confidence helped restore Cole's. "Let's go."

They didn't return to the ballroom, but moved to the opposite end of the corridor. This took them back toward Randolph Street. They came to an intersection and were forced to make a decision on which way to turn.

"This way is east." Cole swung his light to their left.

"We came in that way," Blackie said in a whisper. "I'd say our boy's that way."

They turned west.

Cole's foot hit something soft in the dark. The softness moved.

"What?!" Cole jumped.

His partner's reaction frightened Blackie as well.

Cole's light played along the floor. It picked up the dirty brown fur of an animal moving rapidly away from them.

"Was that a rat?" Blackie said.

"It was too big." Cole attempted to pick it up in the flashlight beam, but it had vanished. As he swung the beam across the floor, he saw tiny red pinpoints of light down at the far end of the corridor. When he swung the light directly at them, a flash of furry movement preceded the animal's disappearance.

"That *was* a rat," Blackie whispered.

"They're a lot of them in here," Cole said, as they again moved forward. "I heard they won't attack people."

"Let's hope you're right."

"Hold it right there, mister!"

They both heard the amplified voice over the loud-speaker. It came from up ahead. They ran toward it.

CHAPTER 96

DECEMBER 1, 1976
10:17 P.M.

Zykus was running blind. The spotlight of the police car had destroyed his night vision. He stumbled back the way he had come, finding his way across the lobby and up the staircase by memory. Twice he slipped and once went down on something sharp, puncturing the flesh in the heel of his hand. This time he managed to keep from crying out.

The enveloping darkness began again to lighten for him, but most of the images he encountered were indistinct. It had taken time to adjust to the darkness when he had first entered the hotel. Now he would again need time. If he could find someplace in here to hole up he could . . .

Suddenly, he became aware of sound in the area he was passing through. Sounds that frightened him rigid. There were soft scraping and clawing noises everywhere. At first, he couldn't tell which direction they were coming from. Then, as he concentrated through his fear, he realized that they were all around him.

He slowed his movements to a walk—then, to barely faster than an infant's crawl. The noises became louder. Then something ran across his feet, while at the same time another something thudded into his back and held on momentarily before skidding off.

The darkness had intensified to the point where he could see nothing, but he was able to feel a presence surrounding him—starting to close in. At that instant, a three-and-a-half-pound rat dropped through the darkness to land on Zykus's head. When he reached up to yank it away, it bit him.

He screamed as he managed to throw it off, but just as quickly another one landed on him, and then another. They were attacking him, and in the dark he couldn't defend himself. Panic seized him and he started to run. He was hampered by the bodies of live rodents underfoot, some of which grabbed and snapped at his legs.

The rat infestation abruptly ceased, and at the instant Zykus felt safe, he ran head-on into a wall. He was knocked flat on his back. Fighting to maintain his consciousness, he attempted to get to his feet. Something cold and wet nudged his cheek and before he could knock it away, the sharp sting of a bite tore his flesh.

"Aieee!" he screamed as he staggered up, holding his bleeding cheek. He stumbled a few feet in confusion, and then the floor was no longer beneath him. He fell through the dark.

CHAPTER 97

Blackie and Cole found the staircase adjacent to the boarded-up entrance. They could see the lights of the police car and the movement of blue uniforms outside, but they had no time to stop. Zykus was in here and he was close. They weren't leaving without him.

"Careful, Larry," Blackie said, as they reached the top of the staircase.

Cole's flashlight had maintained its brilliance, and they were able to see everything in front of them. Blackie hung right on his partner's side, never allowing more than a foot to come between them. They held their guns down at their sides, but were ready to raise them and fire if the busboy appeared. The chase was coming to an end.

Cole stopped. Blackie ran into him before taking a step backward.

"Oh, my God," Cole whispered.

Blackie's reaction was to expel the air from his lungs in one long whistle.

The corridor ahead of them was partially obstructed. The floor above had collapsed, causing another collapse onto the floor below. Girders, pieces of cement, and debris clogged the area, and the reason for the cave-in was not apparent. But it really wasn't of immediate interest to the cops. What drew their attention was the thousands of teeming rats that scrambled through the holes in the upper floors, down onto their level, and into the break below.

"Those are Norway rats," Cole said.

"What?"

"They're called Norway rats. I can tell because they're brown."

The rats were frantically crawling over each other, attempting to get away from the light. They were fleeing onto the lower level, and the corridor was rapidly clearing of the ugly brown bodies.

"Why are there so many of them?" Blackie asked.

"There must be a food source somewhere nearby."

They moved forward cautiously.

"Where's Zykus?" Blackie said. "That scream we heard came from down here."

On cue, the busboy's voice rose out of the hole in the floor. "Help me! Please, help me!"

They reached the edge of the jagged opening and looked down. Zykus straddled a beam that stretched at a hazardous angle from the ceiling beneath their floor down to the level below. As Cole shone the light on him, legions of brown rats scrambled across the floor below.

"You smell that?" Blackie asked.

Cole sniffed the air, but there were so many foul scents in the place it was difficult to distinguish just one. But he did notice that there was a sour sweetness present. "What is that?"

"That's a dead body smell, kid," Blackie said. "And not a fresh one. Let me see your light."

Cole handed it over, and Blackie squatted to swing the beam around below.

"You guys gotta help me!" Zykus whined.

They ignored him.

"Okay," Blackie said. "That's it."

"What have you got?" Cole said, squatting down beside Blackie.

"Follow the beam."

The rats scurried out of the light and the area cleared. That was how he came to see the partial remains of three bodies. The rats had picked the corpses to skeletons.

"Who do you suppose they are?" Cole asked with awe.

"Hey, I'm slipping!" Zykus screamed.

"Shut up, Marty," Blackie snapped. "We'll get to you. There's no way of telling who they are, Larry, but that's your Norway rats' food source."

Cole's voice was deadly serious as he said, "We should give them someone else to eat."

Blackie's head snapped around to look at his partner. "What're you saying?" He had trained the light back on Zykus. The busboy was having a hard time hanging on.

"I'm saying that we should leave him here with the rest of the rats."

"Hey, help me, guys!" Zykus wailed.

"We can't . . . ," Blackie began.

"We can't get him out of there," Cole argued. "We'd need a rope and a hoist to pull him up. We can't go down there with all those rats. Something happens to the flashlight, we'd end up just like those skeletons."

The rodent eyes of the hoard were reflected at the perimeter of the light, as they cautiously reclaimed their feeding ground.

"C'mon, pull me up!" Zykus pleaded. "I can't hold on much longer!"

"What are you saying, Larry? Spell it out." Blackie demanded.

"We made a mistake coming in here after him. We've got to find our way back outside and send for the fire department to get him out of there."

"That could take time."

Cole stood up. "You got any ideas on how the two of us

are supposed to get him out? We try messing around in here and this whole place could come down on us. Then we'd be rat bait just like him."

Blackie remained squatting over the hole. He shined the light down on Zykus. "I want to ask you a couple of things to set the record straight, Marty."

"Help me out! Please! I'll tell you anything you want to know!"

"That won't do, Marty. You've got to tell me now."

"But—"

"Now, Marty!"

"Okay," Zykus said with resignation. "What do you want to know?"

Blackie started with the rapes of the elderly women and moved on to the murder of Dave Higgins. Then he asked about Louise Stallings and Randolph Klein. Zykus confessed to it all.

"Now get me out of here! I can't hold on much longer and the rats are gathering down here again!"

Cole was as silent as a pallbearer. Blackie's face was as grim as a hangman's. "Is there something you haven't told us about, Marty? Maybe something you know that we don't?"

"There's nothing, I tell you!"

"He's lying," Cole said in a funereal whisper. "There's more. He's playing us for chumps."

"My partner says you're lying, Marty," Blackie said, playing with the light to tease the rats teeming at the bottom of the hole. "And you know something, I think he's right. So you'd better come up with something fast."

"There ain't nothing! I swear it!"

Blackie turned the flashlight off, scaring both Zykus and Cole. When he turned it back on, Zykus was talking.

"The broad named Rena. I did her, too." His voice had dropped to a subdued surrender.

"Rena Hartley?" the cops said as one.

"Yeah. She tried to get into my car. She attacked me, man! It was all I could do to get away from her!"

"Her neck was broken, Marty!" Cole shouted down at him.

"She broke it herself! I was just trying to get away."

"Have you heard enough?" Cole said to Blackie.

Blackie let out a sigh. "Yeah. Martin Zykus is a real live menace to society."

"So we go for the fire department?"

"We go for the fire department," Blackie said, handing the flashlight back to Cole.

In the moment that the beam was off him, Zykus screamed. Cole illuminated him again.

"Listen, Marty," Cole said. "Me and Blackie are going outside to get you some help, so don't move and we'll be right back."

With that, they turned away from the hole.

"No! You can't leave me here in the dark! The rats will eat me! No! Come back!"

They kept walking.

When they reached the top of the staircase, they heard a loud scream, followed by a crash.

"We'd better hurry," Blackie said.

"Yeah. We want most of him left to stand trial."

CHAPTER 98

Randolph and Clark Streets looked more like New Year's Eve than a frigid night three weeks before Christmas. Police cars, fire engines, minicam crews, and a truck from the Salvation Army serving coffee and doughnuts brought all traffic in the area to a standstill. People from the late shifts in Loop office buildings, truck drivers making deliveries in the area, and bums from skid row on west Madison crowded the sidewalks, trying to figure out what the cops and smoke eaters were doing.

Battalion Chief Frank McEvoy, wearing a white helmet, turn-out coat, and hip boots, stepped from the abandoned hotel into the glare of lights on Randolph. The wooden partitions that had secured the lobby entrance had been destroyed by fire axes, to facilitate the installation of portable lights inside. These lights were powered by a generator from a hook and ladder truck and gave the area a daylight glow.

McEvoy carried a bloodstained axe over his shoulder. A sharp minicam operator focused on the axe blade as the fireman crossed to a group of policemen huddled around the Salvation Army canteen wagon. Cole and Blackie were waiting anxiously for the fireman.

"That place is a disgrace to the city of Chicago," McEvoy said, picking up a cup of coffee and brandishing his bloodstained fire axe. "The rats"—the fireman swung his axe up as easily as he would a toothpick—"are as big as bulldogs and twice as mean. I had to clobber a couple of the verminous things myself." He swung the axe down, which forced Cole and Blackie to take a step backward. Axe handles had been known to come loose now and then.

"What about Zykus?" Blackie asked.

After exiting the hotel, they'd notified the Chicago Fire Department, which, under the command of Chief McEvoy, had proceeded to efficiently and brutally smash their way into the hotel. After stringing the portable lights, they had disappeared into the bowels of the abandoned edifice. Blackie and Cole had remained outside. Fifteen anxious minutes later, McEvoy had reappeared.

In response to Blackie's question, McEvoy banged his axe on the frozen pavement and said, "There's nothing alive in there now that walks on less than four legs."

"But Zykus can't be dead," Blackie argued. "We only left him for a few minutes."

"Looks like you left him for a few months," McEvoy said. "The rats cleaned the meat off of him and those other two sweet as you please."

"Those skeletons were already there," Cole said. "The man we're looking for was trapped near the spot where we discovered the corpses. Zykus was alive when we came out of there."

"What about the skeletons?" McEvoy said with a frown. "Looks like somebody put big holes in their skulls before they became rat supper."

"We don't know anything about them," Cole said, attempting badly to hide his exasperation. "They've obviously been there for months. We can worry about how they got there later. Now we need to find out what happened to Martin Zykus."

The inside of the Sherman House was brilliantly illuminated by the mobile lights. McEvoy led the way, with the two tactical cops bringing up the rear.

"This was a mall floor," McEvoy said when they reached the area where Cole and Blackie had left Zykus. "Sort of a half-basement arrangement, if you can picture it without all the rat shit and neglect."

At that moment, they could all think of places they'd rather have been. Cole and Blackie held handkerchiefs over their mouths to keep their stomachs from succumbing to the overpowering stench.

"He was up there," Blackie said, pointing to the girder hanging at an angle from the floor above. "Down here was alive with rats."

"Where are they now?" Cole's voice was muffled by the handkerchief.

"Lights scared 'em off," McEvoy sneered. "After all, they're nothing but fucking rats, you know."

"Let me see your flashlight, Larry," Blackie said.

Blackie shone the light off down the corridor into the dark. The red pinpoints of rodent eyes scurried farther into the shadows. "The only place Zykus could have gone was down there."

McEvoy snatched his walkie-talkie from his coat pocket. "Then we'll string more lights."

The second cave-in they found was a place where the basement floor had collapsed into an ancient brick tunnel, which led under Lake Street.

"This is the way the rats get in and out," McEvoy explained.

The air was less foul, but much colder as a steady breeze blew up from the darkness below.

"Where does it go?" Blackie said, being careful not to step too close to the edge.

McEvoy stepped gingerly around the hole. "Has to go

all the way down to the river. Where we are now is close to the original location of the shoreline two hundred years ago. Your man probably went out that way with the rats. It can't be more'n fifteen degrees outside now. If he made it all the way to the river, he'll surely freeze to death. If not, then he's rat bait for sure. By now, he's probably dead."

Blackie and Cole stared down into the hole. They looked at each other, then down again. They knew Battalion Chief Frank McEvoy was wrong. Martin Zykus wasn't dead.

5

"Steven Zalkin is Martin Zykus."

—Larry Cole

CHAPTER 99

Do you think you could drive just a bit faster, Manny?" Commander Cole said, attempting to conceal his irritation.

Manny Sherlock had been pressed into service to drive the commander to his luncheon at the Press Club. Sergeant Silvestri had given Sherlock the order, and before Manny could come up with an excuse, he had been handed the keys to Cole's police car. Now he was driving north on Lake Shore Drive, adhering religiously to the posted forty-five-miles-per-hour speed limit.

In response to Cole's entreaty, Sherlock increased the speed exactly two miles an hour.

As cars continued to zip by them, Cole forced himself to relax. He'd been running around much too uptight lately. But that had been primarily because of Lisa. She was home now, and he could afford to ease up a bit.

He leaned back in the seat and looked out the window at Lake Michigan. There were a few sailboats skimming over the glassy blue surface of the water. It was a real spring day, with the temperatures already hovering around the eighty-degree mark. He was off this weekend. Lisa had mentioned going out of town for a couple of days. He had some time off coming, which he could hook up with his days off. It would be like a mini-vacation. They needed the time together.

But first, he had to successfully conclude the investigation into the explosion and murders at the Temple of Allah. However, as he thought about it, the urgency for him to solve the murders of Abdul Ali Malik and his followers had vanished when Frank Delahanty had been incinerated last night.

The morning papers had screamed the headlines: DELA-HANTY DEAD in the *Chicago Tribune;* COLUMNIST SLAIN! in the *Chicago Sun-Times;* and FRANK DELAHANTY MURDERED WHILE UNDER POLICE PROTECTION in the *Times-Herald.* The front page was surrounded by a black border.

That morning, when Cole arrived at the station, the building had been eerily silent. Not even the phones were ringing. Blackie was at his desk, puffing on a cigar while he read the morning papers. Every item on the first three pages of each of the Chicago dailies was about Delahanty.

"Guess Cap'n Bluto fucked up last night," Blackie said, as he poured Cole's coffee and carried it into the office.

"How did you know about that?"

Blackie set the cup down and took the seat across from his boss. Blackie had left his burning cigar outside.

"It's in all the papers. That news director Moseby and even the superintendent took a couple of swipes at that chucklehead."

"Let me see the articles when you get through with them," Cole said. "I got up late." He thought of Lisa and why he'd been unable to get out of bed on time.

Sherlock made a careful turn off Lake Shore Drive onto Monroe Street. He proceeded at the exact same speed-limit pace toward the Loop. Cole knew he was going to be late, but he didn't think that Schmidt would make an issue of it.

There were too many other things on the first deputy's mind.

The papers had been brutal toward the police. The charges ran the gamut from criminal negligence to criminal conspiracy, depending on which edition the story appeared in. There was mention in the *Times-Herald* of Delahanty's generally critical attitude toward cops. There was a promise by the editor that the famed columnist's last story, which was also uncomplimentary toward "Chicago's Finest," would be printed as part of a salute to Delahanty in the Sunday edition. There was a hint in the editor's message that Delahanty's last column would provide a clue as to the identity of his killer.

The *Times-Herald* went on to mention some of the police officers Delahanty had raked over the coals during his career. The current superintendent of police Chief Riseman, Chief Baldwin, and retired commander Joseph Thomas O'Casey were included. Cole hadn't liked them using O'Casey's name. The Leprechaun was dead. Cole had been a pallbearer at his funeral. It was the first funeral he had shed a tear at since his mother's. O'Casey had not only been a fair boss, but a friend.

Thinking about O'Casey sent Cole's mind roaming back through the years and the times he had spent with the good-natured Leprechaun. He remembered the Christmas parade in 1977 when Cole and Blackie had been pressed into service as Santa's helpers. The memory of Blackie in that skin-tight green costume with the shoes that curled up at the tips made Cole grin.

Then there was the day he had Cole stand up in the roll call room and tell the others about the elderly rape victims. Because of that, Captain O'Neill had gotten mad at him.

Eventually that incident had led to the night down at the Sherman House when Cole and Blackie—

"Is the Press Club on North Michigan Avenue or South

Michigan Avenue, Commander?" Sherlock's question
interrupted Cole's train of thought.

They were traveling north on Michigan toward Madison
Street.

"It's right there," Cole said, pointing at a canopied
entrance a few doors north of the intersection.

"I'll have to go around the block in order to let you off
in front, sir."

God, this kid's uptight, Cole thought. He wondered if
he'd been that way around the brass when he was
Sherlock's age. He certainly hoped not.

"Pull over here, Manny."

Sherlock followed the order so abruptly that he cut off
an oncoming cab. A scream of brakes along with shouted
obscenities greeted the nervous detective's maneuver.

When Cole's heart was out of his throat, he said, "Tell
Sergeant Silvestri that I'll call when I'm ready for someone to pick me up. It will be in about an hour."

"I can come back then, Commander."

"No!" Cole caught himself and said in a more normal
tone, "No, Manny, I've kept you away from your work
with Bronson long enough. Have the sergeant send someone else."

"Yes, sir."

Cole got out of the car and spied a break in traffic. He
was trotting toward the entrance to the Press Club when he
heard the screech of peeling rubber behind him. At the
divider, he turned to see Sherlock hot-rodding the police
car up Michigan Avenue. Cole shook his head and continued across the street.

CHAPTER 100

Cole was directed to the Scrivener's Grill on the eighth floor of the Press Club. He was met at the entrance by a maître d' with a grossly patronizing manner.

"I'm with First Deputy Superintendent Raymond Schmidt of the Chicago Police Department and Mr. Steven Zalkin."

Schmidt's name meant nothing to the pompous little man with the slicked down hair, but Zalkin's lit him up like a Christmas tree plugged into a wall socket.

"Oh yes, sir. Right this way, sir."

Cole was led to a table in an alcove, partially shielded from the rest of the diners. The table was large enough to seat ten. It had been set for three.

The maître d' pulled out a chair for Cole. Two waiters fussed about, filling the cop's water glass and opening the royal-purple velvet drapes to reveal a magnificent view of Grant Park and the western shore of Lake Michigan.

"Can I get you something to drink, sir?" a waiter asked. The maître d' hovered nearby like a vulture over a fresh carcass.

"Orange juice on the rocks," Cole said.

"Yes, sir."

The maître d' remained until the waiter recorded Cole's

drink order on a pad before turning to leave. Cole's voice stopped him. "Am I the first one to arrive?"

"No, sir. Mr. Zalkin went to the men's room. He'll be right back. Enjoy your lunch."

The waiter was back in less than a minute with Cole's orange juice. It was fresh and cold. He took a healthy swallow and turned to admire the view. He recalled a history class he'd taken for his undergraduate degree. The professor had mentioned that at one time the shoreline of Lake Michigan had come all the way up to where Michigan Avenue was today. Cole studied the trees in Grant Park. That area was the result of a landfill after the Chicago Fire in 1871.

Thinking of that history course made Cole recall that he had taken it in the fall of 1976. He had been lucky that the instructor had allowed him to do extra work for credit, because—

"Commander Cole, how are you? I'm Steven Zalkin."

The voice sounded vaguely familiar to Cole, but the image of the man erased this fading echo the moment the cop turned around.

Zalkin reeked of money. It was impossible to estimate the cost of the perfectly tailored gray silk suit he wore, but Cole figured it had to be somewhere in the two-thousand-dollar range. The accessories complemented the ensemble in such a flattering fashion that the policeman was definitely impressed.

Zalkin's handshake was firm and dry with just a hint of formidable strength in the squeeze. He was tanned, blond, and muscular, coming off as a hybrid of Dolph Lundgren and Robert Redford. But there was something familiar about him that eluded Larry Cole.

"Please sit down," Zalkin said, taking the seat facing the window. "I've got some bad news for you, Commander."

"Please, just Larry will be fine."

Zalkin fixed him with a stare of such intensity that Cole

could see the pattern of lines in his irises. "Okay, Larry it will be. Well, the bad news is that Ray Schmidt can't join us. I guess he's got some kind of flap over at police headquarters about what happened last night."

"The press is giving the department quite a going-over because of Delahanty's murder."

Zalkin leaned toward Cole. "May I speak frankly?"

"Of course."

"Frank Delahanty wasn't very well liked among his peers. He was arrogant, boorish, and a lush. A good writer of course, but not much of a human being."

Cole didn't feel comfortable talking about a dead man like this. "He did win the Pulitzer Prize."

"Sure he did." Zalkin leaned back in his chair, snatched his napkin from the tabletop, and signaled for their waiter. "What's that you're having, a screwdriver?"

"Just plain orange juice."

"You a teetotaler, Larry?"

"No. I don't drink on duty."

"Naturally." Zalkin turned to the waiter. "I'll have the same, and you can bring the menus. I don't want to keep the commander tied up too long." His eyes swung back to meet Cole's. "I know he's probably got quite a lot to do today."

The salad was crisp with a creamy house dressing, which Cole found outstanding. The main course, ordered by Zalkin with Cole's acquiescence, was a boneless breast of chicken with a hot fruit sauce and creamed spinach. Cole wasn't sure about the spinach until he tasted it. It was delicious. He looked up to compliment his host on the selection, only to find the millionaire staring at him again. Cole had caught him doing this twice during the salad course.

"I apologize for that crack I made about Delahanty, Larry," Zalkin said. "It was in poor taste."

"Forget it."

"But the guy did make his reputation taking cheap shots at people. However, there was no question that he was a good writer."

Cole kept eating.

"And he didn't care if what he wrote was the truth or not."

"It sounds like you knew Delahanty personally," Cole said, dabbing his lips with a napkin and taking a sip of his orange juice. He noticed that while Zalkin was talking about Delahanty his cheeks had colored just a bit.

"We've met. He wasn't much of a conversationalist, though."

Cole went back to his lunch.

Zalkin stared at him a moment before beginning to eat again.

"Tell me something," Cole said, without looking up.

"Sure."

"Have we ever met before?"

"I don't think so."

"Are you sure?" Cole put his fork down and studied his host. "I noticed you staring at me a couple of times like you were trying to place me or something."

"Was I?" Zalkin said with a hollow laugh. "I'm sorry, but I really wasn't aware of it."

"No sweat, but I was having the same problem with you."

"I don't understand."

Cole detected a bit of nervousness behind the million-dollar front.

"I've seen you before," Cole said. "I know it. I just can't place the when and where."

Zalkin looked down into his plate, speared a morsel of chicken, and chewed it slowly. When he looked back, Cole was staring at him.

"Now you're doing it," Zalkin said.

"Yes, I am," Cole responded with a smile.

The waiter hovered over them with a dessert menu.

"I don't know, Paulo," Zalkin said. "Why don't we let the commander decide."

"*Commandante,*" Paulo said, clicking his heels together in a salute that was as phony as his accent. "May I recommend the fresh strawberries and vanilla ice cream?"

Cole shrugged. "Sounds good to me."

"Excellent choice," Zalkin said. "I'll have the same."

As the waiter made his exit, Zalkin turned back to his guest, but before he could speak Cole said, "You must be very wealthy, Steve."

The self-satisfied smirk that spread across Zalkin's face told Cole that he had hit very close to where the man lived. "Let's just say that I've done all right for myself, Larry."

"Done all right at what?" Cole said.

"I beg your pardon?"

"How did you make your money?" the cop asked bluntly.

A strange look spread across Zalkin's face. It at once displayed amusement, deceit, and an underlying anxiety. Cole remembered that Lou Bronson had said that Zalkin was hiding something. Cole could now see that for himself.

"Most of my fortune came from investments, Larry."

"You must have had quite a lot of money to speculate with."

Zalkin smiled. "You'd be surprised what you can do today with a small amount of cash."

A silence developed between the two men when dessert was served. Cole frantically searched his mind for some clue that would either unlock the knot of misgivings and uncertainty he had about this man or dispel those uncertainties altogether. Zalkin concentrated with particular relish on his strawberries and ice cream and was seemingly oblivious to Cole's presence.

Zalkin finished his dessert and said, "You know, I met a couple of your detectives yesterday."

"Oh?"

"Yeah, a black guy named Bronson and a skinny white kid named Sherlock. They were checking into the death of some soldier who used to hang around my nightclub. They're a couple of pretty smart cops. Complement each other really well, like partners should. I heard someplace that you were real tight with a guy that you used to work with."

"I've had a few partners over the years, Steve."

"No," Zalkin said, nervously drumming his fingers on the table. "I read it somewhere that you'd been in a couple of really hairy cases with one guy. I just can't think of his name."

Cole refused to take the bait.

"Blackie!" Zalkin said. "That was it."

Cole smiled. "We haven't been what you would call 'partners' in a long time, Steve, but we're still close. Look, is there a phone around here I could use to call my office?"

"No sweat." Zalkin snapped his fingers and Paulo appeared instantly. "Bring Commander Cole a telephone."

"Yes, sir," the waiter said, moving away from the table at a dead sprint.

"They give real good service here," Cole said.

"I tip good. I guess you command-guys have to check in every hour or so?"

"No. They know where I am. I just need someone to pick me up."

"Nonsense," Zalkin said. "I can give you a lift."

"I wouldn't want to trouble you." But after the fishing expedition concerning Blackie, the ride was exactly what Cole wanted.

CHAPTER 101

A uniformed parking attendant drove Zalkin's Porsche Cabriolet around in front of the Press Club on Michigan Avenue. The car was silver with a black leather interior. Cole had seen these cars on the streets many times, but had never been in one. Without having to ask, he knew it probably cost more than he made in a year.

Zalkin made a show of handing the attendant a ten-dollar bill.

"Thank you, Mr. Zalkin." The attendant stood dutifully by until his benefactor slid beneath the wheel.

Cole was left to squeeze into the car by himself. He had difficulty adjusting his six-foot frame in the Porsche's seat. There was enough leg room, but getting in and out would take practice.

Zalkin slipped on a pair of aviator sunglasses and was pulling on a pair of black driving gloves when Cole finally got himself adjusted. The windows were down and the sun roof open.

"You'd better fasten your seat belt, Larry," Zalkin said. "It's the law, you know."

Cole couldn't tell if this was a dig or not, but he fastened himself in securely anyway.

Zalkin goosed the engine a couple of times before

letting out the clutch and shifting into first gear. The boom of the exhaust vibrated through the car.

"Hold on," Zalkin said with a smile, revealing a set of perfectly capped white teeth. Then they shot from the curb and through a hole in midday Michigan Avenue traffic. Zalkin switched lanes with a rude disregard for his fellow motorists, bringing blasts from horns and a skeptical frown from his passenger. But he handled the Porsche deftly and maneuvered into the lane to make a left turn on Monroe.

As he shot past the Art Institute into Grant Park, Cole shouted over the engine noise, "Do you always drive like this?"

Zalkin downshifted to take the turn onto Columbus Drive. The force bounced Cole around in the bucket seat, causing the straps of his seat belt to dig painfully into his flesh.

"Like what?" Zalkin's voice barely rose above the scream of the engine.

The traffic on Columbus Drive was considerably lighter than on Michigan Avenue. Zalkin made the light at Congress Parkway in front of Buckingham Fountain. He was not so lucky at Balbo Drive, where he was forced to stop behind a taxi.

Cole found his breathing labored and his palm moist where it had gripped the door handle for support. "Do you always drive like this, is what I said back there." He was glad his voice didn't tremble when he spoke.

"What's the matter, Larry? A little fast driving making you squeamish? I heard you were supposed to be a pretty tough customer."

Cole felt his anger rising, but he wasn't going to let this walking Saks Fifth Avenue dummy get to him. "I don't mind a little fast driving, but not on city streets."

Zalkin laughed. Then the light changed, and they were off again.

At first Cole thought he was going to slow down, but no sooner did the taxi change lanes, clearing a path in front of the Porsche, than Zalkin jammed the accelerator to the floor. As he whipped rapidly through the gears, Cole glanced at the speedometer. The needle hovered at ninety and was rising.

They were traveling south on Lake Shore Drive when Cole ordered, "Slow down!"

"I can't hear you." Zalkin manipulated buttons on the console between them, which shut both windows and the sunroof.

"I said, slow down!" With the wind and traffic noise suddenly cut off, Cole's voice came out a shout. He also noticed a tone of panic there. Zalkin's head turned in his direction. Although the policeman couldn't see his eyes, he knew Zalkin was mocking him.

"Take it easy," Zalkin said. "This thing was made to be driven fast. Has every safety feature available. We could roll completely over at this speed and I bet you wouldn't even get a scratch."

Soldier Field was a blur. They shot past the football stadium and in an instant were approaching the McCormick Place convention center. Ahead traffic was sparse. Every car they passed seemed to be standing still as the Porsche zipped past at twice the posted speed limit.

"Look," Cole's voice was deadly serious. "I want you to slow this car down right now!"

Zalkin did not look at Cole as he accelerated onto the Illinois 55 extension. They came out of the turn traveling west. The car's wheels barely touched the ground.

"So tell me, Larry, you've been a cop what, nineteen, twenty years now?" Zalkin said in a maddeningly conversational tone. "Boy, you must have had a lot of cases in all that time."

It took only scant seconds for the Porsche to cover the

distance between Lake Shore Drive and the entrance to the Dan Ryan Expressway. Cole heard Zalkin's words, but he was watching the tail ends of cars that crept onto the single-lane curving ramp at the posted thirty-five-miles-per-hour speed. As Zalkin and Cole approached in the Porsche, the cars appeared to grow from ant size to full size in the blink of an eye.

With a leer of intense enjoyment, Zalkin downshifted and expertly tapped the brake, slowing the tremendously powerful mechanical beast to a crawl.

"Tell me, Commander—in all those years, did you ever have a man escape on you?"

"I'll tell you what," Cole said, reaching to unsnap his seat belt as the Porsche crept up the ramp with the rest of the traffic, "I'll get out right here. You can—"

"I wouldn't dream of it, Commander!" Zalkin gunned the engine and the Porsche again rocketed forward.

There was an old but well-maintained Cadillac on the ramp in front of them. It was proceeding at a decent pace, but much too slowly for Zalkin. He hit the horn to get the driver's attention before jetting toward the narrow gap between the guardrail and the Cadillac-driver's side. At the last second the Cadillac swerved to the right, banging into the opposite guardrail. Zalkin slipped through the space without a scratch.

Cole was dumbfounded and at that instant knew that the man was indeed insane. Then, Zalkin's driving got worse.

The millionaire crossed the four lanes of the Chinatown feeder ramp to the Dan Ryan Expressway with his foot jammed to the floor of the Porsche and the heel of his hand leaning on the horn. He cut off two cars, one of which side-swiped another. The sideswiped car ended up being rear-ended by a car coming up from behind. Before the multicar accident was over, the Porsche was out of sight.

"What in the hell are you trying to do, man? Get us

killed?" Cole said, bracing himself against the dashboard and roof as best he could in the narrow confines of the small car.

"No, Commander. I just want you to tell me if you've ever had any bad guys get away from you." Zalkin could have been discussing the weather for all the emotion that was in his voice. However, the car was traveling at over 110 miles an hour and accelerating.

"Sure, I've lost suspects," Cole said, watching in horror as the world outside the Porsche became a seamless blur.

"What were their names?"

"What?"

"What were their names, Commander Cole? I need to know."

The anger began bubbling inside Cole to drown his fear. He thought of all that this man would be robbing him of if he killed him in this car.

"There was only one who escaped me," Cole said, reaching beneath his jacket.

"Only one? Excellent. What was his name?" Zalkin's attention was focused on the road in front of him.

"Zykus," Cole said through clenched teeth. "Martin Zykus!" Then Cole jammed the barrel of his automatic against Zalkin's temple. "Now slow down, right now!"

For a brief instant, Zalkin's face split into a grin. Then it dissolved into a mask of stone. He downshifted and began pumping the brakes. They shot under the Fifty-first Street exit sign and up the ramp. At the top, Zalkin halted the car. Cole still held the gun to his head.

"Does this mean I'm under arrest, Commander?"

Cole looked through the sloping back window, expecting a squadron of state police cars to come screaming up the ramp from the expressway in pursuit of the Porsche. The ramp was empty.

Cole removed the gun from Zalkin's head. "Pull over in front of the station."

As the millionaire complied, he said, "Of course, I'll make good on any damages I caused."

"You could have killed someone back there," Cole said.

Zalkin's voice rose in anger. "Thousands of people are killed every year on our expressways, Commander. So what are a few more? Do you see any damage on this car? No. Well then, it's going to be your word against mine that I was doing anything but proceeding in a lawful manner."

"You forgot about our witnesses back there, pal," Cole said, as Zalkin pulled up in front of the station.

"Oh c'mon, Cole. I'll buy them off. You know that I'll give them twice as much as those rattletraps they're driving are worth, so why don't we stop wasting time?"

Cole stared at his crazy host. "What was all this about, anyway?"

Zalkin turned to stare straight ahead. "I don't know what you're talking about. I was just giving you a lift back to work."

Cole studied him. "I'll get a list of those involved in the accidents down there from the state police. I'll expect you to do right by them."

"I give you my word," Zalkin said. "Now, if there's nothing else . . ."

Cole removed the clip from his automatic and ejected the chambered round. He tossed the bullet in Zalkin's lap.

The millionaire fished it out of his crotch. "What's this for?"

Cole got out of the car. "A little memento of this meeting. Something to remember me by if we ever meet again. After all, you came very close to having that piece of lead as a permanent part of your skull."

With a sneer, Steven Zalkin drove away.

CHAPTER 102

When did you find out he was stealing from Astrolab, Corporal?" Lou Bronson asked Cpl. Deborah Winters.

They were in Interrogation Room A on the second floor of Area One. Present were Cap. Robert Watkins, Manny Sherlock, Bronson, and Sgt. Blackie Silvestri. Watkins watched the proceedings with ever-increasing awe, as the attractive young woman in the olive-drab uniform related how SFC. Bryce Carduci made a joke of Astrolab's elaborate security system and took anything he wanted.

"He told me he was stealing the second time he took me out." She kept her eyes down as she talked. "He showed me a big wad of money with lots of hundreds and fifties. For Christmas he took me shopping on Michigan Avenue. He spent over three thousand dollars on me."

"Do you know who he sold the weapons to?" Bronson, serving as sole interrogator, asked.

Debbie Winters shrugged and flipped a few errant hairs off her forehead before saying, "At first, a lot of people."

"What do you mean 'at first'? "

She looked up at Bronson, then quickly back down at her hands. "He used to sell the sidearms to just about anybody. But he asked a lot of money for them and didn't get many takers. He wouldn't sell them any ammunition, so they stopped coming around."

"Who were they?"

"Gang members mostly, I guess." She glanced nervously at Bronson. "They were all black. Bryce said he wouldn't give bullets to the likes of them."

Bronson displayed no reaction. "Who else did he sell to?"

Debbie fidgeted in her seat. "I think he did some business with the man who owned Club Cosmos."

"Do you remember the owner's name?"

She nodded. "It was Steve."

"Do you remember his last name?"

She shook her head in the negative.

"You said you thought he did business with this Steve. Didn't you ever witness any of the sales?"

Again she shook her head in the negative.

"It would be better if you answered me with a 'yes' or 'no,' Corporal. That cuts down the confusion."

"I'm sorry," she said, softly. "No. I never saw him actually sell anything to this Steve, but he would talk about it. Said Steve had a lot of money and didn't mind spending it."

"Do you know what he sold Steve?"

"Everything."

"Could you be more specific?"

"He sold him everything. If Astrolab had it, Bryce said he stole it and sold it to Steve."

"Do you have any idea who might have killed Sergeant Carduci?"

For the first time since the interrogation began, her eyes flared with anger. "A lot of people could have killed him, Officer. I could have done it myself. He was just that kind of man."

"Lou," Blackie said, tapping Bronson on the shoulder.

Together with Sherlock they stepped from the interrogation room.

"I think that gives us enough to get a warrant to search Zalkin's place," Blackie said.

Bronson nodded. "What do you think, Manny?" Bronson surprised his partner with the question.

It took Sherlock a moment to find his voice. "I think we have enough to get a warrant for Zalkin's place, Sarge."

"I thought you were gonna say that, kid," Blackie said with a sneer.

But Bronson noticed his partner had something else on his mind. "Go ahead, Manny. Let's hear it all."

"Well, we can go ahead with the warrant, Lou, but I got a feeling there's a lot more to this than what we've uncovered so far. How do we tie this Zalkin in with the Temple of Allah, Delahanty's death, and Our Lady of Peace?"

"You guys can do that after we house the asshole for possession of stolen property," Blackie said.

"Manny's got a good point, Sarge," Bronson said. "Suppose we do move on Zalkin and come up empty? Corporal Winters never saw Carduci sell him anything, so that will place us right back where we started from and let our boy know we're on to him."

"So what do you recommend, Lou?"

"We go on with the investigation and see if we can get something more concrete on him. Something that'll keep his twenty million and a smart lawyer from springing him before the ink on the warrant is dry."

"I'll have to run this by the boss," Blackie said. "He hasn't called to have someone pick him up yet."

Manny Sherlock looked over Blackie's shoulder. "Sarge, the commander just walked in."

Blackie turned in time to see Cole stomping angrily into his office. "Looks like he's out for bear."

"Who are you telling?" Bronson added.

"You guys get back to little Debbie," Blackie said. "I'm going to see what's wrong with the boss."

Cole was seated behind his desk, staring off into space, when Blackie stepped inside the office.

"Was the Press Club food that bad?"

It took Cole a moment before he realized Blackie was there. He motioned for him to close the door and sit down.

"December 1976," Cole began, "you and I started working together."

"Actually, it was Thanksgiving Day in '76."

"Okay, whatever. We talked about Martin Zykus last night. The last time we saw him was in the Sherman House in December of '76. Somehow he got out of there, and his body was never found. There's still a warrant on file for him downtown, which has never been served. He was never heard from again. At least, not in Chicago."

"I guess I follow you so far."

"Now Zykus," Cole fought to keep anger from taking control of his voice, "used a set of lock picks to get inside Louise Stallings's apartment. He also sold Randolph Klein's jewelry someplace. The question is, where did he sell the jewelry and get the lock picks?"

"Lots of places. You've got to figure every neighborhood had its local fence. Hell, it's the same today."

"But what local fence would have been a snitch for Frank Delahanty?"

Blackie sat up straight. "Abdul Ali Malik—a.k.a. Richard Johnson, also known as Slick Rick Johnson."

"Right. It was about five years ago that Delahanty blew the whistle on Johnson. Wrote about his phony religion scam. Told how he'd been keeping our dearly departed columnist informed of street goings-on for about ten years. Ten years—taking us right back to 1976."

"Yeah," Blackie said. "They sent some reporters out to talk to Johnson, but he clammed up."

There was now excitement in Cole's voice. "Okay, the night we chased Zykus into the Sherman House, we got a tip from the Nineteenth District desk as to where we could find him. Later, I heard Delahanty got the same tip. That's why he wrote that column about Zykus."

Blackie nodded. "It was his way of making peace with the Leprechaun. As I recall, he called Zykus a lot of vile names. But then, Delahanty always called everybody he wrote about a lot of vile names."

"So that gives us the two crimes." Cole held up his fingers. "Both for revenge. Zykus used Abdul Ali Malik as his fence, who rats on him to us and Delahanty. Delahanty writes about Zykus and flips on Malik ten years later. Zykus comes back to Chicago and kills them both."

"Zykus?" Blackie said, looking questioningly at Cole.

The commander nodded. "I had lunch with him today, Blackie. Martin Zykus is Steven Zalkin."

CHAPTER 103

APRIL 19, 1991
3:00 P.M.

Steven Zalkin strained under the four-hundred-pound barbell, lifting it off his chest for the final repetition. His torso was slick with sweat from the heavy workout. As the weight reached its apex, the muscles and sinews of his upper body bulged. He let out a loud groan and dropped the weight in the rack above his head.

Getting off the incline bench, he snatched up a towel and wiped the sweat from his face. His muscles were gorged with blood, giving him a pumped feeling of strength to accompany the sense of well-being that always followed his workouts. At that instant, he felt truly invincible.

Zalkin checked his watch. He had almost two hours before his meeting with the priest at Our Lady of Peace rectory. He had timed it to be right before dinner. That would give him the entire night to do the rest.

He entered the sauna and sat down on a wooden bench, feeling the sweat on his exposed flesh dry as the coals heated.

Fifteen years, he thought, and Cole still frightened him. Oh, Zalkin had put a scare into the cop as well, but Cole had handled it better. That part with the bullet at the end had been sheer artistry. Zalkin chuckled in the silence of the rapidly heating wooden box.

Zalkin had to figure that Cole recognized him by now. Hell, the cop was supposed to. In a way, everything depended on it. However, Zalkin knew how the policeman would react. This was no straight chase of your everyday bad guy. Zalkin's money, his gift to the department, and his friendship with most of the top police brass would cause Detective Commander Cole to proceed cautiously. In twenty-four hours Cole would be ready to move, but by then it would be too late. Zalkin had a much faster timetable.

The sauna was going full blast now, and the perspiration was again starting to flow off the millionaire. Heat and warmth. He opened his hand and felt the air. Before they had worked on his fingers, the frostbite scars had made them looked deformed. Idly, he rubbed the palm of his other hand across his stomach. That was where he had taken the series of rabies shots.

Thirst and heat drove him out of the sauna. Walking from the gym area through the workroom, he thought about the differences between the man he had been and the man he was now. Money could make a lot of difference in the way a person looked, talked, and acted. But was there really any difference between Martin Zykus and Steven Zalkin?

The bathroom was as big as his old northside apartment had been. Zalkin looked at his reflection in one of the frosted-edge full-length mirrors. What he saw there made him smile. Then something—a shadow, or possible defect in the glass—drew him closer.

He wore blue contact lenses, which he popped out, exposing the natural brown color beneath them. Martin Zykus stared back at him.

"Boy."

He spun around, only to realize that what he had heard was not a sound, but a thought.

"You wasn't nothing then, and you still ain't nothing."

At times over the last fifteen years, when Zalkin was depressed or under heavy stress, the voice of Dave Higgins came to him. The last time had been yesterday, when he had been arrested for beating up the truck driver. When he was in prison, Zalkin had thought the words were echoing through his mind to comfort him. But Dave Higgins had never said much of a comforting nature.

Initially, he figured the simple phrases were memories of things Higgins had said before he died. Eventually, however, they started to sound original, and began to come unbidden into his mind. Lately, they came more frequently. Lately as well, Zalkin had begun answering them out loud.

"You're wrong, old man. Look at me. I'm a multimillionaire. I could buy and sell two-bit fry cooks like you ten times a day out of my pocket change."

"Sure you could, boy. But I wasn't no Chicago cop with a .45 in his fist, who was ready to kill you fifteen years ago and will be just as glad to oblige tonight."

"I'll take care of Cole and Silvestri, you old fool. Then Louise is going to be mine."

"You ain't seen her, have you, boy? She's a nun now. A real Holy Roller. She won't give a hoot's damn about your fancy suits, your fancy cars, or all of your filthy money. You can't buy her."

Zalkin grinned. "I won't have to. I've got something else planned for her."

"Okay, boy, let's hear it."

"Just wait a few more hours, old man. You'll see it for yourself."

The voice in Zalkin's mind fell silent for a moment. He thought it was gone. The voice did that sometimes, without warning. Just as suddenly, it was back.

"So, let me get this straight, boy. You're going to take on the Chicago Police Department and God all in one night?"

"That's right. Just me. I'll show them who I am."

"I guess you'll try. Well, if this plan is like all the rest you've had during your worthless life, it's probably screwed up, too."

"It will work. My plans have worked so far against Johnson and Delahanty."

"Yeah, I seen them boys down here. Delahanty looks like a used KKK cross, and Johnson's still trying to pull himself together."

"Make room, old man," Zalkin shouted in the emptiness of his bathroom. "Cole and Silvestri are on the way."

"The only one I'm making room for is you, boy. I got a seat in hell for you right next to me, and I guarantee you'll never be cold again."

"Shut up," Zalkin said.

There was no response.

"I said, shut up!"

Still nothing.

"SHUT UP!" Zalkin snatched a can of shaving cream from the sink counter and hurled it at the mirror. The explosion of glass was as loud as a pistol shot. Shards flew through the air to slice into Zalkin's legs and arms.

When the glass had settled, the voice whispered, *"Right next to me, boy."*

CHAPTER 104

APRIL 19, 1991
3:15 P.M.

The elevator opened on the sixth floor of police head-quarters and First Deputy Superintendent Raymond Schmidt stepped off. The heavyset man stood motionless in the corridor for a moment, as if he were lost or had gotten off on the wrong floor.

A female sergeant approached from the opposite end of the hall. She was so absorbed in a report she was reading that she didn't see Schmidt until she was only a few feet away from him. "Good afternoon, sir."

He stared blankly back at her. She noticed how pale he was. There was a thin sheen of perspiration visible on his forehead.

"Good afternoon," he said in such a low tone of voice that she barely heard him.

The sergeant was dumbfounded. Schmidt was notorious for never speaking to menials, which for him amounted to everyone except the superintendent. She stared at him in shock as he walked past her into his office.

* * *

Lt. Pat Roberts could see that things had not gone well for the first deputy during his meeting with the superintendent. For one, the meeting had been going on since eleven A.M. On the other hand, rumors had been floating around the headquarters building that Schmidt was not only in hot water with the superintendent, but with the mayor as well. Then Roberts saw Schmidt's face.

He had never seen his boss ill, or for that matter, even tired. But now the man looked fit for the undertaker.

Schmidt walked, or more appropriately shuffled, past him. With more concern that he could have thought he could generate for the man, Roberts followed him into the office.

Schmidt went behind his desk and collapsed into the chair. Leaning forward, he placed his elbows on the surface before clutching his forehead with the tips of his thick fingers. His usually square shoulders were rounded, and he gave the appearance of a man many years older.

"Are you okay, boss?" Roberts asked.

Schmidt didn't answer him.

"What's the matter, sir?"

Schmidt looked up as if seeing Roberts for the first time and said, "He demoted me."

The lieutenant sank into one of the chairs in front of Schmidt's desk. "Where did he assign you?"

"I guess to wherever they need a watch commander."

"You're going all the way from being the first deputy to the job of a watch commander? Can he do that?"

Schmidt's bloodshot eyes flashed a little of their old fire. "He can do any goddamned thing that he wants. He is the superintendent of police."

"Yes, sir." Roberts leaped to his feet, properly chastised. "What will you do now?"

"I don't know yet. I'm still the first deputy until Monday. At least for payroll purposes. A lot can happen in that time."

CHAPTER 105

William Riseman sat at his desk, talking to Comdr. Larry Cole on the police auxiliary telephone system. Riseman had heard a lot of strange stories during his career as a police officer and didn't believe that anything was necessarily impossible. However, what he was hearing from the man he considered to be his best field commander strained credibility.

Riseman was idly doodling on a notepad as Cole talked:

> Zalkin—Zykus
> Zykus—Zalkin
> ?????????????

"Hold it a minute, Larry," Riseman said, failing to conceal the irritation in his voice. It had been a long day at headquarters. "You really have nothing concrete connecting Steven Zalkin with the rapist who got away from you and Silvestri fifteen years ago."

There was a knock on Riseman's office door.

"Hold on a minute," he said to Cole, before yelling, "Come in."

In the brief instant before the door opened, Riseman realized that he was riding the edge. He'd been up most of the night on the Chan–Delahanty slayings, he hadn't eaten lunch, and the phone calls, including this one, were starting to give him a headache. He'd learned long ago that getting too strung-out didn't get the job done any better or faster. With a conscious act of will he let his body relax, allowing the tension he felt to dissipate.

Riseman's secretary looked in. "I'm sorry to bother you, boss, but the superintendent wants to see you at 3:45 sharp."

The initial shock made Riseman forget that Cole was on the phone.

"Thanks," he said softly to the secretary. Then he returned to the phone. "Go ahead, Larry."

But when Cole continued his report, Riseman wasn't listening with his full attention. When Cole finally wound up the story the chief said, "You'll need to get something a bit more concrete before I start sounding the alarm on this one, Larry. Keep me posted on your progress."

Hanging up, Riseman hit his intercom button. "Hold all calls until after my meeting with the superintendent."

He leaned back in his chair and tried to relax. He had fifteen minutes to go before the scheduled appointment.

William R. Riseman had been a policeman for thirty-five years. He had a masters degree in psychology from the University of Illinois at Chicago, and had even taught there briefly before becoming a police officer. It had taken him twenty years to go from being a beat cop to chief of detectives. For the last fifteen years he had coveted no other post in the department.

The detective division was his life. He had been married twice. Once to a professor of economics at Illinois, and again to a female police officer. Neither union had lasted longer than three years. Both times his wives had complained that he loved the department more than he did them. Thinking back on it, he had to admit that they were right.

In thirty-five years he had seen his share of superintendents come and go. Some had been better than others.
This current one he rated above average, which—given
that the man had come out of administration as opposed to
a field unit—was high. The administrative-background
factor had Riseman concerned over how the superintendent would react to the pressure following Delahanty's
murder.

He remembered a superintendent a few years back who
had attempted to cover all his mistakes by blaming them
directly on the shortcomings of his command officers. In
each case, the officer blamed was promptly sacked for
incompetence. He hadn't lasted long as Chicago's top cop,
but he had destroyed a lot of careers before he was finally
booted out himself.

Riseman watched the second hand swing rapidly around
past twelve. He had fourteen minutes left.

He got up and went into his closet-sized washroom. He
rolled up his sleeves, loosened his tie, and splashed cold
water on his face. He looked at his reflection in the mirror
above the sink. On his next birthday he would be sixty-one,
two years short of mandatory retirement. He had been
complimented many times before on looking ten years
younger than his chronological age. He still kept himself in
good shape and was as up on current investigative procedure as anyone in big-city law enforcement in the country.
He loved police work, and especially being the chief of
detectives.

He dried his face and checked the clock. He had eleven
minutes. More than enough time to change into a clean shirt.
As he stripped to the waist, he considered the subtle hint that
this was not simply a meeting between the department's
chief executive and a command officer. This was because
Riseman had been given a specific time.

Traditionally, a specific time always signaled a

demotion or a promotion. All command slots within the department were currently filled, making promotions unlikely. If the superintendent had simply wanted to see him, he would have called and had him come down immediately. If the superintendent was busy when Riseman arrived, the chief would simply wait in the outer office until he could be seen. It was the way things were done. Appointments served a more specific purpose.

Wearing a freshly laundered shirt, Riseman knotted his tie and ran a comb through his iron-gray hair. His .38 was holstered on his left side and his gold star, bearing the engraving "Chicago Police Chief of Detectives," was snapped to his belt.

"Give 'em hell," he said to his reflection in the bathroom mirror, but his bravado did not erase the hollow feeling in his gut.

Slipping on his suit jacket, he took one last look around the office and started for the door. On his way out he spoke to every detective he passed, no matter what their rank or status. To Riseman, his subordinates were the real reason for any success he had ever achieved during his tenure as chief of detectives. Any failures he bore the responsibility for alone.

"Good afternoon, Chief," the receptionist in the outer lobby of the superintendent's office greeted him. "You're a couple of minutes early. Would you like to take a seat?"

Riseman managed a weak smile. She was being damned cheerful under the circumstances, but then he realized that she had been here for a few years and had probably seen this kind of thing happen more than once.

He sat down, hitching his pant legs up to protect his trouser creases. According to his watch, he had two minutes and thirty seconds to go.

The intercom on the receptionist's desk buzzed. Riseman jumped.

She gave him an apologetic smile. "Something's wrong with it, Chief. Sounds like a Martian death-ray. Every time it goes off, I think it's going to disintegrate me."

Riseman stood up and carefully straightened his suit jacket. He waited until she said, "You may go in now," before starting for the superintendent's inner office. He walked erect with his head held high.

The superintendent was writing furiously on a yellow legal pad. He was in shirtsleeves and barely looked up when the chief of detectives walked in. He kept writing while motioning with his free hand for Riseman to take one of the chairs across from him.

Riseman sat down and waited.

Thirty seconds later, the superintendent put down his pen and leaned back in his chair. The strain on his face was evident.

"I've just drafted my own press release on Delahanty. Right now that's about all I can do until we can break this thing. Your people haven't come up with anything yet, have they, Bill?"

"Nothing we can really afford to go public with right now, Superintendent," Riseman said evenly.

"I was afraid of that." The superintendent shook his head, which caused Riseman's heart rate to increase. "After last night, we've had to engage in a lot of damage control and we're still going down fast. We can't just say it happened without affixing responsibility. Delahanty's dead and he was under our protection. Even though Chan was killed and Charles is in critical condition, we look bad. Inept. Amateurish."

Riseman listened to the wordy litany with silently raging impatience.

"Well, I had to do something about it. Maybe I should have done something a long time ago, but . . ." The superintendent paused, locked into some memory he refused to share with the chief of detectives. ". . . but I didn't. Now's the time."

The superintendent picked up a typed sheet of paper from his desk. Riseman couldn't see what was on the paper, but he could tell it bore the format of a Personnel Order. The superintendent read, "Effective April 22, 1991, Raymond Schmidt will be returned to his career service rank of captain." He looked up at Riseman. "Also effective on that date, William R. Riseman will be promoted from Chief of Detectives to the rank of First Deputy Superintendent of Police."

Riseman didn't respond.

"Well?" the superintendent said.

"Sir?"

"Do you accept?"

Calmly, Riseman nodded. "Yes, sir. I accept."

CHAPTER 106

APRIL 19, 1991
4:15 P.M.

Sister Mary Louise crossed the courtyard behind the church, heading for the back door of the rectory. In her hand she clutched the message from Father Ken, which was left for her in the school office: "Come to the rectory and meet our benefactor as soon as you can."

The nun felt a knot of apprehension in her stomach. She realized that she hadn't been quite right since Father Ken had mentioned this "benefactor." A benefactor whose last name began with the letter Z.

She let herself in through the back door. The kitchen was empty, but the housekeeper had left Father Ken's dinner on the stove. Sister Mary Louise walked over and lifted the lid on the reheatable metal pan, revealing a broiled steak, mashed potatoes, and green peas. She wondered if the pastor would eat it.

Replacing the lid, she turned to walk into the dining room when she became aware of the silence. If Father Ken had a guest, then she should have been able to hear them talking—unless they were on one of the upper floors. She listened more carefully. She heard nothing.

Slowly, she moved to the wooden door between the kitchen and the dining room. Something, she wasn't sure whether it was a dull thump from far away or the rustle of cloth close up, came from the other side. But the sound was fleeting, and quickly followed by the resumption of silence.

With each passing second she was becoming more and more alarmed. Her primary fear was for Father Ken, but the pounding of her heart revealed her own fear for herself.

Stop this!

She realized that she was simply working herself up for no logical reason. There was nothing to be afraid of in this place she had been walking in and out of for years. There were millions of people with last names beginning with the letter Z, and nightmares were nothing more than bad dreams—which have nothing to do with reality.

Reaching out, she pushed open the door and walked boldly into the dining room.

She thought the room was empty. She started through to the opposite door, which would take her to the front hall. She was halfway across the room when she heard a noise behind her.

Terrified, she spun around.

He was sitting in a chair in the small alcove off the dining room. The midafternoon sun was at such an angle as to throw him into shadow. She only got impressions rather than substance: blond hair, broad shoulders, tanned skin, expensive clothing.

"Good afternoon," he said, standing. She still could not see him clearly.

"Where's Father Ken?" She tried and failed to keep fear out of her voice as she backed toward the hall door.

He didn't move. "He went to get one of the parish photo albums. He said he'd be right back."

She took another step backward. "If you'll please excuse me, I'll go and see what's keeping him."

"You're Sister Mary Louise Stallings, aren't you?"

"Yes." She had made it to the door. She placed her back against the wooden frame.

Before he could say anything, the door opened. The edge slammed into her back, propelling her into the room. Father Ken walked in, carrying a photo album.

"Are you hurt, Sister?" the priest said with concern.

"No." She rubbed her shoulder where the door had struck her. "I'm okay."

"Why were you standing there? If I'd have been in a hurry we could have had a real problem here."

She managed a weak smile, but made no comment.

"Well," Father Ken said, regaining his composure, "come and meet our guest."

The priest led the way around the dining-room table. Slowly, Sister Mary Louise followed. Their guest did not move as they approached.

"Sister Mary Louise Stallings, I'd like to introduce you to Mr. Steven Zalkin."

She raised her hand to shake his. He stepped forward into the light. Taking her hand he smiled and said, "Sister Mary Louise, how nice it is to meet you."

CHAPTER 107

Manny Sherlock pulled into the parking lot behind Area One and left his squad car double-parked in the aisle. He ran as fast as he could to the back door of the station and bounded up the stairs. On the second floor he sprinted toward the commander's office, employing an impressive broken-field run to dodge around obstacles.

Blackie Silvestri was seated at his desk, reviewing reports and chewing on a cigar. When he looked up and saw the long-legged detective bounding in his direction, Blackie frowned. The sergeant found that this was generally his expression whenever he saw the junior officer.

"Sarge, I've got to see the commander right away," Sherlock gasped.

"Take it easy, kid," Blackie said, around the cigar. "All he sent you to do was get an old newspaper clipping."

"I got it," Manny said. "But I found out something else while I was downtown that I know the commander will want to hear about."

"I hope for your sake that whatever it is is damn good."

"So I looked through the microfilm like you told me for Frank Delahanty's column on a guy named Zykus. Well, I found it. It was in the edition for December sixth, 1976."

Cole sat behind his desk, staring blankly at the detective. Blackie Silvestri stood behind Sherlock looking as if he was having an ulcer attack.

"I'm having the page the column appeared on copied when I run into this guy named Carpenter, who I came on the job with. He rides a three-wheeler on Michigan Avenue out of the Eighteenth District and—"

"Sherlock, you're wasting the boss's time!" Blackie said angrily.

"Let him finish, Sarge," Cole said.

Blackie fumed as Sherlock continued.

"So Carpenter tells me that the whole district is buzzing about how the first deputy stormed into the station yesterday and forced this Lieutenant Holland to release a prisoner. I also found out from Carpenter that the released prisoner was none other than Steven Zalkin."

This perked up Cole's and Blackie's interest considerably, but Sherlock was far from through.

"Carpenter even tells me that the second watch lock-up keeper printed Zalkin before Schmidt did the Houdini act for him."

At the mention of "Houdini," Cole's jaw rippled, but he managed to keep his composure.

"After I got the photocopy of Delahanty's column, I hightailed it over to the Eighteenth District and went back to the lock-up. The day watch lock-up keeper was gone, but I asked the afternoon man to take a look around for the prints. He found them in a wastebasket."

Both Cole and Blackie were now very interested.

"I ran the cards on the facsimile machine in Eighteen to the downtown fingerprint computer and drove to headquarters while they were being processed." Sherlock opened the envelope he carried. He pulled out the photostated copy of Frank Delahanty's December 1976 column, "Human Street Vermin," and a Chicago Police Department criminal history sheet. He laid both on Cole's desk.

As Cole picked up the rap sheet, Sherlock explained, "The name belonging to those prints is not Steven Zalkin, but a Stephen M. Zickus."

"Damn!" Cole jumped to his feet. "We've got him."

Blackie came around to look over Cole's shoulder.

The rap sheet had only three entries:

March 9, 1977—Arrested Fort Wayne, Indiana
Charge: Contributing to the sexual delinquency of a minor.
Disposition: Discharged for want of prosecution.
May 21, 1980—Arrested Denver, Colorado.
Charge: Gambling and inmate of a disorderly house.
Disposition: Plea of guilty/fined $50.00
November 28, 1981—Arrested Sacramento, California.
Charge: Aggravated criminal sexual assault.
Disposition: Convicted—sentenced to serve four to
ten years in the California State Penitentiary at San Quentin.
Paroled: July 15, 1987

"Welcome home, Marty," Blackie said.

"Okay, this is enough to go downtown with," Cole said. "Blackie, you start working on the search warrant affidavits. Manny, you did one helluva job on this. You and Bronson are going to be part of the raiding party when we go after Mr. Zalkin, or Zykus, or whatever the hell he wants to be called."

"Thank you, sir," Sherlock said, beaming with every inch of his six-foot-four-inch frame.

"Aren't you forgetting something, boss?" Blackie said.

Cole looked at him quizzically. "Like what?"

"Excuse us a minute, Manny," Blackie said.

Obediently, but still glowing, Sherlock left the office, carefully closing the door behind him.

"What about the nun, Larry?" Blackie said.

"Louise Stallings? What about her?"

"Somebody needs to talk to her about all this," Blackie

said. "And maybe she should have a guard until this is over."

Cole nodded. "Okay, get to work on the affidavits and send Lou Bronson in here."

"You gonna send Bronson to see the nun?"

"Yes, but I'm going, too. I want to explain to Louise what's going on. Since it's Bronson's parish, I intend to leave him there in case Zalkin does show up."

CHAPTER 108

APRIL 19, 1991
4:27 P.M.

And I guess I was as selfish and insensitive as any other businessman," Steven Zalkin was saying. "You can lose sight of who you are and what you are in God's greater scheme of things when you're financially successful. Now, I hope by my contributions to get back in touch with not only my own immortal soul, but also the Lord."

They were seated around the rectory's dining-room table. Zalkin had made a show of clucking over the parish and school albums, which the priest had shown him, while Louise had gone to the kitchen to make coffee. When she returned, Zalkin had launched into his phony rich-man's-soul-baring monologue. He could see that the priest was eating it up, but Louise was staring at him with an intensity bordering on hostility.

"I think that's a very admirable way to feel, Mr. Zalkin," Father Ken said.

Zalkin saw the priest cast a sideways glance at Louise. There was more questioning than reproof in the look.

For a moment the nun's penetrating stare dropped to the silver coffee service. She made a show of refilling Zalkin's and Father Ken's cups before asking, "Are you originally from Chicago?"

The question caught him off guard. "Why, yes, I am. Of course, for the last ten or fifteen years I've done a great deal of traveling."

"What part of town are you from?"

"Sister, please," the priest chuckled nervously. "You sound like a police interrogator."

"Oh, I don't mind answering questions, Father. It helps me get back in touch with my roots." He noticed that she was waiting for his answer. "But somehow I don't think that the part of town I'm from will be the only question Sister Mary Louise will want to ask me. If you don't mind, I'd like to use the washroom before the inquisition begins."

"Right this way, Steve," the black priest said, standing up and heading for the dining-room door.

Zalkin hesitated a moment and looked at Louise. It had been such a long time since he'd been this close to her. And he planned to get a lot closer.

He'd been idly playing with a ballpoint pen with which he drew circles and squares on a pad of paper he'd removed from his pocket. When they had sat down at the dining-room table, he had produced the pen and paper. Now, he clicked the pen twice, placed it beside the pad, and stood up.

Father Ken escorted him to the dining room door. "You go down this hall. The bathroom is the third door on the right."

Zalkin nodded and left the room. He was holding his breath.

When the door swung shut behind their millionaire benefactor, Father Ken whirled on Sister Mary Louise. Rushing
around the table he confronted her.

"What in the name of God are you trying to do, Sister?"
He kept his voice as low as he could. "You're treating a
man who's about to give us a half-million dollars like a
common criminal."

She looked up at him through fatigued eyes. "Father, I
don't believe he is who he presents himself to be. There's
something . . ." She reached up a hand to touch her forehead.

"Louise, aren't you feeling well?" Father Ken asked
with concern. "Maybe that's why you're acting so . . ." A
wave of dizziness swept over him. He reached out and
grabbed the edge of the table for support.

Sister Mary Louise began slumping to the floor, and he
reached out to grab her. But there was no strength left in
his body, and his head felt as if he were wearing a
thousand-pound sweat band. The room dissolved rapidly
into blackness. The priest collapsed to the floor beside
Sister Mary Louise.

Zalkin had merely retreated a few steps down the corridor
outside the dining room. He removed a breathing mask
from his pocket and placed it over his mouth and nose. The
mask had been chemically treated to filter out the aerosol
nerve gas he had released into the atmosphere of the stuffy
room. He waited thirty seconds before returning to the
door and swinging it open. He saw them lying side by side
on the floor.

He slipped the mask's elastic band around the back of his
head before going over to check their pulses. The CZ nerve
gas had to be concentrated in order to work in the area of a

large room. In sufficient doses, it could kill; even in its present diluted dosage, it could cause someone with a bad heart to have an attack. He found both their pulses strong; the priests's however, had a slightly irregular rhythm.

Zalkin stood up and turned off the dispenser hidden within the body of the ballpoint pen he'd been doodling with. He opened two of the windows in the alcove, allowing a breeze to blow into the room. He wasn't worried about them recovering for a while. The effects of the CZ would keep them out for at least an hour, and they would have side effects of wooziness and headaches for at least twenty-four hours. It was because of the aerosol's potency that he kept the mask on.

Zalkin hefted the priest's body over his shoulder and carried him out of the dining room into the hall. Father Ken had given the millionaire a tour of the rectory when he'd arrived; he'd been waiting for Sister Mary Louise before providing the entire tour of the Our Lady of Peace Church and School facility. So it was that Zalkin knew exactly where he was going when he stepped out into the hall and took the second door on the left. This led down into the rectory basement.

The stairs were dark, but Zalkin made his way along well enough by feel. The priest's slender body was little strain for his bodybuilder's strength. He remembered that there was a switch on the wall at about the midway point of the descent. He was now totally immersed in the dark, which caused some of his old phobias to begin acting up. He stopped, balanced the priest precariously on his shoulder, and reached out blindly into the dark. His hand touched something that clung to his fingertips. He jumped—and in doing so, lost control of the priest's body. The unconscious Ken Smith fell into the darkness. The body thumped loudly down the stairs to land at the bottom.

Zalkin, however, was more concerned about what he had touched. He rubbed his fingers to find only the fine strands of a cobweb clinging to his flesh. It took him a moment to bring his breathing back to normal—an effort, because of the mask. Again, he reached out into the dark, and this time found the light switch.

The priest was bleeding from the head when Zalkin found him. He was still breathing, but there was no way of telling the extent of his injuries. To make sure he didn't get any blood on his clothing, Zalkin sat him up and dragged him the rest of the way by the back of his collar.

The idea had come to Zalkin during the rectory tour. The basement was equipped with a small chapel that was artfully appointed with hand-carved statues, a marble altar, a wooden altar railing, and ten wooden pews. The priest explained that the chapel had once been used for daily masses.

Zalkin dumped the priest in the last pew and went back for the nun.

He was just starting across the dining room when he heard voices coming through the windows he had left open to vent the anesthetic.

"We seldom use the front door, Commander," said a voice that sounded familiar to Zalkin. "This place is supposed to be like a home where the kids come in the back door whenever they want."

This was followed by a laugh from someone else. Zalkin knew whose laugh that was.

A smile split his face beneath the breathing mask. Momentarily, he forgot about Sister Mary Louise. Steven Zalkin raced for the back door of the rectory.

CHAPTER 109

APRIL 19, 1991
4:37 P.M.

Larry Cole and Lou Bronson approached the rear door of the rectory. They had reached the back stairs of the two-story house when the lock on the rear door gave an audible click. They stopped and looked up, expecting the door to swing open. When it didn't Bronson started up the stairs. Cole's voice stopped him.

"Take it easy until we find out who's behind that door," Cole said, pulling his automatic.

"It's probably only Father Ken or the housekeeper, boss." Bronson, however, was now whispering.

"Humor me on this one, Lou." Cole climbed the stairs and flattened himself against the wall, out of the line of fire from inside. Bronson, after reluctantly drawing his snub-nosed revolver, took up a position opposite the commander.

Cole reached out and knocked heavily on the door. There was no response from inside.

The distress on Bronson's face was increasing with each passing second. Cole read it as concern for the nun and his celebrated pastor. Cole felt a great deal of the same concern himself.

Carefully, Cole reached down and grasped the doorknob.

It turned easily, and the door swung open into the kitchen beyond.

"This is going to be by the numbers, Lou," he whispered. "I go first and you follow. Understood?"

Bronson nodded. He was a veteran who knew proper backup procedure. He waited until the commander ducked inside moving to the right and then he followed, moving to the left.

The kitchen was spotlessly clean and empty. There were two doors at the far end of the room. Cole moved around the kitchen table, past the stove, to flank one of the doors. Bronson raised his gun to aim at the door. Cole shoved the door open into the dining room. He glanced quickly around the interior and, seeing nothing threatening, was about to turn to the adjacent door leading to what he guessed to be the pantry.

"Commander, look!" Bronson rushed past him into the dining room.

Cole hadn't seen the nun lying on the other side of the dining-room table. He hesitated a moment to glance back at the closed pantry door before following Bronson.

She was lying on her stomach with her head turned to the side. Bronson knelt beside her and checked her pulse. Cole remained alert for any sign of trouble, which he had a feeling was only a short distance away.

"She's still alive," Bronson said. He was breathing heavily. "Looks like she's been drugged . . . or something."

Cole glanced at Sister Mary Louise Stallings and noticed that, except for her habit, she looked exactly the same as she had fifteen years before. The church had been good for her. Cole noticed Bronson sway.

"What's the matter, Lou?"

Bronson stood up, shaking his head from side to side. "Wow, I'm sorry, boss. All of a sudden I don't feel so good."

At that same instant Cole felt a reaction himself, but it

was no more than a slight queasiness he was capable of shrugging off. He noticed that the windows were open, blowing fresh air into the room. He ordered Bronson to go over next to them while he bent to help Sister Mary Louise.

She was dead weight in his arms as he carried her into the alcove. He tried to sit her in a straight-backed chair by a window. But like a puppet whose strings had been cut, she kept collapsing. Finally, Cole was able to prop her up on the floor with her back against a cold radiator. Bronson's head was partially outside the window and he was reviving rapidly.

Then they heard a noise.

First, there was the slamming of the outside door they had entered. This was followed by a faint metallic tinkling sound coming from the kitchen.

Cole checked to make sure Bronson had recovered sufficiently to back him up. Then he headed for the connecting door.

Cole swung the kitchen door open so hard it banged against the wall inside with a loud crash. With Bronson a few steps behind him, he entered the empty room.

Cole noticed the closed pantry door he had failed to check earlier. He raised the .45 and advanced toward it. His foot kicked something which skidded across the linoleum floor and disappeared under the kitchen table. Cole had only caught a glimpse of it, but saw that the object had been a ballpoint pen. Cole looked back up at the door just as a terrible fatigue dropped over him. At the same time, Lou Bronson collapsed.

Cole tried to fight his way through the increasing lethargy, but it was descending on him like a weighted shroud. His gun hand became very heavy, and he was no longer able to hold the weapon up at shoulder level. As his arm dropped involuntarily to his side, the door to the pantry opened.

The policeman's mind fought to bring the weapon back up and fire. However, the kitchen was enclosed and the aerosol he had inhaled potent. After a moment of intense struggle, Cole collapsed backward onto Bronson.

CHAPTER 110

Zalkin dragged the bodies of the two policemen down into the basement chapel before going back for the nun. He carried her gently down the stairs, transfixed by the beauty that had remained unchanged all the years they had been apart.

He examined his handiwork in the subdued lighting of the small chapel. Having Cole was a major bonus for him, and he intended to enjoy it. That is, when the time came.

He walked over to the bench Louise was lying on. He touched the tips of his fingers to the flesh of her cheek. The softness sent a thrill through him. However, a noise from one of the others tore his attention away from her.

Zalkin checked the priest and then Bronson. Both were out cold. It was Cole who had made the noise.

He stood over the policeman. The cop was either having a bad reaction to the nerve gas or was fighting it. Carduci had said that CZ should produce unconsciousness for at least an hour. Cole had been exposed to as much as the others, so he should have been out cold as well. Instead, he was groaning and moving feebly around on the bench of the narrow pew.

Zalkin checked his watch. He needed the hour the gas was supposed to give him. He couldn't be sure Cole would not regain consciousness before he returned. He'd have to make sure the cop stayed put.

He began searching the basement for something to restrain Cole with. There was nothing in the chapel. He found a storage room beneath the staircase. He spied a coil of rope, which he started to pick up, but then stopped. The objects on the small table shoved into the corner drew his attention. He studied them for a moment before forgetting about the rope. He chuckled as he carried the objects back into the chapel.

Steven Zalkin knelt beside Larry Cole. The policeman was unconscious and having a dream, which Zalkin could tell by the rapid eye movement and the way his face contorted. His limbs became motionless as his mind locked his body in sleep.

"I've been thinking about you for a long time, Larry," Zalkin said to his unconscious captive. "I don't think a day has gone by in the last fifteen years when I haven't thought about you or her." He nodded to the pew where Louise Stallings slept.

"I need to let the both of you know how I felt about what you did to me. How much it hurt. How hard it was for me to get myself back together again. But I've got to leave, and you're going to be asleep for a while, so I want to make sure you stay put."

Zalkin reached out and pulled Cole's left arm from beside his body. He repositioned Cole until his hand was flat on the floor with the palm up.

He turned to Cole once more. "I'd say this is going to

hurt a bit, but not right now. I'm sure that later the pain is just going to drive you wild."

Then, with methodical precision, Steven Zalkin drove a ten-penny nail through the palm of the commander's hand, into the wooden floor of the chapel.

CHAPTER 111

APRIL 19, 1991
5:07 P.M.

George Green sat on the front steps of the tenement building across the street from Our Lady of Peace rectory. He had been there since school ended. George had extra homework to do tonight because he had been caught talking in ranks. A hundred words copied by hand from the dictionary. A hundred words from the dictionary beginning with the letter Z. The copying of words was a common punishment; the letters changed as Sister Mary Louise saw fit.

The punishment didn't bother George. He deserved it. There were a couple of times when Sister Mary had caught him bending a rule or two and had not taken any action against him. Once, when he had been a shade tardy getting back from lunch, she had kept him after class and then released him with a stern lecture and a smile. He remembered the smile most of all. Few people had ever smiled at him.

But it wasn't Sister Mary Louise that had him hanging around the schoolgrounds that afternoon. It was instead the silver Porsche parked in front of the rectory. The car had him riveted to the cold stone steps of the ancient tenement.

"George, are you still sitting out here looking at that stupid car?" Shirley Rogers said, sitting down beside him.

"I was just watching it, Shirley."

"Watching it for what?"

"Make sure nobody messes with it."

"George Green," she scolded, "you know nobody around here is going to bother the car of one of Father Kenneth Smith's guests." She turned to look at the silver car. "Look, there's the man whose car you been 'watching.' Why don't you go over there and ask him about it?"

George looked up to see the handsome blond man walk out of the rectory front door. As they watched, he turned and locked the door behind him with a key. Then he started down the steps.

"I wouldn't want to bother him," George said sheepishly. "I'm already in dutch with Sister Mary. She gave me a hundred words."

"Asking him about his car won't get you in trouble. If he's a friend of Father Ken's, he'll be glad to talk to you."

George hesitated.

"You ain't afraid of him are you, George?" Shirley said. A pitchfork could not have galvanized George Green to walk across that street any faster than her words. He came up to the car's owner just as he was unlocking the door.

"Excuse me, sir," George said politely, as Sister Mary Louise had taught him.

The man spun around angrily. "What do you want?"

"I'd just like to ask you a couple of questions about your car."

"My car?" The white man stared at George with open hostility.

"Yes, sir. You see, I'm interested in sports cars. I plan on doing a research paper on them for my term project at the end of the school year. Perhaps you could give me some information about the Porsche I could use for my report."

It was a good speech for George Green, but it was wasted on the driver of the sports car.

"Get lost," the man said.

"Sir?"

"I said get away from me!" Despite George's size, the man took a menacing step toward him. George noticed that he dropped his hand to his waist. The big seventh-grade student's eyes followed the movement and saw the handle of a gun in his belt.

George took a careful step backward. "I'm not looking for any trouble, sir," he managed.

"Then get lost before your fat ass finds more trouble than it ever bargained for."

Without taking his eyes off the man, George backed away. The man got in the sports car, gunned the engine to life, and rocketed away.

Shirley met George in the middle of the street and grabbed his arm protectively. "Why did he curse at you like that? You didn't do nothing but ask him about his stupid car."

A different look had come over George Green's face. A look that had been masked by the culture and education Our Lady of Peace School had exposed him to. A look familiar to residents of the concrete jungle known as the South Side Chicago ghetto. A look that spoke of violence and revenge.

"That motherfucker ain't no friend of Father Ken's," George swore, ignoring Shirley's gasp of surprise at his profanity. "On top of that, he had blood on his shirt, and I'll bet it wasn't his."

Both of Sister Mary Louise's students turned to look at the darkened Our Lady of Peace rectory.

CHAPTER 112

Blackie Silvestri was worried. Larry should have been back by now. The search and arrest warrants for Steven Zalkin had been obtained, and in Cole's absence, Lt. Doug Conrad had jumped in to begin organizing a raiding party for the millionaire's near-Loop factory. This was okay with Blackie, as his mind wouldn't have been on the raid anyway.

Blackie picked up the phone and tried the number of Our Lady of Peace rectory for the third time in the last ten minutes. The phone rang continuously, but was not answered. He hung up and again tried the number for the school. It, too, rang without being answered.

In frustration he slammed the telephone back on its cradle. This caused a number of heads to turn in his direction. He glared back at them.

Blackie knew he had to calm down and think this thing through. Larry should have been back from seeing the nun, and if something had detained him, then he would have at least called. That is, if he could. The thought sent a shiver through Blackie.

He got up and crossed the office bay to the detective squad room. Inside, Conrad was briefing every available detective concerning the planned raid.

". . . felony warrant and a search warrant, so if our boy starts beefing, we cuff him and hustle his ass out of there. Now word has it that he's heavier than whale shit, so we don't want him grabbing the phone and getting some well-intentioned brass-hat paper pusher in the middle of something that's none of their business."

Brief laughter rippled through the small group.

As Conrad went on with the briefing, Blackie counted heads. There were eleven, which was an unusual number. Then he noticed Manny Sherlock. Bronson had gone with Cole. If push came to shove, Blackie would snatch the kid from Conrad for backup if he had to go up to Our Lady of Peace and look for Cole personally. He didn't want to use the kid unless it was absolutely necessary, but with each passing second the necessity became more urgent.

Blackie's thoughts were interrupted by one of the detectives calling to him across the office bay to inform him that the commander's private telephone was ringing. As Blackie was the only one authorized to answer it, he ran across the office, drawing grins from some of his fellow cops.

"Commander Cole's office, Silvestri speaking."

"Blackie?" Lisa Cole said. "What's wrong?"

"Nothing, Lisa. Everything's fine."

"Why are you breathing so hard?"

"I had to run across the office to get the phone."

"Where's Larry?"

Blackie did a good job of keeping the anxiety out of his voice. "He had to go out on this case we're working on. He should be back soon."

"He was supposed to call to tell me what he wanted for dinner tonight, but since he's so busy he probably forgot. I'll just have to surprise him."

"It's always more interesting that way."

"You don't think he'll be working too late do you?"

Blackie fought hard to keep the concern out of his voice. "No. I expect him to walk in the door any minute now. I tell you what, as soon as he gets here I'll have him call you."

"That's okay, Blackie," she said with a sigh. "I'll see him when he gets home."

Blackie hung up the phone and started for the squad room. He intended to grab Sherlock and head to Our Lady of Peace right now. Before he got ten feet, Cole's phone rang again.

"What the hell?"

Blackie retraced his steps.

"Commander Cole's office, Silvestri speaking."

"Take it easy, Sarge," Chief Riseman's voice came across the line. "You sound like you're going to jump through the phone at me."

"I'm sorry, Chief," Blackie said contritely. He rolled his eyes at the ceiling. "I thought you were someone else."

"Well, I'm glad I'm not them. I need to talk to your boss."

"He's not in, Chief," Blackie said. He wondered how many more times he would have to say that before the night was over.

Steven Zalkin walked into the lobby of the Second District police station on the ground floor below the Area One detective headquarters' office. Cole's .45 concealed beneath his jacket, Zalkin carried an attaché case as he approached the sergeant manning the station desk.

The sergeant was a black man with twenty-seven years of service with the department. He had never been known for having a good or even civil disposition, but when he saw the expensively dressed man approaching, his face creased in what could pass for a smile and he said a cordial, "Can I help you, sir?"

"I wonder if I could use your washroom, Sergeant."

"The public washrooms are down the hall on the right."
The sergeant hooked a ballpoint pen over his shoulder.

"Thank you," Zalkin said, following the directions.

Zalkin noticed that foot traffic inside the station was
moderate to slow for such a warm spring evening at an
inner-city police station. He expected things would get a lot
busier as the night wore on. In fact, he knew it was going to
be a very hectic night for the Chicago Police Department.

The thought made him smile.

The washroom had been cleaned recently and the smell
of disinfectant was nearly overpowering. The room was
empty, but Zalkin checked each of the stalls to make sure
he was alone. Satisfied, he entered the last stall, which was
situated next to an exterior wall.

Zalkin fastened the door behind him and placed his
attaché case on top of the toilet tank. Opening the case
revealed three CX-14 detonators—duplicates of the ones
he had used on the Temple of Allah two days ago. He
removed one of the detonators from the case and positioned it against the wall at about eye level for a standing
man of normal height.

The suction cups on the bottom of the detonator housing
fit securely against the brick surface; any attempt at pre-
mature removal would result in an instantaneous explosion. He set the timer at its nine-minute maximum.

He removed a second detonator. Closing the case, he set
the device for eight minutes. Carefully, he stepped from
the stall and walked with a casual urgency to the door leading back to the corridor outside.

He found the hall clear except for two uniformed cops
exiting into the parking lot at the far end. Rapidly, but not
hurriedly, Zalkin walked down the corridor in the direction
of the parking lot exit. About halfway down, opposite the
district roll call room, was a water fountain. Zalkin placed
the attaché case at his feet before bending to take a drink.

In doing so, he checked the traffic in the corridor. There were things going on in various places, but no one was paying him the slightest attention.

With his face over the running water, he lowered the hand holding the detonator. With one movement, he affixed it to the wall beside the cooler tank.

He turned to walk back to the front of the station. At the washroom, he slipped inside again. In less than sixty seconds he again emerged.

The desk sergeant was counting a stack of yellow onion-skin forms. Behind him, seated at desks in an administrative area, sat four blue-uniformed police officers: three older men and a young woman.

With steely patience, Zalkin waited for the sergeant to complete his count, call it to the female officer, and then look up at him. There was less cordiality in the policeman's look now than had been the case before.

"I wonder if you could tell me how to get from here to the Stevenson Expressway?" Zalkin asked.

It was obvious that the sergeant did not relish the task, but he began a thorough explanation of the route. As he did so, Zalkin let the hand holding the freshly primed detonator slide up to the underside of the desk overhang. A slight pressure from Zalkin's hand attached the detonator there securely.

"Thank you, Sergeant," the millionaire said, turning and heading for the front door. "You have a nice day."

The sergeant gave the well-dressed man barely a second's more thought before turning back to his paperwork.

CHAPTER 113

APRIL 19, 1991
6:00 P.M.

Blackie finally got Chief Riseman off Cole's line and headed for the squad room. Lieutenant Conrad was just winding up his briefing. Blackie called him outside.

"I need a man to go over to Our Lady of Peace with me, Doug."

"Sherlock, front and center," Conrad yelled into the squad room.

The young detective appeared instantly.

"Go with Sergeant Silvestri," the lieutenant ordered.

"But what about the raid?"

"Forget that," Conrad said. "I want you to go with the sergeant. He'll tell you what to do."

Dejected, Sherlock followed Blackie across the office. At his desk, Blackie snatched his suit jacket off the back of a chair and started for the stairs.

"You got a car signed out?" Blackie asked as they descended.

"Yes, sir. It's out back in the parking lot."

"Good. We're going to take a little ride."

They reached the main floor and walked past the public washrooms and the water fountain.

"Sarge, could I ask where we're going?"

Blackie was walking rapidly toward the rear exit.

Sherlock increased the length of his long-legged stride to catch up easily.

A Second District patrolman named Dunlap came in the back door just as they were going out. He looked at Sherlock and grinned. "Well, if it ain't Manfred Wolfgang Sherlock, boy detective."

Blackie ignored the patrolman and kept walking, as Sherlock said an annoyed, "Give me a break, Rusty. Not tonight, huh?"

"Oh, off on a big case, Mr. Detective," Dunlap goaded. "Big fucking deal!"

The glass doors closed behind Sherlock, shutting off Dunlap's insults.

"So where is it?" Blackie said, stopping at the edge of the parking lot.

Manny Sherlock stared at the spot where he had left the unmarked squad car. He had parked it in the aisle when he rushed in earlier to give the commander the information on Zalkin. Now the car was gone.

"I left it right here, Sarge."

"Did you leave the keys in it?" Blackie said, trying badly to conceal his exasperation.

"No, I'd never do that. I always take them. . . ." He searched his pockets and came up empty. Suddenly, he said, "Maybe Lou took the car?"

"They took the boss's car," Blackie scowled. "So, no big deal, kid. You left the car in the aisle with the keys in it. You had somebody blocked in. They moved the car. It's got to be around here somewhere. So let's look for it."

"Yes, sir," Sherlock said.

Blackie turned to start a search of the western end of the parking lot, but had only gone a few feet before he realized Sherlock was right behind him. The sergeant spun around angrily. "I don't know if you're bullshitting me or not, Sherlock, but nobody could be this fucking stupid. Now, I haven't got time to play games with you. You search for the car over there and I'll search over here. Understood?"

Sherlock's boyish face wrinkled in a frown. "I just thought you'd need me to help you find the car, Sarge."

"Why? Do I look like I'm blind?"

"No. But you don't know the license plate number or what color it is."

Blackie stared at the beanpole-sized detective for a moment. Then he began to laugh. Sherlock, not quite sure what the sergeant was laughing at, merely smiled.

"You're right," Blackie said between guffaws. "You're absolutely right."

But Manny Sherlock never heard the second "right" Blackie Silvestri uttered, as at that instant a deafening explosion rocked the station and knocked both Blackie and Sherlock to the ground.

CHAPTER 114

APRIL 19, 1991
6:06 P.M.

Officer Rusty Dunlap had compiled one of the most unimpressive careers of any police officer on the Chicago Police Department during his twenty-two years of service. An unintelligent individual, who was generally rude to the public and scornful of more successful department members like Manny Sherlock, Dunlap passed through life collecting paychecks for a job he did very poorly. Of course, he had no way of knowing that this situation was about to be rectified in scant seconds.

Dunlap had enjoyed baiting Sherlock. He couldn't understand how the tall, gangly officer had been promoted to detective with less than three years on the force. Rusty figured he was smarter than Sherlock or any of those other glorified idiots in the detective division because he knew how to get by without doing any work.

He had been called into the station to see the watch commander. He didn't know why, but he was pretty sure it was for another of his screw-ups. However, Rusty didn't care.

On the way down the corridor he stopped for a drink of water. He was still thinking about Sherlock as he bent over the fountain. He noticed the small device attached to the wall. Even if he had recognized it as a potential bomb, he would not have followed proper procedure in dealing with it. Instead, he studied it for a moment, figured it didn't belong there, and proceed to reach down and pull it from the wall.

The explosion completely obliterated both the water fountain and Police Officer Rusty Dunlap.

CHAPTER 115

APRIL 19, 1991
6:07 P.M.

Zalkin sat in the front seat of his new van, counting down the final minutes before the simultaneous explosions of the CX-14 detonation units. He knew they wouldn't have the same impact as the ones he had used at the temple, because the police station was only twenty years old and had been sturdily built. But the small, precision-timed units would cause a great deal of damage inside.

Zalkin had again donned the black motorcycle helmet with the tinted visor he had worn for his assault on the temple. He also wore an iridescent black jumpsuit over his street clothes. He had applied the flame-resistant spray to his helmet, suit, shoes, and gloves before leaving the warehouse. But he'd been forced to use the last of the substance, and there was none left. The same .357 Magnum six-inch barrel Python was strapped to his waist. The speed-loaders were full and ready for action.

He checked the items lying on the floor behind him. There was a high-powered rifle, some fragmentation grenades, the Compact flamethrower, and a light antitank weapon known as a LAW's rocket. Behind his tinted visor, Zalkin's face split into a grin. He planned to use the LAW's rocket to issue the *coup de grâce* to the cops left alive in the station after the CX-14s did their thing.

It was as Zalkin had this thought that Rusty Dunlap pulled the detonator from the wall.

Surprised, Zalkin spun back around in his seat and checked his watch. There were nearly three minutes left before the other units were set to blow.

"Dammit to hell!" Zalkin's words were muffled under the helmet. He realized at once that someone had tampered with the detonator, and that now the surviving cops would be alerted before the other units could explode. He'd have to move *now*.

Zalkin jumped out of the van.

CHAPTER 116

The only fatal casualty caused by the first explosion was Officer Rusty Dunlap. The stone and brick corridor the water fountain was located in was empty at the time of the detonation, and the nearest officer injured was in an administrative office forty-five feet away. She struck her forehead when she fell against a desk, but was able to get up and walk out of the station on her own steam.

The rest of the nineteen cops in the building were unhurt. At least, up to this point. They had no way of knowing about the imminent detonations of the two remaining devices.

"Let's get the hell out of here!" bellowed the desk sergeant who had given directions to Zalkin.

"What happened, Sarge?" one of the officers asked with confusion.

The sergeant noticed the blank expression on the inquirer's face and accurately guessed that he was close to going into shock. "Lamar, get over here and help Milton. We're leaving this building right now."

The other officers assigned to duties on the first floor of the station began moving slowly, but to the sergeant's relief, they were at least moving.

"Somebody check on the captain!"

The sergeant was taking command and the others were responding alertly to his sharply delivered orders. Everyone was covered with dust and there was some blood evident, but only from superficial cuts. They were intent on surviving, and with each passing second their odds of doing so were being rapidly reduced by the descending timers on the explosive devices hidden around them.

"The captain isn't doing too well," the female desk officer called from the entrance to the watch commander's office.

The sergeant rushed into the room and noticed the captain's pale complexion and shallow breathing. "Help me get him to his feet," he said to the female officer.

"Is it wise for us to move him?"

"There's no time to debate this, woman! We'd all better get out of here before this whole place comes down on top of us!"

They each took one of the captain's arms and struggled out of the office with him supported between them. In the corridor, seventy-five feet away from the point of the initial detonation, a number of officers had begun moving toward the front doors of the police station.

The sergeant's voice stopped them. "Not that way."

They turned to stare at him. Their faces were caked with dust and there was more than one questioning look cast his way.

For a moment the sergeant doubted his own decision, but the reason he had made it was because the first explosion had come from the side of the building where the front doors were located.

"Follow me."

Assisting the captain with the policewoman's help, the sergeant led them to the side exit on the east end of the building. The last uniformed officer stepped out into the cool night air just as the last two CX-14 detonators went off.

*　　*　　*

The detectives on the second floor heard and felt the concussive force of the first explosion, but as they were not directly exposed to the blast, no one was hurt.

In the squad room, the ten detectives being briefed by Lieutenant Conrad looked to him for direction.

"Okay, everybody stay put," he said. "I'm going to find out what the hell happened downstairs."

"Shouldn't we be evacuating this building as quickly as possible, boss?" a detective named Andrews said.

"I don't want anybody doing nothing until I say so!" Conrad snapped.

The lieutenant left the squad room and entered the office bay. The detectives followed him. Conrad crossed to the top of the front staircase and looked down. The section of floor he could see below through the banisters was covered with dust and debris. Then dense smoke began drifting up from below.

"Okay, let's head for the back stairs," he directed. "Move quickly, but don't run."

They didn't hesitate. In a few seconds they had all crossed to the staircase Silvestri and Sherlock had descended only moments ago.

Andrews was the first in line, Conrad the last. As soon as the detective's foot touched the top step, the two CX-14 detonators planted on the first floor went off simultaneously. The combined blasts rocked the second floor violently. The staircase Detective Andrews was standing on collapsed beneath him. Screaming, he dropped from view as those following him scurried back into the safety of the office.

The overhead lights flickered and died, plunging them into darkness. Shouts of fear spread across the second floor of the station. Conrad's voice rose above the rest.

"You guys shut up and listen to me!" He waited for silence, which came grudgingly. "The back stairs are gone, but we can still get out the front way."

"How do we know what's waiting for us down there, Lieutenant?" came the shout from a detective, who was very close to hysterics.

"It's the same thing that happened at the Temple of Allah! Nobody got out of there!"

"Hail Mary, full of grace, the Lord is with thee. Blessed—"

"You people shut the fuck up!" the lieutenant roared. "Nobody's going to get out of here alive if we panic. Now listen—"

Someone darted through the dark, brushed past Conrad, and headed for the front stairs. Before the lieutenant could say another word, someone else panicked and ran. The second detective ran into something, cried out, and fell to the floor.

"You people have got to get yourselves together!" the lieutenant pleaded.

"Get out of the way, Lieutenant!" a harsh, angry voice shouted. "I'm getting out of here!"

Conrad realized that trying to reason with them was futile. Instead, he began feeling his way through the dark toward the front staircase. There was confusion raging all around him and he was roughly shoved twice. Then he heard a scream—a scream that died away as it receded rapidly through the dark emptiness at the spot where the front stairs should have been.

Suddenly, there was a second scream originating at the same location. This one was punctuated by a sickeningly audible crunch as flesh and bone met concrete below.

"Those stairs are gone, too!" someone yelled.

"We're all going to die!"

Lt. Doug Conrad retraced his steps. He felt around for a desk, found one, and located the telephone. He picked up the receiver and listened for a dial tone. He almost cried out with relief when he got one. By touch, he dialed 911.

After one ring a male voice said, "Chicago Emergency, Walters."

"This is Area One Detective Division headquarters," Conrad said, keeping his voice as steady as he could. "A series of explosions has gone off inside the station. I don't know what—"

"Who is this speaking?"

Conrad took a breath, ground his teeth together, and said, "This is Lieutenant Conrad, the Violent Crimes unit C.O."

"Now, what did you say is going on there, Lieutenant?"

"Goddammit, I've got a number of police officers dead or dying, the lights are out, and I need fucking help right now, do you understand me? So drop the dumb-assed questions and get me some help A.S.A.P!"

"Please hold."

Conrad felt tears of frustration sting his eyes, as the operator clicked off. In the confusion the lieutenant had forgotten the man's name, but if he survived this night and ever found out who he was, Conrad promised himself he'd kill the son of a bitch.

"Sergeant Murray," another voice came over the line. Before Conrad could say anything, Murray said, "Lieutenant, we've had a number of reports on the explosions at the Area One Police Center. Help is on the way, so sit tight."

Conrad felt his knees go weak. He managed to lean against the desk before he fell down. "You'd better send ambulances and fire equipment. We're trapped on the second floor. Both stairways are gone."

"Stay on the line, Lieutenant," Sergeant Murray said.

Unable to talk anymore, Lt. Doug Conrad dropped the telephone receiver. It banged against the floor, bounding up and down from its coiled cord. Conrad could still hear the sergeant's voice coming over the speaker, but he couldn't make out the words. That, however, didn't matter to him anymore, as he stood alone in the darkness, trembling violently.

CHAPTER 117

APRIL 19, 1991
6:36 P.M.

Manny Sherlock was trying to revive Sergeant Silvestri by gently slapping his cheek. Silvestri, however, was not responding. Sherlock had found the sergeant lying beside a parked car in the lot. Manny had tried to get him up, but Silvestri had been too heavy for him to lift. Finally, he had been forced to drag the sergeant a short distance. He'd gotten him into a sitting position with his back against a squad car bumper. Then, additional blasts had ripped through the station.

At first, Sherlock thought there was only one explosion the second time, but, as he replayed it in his mind, he realized that there had been two blasts simultaneously.

He didn't know what had happened inside, and he didn't know what to do about Silvestri. He wished Lou Bronson were here now. He'd tell him what to do.

The sergeant began stirring, and Manny quickly took his hand away from Silvestri's face. The sergeant was still dazed, but coming around rapidly. Manny was just starting to breathe a sigh of relief when he caught movement out of the corner of his eye.

Manny turned in time to see a man wearing a black motorcycle helmet and dark clothing get out of a dark blue van parked about a hundred feet away. The black-clad figure reached back into the van for a tubular object, which he slung over his shoulder. He slammed the door and walked toward the east parking lot.

Silvestri shook his head to clear the cobwebs. He looked up at Sherlock kneeling over him and said, "What happened?"

"Shhh!" Sherlock held his finger to his lips.

Confused, Blackie said, "What's going on? What are we doing . . . ?"

The sergeant's voice carried easily from their hiding place to the man in black. Half-crouched behind the squad car, Sherlock watched in horror as the dark-clad figure turned to look in their direction.

"It's him, Sarge!" Sherlock whispered frantically. "It's Zalkin. He knows where we are."

Still dazed, Blackie managed to struggle up onto his knees and look over the hood of the car. What he saw made a hard knot of fear form in his throat.

For a moment their strangely dressed adversary stood motionless. Then he lifted the flamethrower and opened fire. A jet of flame zipped across the space separating them and ignited the police car they were crouched behind. The car exploded.

Blackie and Sherlock dodged between cars as they ran through the parking lot skirting the south wall of the station. They were running north through a driveway leading out to Fifty-first Street. Ahead of them the Second District desk crew, with their ailing watch commander, had taken refuge in the east lot among the patrol cars designated for marked units.

As they approached, the desk sergeant recognized Blackie and called, "What're you running from, Silvestri?"

Blackie ran up to them. Sherlock followed, looking back just as the man in the black helmet came around the corner of the building and again opened fire with the flamethrower. The stream of flame stretched from the mouth of the tube to ignite everything in its path for twenty feet. Blackie and Manny took refuge behind a car with three Second District officers. The man in black was adjusting his aim when the cops opened fire on him. Another blast came from the flamethrower, but the cops' fire forced their attacker to take cover behind the building.

"Do you think we hit him?" a breathless Manny Sherlock said.

"I don't know," Blackie said, squinting at the last place they'd seen Zalkin.

The uniformed officers joined the detectives in defending their position. "What in the hell is going on?" one of them asked.

Blackie started to explain when a shadow appeared at the edge of the building. The flashes of gunshots were followed by the sounds of a large-bore handgun discharging. A bullet smashed into the chest of a uniformed cop standing beside Manny. With a strangled scream, the wounded officer dropped to the ground. Two more rounds struck close enough to the concealed cops to make them duck for cover.

"We're sitting ducks," Blackie said, looking into the frightened face of Manny Sherlock. "Zalkin can take us any time he wants."

CHAPTER 118

Soon to be former First Deputy Superintendent Raymond Schmidt was driving the MCV south in the express lanes of the Dan Ryan. He had decided on one final fling with his command vehicle while he was still the first deputy. A simulcast was broadcast over the frequency he was monitoring.

"Units in the Second District and cars on citywide, we have reports of multiple explosions with police officers injured in the Area One Police Center. The fire department is en route, but the cause of the explosions is unknown at this time, so use caution when responding."

Schmidt was already at Sixty-third Street, traveling in the far left-hand lane. Activating the Mars lights, flashing headlights, and high-low frequency siren, he headed for the Seventy-first Street exit.

In response to the emergency lights and siren wail, the last vestiges of rush-hour traffic parted for the big vehicle. At Seventy-first Street, he gunned the motor home up the ramp, wishing he could get more power from the engine.

At the cross street the traffic was clear and Schmidt caught a green light. He entered the intersection too fast, and spun as he tried to make a left turn. The MCV went into a wild skid with the back end coming around fast. Schmidt fought for control. The official motor home turned 180 degrees and began slipping toward the guardrail over the expressway below.

"C'mon, goddammit! C'mon you son of a bitch! Straighten up! Straighten up!"

Schmidt twisted the wheel and turned into the skid. The MCV kept coming around until it had completed 360 degrees and ended up facing east on the overpass. The sirens and lights were still going. Schmidt drove rapidly over the ramp and took a slower turn to take him back down onto the Dan Ryan Expressway. He was less than two minutes from the Second District.

CHAPTER 119

APRIL 19, 1991
6:42 P.M.

Zalkin was enraged. He had expected his attack on the station to go as easily as has been the case with the Temple of Allah and Frank Delahanty. But the cops, particularly Silvestri and Sherlock, were putting up fierce resistance from an entrenched position. Zalkin knew he possessed the firepower to eventually force them from their positions, but that would take time. Steven Zalkin also knew that he was rapidly running out of time. Already he could hear the wail of sirens approaching. Now, he was forced to make a decision as to how he could conclude the attack. He would have to employ the LAW's rocket to dispose of Silvestri and Sherlock.

From his position behind the south wall of the station, Zalkin reloaded the Python and prepared to fire another barrage at the cops. He stuck his head around the edge of the building and sighted on the last spot where he'd seen them. At that instant, Sherlock's head popped up from behind a car.

Leering beneath his visor, Zalkin aimed at the cop and began squeezing the trigger. However, before the killer's weapon discharged, Sherlock fired six bullets at him. Zalkin was shocked when two rounds whined off his helmet. He hadn't expected the skinny detective to be that good with a snub-nosed revolver. Then the killer's right shoulder went numb. Zalkin had been hit!

Zalkin leaned back against the wall and checked the wound. It was bad. There was a hole the size of a quarter in his right deltoid muscle. It was starting to well with blood, and as it did so, he began feeling the pain.

Angrily, he reholstered the Python with some difficulty and unstrapped the LAW's rocket from his back. He had planned to use the weapon on the station, but now Sherlock and the other cops in the parking lot would receive the full brunt of his explosive power. Then, if he had the time, he'd mop things up with the flamethrower.

His arm throbbed unmercifully as he activated the rocket launcher and hefted it onto his wounded shoulder, causing him to cry out. He fumbled for the trigger, found it, and hesitated a moment before exposing himself to fire from the cops. When he was ready, he stepped from behind the wall with the LAW's rocket leveled.

No more rounds came Zalkin's way, and he was adjusting the sight to aim at the car Sherlock had fired from when the MCV came around the corner from the west end of the station parking lot.

The killer was bathed in the spotlights and Mars lights of the huge vehicle. Recognizing his vulnerability, Zalkin spun toward the police van and fired the rocket.

CHAPTER 120

APRIL 19, 1991
6:46 P.M.

The MCV took a direct hit and burst into flames with a deafening explosion. Schmidt was killed instantly. The resulting blast lit up the eastern side of the Area One Police Center with a blinding brilliance. A brilliance that Sherlock and Silvestri's eyes adjusted to in time to see the man in black walk into the wall of flames raging around the destroyed vehicle.

"Let's go," Blackie yelled to Sherlock.

The heat from the MCV was so intense they were forced to swing around the driveway. They reached the spot where the man in black had first confronted them.

"Sarge," Manny said, looking down at the parking lot surface.

Blackie followed his gaze to the trail of blood. "The bastard is hit."

The blue van was visible parked on the street outside the lot. The trail of blood led toward it. Manny started in that direction. Blackie stopped him.

"Not yet, kid. Let's hold it until we get some more guys to give us a hand."

Reluctantly, they began their wait. However, it was a short one, as ninety seconds later the van exploded with a force that hurled scattered parts of it hundreds of feet into the air.

CHAPTER 121

APRIL 19, 1991
6:48 P.M.

George Green and Shirley Rogers rang the doorbell and pounded on the door of the rectory for twenty minutes without receiving an answer. They had then gone around to the back door and ended up with the same results for their trouble.

"They've got to be in there," Shirley said, standing in the darkness at the rear of the building. "Why don't they answer?"

George shook his head. "Something is not right here. That guy in the Porsche locked the front door with a key. Father Ken wouldn't have given no key to a stranger."

"So, what are we going to do now?"

George thought furiously. He had considered kicking down one of the doors, but they looked sturdy enough to stand an assault even from someone of his size. But there was more than one way to get to the other side of a locked door.

He led her to the church side of the rectory. There he pointed up at the partially open dining-room window, which was ten feet above the ground.

"How're you going to get up there?" she said.

"I'm not. You are."

"You must be crazy if you think I'm going to climb up there," she said, taking a step backward.

"I can't do it," he said. "I could no more climb up there than I could fly."

"Well, how am I supposed to do it? I ain't got no wings either."

"I'll help you. Give you a boost."

She glared at him. "Maybe you haven't noticed it, Mr. George Green, but I'm wearing a dress."

He rolled his eyes. "So, I won't look. Now, will you at least try?"

"You're acting like it don't mean nothing. I'm not the kind of girl that puts herself in a position for a boy to take advantage of her."

"Look, woman, I ain't out here to play no silly games with you. Father Ken and Sister Mary could be in real trouble in there and you're out here acting crazy. Now, that man was carrying a gun and had blood on his clothes. How would you feel if they end up dead and we find out later we could have done something to help them?"

This convinced her, but not immediately. "Give me your handkerchief."

"What?"

"I said, give me your handkerchief. I seen those big bandanas you carry in your back pocket. Now give it to me."

After blindfolding him, she allowed him to give her a boost up to the window. She climbed inside the rectory and opened the back door for George.

The rectory was dark. They went from room to room, first on the ground floor, and then the upper floors. As they entered the bathroom on the second floor, he abruptly stopped. "What was that?" He pointed at the heating vent in the floor.

They walked over to it. The sound became louder.

"It's got to be coming from the basement," Shirley said.

CHAPTER 122

APRIL 19, 1991
7:01 P.M.

Sister Mary Louise opened her eyes and stared up at the chapel ceiling. Her disorientation was so great that for long, anxious moments, she could fathom neither where, nor even who, she was. The memory of him flashed through the fog enveloping her brain. This brought her back to reality. Reality, and a headache of such intensity she found it difficult to keep her eyes open.

Fear, however, drove her. Fear, and the memory of what he had done to her fifteen years ago.

She struggled into a sitting position in the pew. For just an instant she thought she was going to be sick to her stomach, but this passed. She looked around and recognized the chapel in the rectory basement. But she couldn't understand why he had brought her here.

Sister Mary Louise stood up too fast and was forced to sit back down hard when a wave of dizziness swept over her. Then she heard someone moaning.

Using the back of the pew for support, she managed to

remain standing. She was forced to close her eyes to stop her head from spinning. When she opened them she saw Father Ken, Detective Bronson, and a man she hadn't seen in nearly fifteen years: Larry Cole. The priest and Bronson were lying in pews; Cole was on the floor near the altar railing. It was Cole who absorbed her total attention.

She struggled to the front of the chapel and leaned over him. She found it impossible to stand on her own for more than a few seconds before the dizziness and blinding pain of her headache buckled her knees. She attempted to sit down in a nearby pew, but before she could do so she collapsed to the floor. She ended up sitting in a pool of blood, which had flowed from the policeman's hand.

The words *beast, monster,* and *defiler* echoed through her drug-tortured brain. God had taught love of neighbor to be equated with love of self, but Louise could feel nothing in her heart but hatred for the man who had done this. The man who now called himself Steven Zalkin, but whom she recognized as Martin Zykus.

There had really never been any doubt in her heart. But she had used her mental faculties to deny the instincts for self-preservation—instincts passed down from the cave-dwelling ancestors of mankind, who knew nothing of logic. When she saw him in the flesh for the first time since those horrible nights in 1976, she knew who he was. Steven Zalkin didn't look anything like Martin Zykus, but she still knew that it was him.

Sister Mary Louise looked over at the priest lying prone on a bench. He was unconscious and bleeding from the head, but she could tell little else about his condition. Father Ken would have to wait. Cole needed her now.

The policeman's eyelids were beginning to flutter, and he was moaning deep in his throat. She couldn't tell if the noise was due to a reaction to the drug he and Detective Bronson had obviously been given by Zykus or the pain from his damaged hand.

She inched forward across the floor, ignoring the blood soaking into her habit. The hand was palm-up, with the fingers splayed open. She could see the head of the nail embedded in the flesh at the center of his palm. Despite the blood, she could see the bruising caused by the hammer driving the nail home. The hand itself had swollen to twice its normal size and was rapidly turning purple. Cole was bathed in sweat and was trying to bring the hand up, which was forcing the head of the nail deeper into his flesh.

Carefully, Louise reached out and touched the fingers. He moaned sharply and opened his eyes to stare at her. But they stayed open for only a moment before shutting again.

She looked around the floor and discovered the hammer Zalkin had used. She stretched for it, being careful not to touch the impaled hand. The former Louise Stallings of Kellam, Iowa, had driven many nails while working on her father's farm. She'd also pulled a few. But she'd never been faced with the task of having to pull a nail from human flesh.

She inverted the hammer and reached for Cole's hand. She opened the fingers as wide as possible to give herself enough room to work. The slightest contact made him groan, and she could tell that he was regaining consciousness rapidly.

She couldn't do it! She was tired, her head ached, and Zalkin could return to kill the others and rape her again at any minute. Yes, she knew in her heart that he intended to assault her. Somehow she had always known that someday he would come back for her.

She fought the urge to flee. To try and get out of this place before he came back. But she knew that she couldn't just leave the others simply to save herself.

She looked around the chapel. Above the tabernacle was a brass figure of the crucified Christ. She managed to make the sign of the cross and say a brief prayer for God to give her strength. Then she leaned forward and wedged the claw of the hammer into the palm, forcing back the fingers. Cole moaned louder. She felt the flesh give beneath the weight of the hammer head. Blood flowed heavily from the palm, as she began searching for the nail head. She concentrated with all her might and ignored the loud groans coming from the policeman. Then she had it.

She pulled and felt the nail give a bit; however, it remained embedded in the hand and anchored to the wooden floor. She pulled harder. It still wouldn't budge. Finally, gritting her teeth and shutting her eyes against the horror of what she was doing, Sister Mary Louise Stallings yanked at the nail head as hard as she could.

The bloody nail made a sickening, wet, popping noise as it came out of Cole's flesh. Larry Cole opened his eyes and stared at her.

CHAPTER 123

APRIL 19, 1991
7:07 P.M.

Zalkin was on fire. When he'd become engulfed in flames from the mobile home, the killer had confidently walked through them, certain that the aerosol spray would protect him. The flames danced off his visor, and he was making plans to retaliate against the cops for his shoulder wound when he suddenly felt the plastic of his helmet starting to burn. Thick smoke began choking him.

Now Zalkin was forced to rush through the wall of

flame, which was infinitely hotter than that of the temple. However, before he could escape the conflagration, he felt his legs and buttocks get hot. He sustained burns so painful he screamed. He emerged into the south parking lot of the Area One Center. Snatching off the helmet erased the acrid odor of burning plastic, which was quickly replaced by the stench of burning hair. He reached up and felt the left side of his face with a gloved hand. In horror, he studied the palm of his glove to see the thin leather surface streaked with blood, pieces of burned flesh, and singed hair.

With a snarl of pain and fury, he struggled across the parking lot in the direction of the van. He looked back and, in the illumination from the burning MCV, he saw Silvestri and Sherlock following the trail of blood he'd left on the surface of the asphalt. They hadn't spied the killer yet.

Zalkin fought a rising panic. He had been trapped by cops before; however, this time he knew that he wouldn't be facing a simple prison sentence. After what had occurred here, he knew that, if they got their hands on him, he was as good as dead.

But luck had been with him so far, and now, despite his wounds and failure to destroy the station with the LAW's rocket, his luck held. He looked back to find that Silvestri and Sherlock had halted their pursuit.

Zalkin slipped behind the van, which served as a momentary hiding place. The hole in his shoulder was bleeding heavily, and if it was allowed to continue, he would soon be too weak to go on—and he wasn't about to abandon his prize back at Our Lady of Peace.

He needed a diversion to give him time to escape. The items he required were in easy reach from where he stood outside the blue van. He left one of them, a CX-14 detonator, on the driver's bucket seat. He set the timer for fifteen seconds. He scrambled away as fast as he could.

He made it fifty feet before the van blew with a force

that knocked him against a parked Buick. The jolt made him cry out.

Cops were showing up fast enough to make an instant mob. Silvestri was approaching the burning van with Sherlock following a short distance behind him, searching the ground with a flashlight. Zalkin silently cursed them, but was forced to put as much distance between himself and what was left of the blue van as he could.

Zalkin had left the Porsche parked in one of the rear rows of the huge Area One parking lot. By the time he got to it, his entire arm was soaked with blood and stabbing pains were running from the tips of his fingers into his chest cavity. He managed to climb inside.

There was a first-aid kit in the glove compartment, but Zalkin didn't have time to use it now. Ignoring the pain, he started the engine and drove out of the parking lot. As he sped north on Wentworth, he drove right past the still-burning van. It was surrounded by cops. In the confusion, none of them noticed the silver Porsche.

CHAPTER 124

APRIL 19, 1991
7:10 P.M.

Larry Cole's left arm ached from the tips of his fingers to his elbow. He couldn't flex his fingers because of the swelling. He was forced to support the wounded hand with his good right hand. He would have probably felt a great deal worse, but then the drug was still making clear thought difficult.

Sister Mary Louise, seated on the bench beside him, had torn off sections of her cotton slip to make a bandage.

Cole looked around the small chapel. Bronson was in a seated position in one of the pews. The detective was bent double, holding his head in his hands. The priest, whom Cole recognized from photographs he had seen of him in the newspapers, was still lying unconscious in another pew. Two teenagers—a heavyset boy and a pretty young girl with a scarred forehead—were standing behind Sister Mary Louise, staring in fascination at the policeman's damaged hand.

There was no sign of Steven Zalkin or, Cole frowned as he had the thought, Martin Zykus.

"We've got to get you a doctor, Larry," the nun said. Her hands trembled as she lifted them to her starkly pale face. "I think we all should go to a hospital."

"We need help," Cole said, finding his mouth so dry his tongue stuck to his teeth when he talked. He moistened his lips, which succeeded in alleviating some of the dryness. "He's got to be around here somewhere."

"You talkin' about the man with the blond hair driving a Porsche?"

Cole and Sister Mary Louise turned to study the hulking George Green.

"He's gone, Sister," he said. "He cursed me out when I asked him about his car. Then he just took off."

"He had a gun, too," Shirley Rogers broke in. "He threatened George with it. That's how he knew he wasn't no friend of Father Ken's."

Cole's head was swimming, and his left hand throbbed like white-hot daggers were piercing his palm with each beat of his heart. He moved his right hand to the place on his left side where he kept his .45. He was merely confirming what he already suspected. It was gone.

"Bronson," Cole called to the detective, who was still bent over on the bench of the church pew.

He didn't answer.

"Lou, wake up!"

The detective struggled to sit up, made it upright, and then slid sideways off the bench onto the floor. He landed hard.

George and Shirley went over and helped the detective back onto the bench.

"He can't help you much, mister," Shirley said. "He's out of it."

"One of you kids see if he still has his gun," Cole said.

George Green checked. "He's got on a holster, but it's empty."

"What do we do now?" Sister Mary Louise asked Cole.

"Where's the telephone?"

"It's upstairs in Father Ken's study."

"Young man," Cole said to George Green, "I need you to go upstairs and call the police."

"Yes, sir," George said, taking off for the stairs with an impressive speed for someone his size.

Shirley remained beside Sister Mary Louise.

"What do you think Zykus is up to?" the nun asked Cole.

"I don't know, Louise—or should I call you Sister Mary Louise?"

"Her name's Sister Mary Louise Stallings," Shirley snapped.

"It's okay, Shirley," the nun said. "The commander and I are old friends. He knew me before I joined the convent."

The student rolled her eyes, displaying quite accurately how she felt about police officers.

"I'll tell you one thing," Cole said, "if I had my gun, I'd feel better about this entire situation."

"I've got a gun," Sister Mary Louise said.

Before Cole could reply, George Green was back. "The phone is dead, Sister. I couldn't even get a dial tone."

"That figures," Cole said. "Where's your gun?"

"In the convent."

"That's on the other side of the church. In the shape we're in, we'll never make it."

"I can get it," Shirley said.

Sister Mary Louise hesitated a moment before shaking her head and saying, "Forget the gun. There's a phone there you can use to call the police."

"Suppose the line's dead like it is over here, Sister?" Shirley argued.

"She's right, Louise," Cole said. "Up until now, Zykus has been very careful."

Finally, the nun produced a ring of keys. She showed Shirley the ones for the top and bottom door locks to the convent. Then she told her where to find the gun.

Shirley took one last look around the chapel, made the sign of the cross, winked at George, and dashed up the stairs.

She didn't hesitate as she crossed through the upstairs hall, the dining room, and kitchen. She made the trip at a dead run, made easier because George had left all the lights on.

Outside, Shirley leaped down the back steps and ran across the courtyard connecting the rectory to the church, the school, and the convent. As she rounded the far corner of the convent and started up the steps to the front door, Zalkin's Porsche skidded to a stop in front of the rectory.

CHAPTER 125

APRIL 19, 1991
7:12 P.M.

The Area One Police Center was in a state of complete chaos. Police cars had responded from not only the Second District but the surrounding Third, Seventh, Ninth, and Twenty-first districts. Seventeen pieces of fire equipment were on the scene, their crews occupied with sporadic fires inside the still-erect but badly damaged station, and the burning vehicles outside. Fire ambulances and stretcher-equipped police squadrols were parked in a line along Fifty-first Street, and were being directed to wherever they were needed by a fire department deputy commissioner.

As of 1900 hours on the night of April 19, the death toll at the Area One Police Center stood at five: three detectives, one patrol officer, and First Deputy Superintendent Raymond Schmidt. This count was based on the bodies recovered from the wreckage, and was not accurate. Officer Rusty Dunlap would become the sixth police victim, but not until he was first listed as missing. This status wouldn't be changed until two days later, when a Streets and Sanitation crew sifting through the wreckage would turn up his scattered remains.

The superintendent's chauffeur-driven Mercury Marquis roared up the ramp from the Dan Ryan Expressway and was waved through the barricades set up across Fifty-first Street. A uniformed sergeant from the Ninth District directed the car into the driveway in front of the station. The superintendent got out of the front seat of the black car. William Riseman came out of the back seat.

A captain from the Third District rushed over to begin reporting information that the superintendent already knew. Riseman interrupted him. "Captain, we have all that. Have someone find Sergeant Silvestri and bring him here right now."

The captain looked curiously at Riseman for just a moment. The chief of detectives wasn't in his chain of command, but with the superintendent standing there he wasn't about to make it an issue.

"Blackie's over at what's left of the perpetrator's van, Chief. I'll have someone go and get him on the double."

"No," the superintendent said. "I want to see that for myself. Where is it, Captain?"

Blackie and Sherlock were forced to stand back while a hook and ladder crew pumped gallons of water onto the still-burning van.

"You think there will be enough of him left to identify, Sarge?" Sherlock asked.

The young detective bounced from one foot to the other, prompting Blackie to inquire if he had an urgent need to go to the bathroom. But after assuring the sergeant that he did not, Sherlock went right back to his constant bounce. Blackie finally decided to ignore him.

"His bones and teeth will withstand the flames, but I doubt if anything else will," Blackie said.

Blackie had not forgotten about Cole, but he couldn't leave here until they knew Zalkin was dead inside the remains of the blue van. Then, as he stared at the flames, Blackie had the sinking feeling that the killer had again escaped.

There was a stirring among the cops and even a few of the firemen present, prompting Blackie and Sherlock to turn away from the van. When he saw the superintendent and Riseman approaching, Sherlock gasped and slipped behind the sergeant.

"How are you, Blackie?" the superintendent said, surprising both Riseman and Sherlock. "It's been a long time."

"Yes, sir, it has. How are your wife and children?"

"Everyone's fine. And Maria and your young ones?"

"They're not so young anymore, but everyone is well."

The superintendent nodded and his expression hardened. The amenities over, his eyes swung to the smoldering hulk of the killer's van. "Give it to me from the top, Blackie."

He did.

A fireman approached the group. Recognizing the Superintendent of Police, he raised a soot-blackened hand to his helmet in a salute, "The fire is still going in that thing, sir, but I thought you'd like to know that there was no one inside."

Blackie tensed.

"You have any idea where Zalkin has gone, Sarge?" Riseman asked.

"I know exactly where he is," Blackie said. "And he's got one helluva head start on us."

CHAPTER 126

Zalkin made a crude bandage for his arm with gauze and tape from the first-aid kit in the Porsche. The blood had stopped flowing heavily, but the front bucket seat and the floor were slippery. The combined pain from his leg and back burns, along with that from his shoulder wound, was beginning to throb with an intensity that made him lightheaded. But his faculties were unimpaired, and the steroid shot he'd taken that morning still had him pumped.

Opening the car door, he stepped onto the street. When he looked at the rectory, Zalkin froze. All the lights were on inside.

He considered and quickly rejected the idea of going back in by way of the front door. He pulled the Magnum, felt the stickiness of his own blood on the grip, and began making his way toward the rear of the building.

"Chicago Emergency, Walters."

"Send the police over to Our Lady of Peace rectory right away!"

"What's the trouble there?"

"A man got into the rectory and drugged Sister Mary and Father Ken. He got two of your cops, too."

"There are policemen there now?"

"That's right. Two of them. . . ."

"Who is this speaking?"

"Why do you need my name?"

"It's just routine procedure, ma'am."

"Listen, Mr. Policeman, some crazy white man nailed one of your fellow cop's hands to the floor of the rectory chapel. Father Ken, Sister Mary, and another cop are too weak to get out of there on their own, so you have to send the police right now!"

"Calm down, young lady, and tell—"

Shirley Rogers slammed the convent telephone back on its cradle. She was so angry that she trembled. She'd never liked police officers, and Sister Mary being friendly with the one who got hurt hadn't changed that. Where she lived, over in the Boulevard projects, people called the police a lot, but didn't get what could be considered a lot of service.

Her second reason for coming to the rectory pushed to the forefront of her mind, and she dashed for the stairs leading to the second floor.

Shirley retrieved the snub-nosed .38 from the bookcase in Sister Mary's room and headed back for the rectory. At the front door of the convent, she stopped. She hefted the revolver and frowned. It wouldn't be smart to go running outside with a gun in her hand. Even if she was only going to the other side of the courtyard, she had called the police. She figured it would be just like the cops to send someone after all those questions. She's seen a movie once where some cops in Los Angeles had shot a teenaged boy who was only carrying a cap pistol in his hand. Shirley didn't intend to become an accident, so she pulled up her sweater and stuck the gun down in the waistband of her skirt. Then she let herself out.

The gun was cold and uncomfortably alien pressed against her side. She was forced to slow her pace considerably as she crossed in front of the convent, passed the school, and headed for the back door of the rectory.

She walked up on the porch and stopped. The back door stood open. She couldn't remember closing it, but she did recall that when she'd left, the kitchen light had been on. Now, the light was out.

She stared at the open door. She touched her side and felt the metal casing of the revolver. She considered pulling it, but quickly discarded the idea. It was possible that George, Sister Mary, or even Father Ken could have come upstairs since she left. She wouldn't want to make an accident out of one of them. She didn't even think about the two cops.

But if they had come up, she thought, why would they turn out the light?

She could see all the way across the kitchen into the dining room. Someone could be hiding behind the kitchen door or even in the pantry. She inched her way across the porch. There was nothing moving inside the kitchen. She stepped inside the rectory.

She stepped in something sticky. She looked down, and at that instant she noticed the odor. She remembered this same smell from the time Mrs. Richards, who lived next door to her family in the housing project, had cut up her husband with a butcher knife. Shirley had been behind her mother when she went to help Mr. Richards, but by the time they arrived, he was very dead. He was also covered with blood. A lot of blood, that had the same smell that was in the kitchen right now.

It had a salty, metallic odor, which collided in her mind with the sight of blood on the floor. Then a dark figure stepped from behind the kitchen door and grabbed her. A thick arm was wrapped around her throat and she was yanked off her feet.

She screamed and struggled to free herself, but she was held fast by someone who was extremely strong.

CHAPTER 127

Father Ken Smith came around last. He had a small head wound, which was not serious.

In a basement sink, Sister Mary Louise had soaked what was left of her slip in cold water. She held the cloth to Father Ken's head.

"You knew Zalkin before?" the priest asked.

"It was fifteen years ago. He raped me."

Father Ken's head snapped around and he looked directly at her. He had moved too fast, and sharp pains shot through his skull. He shut his eyes and waited for the pain to pass before saying, "Why didn't you tell me that before?"

She took the cloth away and busily refolded it. "I wasn't certain that it was him until I saw him."

"How does the policeman fit in?" The priest nodded at Cole, who was walking Lou Bronson up and down the chapel to help him recover from the drug.

"He helped me back then," Louise said. "If I had listened to him, we wouldn't be in this fix now."

"Don't say that, Sister. Everything that happens is God's will."

George Green had been standing by the stairs, waiting for Shirley to return. Suddenly, he turned and crossed to the nun. "Shirley should have been back, Sister. I'm getting worried about her."

"Maybe we should try to get out of here now," Cole said from where he stood with his good arm supporting Bronson. Cole's complexion had turned a sickly gray and there was obvious strain in every move he made, but he was not giving in.

"I agree," Father Ken said, attempting to stand.

George rushed forward to help him. It was at that instant that they heard Shirley scream.

The sound froze them all in place—except George, who rushed across the chapel and thundered up the stairs.

"George, stop!" Sister Mary Louise called to him, but it was too late.

Cole eased Bronson down onto a bench and looked around the room for anything he could use as a weapon. He spied the hammer Zalkin had used to nail his hand to the floor. He picked it up with his good right hand. Feeling his fingers curl around the handle increased his confidence, but did nothing for the pain that had taken sole possession of his left arm.

A single gunshot was followed by a heavy thud from above. Still holding the hammer, Cole started for the stairs. "All of you stay here."

Then Zalkin's voice echoed down to them. "Cole! Do you hear me? I shot the fat boy and I'll do the same to the girl unless you and Louise do exactly what I say."

Cole looked at Louise. A terrified resignation descended over her. Seeing that look made Cole squeeze the handle of the hammer tighter, although he knew it would be worthless against a gun.

"Leave her out of this. It's just between you and me, Zykus."

"Don't be stupid. She's the real reason I came back to Chicago. Not for you. Now you've got five seconds to do what I say or the girl dies. Then I'm going to burn this place to the ground with all of you in it."

Sister Mary Louise crossed the chapel to stand beside Cole. "What do you want from me?" she cried.

"Is that you, babe? Good to hear your voice again. I want you and the black knight to come up here. The priest and Bronson can stay put."

"What about Shirley?" Louise demanded.

"She's my bargaining chip. Nothing will happen to her as long as you and Cole do as I say."

"Send her down and then we'll come up," Cole said.

"You're not giving the orders here, Cole! Now you and Louise get your asses up here or I'll kill Shirley right now."

Without further hesitation, Louise started up the stairs. Cole grabbed her arm.

"Let me go, Larry," she said with a sternness he had never heard from her before. "We've got to go or you know he'll kill her."

"He's probably going to do that anyway."

"I can't take that chance."

The blood was flowing from Zalkin's shoulder again and his back was on fire, but he still kept his forearm wrapped tightly around the black girl's neck. After she screamed, the big black kid had come running upstairs and Zalkin had been forced to shoot him in the chest. Now, George was lying unconscious in a pool of his own blood. He was still breathing, but the wound was making a soft sucking noise, indicating a lung puncture.

But the killer didn't care about him. He wanted Louise and Cole. It was all coming to an end now. Maybe it wasn't exactly like he had planned it, but nothing ever worked out just right.

"You can't make it much longer, boy."

Dave Higgins's disembodied voice made Zalkin flinch.

He pressed the barrel of the Magnum into the side of Shirley's head.

"Shut up!" he shouted.

"I didn't say nothing." The girl's words were heavy with fear.

"I'm not talking to you."

She didn't understand him, but she didn't argue.

Louise came up first. Then Cole. Despite the pain, Zalkin grinned. He released Shirley. The girl leaped from his grasp and ran to embrace the nun.

As the student cried in her arms, Louise held her. "It's okay, honey. It's okay. Everything is going to be fine."

Zalkin sneered. "You know, Louise, you always had that look. I figured that someday you'd be doing charity work or raising little pickaninnies like her."

Shirley glared at him with hatred.

Louise saw George's body on the floor and released Shirley in order to go to him.

"Leave him," Zalkin said.

Louise ignored him.

"I said leave him alone, Louise, or I'll kill the girl right now."

The nun stopped.

Still holding the hammer down at his side, Cole took a step toward Zalkin; however, the drug had slowed the policeman considerably, and the killer easily swung the six-inch-barrel Python up and shot the head off the hammer. The handle was split in two by the round, and Cole dropped the remaining piece of harmless wood to the floor.

Zalkin leveled the gun on the policeman's head. "Stupid, stupid, stupid. I always gave you credit for more smarts than that, Cole. But after all, you're only a cop, so what more could I expect?"

Zalkin cocked the weapon. Cole stared into the killer's eyes.

"If you kill him, you might as well kill all of us," Louise

said, stepping forward and placing her body between Cole and Zalkin. The barrel of the gun touched the crucifix hanging from her neck.

"She's got spunk, ain't she, boy. More woman than you'll ever be a man."

Zalkin tensed at the sound of Higgins's voice in his mind, but said nothing. He backed away, still pointing the gun.

"You must be real hell in the classroom, Louise," Zalkin said. "You even scared me for a minute. But the next time you pull something like that I'll kill all of you starting with the girl."

Louise stood her ground.

"You don't scare her, boy."

"I will," Zalkin said to the voice only he could hear.

"I know you will," Louise said. "But people have died in the service of God before. We'll become martyrs, while you, Mr. Martin Zykus, will burn in hell."

Zalkin reached up and yanked her veil off. Shirley screamed and Cole tensed. Louise's head of curly blond hair was revealed. Tossing the veil away, Zalkin said, "Well, you all might get your wish to go to heaven, but not here. For that, we're going over to the church."

CHAPTER 128

Blackie was behind the wheel of a marked squad car. Two other marked units and three unmarked were following him. With emergency lights and sirens on, they crossed the Second District headed for Washington Park Boulevard and Our Lady of Peace. Manny Sherlock was in the car with Blackie, and the young cop's lips were moving as they shot through intersections and around stopped cars.

"Say one for me while you're at it, kid," Blackie shouted over the wail of the siren. "If Zalkin made it to Our Lady of Peace, they're going to need all the prayers they can get."

"I . . . I wasn't really praying. I guess I don't know how."

Blackie's eyes stayed on the streets in front of him. "Everybody knows how to pray, Sherlock."

The young detective's voice dropped. "I never learned how. We never went to church in my family."

"You don't have to go to church to know how to pray. I bet even guys who say that they're atheists or agnostics do it. When your ass . . ." Blackie paused to think about Cole, "or somebody else's you love is on the line, you'll pray."

Manny nodded. "Could I ask you one question, Sarge?"

"Sure, kid."

"What is an agnostic?"

Blackie exhaled a frustrated sigh. "Not now, Manny. Not now."

CHAPTER 129

Father Ken Smith and Detective Lou Bronson stood at the bottom of the chapel stairs.

"I'm going up," Bronson said weakly.

"That isn't a good idea, Lou," the priest said. "That man will kill you."

They heard the door open and feet pounding down the stairs. They stepped away from the entrance and waited expectantly. Shirley Rogers, her face streaked with tears, stumbled into the chapel.

Father Ken rushed forward to grab her before she collapsed.

"What happened up there, child?"

She was crying.

"He . . . he . . . he shot George and he's . . . taking Sister Mary over . . . to the . . . church!"

"Where's the commander?" Bronson said.

"He's got . . . him, too!"

"What about the *gun?*"

The girl looked at him with red-rimmed eyes, but didn't answer.

"Did you get the gun?"

Frightened at his sharp tone, Shirley buried her face in Father Ken's chest. The priest gave the detective a hard look for shouting at her. Then he patted her shoulder and said, quietly, "Shirley, did you get the gun Sister Mary sent you for?"

"I got the gun, Father."

"Where is it?"

"I slipped it to Sister Mary upstairs. She's got it now." Father Ken's eyes met Lou Bronson's. Each could detect a little hope in the other. Then Bronson headed for the stairs.

CHAPTER 130

APRIL 19, 1991
7:30 P.M.

Larry Cole and Sister Mary Louise Stallings stepped out onto the back porch of the rectory. Zalkin brought up the rear. The policeman and the nun walked side by side in front of him.

Louise had twice considered shooting their captor since Shirley had slipped her the gun back in the rectory. When Zalkin had threatened to kill Cole and she had stepped between them, she had the gun in her deep habit pocket pointed right at his stomach. The moment the barrel of his gun had rested against her crucifix was when she'd come closest, but she had been unable to do it, despite her own personal peril.

The second time had been on the back porch. Now, they were again at his mercy, and if anything happened to Larry she would blame herself. She had considered her personal fate in God's hands for the past fifteen years.

The shadow of the church spires fell across the courtyard, plunging them into shadow. Louise held on to Cole's arm. She was trying to think of a way she could slip Cole the gun without Zalkin seeing it. But with the killer so close, she realized that this would be impossible. So now it was totally up to her.

They reached the side door of the church. Zalkin ordered them to stop. Reluctantly they did so, feeling hollow anger at his control over them.

Louise felt Cole tense beside her. She looked across the courtyard to the breezeway between the school and the convent. Two police cars had pulled up there. The noises of doors being shut and men shouting carried to them. Two more police cars pulled up in front of the rectory.

"Why don't you give up now, Zalkin?" Cole said. "You'll never get out of here in the shape you're in."

A bright spotlight trapped the three of them in its beam. Another, and still a third, were trained on them.

Using Sister Mary Louise as a shield, Zalkin moved to the church door, opened it, and yanked the nun inside behind him. With the door still open he pointed the gun at Cole. "Get inside or you'll die right there."

The commander stepped into the church. Before the door closed behind him, he heard the voice of Blackie Silvestri shout, "Larry, wait!"

CHAPTER 131

The church was immense and dark. They crossed from the side entrance to the center aisle. The only illumination was provided by racks of votive candles burning in front of the three altars. Stoically, the faces of statues stared down at the trio. The place was chilly, which Cole and Sister Mary Louise felt intensely because of the danger they were in.

"Walk up to the altar." Zalkin followed close behind them. They did as they were ordered; they noticed, however, that with each passing second, he was weakening.

"Stop."

They stood at the communion rail in front of a pair of marble gates, which opened into the sanctuary.

"Kneel down."

Cole and Louise glanced at each other before following this command. Then they knelt.

Slowly, Zalkin shuffled around in front of them and leaned against a marble pillar. Half his face was a bloody, blistering mass, and his right arm was dripping blood freely. It seemed impossible for him to remain on his feet much longer, but his gun, which was now pointed at the floor, was still held firmly in his hand.

"Does this place remind you of anything, Cole?" Zalkin's voice came out a wheezing croak.

"Should it?" Cole spoke with an impudence he hadn't realized that he was capable of generating.

Zalkin cracked a grin that turned quickly into a grimace. "The old hotel downtown. Fifteen years ago. You and Silvestri left me there."

Cole remained silent.

Zalkin swung his eyes to Louise. "They ever tell you about that, babe? How they left me down there that night, trapped in a building with a million rats?"

Louise stared solemnly back at him.

"It was funny." He emitted a strangled cough that was intended to be a laugh. "I had them running around in circles, scared of their own shadows. Two big, bad, tough cops. Cole and Silvestri. Real macho men." Zalkin swayed, but managed to right himself before he fell. He came very close to dropping the gun.

His two captives hadn't moved.

"You ever wonder how I got out of there that night?" he asked Cole.

Cole nodded. "We found that old tunnel leading out to the river. We figured that you froze to death, but when your body never turned up we thought you'd fallen in the water and . . ."

When Cole paused, Zalkin's eyes came alive with madness, "And what, Cole?"

The policeman's voice was low but intense. "We figured the rats got you."

A harsh cough rattled deep in Zalkin's chest. Even in the dim available light, they could see that he was sweating profusely. He didn't have much time left, but they didn't think that they could afford to wait him out. "You know something, Cole, you're a pretty smart guy. I mean, for a cop. You were right on all counts. After you and Silvestri abandoned me, the rats went to work. I tried moving

around on that collapsed beam, but I lost my balance and
fell. There must have been thousands of them biting, clawing, tearing at me. I ran and the rats followed. I nearly went
mad in that tunnel. Somehow I found my way out of there,
but they were still on me. I staggered down to the river and
fell in. Even then some of the rats came after me, swimming underwater like fish."

He paused to catch his breath. It disturbed him to find
that neither of his captives was displaying any reaction at
all to his tale.

"Do you know how cold that water was?" he screamed
at them. However, they still didn't react. In a more subdued
tone, he continued. "It was December. I figured that I was
going to die."

Emotionlessly, his captives stared back at him.

"There were some bums keeping warm by a trash-can
fire on the riverbank about a hundred feet west of the tunnel. They saw me flailing around in the water with the rats
still after me and pulled me out. Luckily, they weren't the
types to go calling cops and ambulances. They took me for
one of their own, which I guess at the time I was. Hid me in
a flophouse on West Madison. While you were dragging the
river, Cole, I was recovering on weak vegetable soup, white
bread, and a healthy dose of religion in a place where you
wouldn't even think to look for me. They even got this little
quack Arab doctor to tend my wounds from the rat bites. He
punched fourteen rabies injections into my gut."

Zalkin's face turned hard, and the hatred he felt for
them came through despite the pain. "I was in the mission
when I read Delahanty's column about me. 'Human Street
Vermin,' he called me. What did he know? But then, I was
nobody. Just a bum wanted by the cops. That's when I
decided to get even with everyone who ever crossed me.
Now that leaves only the two of you."

CHAPTER 132

APRIL 19, 1991
7:52 P.M.

There are six entrances into the church," Father Ken Smith said. The priest was seated at the dining room table in the rectory. Seated to his right was the superintendent of police. On his left was First Deputy designate William Riseman. Standing behind the superintendent's chair was Blackie Silvestri. Behind Riseman was Manny Sherlock. An ancient blueprint of the church was spread out on the table in front of them. The legend in the lower right-hand corner read, "Our Lady of Peace Catholic Church—June 1919."

"Those plans show seven entrances, Father," Riseman said.

"This one," Father Ken pointed to a side door at the back of the church, "was bricked over during the Depression. They made a rear sacristy for the bishop out of that part of the vestibule."

"It's a big church," the superintendent said, leaning back wearily in his chair. "Zalkin could have Cole and the nun anywhere inside."

They were all looking to him for a decision as to what direction they should take. At this point, he really wasn't sure what to do and felt his usual decisive judgment deserting him. It had been a long week. A week during which he had had to bear up under ten police officers being slain, a nationally syndicated columnist's death being blamed on his department's incompetence, and his being forced to sack his second in command. Now, one of the pitifully few modern police facilities in the city had been destroyed, and one of his commanders was being held hostage by a madman. The superintendent was tired. He didn't want to make any more decisions that could possibly cost Cole and the nun their lives. All he wanted to do was go home, have a good stiff drink, and lay down the burden of being the chief executive officer of the second largest police department in the country. At least, for a little while.

"May I make a suggestion, Superintendent?" Blackie asked softly.

He nodded.

"The church being such a big place could be an advantage for us as well. We could slip in, locate Zalkin, and take him out."

Riseman stared hard at Silvestri. "Who's 'we'?"

Blackie nodded at Sherlock. "Me and my partner here."

When the superintendent and Riseman turned to stare at him, Sherlock blushed.

CHAPTER 133

Larry Cole's hand was throbbing with an intensity that made concentration impossible. He considered the very real possibility that he and Louise Stallings were going to die for something that had happened fifteen years ago.

Cole's mind began wandering away from the prison of his physical surroundings. He thought about the kind of funeral the department would give him. In his mind, he pictured Lisa in a black dress, standing beside his coffin. His son Butch would be with her.

A lump formed in his throat. Then anger flared. He wasn't dead. Zalkin hadn't won yet.

Zalkin had reached a plateau, which he was maintaining with maddening ease. The bleeding had stopped, and, although he was still leaning heavily against the marble pillar, he felt himself getting marginally stronger as he related the tale he had waited a decade and a half to tell.

"I went over to Indiana with some guys and started knocking around there. I thought about coming back and taking care of you two, but I figured you could wait. I had the time."

"How did you like Fort Wayne, Indiana?" Cole said.

Zalkin frowned. "What?"

"How did you like Fort Wayne, Indiana—or better yet, the Fort Wayne, Indiana jail?"

"Shut up!"

"How about Denver?" Cole pressed.

Zalkin's face contorted in anger. "Keep pushing me, Cole. Keep pushing me."

"But those were only minor busts," Cole continued. "The one you went down hard for was in California. That's when they sent you to prison."

Slowly, Zalkin's gun came up. He stared through the sights at Cole's head. "It's time now, Larry. It is finally time."

Cole's voice was firm. "I've got one last question."

Zalkin kept the gun steady. "Go ahead."

"Where did you get the money?"

The gun didn't waver. A long moment passed. Then Zalkin lowered the Python to his side. "That's a good one, Cole. A real good one. You're going to get a kick out of this. *That's right, old man. I'm going to tell him!*"

Cole and the nun exchanged questioning glances.

Zalkin chuckled softly. "It's Dave Higgins. You remember him, don't you, babe? He was the one that screwed you first that night we followed you from the grocery store."

Louise lowered her head.

"He killed him, too, Louise," Cole said.

"I know," she whispered.

"Well," Zalkin explained, "he talks to me every now and then. It's wild, but it does make life interesting. *I'm gonna tell them! Just give me a chance!*"

"I'm a gambler. Not a card player or dice thrower, but a numbers player. My ma always used to play them when I was a kid. When the lottery came out in Illinois, I played it regularly. The night you and Silvestri chased me into the Sherman House, I'd won five hundred on the instant game." Zalkin laughed. "I was always lucky. At least, at the lottery. *I'm getting to it! Just leave me alone!*

"Everyplace I went, I played the lottery. On the West Coast I was considered some kind of wizard because I always won. It was out there that I hit my jackpot. Six numbers, Cole. I bet you can't guess what they were."

Cole's eyes were locked on Zalkin, but he didn't respond.

"Try one, three, four, eight, twenty-five, and eighty-six. *Give him a chance to figure it all, old man! He's smarter than he looks!*"

Cole said nothing.

"Maybe he's not so smart," Zalkin leered. "Can't figure it out without using all his fingers and toes."

"Martin," Sister Mary Louise said.

"Easy, babe. This is the good part. I won thirty-five million dollars playing those numbers. And you'll never guess where I got them."

"Martin, listen to me," she said, standing up and holding her hands out in front of her as she approached him.

"What're you doing?" He swung the gun up to point at her. "Get back there. Nobody told you to move."

"No, Martin," she said. "There's a policeman behind you in the sacristy off to your right. There's another one over there."

Zalkin's head snapped in that direction in time to see a figure dart behind the sacristy door.

"Louise, don't!" Cole shouted.

"You're dead, Cole!" Zalkin spun back to face the cop, but Louise had stepped in front of him. She was close enough to reach out and clasp the barrel in her hands. He tensed to fire and she shut her eyes.

Cole rolled away from the altar and took shelter beneath a pew.

"I can't kill her, you fool! She's trying to help me!" Zalkin wailed at the disembodied voice in his head. Tears

were now flowing from his eyes to mix with his blood. "You are trying to help me, aren't you, Louise?" he said in a pleading voice.

"Yes," she said. "I'm going to shield you so we can get out of here."

He looked around wildly. "Yes, yes, that's what we'll do. When we get outside, the cops won't dare try anything with you in front of me." He reached out and grabbed her arm. "I always knew that you liked me. I knew it that first night."

"Yes," she said flatly. "Now, stay close to me."

Slowly, Zalkin followed the nun toward the exit.

CHAPTER 134

APRIL 19, 1991
8:05 P.M.

Blackie Silvestri and Manny Sherlock were supplied with bulletproof vests, ten-millimeter automatic pistols, and heavy-duty electric lanterns. Father Ken, Riseman, and two uniformed policemen accompanied them to the outside sacristy door. The entire church-and-school complex was surrounded by cops. Before Silvestri and Sherlock went inside the church, the priest stopped them and gave them his blessing.

"May God go with you," he said as they slipped silently into the darkness of the sacristy.

Riseman and the priest remained there for a few moments.

"I hope no one is killed in there," Father Ken said in a tone that came out sounding like a prayer. "This is God's house in this community. A violent death inside will be a desecration. This area already has enough negative symbols without having the image of Our Lady of Peace being destroyed."

"I don't follow you," Riseman said.

"Someone being killed in there will desecrate the church. We won't be able to use it for religious services until the cardinal can reconsecrate it. I have enough trouble staying afloat down here as it is. I have no idea how the parishioners will react to something like that."

But Riseman was no longer listening to the priest. His problem was not the church, but the cops and the killer inside it.

CHAPTER 135

APRIL 19, 1991
8:07 P.M.

In the sacristy, Blackie and Sherlock split up. They could hear Zalkin's voice easily enough and were able to tell where he was. The plan was to come up on him from two sides. That way, they hoped one of them could get a clear shot at him. They planned to kill him without a second's hesitation.

Blackie crossed to the altar door and listened to Zalkin's ravings outside. Gently, he eased the door open, praying for oiled hinges and locks that wouldn't squeak. His prayers were answered. His heart began to hammer when he saw Zalkin leaning against the marble pillar with Cole and the nun kneeling in front of him.

Blackie pulled the ten-millimeter automatic and looked across the altar to where Sherlock should have been at the other door by now. The skinny detective was barely visible in the darkness, but he was there.

Blackie inched the door open a little farther to enable him to see Cole better. He also wanted Cole to be able to see him. Zalkin had his back to the sacristy doors, and Blackie didn't want either of the hostages to move and end up getting in the way.

The nun's head was down, which was just as well. Blackie didn't want her panicking on him. Then he saw the slight flicker of recognition on Cole's face. *Good!* Blackie thought. Now we're going to bag this bastard. With a motion to Sherlock indicating that he was going to try a shot, Blackie raised the automatic.

Cole began distracting Zalkin, which Blackie didn't like. The killer was getting agitated and Blackie would have preferred him stock-still for a nice shot right through the head.

When Zalkin pointed the six-inch-barrel revolver at Cole, Blackie froze with his finger on the ten-millimeter's trigger. Even if he hit Zalkin, a reflex could cause him to discharge his gun and kill Cole. Tense seconds passed, and finally Zalkin lowered the gun. It was at that instant that Blackie should have taken the shot but something, possibly the nun's head coming up and her looking right at the door he stood behind, made him hesitate. Zalkin began saying something about numbers. Numbers that sounded oddly familiar to Blackie, but which he couldn't afford to concentrate on under the circumstances. Then the nun stood up.

All Blackie could do was watch as she walked toward Zalkin.

CHAPTER 136

Sister Mary Louise Stallings walked rigidly toward the exit, which would return them to the courtyard on the same side of the church through which they had entered. Zalkin's arm was around her. His touch was caressing rather than restrictive, and she could even feel the hot moistness of his sour breath on her cheek. This brought the past back to her with such gut-wrenching suddenness it weakened her knees. Now he had again trespassed into her life and hurt people that she loved. Now he wanted to desecrate the church, which stood as the one symbol of her existence—the church, which had protected her when everything else seemed lost. That, she could not let him do.

When they reached the exit door, Sister Mary Louise knew that, in a few moments, the man she had known fifteen years ago as Martin Zykus was going to die. Once they stepped outside into the world beyond this sanctuary, she was prepared to die with him.

"It's not on the level, boy," the voice raged in Zalkin's head. *"She's setting you up."*

"Shut up!" Zalkin shouted, making Louise go rigid with fear. "I wasn't talking to you, babe," he said by way of apology. "It's Dave. He keeps trying to interfere."

"I understand," she said quietly.

"Don't worry, the cops won't shoot and take the chance of hitting you."

The reached the exit. He stopped her.

"Okay, this is the drill. We walk out together. I'm going to yell for them to kill all the lights or I'll threaten to hurt you, but I won't mean it. In fact, I never meant to hurt you." He tightened his grip on her. "You were all I've been thinking about for the last fifteen years."

"We'd better go," she said.

He hesitated. "Louise?"

She looked at him.

"I just want to thank you for helping me. I know I haven't always done right by you, but that's all going to change. I've got money. Lots of money. You'll live like a queen. You can give up all this mumbo-jumbo bull-shit."

She turned from him and stared blankly at the door in front of her.

"Do you understand?"

She turned to look back at him. The blood flowing from him and his burned, blistered face had turned Steven Zalkin or Martin Zykus into a grotesque figure.

Sister Mary Louise always taught her religion classes that the only true ugliness that existed in God's universe was caused by the mutilation of the spirit by sin. She felt that this man had horribly mutilated his own soul, and that God was providing her an opportunity to look into the true heart of evil.

"I understand," she said.

He leaned forward and kissed her on the lips. She didn't move. When he finished, she turned and walked with him out into the night.

"Hold it right there, Zalkin!" a voice thundered across the courtyard as blinding spotlights captured them in an intense glare.

"You're a fool for coming out here, boy. You're dead meat now for sure."

A few feet outside the church doors, the nun stopped. "You have to surrender now, Martin."

Zalkin swung the Python up and aimed at the glare surrounding them.

"Your only hope is to give up," she continued, speaking quietly. "You can't go any farther. God will forgive you if you are honestly sorry for what you've done and don't attempt to hurt anyone else."

"She's making a fool out of you with this Holy Ghost shit. She walked you right into this. Now you're going to die, Marty, but you've got to take her with you."

At that instant, Zalkin realized that all of this was her fault from the very beginning. Fifteen years ago she had enticed him by begging him not to let Dave hurt her anymore. Then she had sent Cole and Silvestri after him and almost gotten him eaten alive by the rats. Now she had led him out here to die. But he didn't intend to die alone.

"Zalkin!" Larry Cole shouted, as he staggered from the church toward them.

The killer swung his gun to aim at Cole. A single shot rang out.

Sister Mary Louise Stallings fired the bullet from the snub-nosed revolver into Steven Zalkin's heart. The faces of the victim and her former victimizer were less than six inches apart when he died. Louise watched the life go out of his face at the same instant that he released his grip on her and fell to the ground.

For a long time, no movement or sound came from beyond the ring of bright lights rimming the Our Lady of Peace courtyard. Then, the black-clad figure of Father Ken Smith—the white bandage wrapped around his head supplying a sharp contrast to his dark skin—crossed from the area of shadow to where the nun stood alone over Zalkin's body. Larry Cole, Blackie Silvestri, and Manny Sherlock approached her. Then the superintendent of police and William Riseman joined them. From a trickle, the stream of cops, newsmen, and interested others turned into a flood. The human deluge brought its own roar.

Questions were shouted at Sister Mary Louise, which Father Ken tried to deflect. But this didn't bother her. In fact, she was concerned about only one thing.

She looked down at the body of the man who called himself Steven Zalkin, but whom she had known as Martin Zykus. She waited until a doctor arrived on the scene. This doctor had already been inside the rectory and had saved the life of George Green, who had been rushed to University Hospital and was listed in serious but stable condition.

Now, the doctor—a young man with dark hair, who looked hardly older than some of Sister Mary Louise's students—spent precious minutes laboring over Zalkin. Finally, when the doctor was certain that nothing more could be done for him, he turned to those standing over him and said, "He's dead."

"Thank you, Doctor," the nun said before turning to Larry Cole and handing him the .38.

He took it, but made no comment. None of the others around her said anything, and even the press corps had gone eerily silent.

Dry-eyed, her back straight, Sister Mary Louise walked through the mob and went back into the church. Father Ken Smith accompanied her, but no words were exchanged between them. The superintendent gave orders for guards to be posted at the doors to the church so that the nun and priest would not be disturbed.

Inside Our Lady of Peace Catholic Church, Sister Mary Louise Stallings went to the altar. She could still see

Zalkin's blood smeared on the marble pillar. She knelt in the exact same spot she had been in when she was a captive. Father Ken knelt beside her.

Bowing her head, she made the sign of the cross and began, "Oh, my God, I am heartily sorry for having offended thee."

Father Ken joined her in the Act of Contrition.

EPILOGUE

MAY 21, 1991
4:00 P.M.

The ground-breaking ceremony for the new Our Lady of Peace youth center had concluded. The archbishop of Chicago, the mayor, and a host of dignitaries from public, private, and religious life had gathered for a three-o'clock mass in the church, followed by a procession out to the vacant field for the official proceedings. They were blessed with a warm sunny day for the barbecue and picnic following the ceremony.

A tent had been erected, and music blared from speakers arranged around the courtyard. White-hatted chefs tended oil-drum-sized barbecue pits stacked with ribs, chicken, and steak. There were tubs of iced cans of beer for the adults and soft drinks for the kids. Both adults and school children danced in various areas around the complex to music played over a loudspeaker by a local DJ. The cardinal, the mayor, and Father Ken Smith looked on with interest and at times amusement at some of the antics taking place during the festivities.

Picnic tables were set up at the rear of the convent to accommodate the school faculty and their guests. At Sister Mary Louise Stallings's table were the Coles, the Silvestris, Lou Bronson, Manny Sherlock, and Lauren Holmes.

Cole's left hand was in a bandage, making it difficult for him to eat. This made it necessary for Lisa to assist him, which she was doing with great relish. Occasionally, the detective commander's wife was even caught feeding him. Their young son Butch had found a group of kids his age and was off playing.

They were all in a generally festive mood and Sister Mary Louise appeared to be enjoying the party most of all. At times, however, the laughter from this table was too loud, the conversations forced, and the moments of silence protracted. Steven Zalkin, a k a Martin Zykus, was still very much with them, and it would be a long time before his impact on their lives would ease.

"How long will the bandage have to stay on, Larry?" the nun asked.

"I have the dressing changed once a week, so the doctor can check the healing process," Cole said, holding up his bandaged left hand.

"The doctor said he should be as good as new in two months," Lisa added.

Sister Mary Louise turned to look at the festivities. "To think that this celebration came about because of Martin Zykus."

Blackie was leaning back in a lawn chair he had brought with him. His wife was in the chair's companion beside him. Sitting up straight he said, "Come again, Sister?"

The rest of them were also staring quizzically at her.

She shrugged. "Zalkin gave Father Ken a check for half a million dollars. It was good, so we applied it to the youth center fund."

"Can you and Father Ken do that?" Bronson asked.

"Why not? He gave it to us."

"I would say that he owed it to you after all that he did," Lauren Holmes said.

Over the past few weeks, Lauren and Manny had been seeing each other regularly. After their arrival at the church earlier that day, Sister Mary Louise had taken her, along with Lisa and Maria, on a tour of the grounds. Left alone, the men started teasing Manny.

"Now that's going to really be a match made in heaven," Blackie said around a cigar. "Sherlock and Holmes."

"Beautiful," Bronson beamed with pride. Manny was like a son to him.

"In fact, Manny," Cole said, "you look like you've gained some weight since you've been going out with Lauren."

"I have," Sherlock replied glumly.

"So, she's a good cook, Manny," Bronson said. "What's wrong with that?"

"She's not that great a cook, Lou, but I find I eat a lot more when I'm with her."

"Why?" Blackie asked.

"She likes to talk about marriage and having kids. That makes me nervous, so I eat more."

The howls of laughter from the cops made the heads of the cardinal and mayor turn in their direction.

Later, Louise asked, "Tell me, Larry. That night in the church, Zalkin asked you about the numbers he played to win the lottery. Did you ever find out what he meant?"

"Blackie gets the credit for solving that one, Sister. You want to tell her what they were?"

Blackie chewed his cigar and switched it from one side of his mouth to the other. "When we went through Zalkin's place, we found a lot of interesting stuff. Besides using his money for plastic surgery, sharpshooting, and combat-tactics lessons from a court-martialed army colonel, he spent a fortune collecting information about you, me, and Larry, Sister. You could say that his life, even after he won all that money, revolved around us to the point of obsession. Well, without going into a lot of detail, we found that he won the jackpot playing the numbers one, three, four, eight, twenty-five, and eighty-six."

They were all listening closely now.

"Those weren't numbers that Zalkin or Zykus thought up himself. He borrowed them from me and Larry. Sometime back in seventy-six, after we grabbed him and had to let him go, he memorized our badge numbers. Mine was 2586 and Larry's 14083. Zalkin probably rearranged them in a lot of different orders, but if you look, you'll find his one, three, four, eight, twenty-five, and eighty-six right there. He played it and got lucky enough to win thirty-five million dollars."

"We should try those numbers ourselves, Blackie," Maria said.

Blackie reached into his shirt pocket and removed two tickets. "I got yours, too, boss."

"Thanks," Cole said.

They all laughed.

"Well, after going through all this," Manny said, "I'd just like one question answered for me."

They waited.

"Could somebody please tell me what an agnostic is?"